12/21

Hayner PLD/Large Print
Overdues .10/day. Max fine cost of
item. Lost or damaged item: additional
$5 service charge.

THE LAST PROTECTOR

THE LAST PROTECTOR

ANDREW TAYLOR

THORNDIKE PRESS
A part of Gale, a Cengage Company

GALE
A Cengage Company

LIBRARY OF CONGRESS CIP DATA ON FILE.
CATALOGUING IN PUBLICATION FOR THIS BOOK
IS AVAILABLE FROM THE LIBRARY OF CONGRESS.

ISBN-13: 978-1-4328-9278-4 (hardcover alk. paper)

Published in 2021 by arrangement with HarperCollins Publishers Limited

Printed in Mexico
Print Number: 01   Print Year: 2022

For Caroline

For Caroline

THE MAIN CHARACTERS

Infirmary Close, The Savoy

James Marwood, clerk to Joseph William-
son, and to the Board of Red Cloth
Margaret and Sam Witherdine, his servants
Stephen, his footboy

At the sign of the Rose, Henrietta Street

Simon Hakesby, surveyor and architect
Catherine Hakesby, his wife, formerly
Lovett
Jane Ash, her maid
Brennan, Hakesby's draughtsman
Pheebs, the porter

Whitehall

King Charles II
Lord Arlington, Secretary of State
Dudley Gorvin, his clerk

7

Joseph Williamson, Undersecretary of State to Lord Arlington

William Chiffinch, Keeper of the King's Private Closet

George Villiers, second Duke of Buckingham

Ezra Reeves, a mazer-scourer

Ferrus, the mazer-scourer's labourer

Others

Mistress Elizabeth Cromwell, late Lady Protectoress of England (died 1665)

The Reverend Jeremiah White, formerly chaplain to the Lord Protector

Richard Cromwell, late Lord Protector of England, in succession to his father, Oliver Cromwell

Elizabeth Cromwell, Richard's eldest daughter

Mistress Dalton, her godmother

Wanswell, a waterman

Mr Veal, known as the Bishop

Roger Durrell, his servant

Madam Cresswell

Merton: in her employ

Chloris: in her employ

Mary: in her employ

'I shall not say how sad a condition I and my family, nay the nations, are in, for it is better for me to throw myself in the dust and cry before the Lord . . .'

— Richard Cromwell, late Lord Protector of England, in a cypher letter to his brother Henry (the letter is undated but was probably written in May 1659)

CHAPTER ONE

The Walls Run with Blood
Friday, 13 November 1665
The Reverend Jeremiah White took the Lincoln road from Peterborough, riding north through watery sunshine. He was a tall, narrow man, stiff and twig-like, dressed in black. The horse he had hired from the inn was a small, brown creature. White's feet were too close to the ground for dignity.

He had set off in good time, not long after eight of the clock. The journey was no more than six or seven miles, but it took him longer than he had expected. The roads were treacherous after the recent rains, and the mare proved to be a sluggish, sour-tempered jade. He did not reach Northborough until the middle of the afternoon–well after the dinner hour, as his stomach reminded him with steadily increasing insistence.

The gates of the manor were standing

11

open. He clattered under the arch of the gatehouse into the courtyard beyond. The stableman came out of the coach house, touching his cap with one hand and taking the horse's bridle with the other.

'Does she still live?' White asked.

'Aye, sir.' The man looked up at him. 'Though it will be a mercy when God takes her.'

White dismounted. There was a bustle at the main door of the house. Claypole came out with two servants behind him.

'Thank God you're here,' he said. 'Mistress Cromwell has been asking after you all day. She's working herself up to one of her fits. What kept you?'

'The roads were treacherous. I —'

'It doesn't matter now. Come in, come in.'

In his urgency, Claypole almost dragged White into the house, taking him into the great hall to the left of the screens passage, where logs smouldered in the grate. He guided White to a chair. One servant took his cloak. Another knelt before him and drew off his travelling boots.

'Will you see her directly?' Claypole said.

'A morsel to eat first, perhaps,' White suggested.

Claypole glanced at the nearest servant.

'Bread, cheese, whatever there is to be had quickly.' He turned back to White, rubbing his eyes. 'She . . . she was in great pain during the night again, and she was not in her right mind, either.' His mouth trembled. 'She says–she keeps saying . . .'

White took his host's hand. 'She says what?'

Claypole stared at him. 'She says the walls are running with blood.'

'Perhaps she has a fever. Or perhaps God has vouchsafed her a vision of the world to come, though I hope not for her or for you or me. But for now, my friend, there is nothing we can do except try to make the poor lady as comfortable as possible. And, above all, we must pray for her. Do you know why she wants me? Is it the will again?'

'I don't know–I asked her, but she wouldn't say. She can be close and suspicious, even with us, her family.'

The servant brought cold mutton and a jug of ale. White ate and drank a few mouthfuls, but his host's urgency had suppressed his hunger.

'The food must wait,' he said. 'I'd better see her ladyship now.'

The two men went upstairs. On the landing, a maidservant, her face grey with exhaustion, answered Claypole's knock at

13

one of the doors.

'Mistress knows you're here,' she whispered to White. 'She heard you below.'

'Is she in a fit state to receive him?' Claypole said in a low voice.

The maid nodded. 'If it's not for too long. God send it will ease her mind.'

To White's surprise, the bed was empty, though a fire burned on the hearth. The air smelled of herbs and sickness.

'She's in the closet,' the maid murmured to him, pointing to a door in a corner of the room. 'She made me move her there when she heard your horse in the yard. Come, sir.'

Claypole made as if to follow them but she stopped him with a hand on his arm. 'Forgive me, master. She wants to see Mr White alone.'

She held open the door no wider than necessary to allow White to pass through. As soon as he was inside, he heard the clack of the latch.

The closet was tiny—no more than two or three yards square—and crowded with shadowy objects. The walls were panelled. The room had been built out over the porch and it faced north. The windows were small, their lattices set with thick green glass that let in little light. The air was stuffy with the smells of age and sickness. It was very cold.

For an instant, he thought the maid had played a trick on him and the closet was empty. Then, as his eyes adjusted, there came a rustle in one corner. The old lady was there, propped up against pillows and swathed in blankets.

'Mr White,' she said. 'God bless you for coming all this way again. I'm obliged.'

He bowed. 'My wife sends her service to you. She prays for you.'

'Katherine is a good girl.'

'How are you, my lady?'

Mistress Cromwell drew in her breath and whimpered like a dog. He waited; he knew better than to say or do anything. In a moment, when the pain had subsided, she said, 'I'll be in my grave by the end of the month.'

'God's will be done.'

'The workings of God's will seem mysterious indeed, these last five or six years.'

'It is not for us to question Him.' White paused, but she said nothing. 'Is it about the will? Should I send for the lawyer again?'

'No. Not that. Call for a candle, will you? It grows darker and darker.'

He opened the door a crack. Claypole had gone, but the maid was still in the chamber beyond. She had already lighted the candles and she brought him one.

15

'Will mistress take her draught now?' she asked as she handed it to him.

The old woman's ears were sharp. 'No, I will not, you foolish woman,' she said. 'Afterwards.'

He closed the closet door again and set the candle on a bracket in the wall. Mistress Cromwell watched him. It seemed to him that her face was markedly thinner than it had been in the summer, and her body beneath the coverings was no bigger than a child's. She had been a sturdy woman in her prime, with a plump, round face and a brisk, bustling air as she went about the tasks of her household. In the seven years since Oliver's death, she had slowly changed. It was as if time itself was devouring her.

'Sit down, Mr White.'

There was a low stool beside a chest, the only other furnishing in the closet beside the daybed on which she lay. When he sat down, his knees rose towards his chin. You could hardly see the floor.

'I don't care for candles,' she went on. 'It's when I see the blood on the walls. Smell it, too, sometimes. Fresh blood, you see.'

'It is the fever, madam, I assure you. There is no blood.'

She made a low, rattling noise that might have been a laugh. 'No, sir. There is always blood. There has been too much blood altogether. But enough of that for the moment. Will you do something else for me, as well as act as my executor?'

He bowed his head. 'Anything, madam. Anything I can.'

'You and Katherine will not be the losers. There will be something for you when I am gone.' A hand appeared from the blankets, small and wrinkled as a monkey's paw. 'Take this.'

It was an iron key, three inches long and warm to his touch with heat borrowed from its owner.

'Unlock the chest, sir. You will find a bundle of papers inside, on the top. Have the kindness to give them to me.'

He obeyed. The papers were tied together with a broad black ribbon. He glimpsed a dark, rich fabric underneath them; the candle flame glinted on the gold thread that brought the sombre material to life. A relic of the Whitehall days, he thought sadly, wondering what else the chest contained, what other mementoes of other places, of other, better times.

She slipped the ribbon from the papers. 'Hold the candle higher.'

17

She peered at the papers. On one of them he recognized the familiar hand of the old lady's late husband, the Lord Protector himself, Oliver Cromwell of blessed memory. She paused, stroking the paper as if to give it pleasure and comfort. Her lips mumbled rhythmically like a papist telling the beads of her rosary. Words, then phrases, then whole sentences emerged from the muttering:

'Thou are dearer to me than any creature; let that suffice . . . My Dearest, I could not satisfy myself to omit this post, though I have not much to write; yet indeed I love to write to my dear who is very much in my heart. It joys me to hear thy soul prospereth; the Lord increase His favours to thee more and more . . . I love to write to my dear . . . dearer to me than any creature —'

She was wracked with a second spasm of pain, worse than the first. White sat there, still holding the candle, watching the agony twist her features beyond recognition. Automatically he found himself praying aloud, imploring God to ease her suffering in this world and the next. The pain slowly retreated.

'Madam,' he said. 'You're tired and you suffer much. Shall we continue later? I should ask your servant for your draught. It

18

will help you sleep.'

'No,' she said with sudden vigour. 'I shall sleep long enough later.' Her hands went back to the papers. She shuffled through them. 'Ah! This one, Mr White, this is what we need.' She held it up so he could see. The paper was folded like a letter, but there was no name on it. She turned it over, showing him that the folds on the back were secured by three large seals. He made as if to take it, but she snatched it away and clasped it to her breast.

'What would you have me do?' he asked.

'This is for my son,' she said. 'It must reach him with the seals unbroken. Promise me you will guard it with your life. My husband trusted you, and I shall too.'

'You have my word, my lady. If you wish it, I shall set off for Spinney Abbey tomorrow.' Old women, he thought, made such a business out of nothing. But he was relieved to know that the task was as straightforward as this; it would be tedious and tiring, but once it was done, he could find his way home to Katherine without returning here. 'What is it? No more than forty or fifty miles from here across the Fens. It may take me more than a day at this time of year, but —'

Mistress Cromwell waved the letter, cutting him off in mid-sentence. 'No, no, Mr White. You misunderstand me. You must wait until I'm dead and in my grave. And this letter is not for my son Henry. It's for my *elder* son Richard.' Her mouth twisted. 'Tumbledown Dick. Poor Dick. It wasn't his fault.'

He stared at her. 'For Richard? But —'

'He is in France or Italy, I think.' Her mouth split wide, revealing pink gums: either a smile or a grimace of pain. 'Think of it–the second Lord Protector, as he would be still, if God had so wished, in succession to his dear father; but he has not a roof to call his own or a gold piece in his pocket.' The pain stabbed her again. He prayed silently while he waited for it to subside. After a few minutes, she went on: 'You must wait, sir–months, if necessary. They watch us, you know, especially Henry and me, and also Richard's wife. They may search this house when I am dead.'

He thought, dear God, all this will cost a deal of money. He was also fearful for himself. Of all the surviving Cromwells, Richard was the one whom the King's spies would watch most closely. He said, 'How do I find him?'

'You don't.' Mistress Cromwell gave him another glimpse of the pink gums. 'Someone will find you, and you will give that person the letter. With the seals intact.'

White leaned forward. Despite the cold, he felt sweat breaking out on his forehead and under his armpits. 'How will I know him, my lady?'

'Or her. Because the person in question will say these words to you: *The walls run with blood.* And you will say, *Aye, fresh blood.*'

She drifted away from him. Her eyes closed. She rubbed the blanket between forefinger and thumb, slowly and carefully, as though assessing the quality of the material. In a moment or two, even that movement stopped. Her breathing steadied. When he judged she was asleep, he rose and tiptoed to the door.

At the sound of the latch, Mistress Cromwell stirred and said something.

'Madam? What was that?'

'Bid him be kind to poor Ferrus.'

'Ferrus?' he repeated, unsure that he had caught the name correctly. 'Who is Ferrus?'

'I only gave him a penny. I should have given him more.'

Mistress Cromwell murmured something else as she glided into sleep or unconsciousness. It might have been 'Ferrus will help him.' Or it might not.

CHAPTER TWO

The French Style
Thursday, 16 January 1668

That night, Ferrus sleeps with the dog that guards the kitchen yard at the Cockpit. The dog is a large, brindled creature with rough fur and a spiked collar. He is called Windy because that's what he is. Ferrus has known Windy since Windy was a puppy. In those days, Windy was so tiny that Ferrus could hold him in his cupped hands.

Ferrus and Windy don't like each other. But they take each other for granted like rain and sun and nightfall. They keep each other warm on those nights when Ferrus can't sleep in the scullery on account of something he has done wrong. (Cook never allows him to sleep in the kitchen itself, even on the coldest nights, because of the smell.)

Ferrus is chilled to the bone when he wakes. It is still dark. He lies there, huddled against the dog's flank, and pulls his cloak more tightly around him. He listens to the cocks of Whitehall and Westminster crowing on their frosty dunghills. His teeth are aching again but he ignores the pain as best he can. He is hungry. He is almost always hungry. Sometimes he is tempted to eat the food they put out for Windy; but he knows that if he does that, Windy will tear out his throat.

Despite the pain, the cold and the hunger, he likes this time before the light, before the world stirs. He likes its emptiness. He stares at a pinprick of light in the eastern sky and listens to the cocks. He waits for the dawn when it will all begin again.

The first I heard about the duel was on the day itself. I was one of the very few who were aware of it beforehand. My master, Mr Williamson, summoned me into his private room at Scotland Yard shortly after nine o'clock in the morning. He told me to make sure that the door was closed. The door was made of close-fitting oak and the walls were thick. Even so, he beckoned me closer and spoke in an undertone.

'My Lord Shrewsbury has challenged the Duke of Buckingham.'

Startled, I said, 'Won't the King stop them? Does he know?'

Williamson stared at me, and I knew that I had overstepped the mark. 'The King will do as he pleases, Marwood. And you will do as I please.'

'Yes, sir. Of course, sir.'

'They are to fight this afternoon. It's likely to be a bloody business. My lord has decided that the duel will be in the French style, so he and the Duke will both be supported by two seconds.'

Three against three, I thought, slashing at each other with their swords in the name of honour: not so much a duel as a pitched battle. Anything could happen in such a mêlée, anyone could be killed. What worried me was why Williamson was telling me such a dangerous secret.

'Who are the seconds?' I asked.

'My lord has his cousins, Sir John Talbot and Bernard Howard, Lord Arundel's son. The Duke has Sir Robert Holmes and a man called Jenkins, whom I don't know. He's an officer in the Horse Guards.' Williamson paused. 'And a former fencing master.'

In that case, Buckingham had chosen carefully. I had never heard of Jenkins, but his qualifications were obvious. Holmes was well known as a ruthless fighter. He had served as both a soldier and a sailor in his time. On the other hand, Talbot and Howard were both reputed to be fine swordsmen. Talbot was an MP; he frequently attacked Buckingham and his allies in Parliament. He was a close ally of Lord Arlington, William son's superior.

'Can't it be stopped, sir, if so much is known about it? Perhaps the King —'

Williamson frowned at me. 'If that had been possible, we would not be having this conversation.' He went on in a more conciliatory tone: 'Of course the reason for the duel is obvious enough. The only wonder is that my lord has put up with the injury he has suffered for so long.'

As all the world knew, Lord Shrewsbury could hardly have avoided hearing that Buckingham had injured him: the whole town had known for months. The Duke flaunted the fact that Lady Shrewsbury was his latest mistress; so for that matter did she. But I was now quite sure that there was more to this affair than a straying wife and a cuckolded husband.

'I want you to be there,' Williamson said, leaning back in his chair. 'At the duel. To be my eyes.'

My skin crawled. Duels were illegal. Besides, I wanted nothing to do with the quarrels of noblemen. Especially these two:

25

Buckingham and Shrewsbury. 'Sir, they would kill me if —'

'I agree–it would not be convenient to either of us if you were seen,' he interrupted. He opened a drawer in his desk and took out a small wooden box, which he handed to me. 'Open it.'

I obeyed. The box contained a perspective glass made of brass, small enough to slip in a pocket.

'Keep your distance. Once the duel's over, come back as soon as you can and report to me. I want to know who's been killed, who's been wounded. I want to know exactly what happens, and who is there. Not just the combatants. Everyone.'

I made one last effort to avoid the commission. 'Sir, is it wise? The Duke would recognize my face if he chanced to see me. And several members of his household know of my employment at Whitehall.'

Williamson nodded. 'Who do you know among the Duke's people?'

'One is a clergyman named Veal, not that you would know he was in orders if you saw him. He served in the New Model Army, first as a soldier and then as a chaplain. He was given a living during the Commonwealth, but he was later ejected from his benefice. They sometimes call him the

Bishop, because of his calling, though he's not fond of bishops. He has a servant, a brute of a man named Roger, who served with him in the army.' I cleared my throat. 'Neither of them has any cause to like me, any more than their master has.'

'My intelligence is that the Duke uses these two rogues a good deal for his secret dealings. The servant's surname is Durrell. The more I can learn about them both the better. If they are there today, it will be a proof positive of how much the Duke trusts them. But the important thing is the duel itself and what happens to the principals. And I can't emphasize enough that I don't want our interest in the matter to be known.' He coughed, turning his head towards the window and looking down at a team of oxen dragging an overladen coal waggon across the second courtyard at Scotland Yard. 'My interest, that is.'

'Where is the duel to be held, sir?' I asked, noting this hint that Williamson was not acting solely on his own initiative.

'Barn Elms.' He turned back. 'After dinner—two o'clock, according to my information. I'm told that they left the decision about the time and the place until the last moment, to avoid the risk of detection. I don't even know precisely where in Barn

Elms. You had better hire a boat and get there before them. I imagine they must come by river.'

He dismissed me. At the door, however, he called me back. He scowled at me. 'Take great care, Marwood. I don't want to lose you.'

Williamson waved me away and lowered his head over his papers. I supposed I should take his last remark as a twisted compliment.

I had time to return to my lodgings in the Savoy. The weather was milder than it had been last winter, but it was cold enough in all conscience. I had Margaret, my maidservant, send out for a fricassee of veal. While I waited for the dish to arrive, I went up to my bedchamber and put on a second shirt and a thicker waistcoat.

After I had eaten, I put on my heaviest winter cloak and a broad-brimmed hat that I hoped would conceal most of my face. It was now about half-past eleven. I walked down to the Savoy stairs. The tide was up, and several boats were clustered about the landing place, waiting for new fares. Here I had a stroke of good fortune. Among the boats was the pair of oars that belonged to a waterman named Wanswell. I had used him often enough in the past year, usually to take me up the river to Whitehall or Westminster.

'I want to go up to Barn Elms,' I told him. 'And I'll need you to wait for me. Perhaps for a few hours.'

'Picnic, is it, master?' He had a flat, sardonic way of speaking that made it hard to know if he was smiling or sneering inside. His face gave no clue. Exposure to weather had made it a ruddy mask, stiff as old leather. 'Perhaps a bit of singing after you've eaten and drunk your fill?'

'Don't be more of a fool than God made you,' I said.

'I leave that to others, sir.'

I chose not to take offence. The watermen were notorious for their surliness. For my present commission, however, I would rather trust Wanswell than a complete stranger. He had been pressed into the navy in his youth and he had served for a time with Sam Witherdine, Margaret's husband. The two men often spent their leisure drinking together. I asked him how much he would charge.

He spat in the water. 'Seven shillings each way. A shilling an hour waiting time.'

It was an extortionate price. 'But the tide's with you now,' I pointed out. 'And it'll be

29

on the turn by the time we come back.'

'It's six or seven miles up to Barn Elms. The wind's freshening, too.'

'Six shillings.'

'Seven.' Wanswell was no fool. He sensed my urgency. 'All right, sir. Here's what I'll do. I'll take you there. But once the tide turns, I'm off. And whatever happens I'm leaving long before dusk. Which means I want my money when we reach Barn Elms. Take it or leave it, just as you please. It's all one to me.'

I haggled a little more for honour's sake, but he would not give ground. In the end I agreed to his terms. I believed him to be honest enough in his way, and he would think twice about cheating me because of Sam.

We set off, making good time because the wind was with us, as well as the tide. It was most damnably cold on the water, though, with nothing to shield us from the weather, and I wished I had a rug to cover me. The sky was a dark, dull grey, sullen as un-cleaned pewter. There were patches of snow on either bank of the river.

The last time I had been to Barn Elms it had been full summer. The estate lay on a northerly loop of the Thames on the Surrey bank. There was an old mansion there, with

gardens and parkland. The place had become a favoured resort of Londoners in the warm weather. I had never been there in winter but I guessed that, away from the house and the home farm, it would be a desolate spot. The duellists had chosen well.

Wanswell brought me to the landing stage used by the villagers rather than the parties of pleasure from London. An alehouse stood nearby, and it was there he proposed to wait for me.

Time was galloping away—it was already past one o'clock. If the duellists had arrived before me, it would prove difficult to find them in the expanse of gardens, orchards and pastures that formed the estate. My best plan was to keep within sight of the river.

I followed a lane that ran north along the bank, a field or two away from the river itself. Having no alternative, I pressed on for perhaps half a mile, plodding through mud and slushy snow. At this point, the lane veered closer to the water. I paused at a stile to find my bearings and to make sure I was not overlooked. It was then that I saw two or three boats hugging the shore and making for a landing stage about a quarter of a mile upstream. They had four oarsmen apiece, and each of them carried two or

three passengers under the awning at the stern. The passengers were all men, and all wearing dark clothes.

I hung back in the shelter of an ash tree and took out the perspective glass. The party disembarked at the landing stage. The boatmen stayed with their boats. I twisted the brass cylinder to bring the passengers into focus. They were marching in single file towards a spinney that crowned a gentle rise in the ground too slight to be called a hill. I recognized both Sir John Talbot, a tall, red-faced man, and Lord Shrewsbury himself, a thin, stooping figure who struggled to keep up with his kinsman. The third man must be Howard, who was talking earnestly to his lordship as they walked, gesturing with his arm to emphasize what he was saying. The others had the look of servants.

I was about to follow them as discreetly as I could, when another boat appeared on the water. This one came at speed from the opposite bank of the river. It was much larger, a richly painted barge with a dozen or more oarsmen and a cabin made private with leather curtains. Such an ostentatious craft made an instructive contrast with Shrewsbury's three unobtrusive boats. There was a brazier of coals in the stern, and three gentlemen stood beside it warming their

hands. One of them was taller than the others. I knew who he was before I fixed the glass on him and made out the florid features of the Duke of Buckingham.

Among the other passengers were two men standing on the other side of the cabin, near the oarsmen. Their faces were shaded by their hats. Both were big men, one thin and tall; the other more than making up for his relative lack of height by his breadth. They were almost certainly the men I had encountered last autumn, when I had had certain difficulties with Buckingham: his confidential servants, the Reverend Mr Veal and Roger Durrell.

While the Duke's party were disembarking, I moved away from the ash tree, following a line of hedgerow towards the spinney. I concealed myself among the trees. Buckingham and his followers marched away from the river, making no attempt to conceal themselves; I heard one of them laughing, as if he were on a jaunt.

By this time the Shrewsbury party had vanished into the spinney. When the trees had swallowed Buckingham's party as well, I followed cautiously. The one advantage of spying on members of the aristocracy was that they were so absorbed in their own affairs, so shrouded in a sense of their overwhelming importance in God's creation, that they tended to be careless of what was going on around them. They (or more probably their advisors) had taken the precaution of choosing this secluded spot for the duel; but, once here, it did not occur to them to take particular precautions against being observed.

By the time I reached the spinney, the duellists and their supporters were out of sight, but I heard the sound of voices in the distance. There was a path through the trees, the soft ground churned up by the passage of a dozen or so people. I advanced slowly among the leafless trees, a mix of birch, ash saplings and the occasional oak. Though the path was clear, it was obvious from the tangled undergrowth that the spinney had not been coppiced for some years.

I was aware of a leaden sensation in my belly, together with an inconvenient urge to empty my bowels. I walked even more slowly than before. Unlike the gentlemen ahead, I was not the stuff of which heroes are made. I could imagine, all too easily, what the duellists and their entourage would do to me if they found me here.

The voices ahead were louder. Then came a deep and throaty shout, a word of command. It was followed by the clash of steel, fast, furious and shockingly harsh. All this time I was continuing to advance. The path rounded a corner and suddenly they were all in front of me.

The spinney was bounded by a low line of bushes that once had been a hedge. The path passed through a wide gap and into a small field, a close perhaps used for confining stock. Beyond it were more trees and more hedges, which cut off the view of what lay beyond.

The six swordsmen were going at each other in a blur of movement, grunting, shouting and stamping. The others had gathered in two camps, one on each side of the close. It was fortunate that everyone's attention was drawn exclusively to the duel, otherwise I must have been seen at once. But they had eyes for nothing else.

I took in this picture in a fragment of a moment. At the same time I leapt backwards, skidding on the mud, in my effort to avoid being seen. As it was, I stumbled, almost falling into a vast yew tree beside the path. The tree swallowed me up: it was hollow inside, for its centre had been eaten away by time, leaving a sturdy palisade of offshoots and bark, thickly covered with evergreen foliage. I slowly parted two of the branches on the side of the yew nearest the field. At this point, the tree had invaded the hedgerow, and my spyhole gave me a view of the duel.

The swordsmen had put off their cloaks and hats, removed their coats and tucked up the cuffs of their shirt sleeves. Buckingham had removed his hat and golden peruke. His shaven scalp was pinker than a lobster in the pot. He towered over Shrewsbury, who was breathing hard and retreating before the onslaught of the Duke's thrusts. The other four were hacking and slashing with the abandon of madmen. There was no science to this–no elegant dance of thrust, parry and riposte: this was as bloody and brutal as a pitched battle between rival packs of apprentices in Moorfields. In such a brawl, weight, muscle and length of arm were more important than skill or agility.

Screaming in triumph, Buckingham ran Shrewsbury through in the chest, driving the blade up into the right shoulder. The Earl dropped his sword and fell to the ground. The Duke tugged his sword free.

Holmes and Talbot were evenly matched, giving each other blow for blow, so Buckingham swung to his right to aid Jenkins, who was hard pressed by Howard. Howard saw the danger. Snarling, he flicked away the Duke's blade, putting him off balance and causing him to lurch towards Jenkins. The latter, his sword arm impeded by Buckingham, tried to recover. But he was too late. In a fluid, unexpectedly graceful movement, Howard switched his attack from the Duke and drove his blade into Jenkin's left side. The young soldier cried out and fell.

The duel was over as abruptly as it had begun. The bystanders rushed forward, shouting. The four remaining swordsmen stood suddenly still, their blades hanging towards the ground; they were open-mouthed, red-faced, panting like bellows; their expressions were confused and embarrassed, as if they had been unexpectedly caught out in an act of folly.

One man, a physician perhaps, knelt beside Shrewsbury and felt for his pulse. Blood was pumping on to the grass. The Earl made a feeble attempt to stand, his left arm flailing for purchase on the ground; one of his servants pressed him back down and tore off his own cloak to cover his master.

Jenkins lay silent and unmoving. Mr Veal was bending over him and shaking his head at a question from Buckingham. 'Dead, Your Grace,' I heard him say. 'The poor brave fellow.'

'Oh God's blood,' Buckingham said, mopping the sweat from his scalp with his sleeve.

'And now?' Veal said, in a lower voice I could hardly catch.

'Dog and bitch . . .' said the Duke.

That was what it sounded like, but as the words were fainter and more muffled than before, I wasn't at all sure I had heard him accurately. He might have been saying 'something which . . .' or 'the wound needs a stitch' or a dozen other phrases. He was still speaking, but I could no longer hear any of the words, only see his lips moving, and his arm gesturing to the two men lying on the ground with the blood soaking into their shirts.

In a moment or two, both parties would be returning to the boats. It was time for me to leave. I retreated through the spinney and made the best speed I could, running and walking, down to the lane. The tide was high, and it was still light, so with luck Wanswell would be waiting at the alehouse. I glanced towards the river, where the boats were moored alongside the Barn Elms stairs.

To my horror, one of Buckingham's boatmen was pointing in my direction. Ignoring the stitch in my side, I pushed myself to walk faster, praying that the boatmen would take me for a passing farmworker.

The alehouse by the landing place was crowded with men who made their living on and from the river. Several of them turned to scowl at me as I blundered into the smoke-filled, low-ceilinged room. Wanswell was one of the men drinking at the long table by the window.

'Come–we must go,' I said.

He raised his head. 'Must we, master?' He appealed to the company at large. 'Must we, boys?'

'No,' someone said loudly. 'You're as free a man as any in London. Have a drink instead. Let's all have a drink.'

His fellows agreed with a clatter of mugs and bottles on the table.

I brought my head down to the level of Wanswell's. 'Another five shillings if we go now,' I said pleasantly. 'Or I start walking to Putney, and you lose your return fare as well as your shilling-an-hour charge for waiting.'

He accepted the offer, though for pride's sake he took his time finishing his ale. I led the way outside, with the waterman staggering behind me. The delay had cost me five minutes, and that was too much. Roger Durrell, Mr Veal's servant, was pounding down the lane towards the alehouse. Despite his bulk, he was capable of a surprising turn of speed. When he saw me, he stopped thirty yards away, his hand dropping to the hilt of his old cavalry sword.

'God's arse, if it ain't Marwood,' he said. He had a sonorous, phlegm-filled voice. 'That will interest Mr Veal. So those web-footed watermen were right after all. You come along with me, sir, eh?'

Wanswell staggered to my side. 'Who you calling web-footed?'

'Save your breath, numbskull.'

'Me? A numbskull? I'll rip your guts out for that, you fat bag of wind.'

Durrell looked at the small squat man and burst out laughing. 'Quite the little game-cock, ain't you?'

Wanswell held his gaze for a moment. Then he spat, shrugged and retreated to the alehouse, abandoning me to my fate.

Durrell advanced slowly towards me. I backed away along the path to the river, with a half-baked idea in my head that I might leap into a boat and escape him that way.

The alehouse door opened again, and Wanswell returned. He was carrying a staff shod with iron. Behind him came six or seven of his fellows. One of them had an axe over his shoulder. Another had a bill-hook with which he was slashing the air before him.

'That's him,' Wanswell said, shaking his staff at Durrell. 'That's the poxy windfucker. He's the one calling us web-footed fools. Fat whoreson.'

The watermen advanced towards him in a solid, menacing phalanx. Durrell ripped out his sword. He stood there irresolutely. Then he turned tail and walked rapidly back the way he had come.

The clock over the guardhouse stairs struck five.

When Mr Undersecretary Williamson had dismissed his clerk Marwood, he allowed himself a moment to consider what he had learned, and the most advantageous way to present it to my Lord Arlington. Then he rose from his chair, put on his cloak and walked through Scotland Yard into Whitehall itself. Rain drifted from a dark sky heavy with clouds. Twilight was creeping through the palace. He made his way to Lord Arlington's office overlooking the Privy Garden and requested the honour of an interview with his lordship.

The clerk returned almost immediately and ushered him into the Secretary's presence. The curtains were drawn and the candles lit. Arlington acknowledged Williamson's greeting with a stately inclination of his head; he had spent four years representing the King in Spain, and he had brought back with him the manners of the Spanish court, as well as its language.

'There's news?' he demanded.

'Yes, my lord. I had a witness to the whole affair.'

'What happened?'

'They met in a close at Barn Elms. It did not turn out as we might have wished. Buckingham wounded my Lord Shrewsbury.'

'Mortally?'

'We don't know yet. The blade went into the right side of his chest and came out at the shoulder. He fell to the ground. There was a good deal of blood. Apparently he was still conscious, but unable to stand.'

'It's most unfortunate,' Arlington said. 'I must tell the King at once.' But he stayed in his chair, staring at the fire and showing no apparent signs of urgency. 'I thought that Talbot and Howard would take care of matters, I really did. They hate Buckingham enough. Was anyone else hurt? Or killed?'

'Jenkins. Once my lord was down, the Duke got in the way of Jenkins' sword arm, and that's when Howard ran him through.' Williamson pursed his lips. 'He's dead.'

Arlington considered the information.

Williamson waited, accustomed to his superior's silences and knowing better than to interrupt. The Secretary always wore a narrow strip of black plaster across his nose, which Williamson privately thought a ridiculous affectation. The plaster was supposed to cover the scar of a wound sustained when Arlington had fought for the King in one of the early battles of the Civil War. People said its only purpose was to remind the world of his loyalty to the crown in the late wars. But they didn't say it to his face.

'It's a great misfortune.' Arlington frowned and then brightened. 'Though of course there is a silver lining: we have a dead man, after all, and Shrewsbury wounded, if not worse: it cannot bode well for the four that survived unharmed. They must go into hiding, even flee the country.'

'It depends on how the King responds,' Williamson said.

'Indeed.'

'My lord, you know as well as I do that the King needs Buckingham's services at present. He can't manage Parliament without him.'

'But he can't ignore what's happened, either. Such a flagrant breaking of the law. It must be manslaughter at the very least, with Buckingham at the heart of it, even if

he did not deal the fatal blow himself. Who was your witness, by the way? We may need his testimony.'

'My clerk Marwood.'

Arlington met Williamson's eyes. 'Ah. I know the name.'

'I regret to say that one of Buckingham's creatures saw him in the neighbourhood. A broken-down trooper from Cromwell's horse. The rogue recognized him and tried to detain him. Marwood gave him the slip, but the fact he was there will get back to the Duke.'

'That's a pity. Do you trust him? Marwood, I mean.'

'I believe so, my lord. He's served us well in the past. He's a careful man, and he knows the value of his place with me. His father was a Fifth Monarchist, but he himself has none of that dangerous nonsense about him.' Williamson hesitated. 'The King has employed him too, once or twice, through Mr Chiffinch, which I cannot say I like, though the King was much pleased with Marwood's service. He gave him the clerkship of the Board of Red Cloth as a reward.'

Arlington stared up at the fresco on the ceiling. It showed the Banquet of the Gods, with Jupiter bearing a marked resemblance

to King Charles II. 'I think you're probably right about Buckingham—in the next week or two, there will be a great deal of fuss and then a royal pardon, at least for him. The King opens Parliament on the sixth of February, so he needs the Duke in harness by then. He has to be, if he is to carry out his promise and persuade the Commons to grant the King the money he needs for the navy.'

'If . . .' said Williamson.

Arlington tapped his fingertips on the table before him, as if playing a flourish of notes on the keyboard of a clavichord. Probably a jig, Williamson thought sourly. The Secretary had a vulgar taste for them. Williamson himself sneered at jigs. His own tastes were more sophisticated. He loved the work of the new French and Italian composers, and particularly the unfairly beautiful harmonies of papist choral music.

'Exactly,' his lordship said at last. 'You see the situation as I do.'

He smiled. Williamson could not avoid smiling back. The Undersecretary distrusted charm above all things—in the last few years, its dangers had been amply demonstrated by the King himself, who could have charmed the angels out of heaven if he had set his mind to it, and then handed them in chains to the Devil if the Devil had been willing to pay the right price and keep his mouth shut about the transaction.

'In time Buckingham will damn himself in the King's eyes,' Arlington went on. 'He's a firecracker, dangerous when he catches a spark because you can never tell which way he will jump. But give him a steady job of work to do and he will soon show his want of application, his inability to match deeds to word. He can no more manage the House of Commons for the King than my daughter could. In the meantime, though, we have another difficulty, don't we?'

Williamson said nothing. Arlington was always seeing difficulties, and for once he had no idea which one his lordship meant.

Arlington lowered his voice. 'My Lord Shrewsbury has been complaisant about his cuckold's horns for nearly two years. Her ladyship and Buckingham have let the world know of their passion for one another, so Shrewsbury must have known about it from the first. Which means that Buckingham must be wondering, why now, why after all this time should my lord have challenged him? And in the French style, too, with three against three, which makes it so likely that a great deal of blood will be spilt. And with Talbot as one of his seconds, who is one of the Duke's greatest enemies not just in Parliament but in the whole of London. And my supporter.'

'You think, my lord, His Grace may suspect that . . .'

'That we had a hand in it,' Arlington said. 'Yes. Not that it was a bad idea in itself.'

He and Williamson had persuaded Talbot to work on the cuckold's sense of grievance and issue the challenge to the Duke. If they had fought one against one, the smaller, older Shrewsbury would have been at a disadvantage against Buckingham. But a duel in the French style had offered the Earl a chance to tilt the odds in his favour. Obviously it had been a risky business from the outset but, had it come off, the rewards would have been immense. Arlington's most powerful political rival would have been either disgraced or dead, and through a tragic train of circumstances that had no apparent connection to Arlington.

'I always had my doubts that the plan would work,' he continued. 'Still . . .'

Williamson clamped his lips together. The scheme had been Arlington's from start to finish.

'Buckingham already has no reason to like us,' the Secretary went on. 'This will make him hate us. And, if I'm any judge of

47

character, it will also make him want to make fools of us.' His fingers danced on the table; another damned jig, no doubt. 'He will want his revenge. But how will he set about it?'

CHAPTER THREE

A Friend from the Country
Friday, 17–Sunday, 19 January 1668
Master kicks Ferrus awake. He has fallen asleep over his empty bowl. The bowl slipped from his hands. It's upside down on the flagstones.

Ferrus was sitting on the floor, leaning against the wall by the door to the yard. The toe of Master's boot lands just above Ferrus's elbow. The impact pushes him over. He lies on the threshold, covering his face with his hands. He curls himself into a ball.

Hedgepig, he thinks. He likes hedgepigs. Sometimes they come into the yard from the park, hoping for kitchen scraps. When Windy tried to kill one, the hedgepig rolled itself into a bundle of spikes and the spikes hurt Windy's nose. In a while, Windy grew bored and left the hedgepig alone. Time

49

passed. The hedgepig uncurled and crept away.

Another kick lands, this one on Ferrus's thigh. He cries out, because Master likes that, but the pain is bearable.

Time passes.

Ferrus is hedgepig.

At ten o'clock in the morning on Friday, Mistress Hakesby was at Burton's the instrument-maker's shop at the sign of the Bear's Head, which was a few doors along from the Devil Tavern in Fleet Street. She was attended by her maid, a thirteen-year-old girl named Jane Ash, who was more of a hindrance than a help. But Mr Hakesby did not think it proper for his wife to go about town by herself, and Jane was the price that Cat had to pay for a degree of independence.

Mr Burton opened the box with a flourish. 'There, mistress,' he said with the air of a man giving a treat to a child, 'this is what your husband ordered. Imported especially from France.'

Cat lifted the brass instrument from the box. A magnetic compass was set within the semicircular arc, which was marked in degrees. Below it was an alidade capable of rotation around the semicircle. It was

50

designed for the precise measurement of angles. She carried it to the doorway, where the light was better. She turned it over in her hands.

'The French call it a graphometer,' Mr Burton said. 'But I prefer the good old English term of semicircle. Be that as it may, tell Mr Hakesby that he will find it improves the accuracy of his surveys a thousandfold. It may seem expensive but, at times like these, with so much building going on, so many measurements to be taken, he will find it a most valuable investment. One can do nothing without accurate angles.'

'No,' said Cat.

'What?'

'This won't do, Mr Burton.'

'Mistress Hakesby, I think we must let your husband be the best judge of that, and I'm quite sure he will agree with me —'

'I said it won't do.' Cat came back into the shop and laid the graphometer on the counter. 'Look, the alidade does not rotate as cleanly as it should. I'm not satisfied with the engraving of the degrees either. The workmanship is poor.'

Mr Burton drew himself to his full height. He towered a good nine inches above Cat. 'I can assure you that —'

'I have seen better elsewhere, thank you. I wish you had sent to Antwerp for it, sir. Their instruments are infinitely superior.'

'I–I shall write to Mr Hakesby about this. Or call on him. I think you —'

'By all means, Mr Burton. Goodbye.'

'Won't master mind?' Jane said timidly when they were outside again. 'If Mr Burton goes to him and —'

'Your master will agree with me,' Cat said sharply. She glanced at Jane's frightened face and went on more gently. 'The instrument is not what it should be. He will know that better than I do.'

'Catherine!' A woman called. 'Catherine Lovett!'

Startled, Cat swung round. A hackney coach was drawn up by the line of posts that kept those on foot apart from the traffic on the roadway. A woman had pulled aside the leather curtain and was smiling tentatively at Cat.

'It is Catherine Lovett, isn't it?'

'It was,' Cat said, her voice wary. 'I'm Catherine Hakesby now.'

The woman was well dressed, indeed a little overdressed, though not in the height of fashion. She was very young, with plump, pink cheeks and small eyes. Something about the eager face was half-familiar.

52

'Forgive me, I —'

'You don't know me?' The woman looked mortified for a moment, but then the expression was smoothed away and the eagerness returned. 'We've all changed, but you not so much as I perhaps. Shall I give you a clue?' She beckoned Cat closer. 'Cast your mind back ten years or so,' she whispered. 'Elizabeth.' She hesitated. 'Elizabeth from Whitehall. We used to play together.'

It was her grandfather's long, straight nose that gave Cat the clue she needed, that and the wide mouth. 'Elizabeth,' she said slowly, recognition dawning. 'Elizabeth Cromwell.'

'You were so kind,' Elizabeth said. 'Those endless games of shuttlecock. And you would tell me stories, and build me houses made of twigs.'

'Yes,' Cat said. 'I remember. Where — ?'

'Am I living now? We're down in Hampshire, at Hursley, my father's house. But he can't be with us there . . .' Elizabeth broke off. The eagerness and the smiles had vanished. She looked unhappy. Then: 'And you, too. I–I was sorry to hear about your father's death, and your uncle's.' She grimaced. 'So many changes, and not all for the better. But you're married, then–how wonderful that must be. Hakesby, did you say? Do you live in London?'

'Yes. Mr Hakesby's a surveyor. He designs and builds houses. Forgive me, but he's waiting and I should go.'

'But I can't lose sight of my old playmate.' Elizabeth pouted, summoning up the ghost of the child she had once been. 'Not now, when I've just found you again. Where do you lodge? We can take you there.'

'Henrietta Street by Covent Garden,' Cat said. 'I'll be there faster if I walk.' She could see another young woman in the hackney and an older man. 'Besides, you won't have room for both of us.'

Elizabeth looked disconcerted. 'But I cannot let you go like this. You must dine with us, and Mr Hakesby too. I'm staying at my godmother's by Hatton Garden. You will, won't you?'

'It's kind of you but —'

'I shall write to you at the sign of the Rose this very afternoon, and name a day. I want to meet your husband. I'm sure he's a most admirable gentleman.'

Cat kept a smile on her face, but privately she writhed with embarrassment. 'I can't promise that we shall be able to come. He has not been well, and he does not go out a great deal, except in the way of business.'

Without warning, Elizabeth lunged forward, steadying herself by holding the strap

54

that retained the curtain. She tried to plant a kiss on Cat's cheek. Instead she pushed the brim of her hat into Cat's eye. Cat recoiled with a cry of mingled pain and surprise.

'I'm so sorry,' Elizabeth said. 'I was always so clumsy. Pray forgive me.'

'It's nothing,' she said, aware her eye was watering.

The younger woman looked so miserable that Cat could not be cross with her. She remembered the clumsiness well enough: Elizabeth had been a child who was always spilling her milk and tripping over her skirts. She still was not much more than a child. She was younger than Cat, and could be no more than seventeen or eighteen.

'And you'll dine with us?' Elizabeth said, her cheeks pinker than ever. 'I haven't put you off with my blundering? Catherine, please say you will.'

'Yes, if you wish it,' Cat said, moved by pity. 'With pleasure.'

'Catty. Do you remember? I called you Catty and you called me Betty.'

'Cromwell?' Hakesby said, frowning. 'Is this a piece of drollery?'

In his irritation, he spoke more loudly than usual, and Brennan the draughtsman

55

looked up from his stool on the other side of the Drawing Office.

'No, sir,' Cat said quietly, trying to control her irritation. 'Elizabeth Cromwell.'

'Really? Were you not aware that her highness the Protectoress died three years ago?' At times, when his illness was upon him, Hakesby affected a bitter, satirical tone. 'Or do you mean her daughter Elizabeth, my Lady Claypole? She's been dead for even longer. What nonsense is —'

'I mean Oliver's granddaughter, sir. The eldest child of Richard, the last Protector. I used to play with her as a child.'

Hakesby stared at his wife, with his mouth open. His nose was red and it had a drop of moisture on the end. He was suffering from a cold, which made worse a temper that was increasingly uncertain at the best of times. It was his illness that made him unpredictable and often cross; he had not always been like this. It was unfortunate that he was not only irritable this morning but relatively vigorous as well. He said: 'You . . . you knew the Protector and his family?'

'My father was much in Oliver's company, and he knew Richard, too, though he was more friendly with Henry, Richard's brother. Sometimes my father would take me to Whitehall with him.'

When Cat thought of it, which was rarely, her memories of those days seemed to belong to someone else. It seemed unreal to her, the young wife of an elderly surveyor, that she had once been an heiress, and that her parents had been intimate with the Cromwells. Her father had been one of the wealthiest stonemasons in London, and her mother had been allied to the Eyres, substantial Suffolk gentry. The Lovetts and the Eyres had been staunch supporters of Parliament in the wars against the King, and later of the Cromwells. Thomas Lovett had been one of the regicides who had signed the death warrant of Charles I.

'If the truth be told, I wish Oliver were still alive,' Hakesby muttered.

'Hush, sir.'

'I know the King is back,' Hakesby said, 'and naturally we are his loyal subjects. But it was better in the old days, when we were ruled by godly men, and England held its head up high among the nations of Europe. All that was Oliver's doing.'

'The times have changed, sir. Oliver is gone, and so is his son. And Mistress Elizabeth is eager to resume her acquaintance with me.'

'Well, why not?' Hakesby straightened in his chair.

57

'She says she will ask us to dine with her at her godmother's house in Hatton Garden. She is staying there for a while.'

Hakesby wiped the drop from his nose with the sleeve of his shirt. 'We shall accept. I shall be honoured to dine with her.'

'I'm not sure it would be wise. Though the Protector's family are allowed to live peacefully in England, it would not be sensible for you to be seen with them. They are not encouraged to show themselves in London.'

'Who are you to tell me what's wise?' Hakesby scowled at her. 'Have you forgotten I'm your husband, and the duty you owe to me?'

'No, sir. I never forget that.'

There was a silence between them. Cat heard Brennan's pen scratching on the paper, as he indited a list of the scaffolding and other timber that would be required for the next stage of the Dragon Yard commission, which was the major project they had in hand at present. The draughtsman could hardly have avoided hearing Hakesby's side of the conversation, and probably some of hers.

Hakesby closed his eyes. Waves of weariness often swept over him without warning. Cat waited, hoping he would doze off.

But his eyes snapped open. 'She knows where to find us? Here at the sign of the Rose?'

'Mistress Cromwell?'

'Who else could I mean?'

'Yes, sir, she does know where to find us.' *Here at the sign of the Rose.*

The eyes closed again, and soon Hakesby's breathing had slowed and steadied. His mouth fell open again. He began to snore.

'What about the chimney stacks, mistress?' Brennan asked in a low voice. 'Should we order extra props for the inner frames?'

Cat said absently, 'As you think best.'

She still stood beside her husband's chair, though there were a dozen tasks waiting to be done. Elizabeth Cromwell had known where to find them because Cat had told her: in Henrietta Street by Covent Garden. But how had Elizabeth known that they were living in the house at the sign of the Rose?

'Have you heard the news?' Brennan said when he arrived at the Drawing Office on Saturday morning. 'There was a terrible duel at Barn Elms on Thursday. The whole town is talking about it.'

'Who was fighting?' Cat asked.

'My Lord Shrewsbury and the Duke of

Buckingham.' He grinned, baring his teeth, which made him look even more like a moulting fox than usual. 'Not hard to find the reason.'

'What? What reason?' Hakesby said, cupping his ear, though there was nothing wrong with his hearing. 'Speak up, man.'

'Why, master, the whole world knows that my lady sees more of the Duke than her own husband. By night as well as day, if you take my meaning.'

'The court has become a cesspit of sin,' Hakesby said. 'These nobles are like alley cats on heat, for all their finery. This would never have been allowed to happen under Oliver.'

'Hush, sir,' Cat said quietly. Her encounter with Elizabeth Cromwell yesterday had opened the floodgates of her husband's memory, and released a great tide of nostalgia for the Commonwealth and Cromwell.

'But it's true. And sooner or later the devil will give them their due.'

'It wasn't just them that fought, sir,' Brennan said, still bursting with news. 'They each had two gentlemen to support them. One of them was killed, man called Jenkins, and Lord Shrewsbury lies badly wounded and like to die. And the others are in hiding, including the Duke.'

'In my opinion —'

Fortunately there came a knock at the door, which stopped Hakesby in mid-flow. It was the porter's boy with two letters in his hand. Hakesby took them both and examined them.

'Ah–this is from Dr Wren in Oxford; I wonder what he wants.' He glanced at the other and looked up at Cat. 'And this is for you. Not another wretched bill?'

She took the letter from him. He unfolded Wren's.

'How interesting,' he burst out. 'Indeed, how gratifying. He writes that Mr Howard has offered the Royal Society a plot of land in the garden at Arundel House. It's for them to build a house for their meetings and experiments, with laboratories and an observatory and so forth. Nothing's settled yet, but Dr Wren wishes to make a preliminary design. He wonders if I would be willing to assist him.'

'Nothing's settled?' Cat said. 'So it may not go ahead?'

Hakesby dismissed her question with a wave of his hand. 'What a challenge a building like that would be. Our reputation in the world would rise if we were seen to be engaged in it.' He glanced down at the letter. 'To begin with, Wren asks if I would be

61

able to survey the land for him, and send him a detailed plan of the plot. If I agree, he will send to Mr Howard for a letter of authorization.'

'Is there money promised for the scheme? Or even for the survey?'

'Money won't be a difficulty.'

'Money *is* a difficulty, sir.' Cat kept their accounts and knew to a farthing what was due and what was owed. 'We cannot afford to work for free.'

Her husband frowned. 'No doubt there will be a subscription for the building in due course. The Society's members will contribute generously, and probably the King himself.'

Cat thought it unlikely. Money for new projects was always a problem, particularly in a city where half the buildings were in ruins and everyone was trying to rebuild. Add to that a shortage of materials and skilled craftsmen, and the odds against the Arundel House scheme seemed even worse.

'It is to be called Solomon's House,' Hakesby said. 'How fitting.'

'Why?'

'Do you not know Bacon's *New Atlantis*?' Hakesby was growing excited. 'He envisaged a great college dedicated to the expansion of our knowledge, and the foundation of the Royal Society was conceived as a great step towards it. But note this'–here he waved his finger at her–'Bacon called it Solomon's House because King Solomon is the wisest man in the Bible. The Royal Society's discoveries are worth nothing if they do not bring wisdom as well as knowledge.'

Cat turned away to open her own letter. She was quietly furious. Their accounts were in better shape than they had been before her marriage, but Hakesby had accumulated a load of debt beforehand, and the interest on this was a steady drain on their income, which was already under threat because of his declining health. All in all, it would be folly for Hakesby's Drawing Office to undertake risky, speculative work without payment. Where was the wisdom in that? She broke the seal and unfolded the paper.

'Who's your letter from?' Hakesby demanded. 'Is it the coal merchant again? Come, stand by me so I can see.'

As Cat had feared, the letter was from Elizabeth Cromwell. Writing in a round, clumsy hand, Elizabeth began by blessing God for reuniting her with the bosom friend of her youth and went on to make several observations about the workings of God's providence. At last she moved on to her purpose: her godmother, Mistress Dalton, had asked her to send a most pressing invitation to Mistress Hakesby and her husband. Would they possibly be free to dine with them tomorrow, on this very Sunday? Elizabeth knew that it was short notice, she went on, but nothing could give her more pleasure than seeing them as soon as possible. She ended by sending her respectful salutations to Mr Hakesby and her fondest love to Cat.

'It's from Mistress Cromwell, sir.'

'Really?' Hakesby said. 'What a day this is–letters from Dr Wren and Mistress Cromwell by the same post. When are we to dine there?'

'She asks us for tomorrow, sir. But it is not entirely convenient, because —'

'Nonsense, my dear. Let me see the letter.' He almost snatched it from her hand. He read it quickly. In an access of good humour, he beamed at Cat. 'How very civil. "Fondest love", eh? You shall write to her at once, and say that nothing would be more agreeable than to dine with them. Then look out my best suit and send for the barber directly. I must have a shave.'

When the letter had been sent to Elizabeth Cromwell, and Hakesby's suit sent downstairs to be cleaned of food stains, and the

64

barber had come at last, Cat was able to return to work. She discussed and finalized the Dragon Yard timber order with Brennan. After that, she had a great deal of copying to do, for both the foreman of the builders and the future owner required sets of plans of one of the larger houses in Dragon Yard; it was to have a number of modifications, including a music room at the back and a walkway on the leads of the roof.

The copying was close, mechanical work. Usually Cat enjoyed it, for there was pleasure in seeing the lines spreading across the paper, following the patterns that she and Hakesby had created: the lines that would soon be fixed for generations in brick and stone, timber and tile. Copying also left room for her mind to roam free, resolving current problems or, best of all, dreaming of fantastical designs for buildings that she would never see built.

Not this morning, however. Elizabeth Cromwell intruded into Cat's thoughts; Elizabeth with her plump cheeks and slit-like eyes, her abrupt, uncontrolled movements and her overeager manner. As a child, she had been like an overgrown puppy, Cat thought, unschooled in manners and desperate to be loved. She was still like that as a young woman. She had been sly as a child, and perhaps that too was unchanged.

Was she also lonely? She had greeted Cat as if they had been the closest of friends; but Cat, who was several years older, had not played with her at Whitehall more than half a dozen times, spread out over two or three years. Elizabeth had been lonely then. Her mother had exercised little direct control over her. Her father had been much occupied and often absent, especially when he had succeeded his father as Lord Protector. For much of the time Elizabeth had been left in the care of servants.

Cat remembered playing shuttlecock in the big garden by the Cockpit, and Elizabeth tripping over a low hedge and wailing for her maid; and, on another occasion, her losing a match and throwing her racket on the ground and stamping on it.

The Cockpit lodging, where Elizabeth had lived, was separated from the main palace of Whitehall by the road to Westminster. But on one occasion the pair of them had bowled a hoop above the gateway that bridged the road and down the Privy Gallery towards the door leading to the former royal apartments. Outraged servants had driven them back into their private quarters. Elizabeth had blamed Cat for that episode, though she herself had been the instigator, and Cat had been the one who received the whipping.

Cat had never seen the inside of the royal apartments, where Oliver had lived in state until his death, a king in all but name. His son Richard, Elizabeth's father, had moved into the apartments in his turn when he became Lord Protector; but his reign had lasted less than nine months. Elizabeth had once whispered to her that her grandfather liked to have pictures of naked ladies in his bedroom, pictures that had once belonged to the King whose head they had chopped off in front of the Banqueting House.

For a while, the new Protector's eldest daughter had been effectively a princess of England, a desirable match for any man. But what was she these days?

After the Restoration, Oliver's bones had been dug up from his grave. His head had been impaled on a spike above Westminster Hall, where it was thickly smeared with bird shit and twitched at the mercy of every breath of wind, a decaying reminder of the blasphemy of murdering a king anointed by God. Charles II had been merciful to Oliver's family. Richard, no longer Lord Protector, had proclaimed his loyalty to the crown and gone into voluntary exile. His wife and children were rarely seen in public.

They were not encouraged to show themselves in London. The name of Cromwell was still powerful: a reminder of past glories, and a rallying point for those with present grievances.

Cat did not want to go to dinner with Elizabeth Cromwell and her godmother, for it could do her no good. She did not want to introduce her ailing, elderly husband to a young woman whose father and grandfather had ruled England. If she was brutally honest with herself, she was ashamed of Simon Hakesby, who had given her his name, his house and his occupation; and she was even more ashamed of herself for being ashamed.

And then there was that other matter, the other reason why she did not want to go to the house near Hatton Garden: how was it that Elizabeth in her hackney had been waiting in Fleet Street outside the instrument makers? Above all, how had she known that Cat lived at the sign of the Rose?

She wished she could discuss this last matter with someone. Neither her husband nor Brennan would do, for different reasons. Out of the blue, she wondered what James Marwood would say if she were to tell him about it.

Which was of course impossible.

Mr Hakesby was painfully anxious that they should create the right impression on their hosts. He had to be dissuaded from hiring a private coach from the livery stable at the Mitre. Before he could change his mind, Cat sent the porter's boy for a hackney, which would cost a fraction of the price.

She had never seen her husband in such a state, and it surprised her. He was not a man who was usually impressed by wealth or birth. But for him, it seemed, a Cromwell was different. To dine with a young lady who was Lord Protector Richard Cromwell's daughter, whom the great Oliver himself had no doubt dandled upon his knee: well, that would indeed be a notable encounter.

They made good time—it was a crisp, cold day, and the ground was hard. Hatton Garden itself was a street of modern houses, but the coach set them down at the gateway of a much older building to the east of it. A porter opened the gate to their knock and admitted them to a paved courtyard beyond. There was a waterless fountain in the middle, and beyond it a shabby house with a roof of sagging tiles speckled with moss.

A few yards in front of them, an elderly man was picking his way towards the door of the main house. He was leaning on the arm of a manservant and tapping the ground with a stick he held in his other hand. He turned his head at the sound of the Hakesbys' footsteps. He was wearing a large felt hat and a pair of glasses set with thick green glass.

'Who's that?'

'The guests, master,' said the servant holding his arm.

'Good day, sir,' said Hakesby, who was also leaning on a stick. 'My name is Hakesby.' He peered at the man and then said, enunciating the words very clearly in case the man was deaf as well as blind or at least partially sighted, 'And this is my wife.'

'Your servant, sir,' Cat said.

The man bent his head. 'Ah yes—my cousin told me you were dining with us. John Cranmore, sir, at your service.' The voice was cultivated but hoarse, as if Cranmore were on the verge of losing his voice. Added to this, his beard and moustache, which he wore in the style favoured by the late king, needed trimming; stray hairs trailed over his lips and increased the difficulty of understanding what he was saying. 'Pray go ahead of me. I proceed at a snail's pace, and the

70

weather's too cold for lingering.'

The Hakesbys made their way to the door. It opened before they reached it, and another servant led them into a hall with tall pointed windows and blackened roof timbers high above their heads. The air was chilly, despite the small fire of logs that burned in an enormous grate. He took their cloaks and ushered them to a doorway set in the side wall of a low dais at the far end.

This led to a much warmer parlour, where Elizabeth Cromwell was reading aloud from a volume of sermons to a plainly dressed lady in middle age. Elizabeth rose as soon as they entered and, putting aside the book, came quickly to greet them.

'My dearest Catherine, how kind of you to come, and so soon.' She embraced her, which took Cat by surprise, and then turned to Hakesby, who bowed unsteadily. 'And this must be . . .'

'My husband,' Cat said. 'Mr Hakesby.'

'Madam,' he said in a voice that creaked with emotion, 'I am honoured to make your acquaintance.'

'You flatter me, sir,' Elizabeth said awkwardly, as if the making and receiving of compliments did not come naturally to her. She turned back to the older lady, who had risen to her feet. 'And this is my dear

71

godmother Mistress Dalton, whose house this is.'

The introductions were barely over when the door opened again and the servant led in the man they had met in the courtyard.

'My cousin Cranmore, up from the country to see his physicians,' said Mistress Dalton, staring at the floor.

'We have already met, madam,' Hakesby said. 'We passed one another in the courtyard.'

Mistress Dalton lowered her voice, though her words must still have been audible to Cranmore. 'He is practically blind, poor man, and to make matters worse, the light hurts his eyes most cruelly.'

'A terrible affliction,' Hakesby said loudly. 'How long have you been in this condition, sir?'

Cranmore turned his head towards the sound of Hakesby's voice. 'Too long, sir, too long. My sight began to go when I was a young man. But in these last few years it has worsened rapidly until I'm in the state you see me now.'

'Can the occulists help? Or a physician?'

'They say they can, and they take their fees. I smear my eyes with their ointments, but I've yet to notice any improvement.'

A servant led them into dinner, which was

served in the next room. The food was plain though plentiful, probably sent in from a nearby tavern. There was no wine, only water and small beer on the table.

Cat and Mr Cranmore spoke little, leaving most of the conversation to others. Hakesby's unusual vigour continued. His cheeks were ruddy, and his movements less tremulous than they had been yesterday. It was as if the excitement of the occasion, the honour of dining with the Protector's flesh and blood, had effected a miraculous cure.

Mistress Dalton and Elizabeth Cromwell were attentive to him. They asked about his work, showing a remarkable appetite for information about the Dragon Yard contract and about his collaboration with Dr Wren on the plans for a new St Paul's Cathedral to replace the one destroyed in the Fire. It was by no means certain, he told them, that the project would go ahead. There were those who argued that restoring the cathedral would be better than replacing it–far cheaper and more quickly achieved.

'It is nonsense,' Hakesby said, showering crumbs over the table. 'The old cathedral was practically ruinous even before the Fire. A new St Paul's would be the glory of London for centuries to come.'

'What a God-given talent it must be,' Elizabeth Cromwell said, 'to conjure great buildings to rise from the ashes. And to work on St Paul's itself–why, it is the very heart and soul of the City.'

'I sometimes fear I shan't see a single stone put in place in my lifetime,' Hakesby said, beaming with pleasure at the compliment and spilling sauce over his shirt cuff. 'The King doesn't agree with the Court of Aldermen, the Aldermen are at loggerheads with the Dean and Chapter, and the Bishop thinks that no one has a right to an opinion but himself. But the greatest problem of all is the want of money. A cathedral worthy of London will take tens of thousands of pounds to build.'

'Very true, sir,' Mistress Dalton said. 'But in the end is not the money always found for these great buildings? Take Whitehall, for example. I shudder to think what the Banqueting House must have cost, but somehow King James raised the money to do it.' Her lips tightened to a thin line of disapproval, and then relaxed as she went on: 'But perhaps you were not in London then, sir.'

'Indeed I was, Mistress Dalton. At the time I was apprenticed to a surveyor who did much work for Inigo Jones. I learned much at Whitehall, and from Mr Jones.'

Elizabeth, who was sitting next to him, asked, 'Did you work there again, sir?'

'Oh yes. I was much at Whitehall in your grandfather's time. And your father's.'

'Then you probably saw me as a little girl, playing some childish game, and didn't even notice me.'

'That would have been impossible, madam,' Hakesby said, looking flustered. 'I– I'm sure that even then your–your —'

'Perhaps you saw me as well, sir,' Cat said, to save her husband the embarrassment of finding the words for the compliment he obviously thought was necessary. 'As I told you, Elizabeth and I sometimes played at Whitehall together.' She shot a glance at Elizabeth. 'Bowling a hoop.'

'That palace is such a rabbit warren,' Mistress Dalton said, frowning at Mr Cranmore, as if Whitehall's architectural confusion were morally reprehensible and he were somehow to blame.

Mr Cranmore cleared his throat but said nothing.

'Did you visit Whitehall much yourself, sir?' Cat asked, feeling the poor gentleman was being ignored.

He turned his head in her direction. Within each lens of the green glasses were tiny, distorted reflections of the window

75

behind her. 'Rarely,' he said in his soft, slushy voice. He rubbed his fingertip on the table, as though trying to erase an invisible spot. Something stirred in the depths of Cat's memory. 'Indeed,' he went on after a pause, 'I rarely come to London, if I can help it.'

'Where do you live, sir?'

But Cat was too late. As she spoke, Cranmore stuffed a morsel of bread into his mouth, effectively stopping the conversation.

'I used to know the palace well,' Elizabeth said to Hakesby. 'Where else did you work there?'

He turned back to her. 'On the royal apartments before your grandfather became Lord Protector and moved into them himself; naturally he wanted alterations made. But mainly I worked on the Cockpit buildings—your grandparents lodged there a few years before.'

'Oh, I remember! I visited my grandmother there when I was still in leading strings. And later on, of course, we lived in the Cockpit ourselves for a time. How I loved the place! Catty and I played shuttlecock in the garden and ran wild in the park.' She appealed to Cat, who could not remember Elizabeth ever calling her Catty, any more than she could remember calling Elizabeth Betty. 'Did we not, my love? Do you remember?'

'Not very well,' Cat said.

'Well, I do. Happy, blessed times.' She swung back to Hakesby and put her hand on his sleeve, a gesture that made his face light up as if he had been touched by an angel. 'But there's such a strange thing. My memories of the Cockpit are dreadfully confused. The layout of the lodging changed so much in my childhood. It confuses my infant memories, for I cannot overlay them on the later ones.' She withdrew her hand. 'Am I very foolish to think of these things, sir?'

'Not in the slightest,' Hakesby said. 'It is perfectly natural to wish to–to remember those places where we have been happy. Old buildings contain the history of those who used to live in them.' He looked across the table at Cat. 'Is it not so?'

'No doubt, sir.'

'For example,' Mistress Dalton said, looking at Hakesby, 'was there not a chamber with a painted ceiling? It used to open into the passage from King Street in the old days, I think.'

'We used to play there when it was wet,' Elizabeth said. 'Do you recall it, Cat?'

Hakesby looked unhappy. 'I can't bring it to mind, Mistress.'

'If only,' Elizabeth said in a soft voice, bringing her lips closer to Hakesby's ear, 'if only . . .'

'If only what, madam?'

She smiled at him. 'If only there were plans of the Cockpit as it was then, in those days. I don't suppose by any lucky chance you have any still?'

Hakesby nodded. 'Yes, quite possibly.' He drew himself up in his chair. 'I try to make it a rule to keep copies of my plans and surveys. Sometimes one can show a design to prospective clients, or sometimes it's useful as a memorandum to remind oneself of a detail here or a detail there that might be —'

Mistress Dalton coughed. 'Elizabeth, my love, you mustn't pester Mr Hakesby. He's our guest, and I cannot allow it.'

'It is no trouble, madam,' Hakesby said. 'None in the world.' He turned back to Elizabeth. 'If it would please you, I shall see if I can lay my hand on the Cockpit survey, and the plans for the work we did for your grandfather and later for your father. Then you will be able to overlay them with your memories.'

'Oh sir,' Elizabeth said, peering at him

with her bright little eyes, 'that would be so very obliging of you.'

Mr Cranmore stirred in his chair. Cat glanced towards him. He was rubbing the invisible spot on the table again. Something shifted in her memory. She sucked in her breath sharply, aghast at the possibility that had opened up before her.

'Are you quite well, my dear?' Elizabeth murmured, leaning forward, all sympathy and smiles and narrow eyes. She lowered her voice to a whisper. 'A spasm? We women suffer so, do we not, and the gentlemen have not the slightest understanding of it.'

CHAPTER FOUR

Freshly Killed Pigeons
Saturday, 18 January–Sunday, 2 February
1668

When cook isn't looking, the scullery maids come into the kitchen yard to meet stable-boys. The boys bring the maids ribbons. The boys fondle the girls and the girls giggle. The boys put their hands up the maids' skirts and make them squeal.

Ferrus lies in Windy's kennel and waits for Master to call him. The later Master comes in the morning, the more drunk he was last night. Master sleeps in Scotland Yard. But Ferrus sleeps here, on the Cockpit side of the palace. He doesn't know why, but that is how it has always been, for ever and ever, even before Mistress Crummle came to live here.

The maids and the stableboys chatter like birds. The gentles have been fighting each other over the river. One's dead. A lord is

80

like to die of his wounds. Perhaps the King will chop off the heads of the others. It's the Duke's fault, they say: not their duke, my lord, the fat old soldier who sometimes lodges at the Cockpit: another duke.

Kill, kill, kill, Ferrus thinks, let them all kill each other.

I was much shaken by the duel. I had witnessed the killing of one man and the wounding, perhaps fatal, of another. Without the assistance of Wanswell and his fellow watermen, I might have suffered violence or worse myself. I had already seen too much violent death in my life, and I still had not become accustomed to it. I was a clerk by trade, after all, not a soldier.

Afterwards, I slept badly, and drank too much wine in the hope of numbing my senses and blurring my memory. What made it even more unsettling was my suspicion that this business wasn't over as far as I was concerned. Buckingham and his servants now had even more reason to dislike me. Jenkins was dead, and Shrewsbury wounded. Buckingham and the other three were in hiding. But that would not stop the Duke from directing his affairs and managing his hatreds.

On Saturday afternoon, Mr Williamson

called me to his private room in Scotland Yard. He told me that, despite his wound, my Lord Shrewsbury was to be moved from the house in Chelsea where he had been since the duel.

'They're taking him to Arundel House,' he said. 'A risky business–I would have thought that jolting him about could reopen the wound. Presumably they'll go most of the way by river, and pray the weather is kind. His people must think he will be safer among his kin. The Howards look after their own. And of course they're all papists together.'

Arundel House was between the Strand and the river, a stone's throw from my own lodging at the Savoy. It was another rambling mansion, and its best days were long since gone. Many of these riverside palaces were being rebuilt or sold piecemeal for redevelopment. No doubt Arundel House would go the way of the others, probably sooner rather than later. I had heard that the Howards had offered part of the garden to the Royal Society, for them to build their headquarters. Perhaps that would be the start of it.

'They say my lord is mending well,' Williamson went on. 'Which is why I want you to go there tomorrow after dinner, once he's

82

settled into his new quarters. They will be expecting you. You will give him a letter from Lord Arlington–merely a few words to wish him well; a courtesy.'

'But if the Duke of Buckingham is having Arundel House watched,' I said, 'would it be wiser to send someone who would not be recognized?'

Williamson gave me a hard stare. 'If I want your advice, Marwood, I'll ask for it. While you're there, see how my lord does. I want your opinion of his condition.'

'I'm no physician, sir. I —'

'I'm aware of that. But you're not altogether stupid either. And there's something else you can do. Lord Arlington has a message for Lord Shrewsbury as well, and he doesn't want it committed to paper. If you get the opportunity for a private word, tell him that Lord Arlington stands in his debt, and that he promises the Duke will pay dearly for what he has done. But be discreet in all things, and urge my lord to be the same. If you can't find the opportunity to pass on the message without being heard, leave it.' He gave me another stare. 'But I am sure you will contrive it somehow.'

He dismissed me, but as I was leaving he called me back.

'Have you heard the rumour about my Lady Shrewsbury?'

I shook my head.

'They say she was at the duel herself. She was disguised as a page boy and stood among the Duke's servants. And afterwards she lay with him. He was still wearing his shirt. It was stained with her poor husband's blood.'

'But I saw no page boy there, sir. Nor any blood on the Duke's shirt.'

Williamson moistened his lips. 'What a pity. But it's a useful story to have about town, nevertheless.'

After dinner on Sunday, I walked across from my lodging in the Savoy and presented myself at Arundel House. I gave my name at the gate, where there were two servants dressed in the Howard livery and armed with swords; Lord Shrewsbury's hosts were taking precautions.

The entrance courtyard was large but unimpressive. It was lined with old buildings, many of which were unexpectedly humble. There was also an ancient hall of crumbling stone, with a ramshackle lantern on its roof. A manservant took me across the court to a tall range of buildings west of the hall, where the family had its apartments.

Here the grandeur was more in evidence. The place was crowded, for like all great people the Howards surrounded themselves with retainers, dependants and relations as a mark of their importance. I was led upstairs to a chamber overlooking the garden and the river beyond. It was empty. The walls were hung with tapestries. Halfway down one of the longer sides, a small coal fire burned sullenly in a large and elaborately carved marble fireplace. It made little difference, for the air was cold and damp.

The servant asked me to wait while he enquired if his lordship was well enough to see me. I stood by one of the windows. The garden was strewn with statuary in poor repair. To the right, a long gallery stretched down to the river, with a battlemented viewing platform at the end. The trees and bushes swayed in a stiff easterly breeze. Beyond the garden lay the bleak prospect of the Thames in winter at low tide. The sky, the water and the mud were shades of grey.

I turned to face the room. An oak armchair with a high back stood facing the hearth. As I approached it, hoping to warm my hands, I discovered that I was not after all alone. A hand was resting on the arm of the chair. At the sound of my footsteps, a periwigged head appeared, and beneath it was a familiar face.

'Marwood,' Mr Chiffinch said. 'I might have known.'

I bowed, thinking furiously as I did so. William Chiffinch was the Keeper of the King's Private Closet, and a man whom the King employed about his most secret business. He and I knew each other better than either of us liked, for once or twice it had pleased the King to employ me; Chiffinch had acted as the middleman for such commissions. Mr Williamson and Mr Chiffinch disliked each other, and they both particularly disliked the fact that they were occasionally obliged to share my services.

'What are you doing here?'

'Mr Williamson sent me to enquire after my lord's health. To see how he did after his journey here.'

Chiffinch rubbed his lips, which were stained a reddish purple with the wine he had taken at dinner. 'I see.'

His head vanished abruptly. I heard him sigh. I stood closer to the fire, taking care not to block its heat from him.

'The master has a word with the servant,' Chiffinch said suddenly, 'the servant sends the boy.'

I said nothing. His meaning was clear enough: Lord Arlington had ordered Williamson to send a message to Shrewsbury, and Williamson had given me the task.

'In this case,' Chiffinch went on, staring at me, 'the master has a most particular interest in my lord's health, does he not? Since he was responsible for this . . . this absurd revelry in the first place.'

I had thought from the first that there was more to this business than Williamson had seen fit to tell me. Now I knew for certain. Chiffinch had overestimated my knowledge of the matter. He had as good as told me that Arlington was behind the duel. Once I knew that, the rest fell into place: Lady Shrewsbury's infidelity was merely the pretext for this; Arlington and his ally Talbot had encouraged the duel in the hope of killing Buckingham, their principal political enemy, or at least disgracing him and undermining his power.

If Chiffinch knew this, then the King must as well. He had probably sent Chiffinch here to assess not only Shrewsbury's health but his state of mind. It was a delicate matter. The King needed the services of both Arlington and Buckingham to get his business through Parliament.

A door opened at the far end of the room, and a manservant appeared. He bowed to Chiffinch. 'You may attend my lord now, sir.'

They kept me waiting another hour. I took Chiffinch's place in the chair and wrapped myself in my cloak. At last the servant returned and asked me, civilly enough, to follow him.

He led me through the doorway and up a private stair to the floor above. Here, I guessed, were the apartments occupied by the Howards and their intimates, where the public were not usually admitted. He took me through room after room furnished with paintings, tapestries and with the battered marbles of antiquity. He showed me into a bedchamber, a vast but stuffy room. The air was cold.

My eyes went at once towards the bed, which was set in an alcove beneath a gilded arch that bore the arms of the Howards. The curtains were drawn back. Lord Shrewsbury lay with his eyes closed. He was propped against the pillows, and his body seemed reduced to the size of a child's beneath the heap of bedclothes.

A papist priest knelt beside the bed at a prie-dieu, muttering his prayers and telling his rosary, while a maidservant was tiptoeing away, carrying a bedpan. Two physicians were conferring in low voices by the window, their robes drawn tightly about them against the cold. A great fire burned in the hearth but most of its heat went upwards and warmed the chimney and the sky above.

A gentleman approached me and introduced himself as Francis Weld, a member of Lord Shrewsbury's household. 'It's kind of Lord Arlington to send you,' he said in a dry, uninflected voice that made it impossible to detect if there was an element of irony behind the words. 'Pray don't stay long–Mr Chiffinch's visit has tired my master.'

'How is he today?'

'He rallied astonishingly yesterday morning, which is why we took the risk of bringing him here from Chelsea. He seemed to suffer no ill effects from the journey during the evening–he made a good supper and talked for nearly an hour with Mr Howard. But this morning he was weak and feverish again. The wound's infected. They've bled him, but it seems not to have helped.' Weld nodded towards the doctors. 'They are talking of applying a brace of pigeons if he grows much worse. Possibly more.'

'I'm sorry to hear it,' I said. 'Is he really that ill?'

'Not yet, I hope. And he would not hear of it when they mentioned the idea to him. But if he grows worse in the night . . .'

This was alarming news. Dead pigeons were considered one of the last remedies at a doctor's disposal. They were often used in cases of plague and other noxious fevers. Live birds were brought into the sickroom. Their necks were wrung and, while they were still warm, their breasts were slit open and applied to the patient's skin, usually to the soles of the feet. In this case, perhaps, they would apply them directly to the infected wound. It was a messy business, I had heard, and often unsuccessful.

'I've a private message from Lord Arlington.' I turned towards the figure on the bed. 'May I try to speak to him?'

Weld pursed his lips. 'Let me find out if he's awake.'

He crossed the room to the bed. I followed, a pace or two behind. The priest fell silent as Weld bent over the figure on the bed and whispered a few words.

Lord Shrewsbury's eyelids fluttered, and he said in a low, distinct voice, 'If I must.'

His pale hand twitched on the coverlet. He lifted a finger and beckoned me to approach. Weld introduced me.

I bowed. 'I'm sorry to see your lordship so ill.'

His face was thin, the pale skin stretched tightly over the bony ridges and hollows of the skull. Drops of sweat caught the light. His chin was black with stubble.

'You come from my Lord Arlington?' he said.

'Yes, my lord. I have a letter from him.' I came closer. 'And a message.'

A burst of energy transformed him. 'Leave us a moment,' he said to Weld. He turned his head towards the priest. 'As for you, stop your damned mumbling and pray for me somewhere else.' He pointed his finger at me. 'The letter.'

I gave it to him. He broke the seal and unfolded it. I could not read the contents but I saw there were only a few lines. He crumpled it up and pushed it aside; it fell to the floor.

'My head hurts,' he said. 'I'm thirsty . . . what's this message?'

I brought my head closer to his. 'My lord says he stands in your debt, and he assures you that the Duke of Buckingham will pay for the injuries he has done you. In the meantime, he begs you to be discreet.'

'Discreet? When the fever is upon me, they say I prattle like a child. If I do, I know not

91

what I say.' He was growing excited, and talking had brought an unhealthy flush to his cheeks. 'And my head hurts. I wish the Duke was in his grave, and dishonoured as well as dead. And my wife with him.'

I felt an unexpected pity. There was a cup containing a brown liquid on the bed table. I held it to his lips and he took a few sips. Some of the liquid ran down his chin.

'Where's he now?' he said, pushing aside the cup.

I dabbed his face with a napkin. 'Who, my lord?'

'That devil Buckingham, of course.'

'No one knows. He is in hiding.'

'Probably with my bitch of a wife.'

I was aware that Weld was approaching the bed on the far side, so his master would not see him. He was making gestures, urging me to cut short the conversation.

Shrewsbury's voice was rising. 'I heard the rogue talking to that man of his, the long, thin one, when I was on the ground. He must have made his plans already. The dog going to the bitch, the whoreson dog lying with the punkish bitch, rutting in their foulness in their yard. The dog, the bitch, the dog and the bitch, the —'

'My lord,' Weld said, moving forward and laying his hand on his master's arm, 'my lord, you must not overtire yourself.' He lifted his head and mouthed at me across the bed: 'Go. Go now.'

The physicians had abandoned their conference and were staring at us. I had no choice but to withdraw. I bowed to the man on the bed and walked away.

'The dog and the bitch,' Shrewsbury said behind me, his voice faint but urgent. 'Dog and bitch.'

After the fetid atmosphere of the bed-chamber, it was a relief to be in the open air again. I crossed the courtyard, making for the north gate. My mind was busy with the implications of my interview. Two points stood out: my lord was in great anguish of mind, and the infected wound lessened his chance of making a recovery.

The court was busy, even on a Sunday afternoon. A coach was unloading its passengers, and a knot of servants were squabbling in one corner. Three boys were urging on a fight between a pair of mismatched dogs, one a mastiff bitch, the other some sort of terrier, who was desperately trying to compensate with its agility for its lack of strength. I knew how the terrier felt.

My mind still full of the wounded man, I stopped to watch the fight. The two snarling dogs set me thinking about Shrewsbury's rambling remarks as I was leaving. Clearly his fever had been rising, and he might not have known what he was saying. Veal had been in attendance on the Duke at the duel, and the long, thin man the Earl had mentioned could have been him. Then what were these plans? Did the whoreson dog and the punkish bitch refer to Buckingham and Lady Shrewsbury, or had there been some other meaning? Or was Shrewsbury's mind so disordered that the words had been no more than meaningless fragments thrown out by his feverish imaginings?

The dog and bitch, I muttered under my breath, the dog and bitch. I remembered the duel last Thursday all too clearly. The dog and the bitch. I'd thought that Buckingham had said those words to Veal: dog, bitch. But I wasn't any more sure of that now than I had been then. I had had other things on my mind at the time: the two men lying on the ground in their blood-soaked shirts; and above all my desperate need to put as much distance as possible between Barn Elms and myself. I had been on the verge of panic. I couldn't trust my own memory.

The snarling and snapping intensified. The terrier broke away and ran between my legs, nearly oversetting me. The mastiff was slow off the mark, which gave the terrier time to reach an open window of a store at the end of the stables. It scrabbled over the stone sill and vanished inside. The mastiff gave chase but was brought up short outside the window frame, which was too small for it to pass through. It put its front paws on the sill and sniffed it, whining all the while. The little dog had got away scot-free.

I walked through the gateway and made my way slowly up to the Strand. I glimpsed a big, broad fellow at the top of the lane, with the sheath of a heavy sword swinging by his side. He had his back to me, and other people hindered my view. I hastily stepped into a doorway. Was it Roger Durrell, the man who had tried to detain me by force as I left Barn Elms after the duel? I wondered if he had seen me entering Arundel House.

I looked out, shading my face with my hat. I was just in time to see him going into an alehouse on the other side of the Strand.

I lingered in the lane for a moment longer. It was perfectly possible that Buckingham had set a watch on the house. He had good reason to. If Shrewsbury died, he could be arrested for murder. If it had been Durrell going into the alehouse, his master Veal might be in there too, the man they called the Bishop. I knew Mr Williamson and Lord Arlington would be interested, and perhaps they would decide to set their own watchers to watch Buckingham's.

But I didn't intend to test the truth of the theory myself. This was cowardice partly disguised as prudence. Veal could be ruthless if his conscience encouraged him, as it often seemed to do, but he was a clergyman of sorts, albeit one who had been ejected from his living. I was more afraid of his servant, Roger Durrell. I seriously doubted that Durrell was troubled by anything resembling a conscience.

I walked the short distance back to the Savoy, which was separated from Arundel House only by the sprawling courtyards of Somerset House. My lodging, a small house with a yard, was off a narrow lane called Infirmary Close. It suited me well enough, though in the warmer weather the Savoy's overfull graveyard, which lay behind the house, was not a pleasant neighbour.

My servant Sam Witherdine answered the door to my knock. He was a pensioned-off sailor who had lost his right leg below the knee; but he was miraculously agile, despite this. He had proved his loyalty to me more than once, though he had a weakness for strong ale and sometimes let his tongue run away with him.

He took my cloak and hat. 'Do you go out again, master?'

'I don't know.' I went into the parlour where there was a fire. 'Fetch Stephen, will you? I want to speak to both of you.'

He knuckled his forehead in the way sailors did and went away, leaving me to warm my hands. The dog and the bitch, I thought, the dog and the bitch. I couldn't rid myself of the feeling that the words meant something significant, that they were more than the desperate insults that a cuckold applied to his tormentors.

The servants clattered up the stairs from the kitchen–Stephen at a run, and Sam's heavier, hirpling steps. The boy waited in the hall, letting Sam precede him into the parlour. Stephen followed warily.

'I've a task for you both,' I said. 'Go to the alehouse by the lane to Arundel House.' I glanced at Sam. 'You know the one I mean?'

'Sign of the Silver Crescent, sir,' he said promptly. 'Mr Fawley has it, though in truth it's Mrs Fawley who runs the place. High prices, and she waters the ale after you've had a few.'

'I take it they know you in there?'

Sam smiled, almost coyly. 'Well, sir, you might be right there, or you might be wrong, but I doubt it's the latter.'

'Very well. Stephen—come here where I can see you.'

The boy, who had been standing behind Sam, came forward and stood before me. We did not know his age but I put him at about eleven years old. He had lived in my household since last autumn, when his previous owner, my Lady Quincy, had given him to me. Stephen was an African who had served great ladies as a page until he lost his childish beauty and grew too old and too diseased for them. In theory, I supposed, I owned him as I did any other of my chattels, for he was a slave whose ownership had been transferred to me. But I did not much like the idea of possessing another human being so I treated him as I would have done any boy who had come to my house to serve me.

When I had first known him, Stephen had been afflicted with the King's Evil; the disease, known as scrofula, had covered his face and neck with angry, painful swellings. Since the King had touched him in a private healing ceremony two months ago, however, the swellings had gradually diminished, and there was now hardly any trace of them. The efficacy of the royal touch in curing scrofula was, we were told, a sure and certain proof that our sovereign had been appointed by God Himself to rule over us. I was not a man who had much taste for miracles and other wonders contrary to nature. I did not know what to think of the improvement to Stephen's condition, but I was glad of it, for his sake.

'Do you remember when we first met, we were in the Fens beyond Cambridge?'

'Aye, master.'

'And one night, you were in the garden, and a bad man took you away in a boat and left you on an island.'

He began to tremble.

'And I came to find you on the island, and all was well again,' I reminded him.

He nodded.

'I know it was dark, but do you remember there were two men there–the one who took you from the garden, and the one he brought you to, who ordered the first man to leave you on the island? Would you recognize their voices if you heard them again?'

'I don't know, sir. Perhaps.'

'The man who took you is a big, fat, greasy fellow. He's called Roger Durrell. He wears a sword. His master's a tall, thin man.

He usually wears a sword, too, and the last time I saw him he had a long brown coat. His name's Veal. Sometimes they call him the Bishop.' I turned to Sam. 'You've met Durrell before. He waylaid me as I was coming home one evening in September, and you came to meet me in the nick of time. Do you remember?'

'That fellow? Aye. I didn't get a good look at him, but I heard him well enough—he sounded like he had a mouth full of snot.'

'That's the one. And his master's a northerner, a Yorkshireman, and you can hear it in his voice. I want the pair of you to go to the sign of the Silver Crescent to fetch me a jug of ale.' I gave Sam a shilling. 'Stephen goes with you to carry it. Don't linger, but keep your eyes and ears open. If there's anyone like those two men in there, I want to know. But don't run any risks.'

Shortly afterwards, I heard them leaving the house. The light was fading from the afternoon. I lit candles and tried to read. But I could not concentrate. The words danced in front of my eyes. I read and reread sentences, forgetting their beginnings before I reached their ends. As time crawled past, I began to wish that I had not sent Sam and Stephen, but had gone myself instead. My decision now seemed more cowardly than prudent. It was possible that Durrell had recognized Sam or Stephen, I thought, though as far as I knew he had seen neither of them by daylight. I clung to the fact that Stephen was much changed since joining my household. His swellings had subsided and Margaret's food had filled him out. He dressed differently too, more plainly than when he had worn his mistress's livery. But I could not suppress the niggling worry that I was wrong.

In the end, I gave up and called for my cloak. It was nearly an hour since the pair of them had left the house. I took my heaviest stick, which was tipped with iron, and went up to the Strand. It took me only a moment to reach the alehouse.

As soon as I opened the door I heard Sam. His voice rolled over me, along with the warm, ale-flavoured fug. He was singing one of the interminable ballads he had learned at sea. As I entered, the verse gave way to the chorus, and half the customers in the house joined in, banging their mugs on the table to mark time.

Stephen was crouching in the corner nearest the door and furthest from the fire. He was almost invisible in the gloom. He was the only one who noticed me. I dropped the latch and bent down so he could speak in my ear.

'They were there when we came, master,' he said, 'those two men. Talking with Mr Fawley. They left a few minutes later, while Sam was getting the ale.'

'They didn't mark you coming in? They took no notice of either of you?'

He shook his head. I was too relieved to be angry with Sam. It didn't take much imagination to see that he had decided to take some refreshment while the jug was being filled, and that the refreshment had bred an appetite for further refreshment, with the usual result.

But Stephen hadn't finished. 'They were with another man. In a doctor's robe . . . And as they were leaving, he took out his purse and threw Mr Fawley a piece of gold. He said there was to be ale for all the company, and they cheered him as he left.'

The song was coming to its raucous end. I was about to send Stephen over to Sam when the boy touched my sleeve. I bent down again.

'I've seen him before, master,' he said.

'The doctor?'

'When I was at her ladyship's. He wasn't a doctor then. He was a great lord, like a prince, with a nose like a beak and golden peruke.'

A jolt went through me. I should have guessed at the mention of the flamboyant gesture with the gold. I said, 'The Duke of Buckingham?'

I wasn't able to report to Mr Williamson until the following morning. He came over to Scotland Yard and saw me in his private room. I told him how Lord Shrewsbury had been, and about the presence of Buckingham and his servants in an alehouse within a stone's throw of Arundel House.

'The barefaced impudence,' Williamson said, tight-lipped with disdain. 'And disguised as a doctor, too. He has no sense of the dignity due to his own station. The man's no better than a mountebank.'

'Do you want me to do anything, sir?' I asked.

Williamson did not usually allow himself to betray his emotions, or at least not to me. He calmed himself with a visible effort. 'No, not you—he knows who you are. No, we'll put a watch on the sign of the Silver Crescent, and pray he comes back. There's not much else we can do.'

The days passed. Buckingham was too clever to reappear. Almost certainly, he was still somewhere in London, for he had many friends and sympathizers to shelter him, as well as gold enough to smooth his way and to shut mouths that might be tempted to blab.

He must have known that time was on his side. Parliament was due to reopen in little more than a fortnight, on 6 February, and the King needed all the support he could get, including Buckingham's, if he was to have the money he needed from the Lords and Commons, let alone the other bills he wanted passed. One of them, the Comprehension Bill, was a proposal to allow Dissenters freedom of worship, which was of particular interest to the Duke. He had cultivated the Dissenters, many of whom were both wealthy and influential.

Meanwhile, Williamson received daily reports from Arundel House. On the Tuesday morning after my visit, he sent me back there to enquire in person. This time, I was not admitted to Lord Shrewsbury's bedchamber. Instead, Mr Weld came down to speak to me.

'There's nothing of consequence to tell you, sir,' he told me. 'My lord was given the pigeons last night. He's no worse this morning, which must be accounted a gain, but no better. His doctors say that the pigeons take a day or two to have their beneficial effect. In the meantime, they have prescribed perfect quiet.'

Two days later, I called again. On this occasion the news was better. Lord Shrewsbury's fever had diminished, and his physicians were cautiously optimistic about his prognosis; Mr Weld told me that they attributed this to the prompt application of the dead pigeons. He was still very weak, but it was a sign of their optimism that his case had been left to the management of a single chirurgeon.

'Pity,' Williamson muttered when he heard the news. 'If my lord had died, Buckingham would have found it hard to wriggle out of a charge of murder.'

On the 27 January, when Shrewsbury was considered out of danger, the King sent him a royal pardon for accidentally causing Lieutenant Jenkins' death; he was clearly anxious that the Earl's enemies should have no legal means of attacking him now his health was improving. More controversially, the King also pardoned Buckingham and his seconds. He did this by warrants authorized by his own signature alone, rather than following the usual procedure of issuing pardons through the Lord Privy Seal, which might not have been so easy for him, or so swift. He tried to smudge the bad impression this made in the City by appointing a committee of his Council to suppress duelling. But everyone knew that the committee had no power to change anything. You could no more stop gentlemen fighting each other than you could stop rain falling from the sky.

The business was most irregular, Mr Williamson told me, shaking his head, and no good would come of it. After all, none of the parties had been charged for their part in the duel, let alone sentenced, so how could they be pardoned for something they had not been convicted of? Williamson was a man who liked matters to be arranged according to form and precedent. His irritation made him unusually communicative.

'The King told the council that he issued the pardons because of the "eminent services" done by the survivors of this bloody affair.' Williamson shook his head. ' "Eminent services"! It's but a fig leaf, Marwood, and it will convince no one. My Lord Arlington says Buckingham sneaked like a thief into the Duke of Albemarle's lodgings to receive his pardon.'

Thursday, 30 January was the anniversary of the late king's execution on the scaffold in Whitehall, and therefore a solemn fast day for all of us. But on the following day,

106

Lord Arlington told Williamson that Buckingham's name had been added to the Select Committee for Foreign Affairs, which met weekly on Mondays to deal with the most important and most delicate matters of policy. The committee formed the inner circle of government, and Williamson was predictably furious at the news–which was why he let it slip to me, for the matter was meant to be confidential.

'The King could hardly have chosen a more effective way to show his support of the Duke. And it flies in the face of Lord Arlington's advice.'

Two days later, on Sunday morning, Mr Williamson summoned me to Whitehall; he was dining with Lord Shrewsbury's gentleman, Mr Weld, at midday, and he said it might be useful for me to join them as I had already met him.

I was early. Mr Williamson was attending the service in the Chapel Royal. While I waited for him, I paced up and down the Matted Gallery, where we were also to meet Mr Weld.

The doors to the King's apartments opened, and a group of gentlemen emerged, talking among themselves. In their centre was the Duke of Buckingham, strolling arm-in-arm with Sir Charles Sedley, and laughing at something the latter had said. He seemed to have not a care in the world.

I drew back into the nearest window embrasure. But I was too late. Buckingham had seen me. He paused in his progress along the gallery, and his friends did the same, for he was clearly their leader. He pointed a beringed finger in my direction.

'Charles,' he said loudly. 'Mark that fellow there, the one with the scars on his face. He's a worm, you know, Williamson's tame worm. Don't hesitate to trample him underfoot if he gets in your way.'

The gentlemen around him laughed, or rather sniggered. I felt the blood rushing to my cheeks. For a moment, Buckingham stared down at me, making the most of his great height. With his golden hair, his rich clothing and his well-marked features, he looked more kingly than the King himself.

I willed myself to hold his gaze without flinching. At last he walked on with his friends.

'The worm's father was a traitor and a fanatic,' I heard him say in a carrying voice. 'His name is Marwood. But I hereby baptize him Marworm.'

CHAPTER FIVE

The Solomon House
Monday, 3–Wednesday, 5 February 1668
Yesterday, Sunday, was full of church bells, so this must be Monday, mumbleday.

Master mumbles curses, better than kicks, as they go down, down, down into the rat-filled dark. Master first, lantern swinging in one hand, pole with hook in the other. In his belt the axe.

Ferrus behind Master, carrying the big bag with the brushes and more poles. The shovel strapped on his back. Up comes the smell and the rustling to meet them.

A rat runs over Master's boot and then up the steps and between Ferrus's legs. Windy likes rats but they don't like him. Windy takes them in his jaws and waves them in the air until they are dead.

Near to the foot of the steps, Master stands aside, pressing his back against the wall. He raises the lantern to shoulder height and waves the pole. Ferrus passes him.

Down here, Ferrus goes first. Always. Scribble-scrabble. Worm wriggle. Fill the bucket, pass it back.

Sodden, stinking heap fills the sewer. Blocking the run. Sometimes servants throw the ashes into the privy. Stuck. Ferrus stuck. Shovel stuck.

Ferrus bends this way and that. Ferrus wriggles.

Master swearing and shouting. Oh bad.

Still stuck.

Pain in the arse. Oh, Master uses pole, the pointy end that hurts. Ferrus squeals and thrashes and scribble-scrabbles.

A sucking, stinky noise.

Ferrus is free.

As day succeeded day, and one week was followed by the next, no letter came from the house in Hatton Garden, and there was no attempt to arrange another meeting. Cat began to hope that they had seen the last of Elizabeth Cromwell and the man introduced as Mr Cranmore.

Since their visit to Mistress Dalton's house, Cat tried more than once to sound out her husband about Elizabeth's curious interest in the plans of the Cockpit that

110

Hakesby had made during the Common-wealth and the Protectorate. But he would not discuss it with her. It was not that he denied her point-blank, or ordered her to be silent as a husband had a perfect right to do. He did not swear at her or throw his pen at her. He simply ignored her questions, or deflected them, or found it imperative to shuffle off and do something else.

What made it so much more difficult was the delicate matter of Mr Cranmore and his habit of rubbing at the table with his finger-tip when he was deep in thought. Children noticed such peculiarities; and because their infant memories had as yet acquired so little to fill them, they tended to remember them. As a child, Cat, sitting at the bottom of the table with Elizabeth, had stared at Richard Cromwell, Elizabeth's father, at the head: she had noticed the trick he had with his fingertip; she had wondered at it, with a child's niggling curiosity, and she had remembered it.

Once the bridge had been thrown across the gap between the past and the present, the rest followed. How better to disguise yourself than with thick tinted glasses and a beard, with the movements of age and infirmity, and with ashes rubbed into your hair to make it greyer than it was. The appearance of Mr Cranmore fitted neatly over her memory of Richard Cromwell: the late Lord Protector of England reduced to playing the part of a doddering, prematurely old man who could hardly see the plate before him.

Why had Cromwell crept back to England in disguise, where he could be arrested at any time for debt, if not for treason? What did he really want from Mr Hakesby? The answers to the questions didn't matter in themselves, not to Cat. Sometimes it was better not to know.

All that really mattered was keeping her husband away from the Protector and his daughter. Hakesby had grown so erratic in his behaviour of late, so obstinate in pursuing his freaks and fancies, that there was no knowing what he might do if the whim took him.

Until their marriage, Cat had not realized that there was a devious side to her husband.

He worked by stealth. A fortnight after the Hatton Garden dinner, she woke in the middle of the night and found herself alone in bed. She heard sounds of movement above her head, up in the attic where the Drawing Office was. There were footsteps and what sounded like the dragging of something across the floor, not in the main office but in the closet next to it.

She twitched aside the bed curtain. The chamber was in darkness. There was a draught, which meant that the door to the landing was ajar.

She waited. After a while, Hakesby came slowly down the stairs and into the bed-chamber. Breathing heavily, he shuffled across the floor. Keys chinked as he replaced them on the hook on the bedpost. He was a man who liked keys and locks.

He pushed aside the curtain and clambered into bed. As he raised the covers, cold air eddied around Cat's body. She pretended to be asleep, forcing herself to breathe slowly and regularly. Her husband placed his hands on her thigh: not from lust, she knew, but in the hope of stealing her warmth. His old blood ran thin and slow.

In the morning Cat rose early and went upstairs, her slippered feet making little noise. It was still dark but that mattered not; she knew her way blindfold in the Drawing Office. She found a candle and a tinder box on the shelf on the left of the door. After she had fumbled with flint and steel, the big room filled with a wavering yellow light. It spread like liquid towards the corners where the shadows lay. She tiptoed into the office closet, which was used for storage. It also contained the commode reserved for Mr Hakesby's use. He had two commodes–one here, the other on the floor below in the private lodging.

She crouched and examined the floor. The commode was not at its usual angle to the window. Two of the boxes stacked behind it were out of line. When she looked closely, she saw the dust on their lids had been disturbed. They were old boxes, clumsily made but strong, each bound with iron hoops and each locked. She tried to open them, but the lids didn't move.

It was clear enough what her husband had been doing, Cat thought, but not whether he had found what he was looking for. Shivering, she wrapped her bedgown around her and considered. Suppose her husband had been looking for the Cockpit plans, and suppose he had found them, what would he have done with them?

To her horror, she heard the creak of the door below, followed by slow steps on the stairs. She stood up quickly and tiptoed into the main room, latching the closet door behind her. The door from the landing place opened, and the stooped figure of her husband, candle in hand, filled the doorway.

'You've risen early,' he said.

'I couldn't sleep.'

Hakesby looked at her and, old and tremulous as he was, he was formidable. 'No. Nor I. Make up the fire, will you, and warm some milk.'

She turned to obey. She knelt by the hearth and riddled the ash, exposing the glowing coals. She took a handful of wood shavings from the pot by the coal scuttle and threw them on the fire. She blew until the shavings caught fire, and then added kindling, frugally, piece by piece. The porter's boy was supposed to bring up the kindling with the coal, but he never brought enough.

Pale flames rose, hesitantly at first, but rapidly gathering strength. One day, Cat thought, my husband will be dead and in his grave. Then she felt guilty for allowing to herself to think of such a thing.

'Were you looking for the Cockpit plans?' her husband said.

She said nothing.

'Why? They are nothing to do with you.'

She picked up the tongs and placed a small piece of coal on to the kindling. 'I think a Cromwell is dangerous company for people such as us. Any Cromwell. Even Elizabeth.' She dared not tell him about the real identity of Mr Cranmore. 'I don't trust her.'

'I am master in my house, and God has placed you under me. You owe me obedience, not questions.'

Cat picked up another piece of coal and dropped it into the fire.

'The boy brought me a letter when you were ordering our dinner yesterday,' Hakesby said. 'Mistress Cromwell will call here on Wednesday morning at eleven o'clock.'

She turned her head. He was frowning at her.

'We will receive her privately in the parlour,' he said. 'Make the place fit to receive her.'

The following day, the first Tuesday in February, another letter arrived, this one from Mr Howard at Arundel House. Dr Wren had written to him, and Mr Howard was graciously pleased to permit Mr Hakesby to make a preliminary survey of the plot of ground designated for the Royal Society's Solomon House. The steward would give orders that he was to be admitted.

'Brennan could go in your place if you wish, sir,' Cat said, thinking of the lost hours

116

of work if they all went, particularly if her husband exhausted himself at Arundel House.

'I'm quite well enough to go,' Hakesby snapped. He had been particularly irritable with her since their encounter in his closet in the early hours of yesterday morning. 'It's of great importance to see the site oneself if one is to design a building for it.'

'But it's raining. If you wish, I could accompany Brennan myself.'

'Didn't you hear me? I shall go in person. Besides, Mr Howard's letter mentions me by name. He will no doubt be expecting me to be there.'

In the end, all three of them went to Arundel House that morning, despite the rain. At least Hakesby's health was in general better than it had been. The improvement, Cat suspected, had coincided with his excitement over their visit to Mistress Dalton's; she hoped it would last.

Now his imagination had been seized by the Solomon House scheme. Wren had talked of designing a building uniquely adapted to the scientific enquiries of the Society, the like of which would astonish the whole of Europe. Add to that its location in the garden of one of the great houses of London, Hakesby said, and the prestige that would accrue from being associated with the project would lead to a flood of commissions. It would indeed be exciting, Cat thought, if it ever came to anything. But she could not help feeling, not for the first time, that Dr Wren was taking advantage of her husband's good nature.

At the gate of Arundel House, the porter asked them to wait while he sent word to the steward.

The steward kept them waiting, and then sent an assistant, a short, round man whose eyes seemed perpetually wide with surprise. 'Mr Hakesby?' His eyes moved from Hakesby to Brennan, and then to Cat. He frowned, as if surprised by the sight of a woman in the party. 'My master told me to expect you. Before we go any further, I must ask you not to make any disturbance as you go about your job.'

Mr Hakesby drew himself up to his full height. 'Sir, I am not accustomed to creating a disturbance.'

'My Lord Shrewsbury is lying gravely ill here. He grows better, day by day, God be thanked, but Mr Howard is anxious that there should be no unseemly din or sudden racket.'

'Of course, sir,' Cat said, forcing herself to smile at him.

The man ignored her. 'And another thing. The part of the garden you will visit has been enclosed with a fence, and you will need this key for its gate. Pray bring it to the steward's office when you leave.' He pointed across the courtyard to a modern lodging on its eastern side. 'Through the door and to the left.'

He turned to a servant he had brought with him. 'Take Mr Hakesby and his party to the garden door.' He glanced back at Hakesby. 'Pray do your work as quickly as possible.'

The servant led them with a fine air of disdain out of the entrance quadrangle and through a courtyard to the west. Beyond it lay the site that was to be measured. The main gardens were to the south of the mansion, along the banks of the Thames, but the plot for the Royal Society was at the north-west corner of the house and set upon a terrace. Its western boundary was the high wall separating the Arundel property from the lane running from the Strand down to the river, where there was a public landing place by the water tower.

The servant unlocked the door in the paling, gave Hakesby the key, and left them. The three of them went into the enclosure. Once part of a formal garden, the area had clearly been neglected for some years. The bushes had grown to wild and tangled shapes, and the paths were strewn with muddy puddles and unkempt with last year's weeds. On the far side was a stone wall topped with spikes.

Hakesby looked about him. 'I see why they have chosen this place,' he said. 'It's well away from the river, and I doubt they've done much with it for years. Why, it's little better than a parcel of waste ground.'

'It's smaller than I expected,' Cat said.

'I'm sure we can contrive something, nonetheless.' He gave her a smile that took her by surprise and turned to stare at the boundary wall. 'We could have a separate access by the lane, perhaps, for the Royal Society to come and go. That way they would avoid inconveniencing the Howards and their household.'

The rain was falling gently but steadily. Hakesby sheltered under a tree while Cat and Brennan measured the ground and calculated its relationship to the surrounding buildings.

Cat noted the measurements that Brennan called out to her. The overall dimensions of the site were a hundred feet by forty, thirty-three paces by thirteen. The plot lay at the north end of the long gallery that ran south to the river; but there were no windows directly overlooking it.

The work absorbed her. Despite herself, her imagination stirred, and she found herself thinking of how she would build the Solomon House, if the decisions were hers to make. Clearly, the principal windows should face south, towards the river, to have the most advantage from the light. The observatory should be built at the western end, as far as possible from the tall range of apartments that joined the long gallery at right angles.

It was nearly dinner time before they were finished, because Hakesby wanted her to make rough sketches of the elevations of the surrounding buildings. By this time he was flagging, and the symptoms of his ague or shaking palsy were growing more marked. After they had finished, as they were walking across the nearer courtyard, the three of them arm in arm with Hakesby in the middle, he announced that he wished to be taken at once to the nearest privy.

Cat and Brennan exchanged glances. The movements of Hakesby's bowels were sacrosanct and unpredictable. A clock began to strike midday.

'At once,' her husband repeated, with a

note of panic in his voice.

'Will you take him?' Cat said to Brennan. She nodded towards an outhouse tucked in the corner of the court. 'Try there. I'll give the key back to the steward, and meet you in the front court by the archway to the lane. We'll find a hackney in the Strand.'

She left Brennan to escort his master to the necessary house. Hakesby's absence, even for a moment, made her feel lighter and younger. She almost ran into the passage to the court beyond, earning a curious glance from a pair of maidservants who were gossiping out of the rain.

Cat returned the site key to the steward's office, and walked at a more decorous pace towards the main gateway. Hakesby and Brennan had not yet arrived, which did not surprise her. To the left of the gate, a covered flight of steps led up to a first-floor entrance. The rain was falling more heavily, so she took shelter in the space beneath the steps. She set her back against the wall, drew her cloak more tightly around her and idly watched the people passing to and fro.

Two gentlemen emerged from a doorway on the south side of the court, where the main range of the family's apartments were; on the other side, the windows looked over the gardens and the river. The men were talking earnestly, and walked slowly towards the gateway, their broad hats close together. As they drew near, the one on the left looked up and she recognized him with a jolt of surprise. It was James Marwood.

At almost the same moment, he caught sight of her. He said a word to his companion, who turned away. Marwood changed his course and walked towards Cat. He stopped a few yards from her and bowed. 'Mistress Hakesby. I hope you're in good health.'

'Thank you, sir, yes.'

For a moment they stared at each other. When she had seen him four months earlier, he had looked haggard, and indeed with reason. Now he seemed in good spirits; he was better dressed than before, too. All in all, she thought with a touch of amusement, he looked quite the rising man of affairs.

Marwood was examining her too. 'What are you doing at Arundel House?'

'I might ask you the same thing.'

'I've business here.'

'So have I.'

Disarmingly, he smiled. 'In fact, my master Mr Williamson sent me to enquire how Lord Shrewsbury does.'

'After that wretched duel?'

'Yes. My lord is recovering.'

'I'm glad to hear it.'

'And you? Why are you here?'

'Mr Hakesby has been surveying a piece of the garden. The Howards have offered it to the Royal Society for their meeting house.'

Marwood's eyes flickered as if he were resisting the temptation to look about him for her husband. The scar tissue on the left-hand side of his face was less angry than it had been a few months ago, less obvious to the eye.

'My husband is easing nature,' she said primly, answering the question he hadn't asked. 'Brennan is with him. I am to meet them here when they are done.'

'And are you all thriving in Henrietta Street?'

'There's work enough, if that's what you mean. Though the payments come more slowly than I would like.'

A short but awkward silence fell like a stone between them.

He said, 'And Mr Hakesby's health?'

'Very well,' she answered automatically. But then she found herself blurting out something closer to the truth. 'In truth, he grows no younger, sir, and he has his good days and his bad days.'

'Yes,' Marwood said. 'I understand.'

Cat thought he did. That was the quality she expected least from him and liked most: that he generally seemed to understand what she was about, or at least to accept her for what she was.

For a moment or two neither of them spoke, but this was a more comfortable silence than before. They stood side by side, looking out at the rain and at people scurrying from doorway to doorway. She was suddenly tempted to lay before him the matter of Elizabeth Cromwell, and ask his opinion about what she should do. She could hardly confide in Hakesby, and she did not entirely trust Brennan.

But Marwood was different. At their first meeting, during the Great Fire eighteen months ago, circumstances had briefly thrown them together and made them unwilling allies in a dangerous affair that involved Cat's late father, the notorious regicide Thomas Lovett. Since then there had been two other episodes, when each had been in a position to help the other. They had survived great peril together too, and had kept each other's secrets. That had bred trust between them, if not friendship.

She knew that Marwood could keep his mouth shut. Besides, he was much at Whitehall, and was probably better aware than she of how the government currently viewed the Cromwell family. There was also the point that, if the worst came to the worst and there was a sinister motive behind Elizabeth's actions, the authorities might see it as a point in Cat's favour that she had asked Marwood's advice about what to do.

Before she could speak, though, he turned to her and said, 'Do you remember when we last met?'

She felt the colour rising to her face. 'Of course I do.'

'I warned you against two men who wish me harm. A tall and very thin one, and his servant who is a big, gross fellow. They both wear swords. The tall one is named Veal. The other one is called Roger Durrell.'

'I remember. I saw them once, in Love Lane.' She bit her lip, for it had not been a happy occasion.

'They're the Duke of Buckingham's creatures. They're watching this house.'

'Why?' As she was speaking, she guessed the answer to her question. 'Lord Shrewsbury.'

'Yes. They wish me harm. If you see them again, would you write to me privately at the Savoy and let me know?'

'Very well. Why do they wish you harm?'

Marwood shrugged. 'Because their master does.'

Surprised, Cat looked at him. 'You've offended the Duke? How?'

'It doesn't matter.'

'There's something you can do for me, too.'

'Name it.'

'I met an old acquaintance the —'

'Is that Marwood?'

At the sound of Hakesby's voice, Cat turned sharply, a sudden, irrational surge of guilt shooting through her. Her husband and Brennan were framed in the archway leading to the passage.

Marwood was already moving towards them. 'It is indeed, sir. What a pleasant chance this is, this encounter. How are you?'

He's learned to be as smooth as butter, Cat thought. But then Marwood had always been a quick learner.

'To tell the truth, sir, I wish I were better,' Hakesby said. 'It's the damp weather–I find I cannot tolerate it. I must go back to our lodgings.' He was so wrapped in his own problems, Cat realized, that he had little time for outsiders except insofar as they affected his comfort. 'I need a hackney. Would you fetch one for me? You would stand a

127

better chance of success than poor Brennan here.'

This was tactless but true. Hackneys were in short supply in wet weather, particularly in the Strand. Marwood's prosperous appearance suggested a full purse, whereas Brennan looked no more than he was: a plainly dressed artisan who did not usually take hackneys.

'Of course, sir,' Marwood said. If he was surprised by Hakesby's condition he did not show it. 'I'll go up to the street, and leave you to follow at your convenience.'

Marwood took his leave. With a sour face, Brennan watched him go. She took Hakesby's arm and followed more slowly, with Brennan supporting him on the other side. When they reached the street, they found Marwood negotiating with the driver.

He pulled aside the curtain for them. Cat mounted the step first.

'Don't let the fellow charge you again,' he murmured to her as she climbed into the coach. 'He's had his fare, and he knows where to go.'

'You must let us repay you.'

'Not now.'

He turned aside to help Brennan manoeuvre the old man into the coach. He did not linger to say farewell but walked away, westwards towards the Savoy or perhaps Whitehall.

Hakesby kept up a stream of complaint on their way back to Henrietta Street. Their progress was slow, with many stops, because of the traffic. But at least, Cat thought, he was sitting down; it would have been worse for them all if he had had to stand much longer or walk for any length of time.

When the hackney came to a halt outside their house in Henrietta Street. Brennan scrambled out to alert the porter. Cat followed more slowly with her husband, while their driver watched from the box, with a studiously uninterested expression on his face.

Brennan and the porter helped Hakesby into the house. Cat followed. On the step, she glanced back. A large man was walking up the road in the same direction as they had taken. He was shabbily dressed, and a heavy sword hung by his side. The sword's sheath was swinging from side to side, banging against the legs of passers-by.

For an instant, their eyes met. He examined her briefly, his gaze running up and down in that familiar masculine way that contrived to be impersonal, invasive and insulting, all at the same time. He swaggered across the road and entered St Paul's churchyard on the other side.

It was the man she had seen all those months ago in Love Lane, the man Marwood had said might be watching Arundel House. Roger Durrell. In which case, he had probably seen them together in the Strand. He had followed their coach as it struggled through the traffic, as sluggish as Mr Hakesby's bowels, and at last turned into Henrietta Street. And now he knew where she and Hakesby lived.

But why had Durrell followed them? It was only as she was climbing the stairs in their house that the obvious answer came to her: because she had been talking to James Marwood.

The rest of Tuesday was taken up with preparations for Elizabeth Cromwell's visit in the morning. With Hakesby fussing around them, Cat and the maid prepared the parlour below the Drawing Office. They washed and scrubbed, dusted and polished. They ordered biscuits and sweetmeats to tempt Mistress Cromwell's appetite and wine to delight her palate. At Hakesby's insistence, they even placed a provisional order for a dinner to be sent in from a neighbouring tavern.

'After all,' he said, 'it's possible that she

might condescend to dine with us.'

He could hardly have been more concerned, or more excited, if a member of the royal family had been due to visit Henrietta Street. But in a way, Cat thought, that was precisely how the occasion seemed to him. For all his pretended loyalty to the King, her husband believed that the Cromwells were more worthy of veneration than the Stuarts had ever been. In one sense he was right: Oliver had managed to rule England with a firmer hand than either the king who had lost his head or the one who now sat on the throne.

When Hakesby went upstairs to deal with a query from Brennan, Cat scribbled a note to Marwood, telling him about Durrell, Buckingham's servant, whom she had seen in the street. She sent it to the Savoy by the porter's boy. She hoped the boy might return from Infirmary Close with a reply, or even that Marwood himself might call. If she were lucky, they might have a chance for private conversation, and she could discuss the matter of Elizabeth Cromwell with him.

But when the boy came back, he told her that Mr Marwood had not been at the house, and he had left her letter with the servant.

■ ■ ■ ■

That night, Hakesby slept more restlessly than usual. Cat lay awake by his side, counting the hours. When at last the morning came, she and the maid helped her husband dress in his best suit, the one he had worn when they dined at Hatton Garden. After breakfast, he went to his closet. When he emerged he was carrying a scuffed leather folder. Cat settled him in the elbow chair by the parlour fire.

'You must set Mistress Dalton's chair by the fire too,' he said, 'as well as Mistress Cromwell's.'

'Yes, sir,' she said, 'and we shall. But first, sit here and rest.'

To her relief, he obeyed. But he would not relinquish his grip on the folder. He cradled it in his arms like a baby. Even when he dozed off, the dribble running from one corner of his mouth, he did not let the folder slip.

It was not until a quarter-past eleven that the porter's boy came running up the stairs to say that a hackney had drawn up outside the street door. With some difficulty, Cat induced Mr Hakesby to remain where he was, while she and Brennan went downstairs to usher the ladies up to the parlour.

Guided by the boy, however, Elizabeth Cromwell was already mounting the stairs. 'Catty!' she cried, putting on a spurt of speed. 'Dearest! It seems an age since I saw you!'

The person behind her wasn't Mistress Dalton, after all. It was her father.

On the half-landing, Elizabeth embraced Cat with such force that her cheekbone jarred against Cat's mouth, forcing her to bite her tongue. She curtsied to Cromwell in his guise as Mr Cranmore, who peered at her and gripped the bannister rail with both hands.

'Mistress Hakesby?' he said uncertainly, as if unsure it was her. 'Your servant, madam.'

'You are welcome indeed, sir,' she said mechanically. 'My husband is upstairs. He begs your pardon for not coming down to greet you—his health is indifferent today.'

'Mr Cranmore has been so obliging,' Elizabeth said loudly. 'Mistress Dalton has a chill on her stomach, and he graciously offered to escort me in her place.'

Cat introduced Brennan. Sulky-faced, he sent Elizabeth a swift, sly glance as if assessing her charms, and then looked down at his feet. In a flutter of compliments, the four of them walked slowly up to the next floor, where the Hakesbys' apartments were. Brennan opened the parlour door, bowed and left them.

Hakesby had already struggled to his feet. He gave the newcomers a shaky bow and muttered something about being honoured by Mistress Cromwell's condescension.

'None of that, sir,' she cried with an arch note in her voice. 'We are all friends here, I hope.'

The maid carried away the visitors' cloaks. It took several flustered minutes to settle their guests to Mr Hakesby's satisfaction, and to provide them with the refreshments he felt essential to their happiness as his guests and his honour as their host.

Under cover of this, Elizabeth leaned her head so close to Cat that she felt the other woman's breath on her cheek.

'Would you send your maid away when this is done? There is a matter we would like to discuss . . . in confidence.'

I am sure you would, Cat thought as she smiled and nodded. And so would your father.

When the four of them were alone, there was a moment's silence. Elizabeth glanced at the parlour door, making sure that the maid had latched it properly when she left. She was more richly dressed than before, as if reminding them all of the position she had once held in the world. Mr Hakesby could not help giving her admiring glances in a manner he fondly believed to be discreet.

Mr Cranmore removed his green glasses and rose to his feet. 'Sir,' he said to Hakesby. 'And you, madam.' He turned to Cat. 'I'm afraid we haven't been altogether open with you. If I may, I should like to make amends.'

Hakesby stopped fumbling with the strap of his satchel. He looked bewildered. 'But I don't understand, sir. The plans — ?'

'Forgive me—one moment.' Their guest's voice was quiet, but it had become more assured; he had lost his stoop; and his face without the glasses looked younger. 'Here in London, I am in a delicate position, though I have done nothing wrong, as God is my witness.'

'Nothing wrong?' Hakesby echoed. 'Then why — ?'

'I have committed no crime, sir, I assure you, and I mean you no harm. But before I took you fully into my confidence, I thought it best–for all of us, I mean–to see you at close quarters, without your knowing my identity.' He dropped the glasses on the table. 'Though God knows my troubles have changed me so much I need hardly have troubled to disguise myself.'

'Mr Cromwell,' Cat said.

He glanced at her. 'Yes, Mistress Hakesby, you have it in one.' He turned back to Hakesby, who was trembling, his mouth wide open. 'Pray don't be disturbed, sir. There is no need for concern.'

'My lord,' Hakesby said faintly. 'Your— your highness.'

'I beg you, sir—none of that. I am a private gentleman now, and I have been these ten years. Nor have I ever sought to be anything else.' He paused to clear his throat. 'And I am as loyal to the King as any man.'

Elizabeth took his hand in both of hers. 'My dear father.' She glanced at Hakesby. 'He can't bear to be parted from his family. He hasn't seen any of us for nearly eight years.'

Cromwell smiled down at her. 'Nowadays, I want nothing more than my family and the means to live quietly as a gentleman in modest comfort. Indeed, that's what I've always wanted.'

Cat stared at him, trying to combine what she saw with the glimpses of Elizabeth's father that she recalled from childhood. It wasn't easy. The beard and moustache were partly responsible for that, together with the passage of time. The wrinkles and the grey hair were real enough. But she fancied that there was a slight resemblance to Oliver, Richard Cromwell's father, in the nose and the set of the mouth.

'I saw you at Whitehall in the old days, sir,' Hakesby said. 'And sometimes in the City. You wouldn't remember me.'

Cromwell smiled at him. 'You know the saying, Mr Hakesby. More know Tom Fool than Tom Fool knows. The loss is mine.'

It was a courteous speech. Cat almost warmed to the man. She liked the fact that he had not tried to conceal his identity from them any longer. But the danger his presence might cause them struck her afresh. Moreover, there was no reason to assume that he was trustworthy. The Cromwells' behaviour had been too devious to encourage trust.

Then, with a speed that dizzied her, she grasped the implications of their visit. 'What is this, sir–this meeting that you and Elizabeth have contrived? That's what you did, isn't it? You desired to meet my husband. You found out where we lived. You or Elizabeth discovered that he was married, and that I was his wife. And Elizabeth would have told you that she and I had been

137

playmates in the old days, when you knew my father. And —'

'Catherine!' Hakesby interrupted. 'You must not speak so rudely to Mr Cromwell. It is not fitting.'

'Nor is this ploy of theirs, sir,' she snapped. She turned back to Cromwell. 'And so you found out where we lived and you set Elizabeth to work. She followed me and pretended to meet me by chance in Fleet Street.'

Cromwell had the grace to look shamefaced. 'You are right to be angry. But the fault is mine, not Elizabeth's. I fear that these last years have made me suspicious and over-cautious. I take no one and nothing for granted. I'm sensible that I've put you in a difficult position, and I'm sorry for it.'

'Not at all, sir,' Hakesby said. 'But–honoured though I am–I confess I don't understand why you should want my acquaintance.'

'The Cockpit plans,' Cat said. 'What else could it be?'

'Yes.' Cromwell spoke calmly but the fixity of his expression hinted at tension inside. He gestured towards the leather folder on the table at Hakesby's elbow. 'I assume they are there.'

'Why do you want them?' Cat said.

He sat back in his chair. 'If I tell you, I must trust you.'

'If you honour us with your trust, sir,' Hakesby said, 'you will not be disappointed. You have my oath on that.'

'In the past, sir, I trusted people I should not have trusted.' He stared at Cat and shrugged. 'But it seems I've no choice in the matter. Will you do me the kindness of promising this will go no further than the four of us? I give you my solemn word that this business threatens no one's life or liberty. There's nothing treasonable in it or in any way criminal.'

'I have no doubt of it, sir,' Hakesby said, holding out the folder to him.

Cat snatched it from his hand.

'Wife!'

Hakesby's face flushed with anger. He raised his hand to strike her.

Cromwell moved between them, his hands spread wide, palms upwards: a peacemaker's gesture. 'Pray don't let me be the cause of a quarrel. Let's forget this conversation ever happened. Elizabeth and I will leave you in peace. Come, Daughter.'

'No,' Cat said. 'Tell us why you want these plans. If I've no good reason to tell anyone, then I won't.'

'You will do as I say, madam,' Hakesby said faintly.

Cromwell smiled at them, as if nothing were amiss and they were all friends together. He sat down again and took a sip of wine. 'My dear mother died,' he said. 'Did you hear?'

Hakesby nodded. 'Several years ago, I think?'

'Yes—in the November of 1665. She had been living in retirement at my brother-in-law's house in Northborough. She was very ill towards the end, and wracked with pain. It wasn't just her body that sickened. Her heart did, too. She didn't care a straw about no longer being Her Highness the Lady Protectoress. But she missed my father terribly. I believe she would have been happy with him in a farmhouse.'

Cromwell paused and looked down at his lap. Muscles twitched at the corners of his mouth. Either he was a very fine actor, Cat thought, or he was telling the truth.

'Before she died,' he continued, 'she called Mr White to her.' He turned to Hakesby. 'Did you ever meet him, sir? One of my father's chaplains.'

Hakesby frowned. 'Yes . . . a young man. Wasn't there some—some story about him?'

'Aye—people always remember that. They

140

said he was making sheep's eyes at my sister Frances. She liked him well enough, but my father found out, and it would not do. He had him married off to one of Frances's maids instead, which answered very well and killed the scandal. But White's a good man, for all that, and sound in his religion too, and my father liked him. So did my mother, and he did not desert us when the King returned. She made Mr White the executor of her will. And, just before she died, she gave him a letter for me. By then, the poor lady was seeing visions. She thought the walls of her chamber ran with blood.'

'Sir, must you say so much?' Elizabeth said. 'Is this wise?'

'If they are to trust me, my dear,' her father said gently, 'I must trust them.' He turned back to Hakesby. 'I was in Switzerland then, but a fortnight later my wife sent a servant secretly to Mr White. My mother had given her a password for the servant to say, *The walls run with blood,* and White surrendered the letter to his keeping. Then it had to be smuggled out of England. It took months for it to reach me, and when I had it, I lacked the funds to do anything. Is it not ironical?'

'The funds to do what?' said Cat, who was

141

beginning to lose patience. She was scared, which tended to make her short-tempered.

'Why, to act on what my mother told me in that last letter. She knew my position—that I was crippled by debt. That was none of my own fault, by the way—these debts are the thousands of pounds I was obliged to borrow when I was Lord Protector. I didn't need the money for my own sake, mark you, but to fulfil the duties of my position, a position I neither sought nor wanted. And when I resigned, Parliament promised me that my debts would be paid, and they granted me a pension for life as well. But then the King returned, and the old Parliament was dissolved, and there was a new Parliament that had no wish to fulfil the promises that the Commonwealth had made to me.'

'But you have an estate of your own, haven't you?' Cat said. 'Couldn't you have managed with your private revenues?'

Cromwell shook his head. 'I have but a life interest in the estate, and no other income. The estate is much embarrassed. My family is large and needs to be supported. My creditors would pursue me to the ends of the earth if they could. That's why I have to live in exile, rather than quietly in my own house among my own people. And the King is more than content that it should be so. I cannot trouble the peace of his kingdom if I'm on the continent. If he banished me himself, he would seem cruel and tyrannical, and he would anger those who think fondly of the old days.'

'You tell us all this?' Cat said slowly. 'You must realize —'

'That a word from Mr Hakesby or yourself could ruin me utterly? Of course. If my creditors discover I am in London, they will have me taken up for debt at once. And the King will be forced to act. So, madam, I have placed myself in the hands of you and your husband.'

Hakesby said, 'I would gladly serve you in any way I could, sir, for your father's sake– and for yours.'

'Thank you, sir.' Cromwell glanced at Cat. 'So?'

'This letter,' she said. 'What has this to do with the Cockpit?'

'As your husband knows, my parents had lodgings there for the better part of four years. When my father was elevated to Lord Protector, they moved into the royal apartments at Whitehall. But part of the Cockpit was retained for their use, and it remained so in my mother's widowhood. She had a fondness for the place. It was a little apart from all the lies and flatteries of the Court. She liked that she could walk from her garden into St James's Park and stroll there quite unknown.'

Cromwell has a pleasant voice, Cat thought, though perhaps he likes the sound of it too much. She cleared her throat, hoping he would take the hint and come to the point. Her husband frowned at her, but Cromwell took no apparent notice.

'When the King was restored, my mother had another set of troubles. Malicious people accused her of stealing royal possessions. They professed to believe she had profited by her position.'

'Poor lady,' Hakesby said. 'I remember. There were cruel, libellous pamphlets.'

'She was accused of having them with her or of concealing them in the hope of collecting them later.' Cromwell frowned at them. 'Small things. Gold, jewels and the like; easily portable. It was quite baseless. A foul libel.' He hesitated. 'But . . .'

Ah, Cat thought, I knew there would be a 'but'. Richard Cromwell rubbed the invisible spot on the table beside him; the old habit that had betrayed his identity to her.

'It's true that my mother concealed something valuable before she left Whitehall. But it was her own, not the King's. I must

144

emphasize that. The times were troubled and uncertain, and she feared with good reason that it would be taken from her if she tried to carry it away with her. I'm sure she was right in that. In her last letter, she told me the whole story. She also told me where to find it. That's why I'm here.'

'*It?*' Cat said. 'What is this *it?*'

'That need not concern you, madam,' Cromwell snapped. There was a pause. Then he smiled at her, trying to soften the bluntness of the refusal. 'All you need to understand is that it is not a large object, and it belongs to me.'

Hakesby tapped the leather folder. 'And this . . . ?'

'Yes, sir. Those plans may help me find what is mine. If you would be so kind as to let me have a sight of them.'

'They may not mean a great deal to you.'

'Then perhaps you will be my guide. I can think of no better one.'

Hakesby bowed his head. 'Willingly.'

The compliment brought spots of colour to his cheeks. He tried to unlace the fastening that secured the folder, but his fingers would not do the work required of them. Cat took it from him and undid the string. She removed the papers inside and laid them on the table. The others clustered round.

Cromwell frowned. 'Which way up is this? I don't understand.'

'The Cockpit is a strange place,' Hakesby said, his voice suddenly strong and authoritative, like a preacher's in his own pulpit. 'Faith, sir, I believe there is nothing quite like it on this earth.'

When he had taken too much wine of an evening, Hakesby would sometimes talk to Cat of his work and his dreams. His willingness to impart his knowledge, whatever his motive, was the quality she valued the most about him. Months ago, he had told her about the Cockpit.

'Henry VIII was responsible for the whole sorry hotchpotch,' he cried.

Hakesby had no objection to the old King's taking the riverside mansion of Cardinal Wolsey for himself and making it into a palace from which he could govern his realm. After all, Wolsey had been a papist, and a corrupt one at that. Whitehall's situation was convenient for the country's ruler, whether or not he wore a crown: it was beside the river, and conveniently placed between Westminster on the one hand, and the City and the Tower on the other.

It was, however, by modern standards a mean and impractical group of buildings, both ugly and old-fashioned. But, Hakesby said, given money and a good architect, all that could be remedied. Inigo Jones had shown the way with the Banqueting House. Tear down everything else and rebuild, with the Banqueting House as one's model, and one could not go far wrong.

The Cockpit was different. It had been a problem from the start. The reason for this was King Street, the public thoroughfare running from Charing Cross to Westminster. Henry VIII could defy His Holiness the Pope and behead two wives, but he found himself unable to close King Street. The laws of his kingdom would not allow it, and nor would his subjects.

King Street separated the main palace by the river from St James's Park and from the pleasures of the chase. Accordingly, the King had commanded two gatehouses to be built across King Street. They served as bridges as well as gates, for they allowed him and his courtiers to pass above the roadway from his palace to his park.

And not just to his park and his hunting. This was a king who loved sport of all kind. On the park side, on the west side of King Street, he built for himself a tiltyard for jousting, courts (both open and covered) for tennis and similar games, and a vast covered cockpit for the splendid sport of placing bets and shouting like hysterical madmen while watching two small, fierce birds rip each other to shreds. There were lodgings and gardens too, for courtiers and officials, and chambers for private assignations and entertainments. There was no method to it all. Nothing mattered except the King's convenience, the King's whims, and the King's ability to raise the money needed to gratify them.

Since then, Hakesby had told Cat more than once, the Cockpit and the muddle of surrounding buildings around it had gone from bad to worse, as had the rest of Whitehall. Successive monarchs had added this, taken away that, and generations of courtiers had come and gone, each trying to make changes for their own selfish reasons.

The more his body and mind decayed, the more Hakesby clung to the principle of order and the desirability of good design. 'If I were God,' he had once told Cat on an evening when he had taken more wine than usual, 'I should tear down the whole place, both Whitehall by the river and the Cockpit by the park. I should close that cursed road for ever and build a palace that would make the King of France weep bitter tears of envy.'

He had begun to weep himself then.

'Sir,' Cat said. 'You mustn't distress yourself. It is a most glorious vision.'

Hakesby turned his moist-eyed, shiny-nosed, tear-stained face to her. 'But where would we find a sovereign fit for such a palace? Only God himself would be worthy of it.'

To Mr Hakesby's delight and Cat's annoyance, the Cromwells dined with them. The tavern dinner, overpriced and overcooked, came and went. While they were eating, drinking and talking, the windows darkened into the early dusk of a dull day in February.

Afterwards, the table was cleared and Hakesby called for candles. Their flickering light drew the four of them together, enclosing them, making them conspirators. At Hakesby's nod, Cat took the plans from the folder again and laid them on the table. There were four sheets of paper. Placed together they formed a survey of the Cockpit and the surrounding buildings as far north as the Holbein Gate and the Tiltyard. Tangles of notes rioted in their margins.

One sheet had greasy thumbprints on each side. Another was stained with wine. They were working plans, partly drawn in faded ink, partly in pencil; they had been intended for site work, not to impress a client.

Given a set of plans, Hakesby was transformed. He spoke with certainty and clarity, his words weighted with decades of experience. Cat had never loved her husband as a wife should, but this was a part of him she respected so greatly that it amounted to something that strangely resembled love.

'Turn it,' he commanded her, 'so Mr Cromwell is looking at it towards the west; he will find that easier to grasp. Do you see, sir, there is King Street, with the Privy Garden below, that is to the east. To the north–that is to your right–you see the Holbein Gate. And above–a little to the left, sir, if you please–there, mark that building, the square enclosing an octagon: that is the Cockpit itself. And beyond it lies St James's Park. To the south of *that*'–his forefinger stabbed the paper to the left of the Cockpit–'you see the lodgings that your family had during the Commonwealth. The apartments are much changed, I believe, since the Duke of Albemarle has had them. They have been remodelled and extended.'

'Pray, sir, is that the garden where Catty and I played as children?' Elizabeth said, pointing.

Cat thought uncharitably that there had been no need for Elizabeth's question, and that she had probably asked it only because nobody had paid her any attention for the previous half hour.

'Very likely,' Hakesby said without much interest; his attention was on Cromwell himself. 'If my memory serves, the principal parlour was there, facing south and extending into a bay: does that allow you to get your bearings?'

Cromwell leaned over the table and moved one of the candles so that its light shone more directly on the paper. 'And the closet I mentioned?'

'Over there. In the corner. You see the dotted line beneath? It marks the course of the culverted stream.' Hakesby's forefinger traced the line across the garden and into the park beyond, and then past the edge of the paper and on to the table itself. 'There—you see? It flows—or it used to flow—into a brook that drains under the road. Then it passes under the bowling green to about *there*'—the finger stabbed the table again—'where it discharges into the Thames.'

Cromwell frowned. 'I cannot quite see . . .'

He took out a paper from his coat, which Cat assumed was the letter from his mother. 'This talks of a shed in a corner of the garden. As well as the closet.'

'Indeed, sir.' Hakesby's finger hovered over the garden again. 'The outhouse was in a fenced-off part used at the time as a kitchen garden. That line there must mark the paling around the enclosure. If I interpret your letter correctly, inside the shed there was an opening which provided access to the sewer for maintenance purposes. Covered by a slab of stone, perhaps, or planking. It was probably judged that to have it in the closet itself, or elsewhere in the lodging, would not be convenient– cleaning sewers is a noisome business at the best of times . . . and indeed the mazer scourers who frequent them are not pleasant company in a confined space.'

Elizabeth wrinkled her nose. 'But why would my grandmother choose such a foul spot to hide something?'

'Precisely because so few go there, mistress,' Hakesby said. 'And those that do, go to clear an obstruction or shore up a wall. Then they escape as soon as they can. The fumes can be worse than noisome: without a current of fresh air to move them along, they can thicken and kill.'

'Did you inspect this particular sewer yourself, sir?' Cromwell asked.

'Probably not.' Hakesby glanced across the table at him. 'We knew the approximate line from previous surveys. I cannot recall, but I suspect I would have had a workman make sure that the sewage was moving freely. The sewer must have been dug about the same time as the Cockpit itself. That probably means it's brick-lined and about four feet high. If the bottom is clear enough and the sewage level not too high, an agile man should be able to move through it at a crouch. The scourers tend to be small and wiry as a breed for that very reason.'

Crowell sat back in his chair. 'It seems straightforward enough. According to my mother, a box is concealed in an alcove in the sewer wall somewhere between the shed and the privy off the parlour. A mark cut into the brickwork reveals the place. Of course, the problem we now face is how to get there. We can hardly expect the Duke of Albemarle to welcome us with open arms.'

'Isn't there another difficulty, sir?' Cat said. 'The passing of time.'

Hakesby gave her an approving nod. 'Indeed. These plans were made near twenty years ago. Almost certainly the parlour and its closet are no longer there, or else they are so buried in the new work that they might never have existed. As for the shed and kitchen garden, they must be long gone.'

Cromwell glanced at his daughter. 'Then— has all this been in vain? Is there nothing we can do?'

'I didn't say that, sir.' Hakesby looked happier than Cat had seen him for months. 'Working on these old buildings is an art in itself. The secret is knowing how to gather the information one needs. In this case, we shall require the services of an expert.'

Elizabeth pouted. 'An expert in what?'

'Mazers, madam. When it is a matter of sewage, who better to ask than a mazer scourer?' He stopped abruptly, and his face fell. 'But all this may well cost a deal of money. In these venal times of ours, every thing and every man has its price.'

'God will find a way,' Cromwell said. Frowning, he rubbed his forefinger on the tabletop, erasing something that only he could see. 'I hope. I pray.'

Pheebs, who kept the street door at the sign of the Rose, considered himself a broad-minded man who did to others as they did to him. His position as porter gave him a roof over his head—he usually slept in the hall on a palliasse stuffed with straw–and a small weekly wage. He earned considerably more than his wage through gratuities from the tenants and from their visitors, and from certain mutually beneficial arrangements with nearby tradesmen and hackney coachmen.

Over the years Pheebs had developed an extensive store of knowledge about those who came and went–not just through the door he guarded but also those who passed to and fro along Henrietta Street. Yesterday, for example, he had marked a large, gross man who had walked–or rather moved in a menacing waddle, with an old cavalry sword swinging from side to side to the peril of the legs of other passers-by–up and down the road at about the time the Hakesbys and Brennan had arrived in a hackney coach.

Mr Hakesby had been exhausted, and the boy had helped Brennan take the old man upstairs. Mistress Hakesby had given Pheebs sixpence for his trouble. She had grown into a fine young woman, he considered, quite wasted on her husband. If only she would take a little trouble with herself she might almost be called pretty.

The big fellow had waddled down the street an hour later. He paused to ask

Pheebs for directions to Drury Lane. In the way of idle conversation, he had asked who lived here at the sign of the Rose. Pheebs, his tongue greased by another sixpence, saw no harm in telling him, for if he did not, then others would.

That same evening, Pheebs had wetted his whistle in the alehouse by Half Moon Passage where the neighbourhood's porters and chairmen gathered. The porter of a nearby house told him that the man had been asking him questions about the sign of the Rose. He had promised the porter's nephew a couple of shillings if he reported who visited the house. He was, the porter said, particularly interested in hearing if a prosperous-looking young man named Marwood had paid the Hakesbys a visit. The left-hand side of Marwood's face was badly scarred by fire, the fat man had said, though his periwig concealed the worst of it.

All this explained why Pheebs was not altogether surprised to see the man loitering outside the house again today. It was late in the afternoon, and he was standing by a brazier on the other side of the road, warming his hands over the coals and talking to a workman.

The Hakesbys had guests for dinner–another old man and another young woman:

potential clients, perhaps; the Hakesbys did not entertain much. Pheebs had admitted them himself. In the middle of the afternoon, Pheebs's boy was sent to fetch a hackney for the visitors.

Shortly afterwards, the Hakesbys ushered their guests downstairs in person, which suggested they must be people of consequence, though the man in particular looked like an old farmer who had had too many bad harvests. The farmer had been wearing green glasses when he arrived, but now he had left them off. The young woman was well enough, though; barely more than a girl but quite the fine lady. She had seemed deeply attached to Mistress Hakesby. The four of them stood in the doorway, looking up the street at the approaching coach.

All this Pheebs marked and inwardly digested with the lofty objectivity that his position required. He had also noted how the man on the other side of the road responded to the sight of the Hakesbys and their two guests in the doorway of the sign of the Rose. He broke off what he was saying to the workman. His arms dropped to his sides. One hand gripped the hilt of his sword.

He had looked, Pheebs thought, not just surprised. He looked as if he couldn't believe the evidence of his eyes. Indeed, he looked, Pheebs thought, filing the knowledge away in case it came in useful later, as if he had seen a ghost.

CHAPTER SIX

For Ye Are All Sinners
Tuesday, 4–Saturday, 8 February 1668

That night Ferrus sleeps in the scullery by the yard door. Pain touches him. Stabs his hand. He smells burning hair. Roasting meat.

A girl giggles.

Someone screams like a pig on the slab. It's him, Ferrus. He jerks awake, pulls himself up, arms flailing. A footman stoops over him. The fair-haired one the maids like. Devil-face. He grins.

Ferrus squeals.

In the yard, Windy barks.

Nightmare, footman says, you always having nightmares and shitting yourself. Bag of stinking, poxy terrors you are, disturbing good Christian souls at night.

On Tuesday evening I was detained at Scotland Yard until almost midnight. When

I returned to my lodging in the Savoy, a sleepy and irritable Sam admitted me to the house. Margaret and Stephen had long since gone to bed.

'Any news?' I asked.

'If there is, no one told me,' he said, adding 'sir' just as I was about to reprimand him for insolence. He turned aside to light a candle for me from his own. 'Except, now I call it to mind, there's a letter, master. A boy brought it round this afternoon.'

'From?'

'Wouldn't know, sir, would I? Being unlettered and all.' I couldn't see his face but there was a hint of mockery in his voice. 'Margaret said it looked like Mistress Hakesby's hand.'

'Bring it to the parlour,' I said. 'And make up the fire. Then you can go to bed.'

Sam obeyed, making an unnecessary amount of noise with his crutch and his stump as he hobbled off. I was tempted to snap at him but something held me back. He and I knew each other well–he had been in my service for over a year now. He wasn't drunk, which could make him impudent. But his amputated leg sometimes caused him considerable pain, and he deserved better from me than a reprimand. All things considered, he had been a faithful servant.

When Sam had left me alone, I sat by the fire and opened Cat's note. I confess I was pleasurably excited at the prospect of reading it, though for no reason; weariness made me foolish. At Arundel House, just before Hakesby interrupted us, she had been about to ask me for something. I assumed the letter would have some connection with that.

I was wrong. The letter had nothing to do with that. To my alarm, she wrote that she had seen Roger Durrell, Veal's servant, in Henrietta Street when they had returned from Arundel House that morning. The coincidence was too great for comfort: in other words, I didn't believe it was a coincidence at all.

I knew that the Duke of Buckingham had set Veal and Durrell to watch the comings and goings at Arundel House. There was a good chance that they had seen me there on at least one occasion. That would have interested but not surprised them; after all, they knew that I was clerk to Mr Williamson, and Williamson was Lord Arlington's Undersecretary.

What worried me now was that they might well have seen me talking to Cat and Hakesby. In which case, their curiosity would have been aroused. Why else would Durrell have taken the trouble to find out where the Hakesbys lived? As far as I knew, they had not previously known who they were, or their connection to me. But if Durrell had followed their hackney to Henrietta Street, they must be well on the way to finding out.

Was I reading too much into the situation? I was too tired to think clearly, and melancholy with it. Seeing Cat earlier in the day had troubled me and so, for some unfathomable reason, had this letter from her. It was one thing to know that she was now Mistress Hakesby, married to a man who could almost have been her grandfather. It was quite another to see them together. Man and wife.

Now here was this new problem. My imagination ran riot, and I lacked the will to restrain it. My doubts bred further doubts, and my worries and fears multiplied to a point that, if made flesh, they could have populated half of London.

It was far too late for me to call at the Drawing Office. No one would thank me for rousing the entire house after midnight. Besides, it might be unsafe to give Buckingham and his servants any reason to believe that there was more than a casual connection between the Hakesbys and myself. As it stood, Veal and Durrell might think that my encounter with them at Arundel House was of no importance, that perhaps I had seen the surveyor's pretty wife waiting in the court and decided to try the effect of a little gallantry.

Gradually I forced my restless mind to consider the matter rationally. There was no cause for alarm, no reason why the Hakesbys should be in danger. Buckingham and his hirelings had bigger fish to fry.

By degrees I became calmer. Before I went to bed that night, I unlocked my desk and wrote a short reply to Cat, thanking her for the information and asking her to let me know if she saw Veal or Durrell again. I added as a postscript that if we chanced to encounter each other elsewhere, perhaps it would be safer if we pretended to be strangers.

This was true, but not the whole truth. I was honest enough to admit to myself that I did not want to see Cat Hakesby again in person if I could help it. She unsettled me. Desire is like a horse, I told myself: it will run away with us if we do not learn to restrain it with bridle and bit.

I sealed my letter to her and left it on the parlour mantelpiece, intending to order Stephen to take it round to Henrietta Street. But in the morning Sam failed to call me at my usual time, and I was late rising. I swore at Sam, dressed in haste and rushed from the house.

The letter I had written to Cat had flown out of my mind. It remained on the parlour mantelpiece, and it was still waiting for me when I returned late in the evening.

On Thursday 6 February, the King opened Parliament.

'Let us hope he's not disappointed, Marwood,' Mr Williamson said to me that morning, when I met him in the Matted Gallery. 'The Duke of Buckingham promised him the moon, but it's just possible that His Grace won't be able to provide him with it.'

In this case, the moon consisted of sufficient funds to rebuild the navy, pay for the government, and allow the King to live as he believed a monarch should. It included a Comprehension Act that would allow the country's Nonconformists to worship freely and, as a natural consequence, be wholeheartedly loyal to their king.

Buckingham's problem was that Parliament was dominated by gentlemen who were far more attached to the Church of England than was the King, its titular head; or so they and their friends the bishops claimed. They were even more attached to their own interests; more money for the King's government would require increased taxation to raise it, and the burden of that would fall at least partly on themselves.

In my darker moods, I believed that both houses of Parliament were filled with men who cared nothing for the common good. Principle had flown out of the window. Come what may, some would vote for the bills put forward by the King's men because their own careers depended on the government's favour. Some would vote against, because they hated kings, or they hated this king, or they longed for the good old days when a Cromwell ruled in Whitehall and England was a godly land. Others simply voted for whatever side promised them most or damaged them least.

Politics is nothing but a game played by greedy men and fools, by saints and monsters.

'Talking of the Duke of Buckingham,' Williamson said, 'that reminds me. He's holding a day of prayer and penance at Wallingford House tomorrow. A day of humiliation.'

'Prayer and penance?' I said. '*Humiliation? The Duke?*'

'There is no end to God's miracles,'

Williamson said. It was the nearest I had heard him come to making a joke, though you could not have told that from his face. 'He has invited a number of clergymen to join him for a day of humiliation to atone for our sins. He has also asked various gentlemen of his acquaintance. Indeed, he even sent Lord Arlington an invitation.'

This was unmistakably a jest, the sort of jest that is merely an insult in disguise. Arlington was not just Buckingham's political enemy: they were opposed in religion too.

'Of course my lord won't go.' Williamson stared at me. 'But he has decided he will send an emissary to represent him at Wallingford House instead. He commands you to go in his place.'

'But sir, the Duke dislikes me intensely.'

'I believe Lord Arlington is aware of that, Marwood.'

Naturally he was. Arlington, I realized belatedly, had answered Buckingham's jest with one of his own.

In the early evening of Thursday, 6 February, two men came with the dusk to the house in Hatton Garden. The porter had just unbarred the wicket to admit the maid, whom Mistress Dalton had sent out earlier to fetch a pair of gloves she had ordered.

The two men appeared from the shadows and pushed their way inside at her heels.

'Nothing to worry about, fellow,' the taller of the two men said. He was rake-thin and spoke with a Yorkshire accent. 'Your mistress will be glad to see us.'

The porter was unconvinced. But the crown piece the man gave him was a good reason to hold his peace, and the fact that both men were armed was another. Meanwhile, the second man, who was almost as wide as he was tall, took the arm of the maid and with ponderous gallantry volunteered to carry her minuscule parcel.

Inside the house, Mistress Dalton, who was no coward, tried to bar their way. The tall man bowed politely to her. He begged her pardon for their intrusion. Then, lowering his voice so only she could hear, he whispered that he had brought a message for her honoured guest, a piece of good news that he would be pleased to hear.

Mistress Dalton was not to be won over so easily. But her attempt to argue was made useless by the opening of the parlour door and the arrival of the guest himself. He was carrying a book in one hand, his forefinger marking the place, and wearing his glasses with the thick green lenses.

The servant released the maid, drew

himself up and sketched a vaguely military salute. 'Trooper Durrell, sir.'

Cromwell looked blankly at him.

The tall man bowed low. 'Your highness,' he said.

'Not that,' Cromwell said sharply. 'None of such foolishness. Who are you?'

'As you wish, sir. My name is Veal. I have a letter for you.'

He took it from his pocket and handed it to Cromwell, who removed his glasses and carried it across the hall to a dresser where two candles stood. He examined the seal by their light and raised his eyebrows. He tore open the letter and read it quickly. The paper trembled in his hand so he laid it on the dresser between the candles.

Afterwards, he looked up. 'If I decline the Duke's invitation?'

Veal gave a shake of his head. He said nothing. He bowed.

Cromwell realized that he had no choice in the matter. Either he accompanied these men to Wallingford House or they would force him to do so. In the unlikely event of failure, they would report his presence in London to the authorities, which would bring disaster down on his head, and probably on Mistress Dalton's and Elizabeth's as well.

On the other hand, this letter might prove a stroke of good fortune. A friend at Court could solve a number of his problems. He balanced the options and came to a decision.

'You must not disturb yourself, madam,' Cromwell said to Mistress Dalton. 'These men are friends, or at least the friends of friends.' Then, to Veal: 'You had better take me to your master.'

The coach was a private one, shabby and undistinguished, with nothing on the outside to suggest its owner.

'How did you find me?' Cromwell asked as they drove down to Holborn.

'It was the purest chance, sir,' Veal said. 'Or rather Providence ordained it. Roger here happened to catch sight of you in the street. He knew you at once.'

'Trooper Durrell as was, Your Honour,' Roger Durrell said in a voice like liquid mud. 'Lord General Fairfax's lifeguard. Had the honour to serve under you in '48. Saw Your Honour again at Whitehall in '57. Never forget a face, sir.'

'I only served in the army for a few months,' Cromwell said. 'I'm surprised anyone had time to remember me. And it's twenty years ago.'

'Roger told me he had seen you,' Veal continued, ignoring this, 'and I told His Grace, whom we both have the honour to serve in a confidential capacity. And he sent us to you at once.'

'If Durrell here recognized me, others might,' Cromwell said, voicing a worry that had been growing in his mind. 'I'd hoped I was sufficiently changed to pass without notice.'

'As you are, sir, when you wear those green glasses. But remember–Roger caught sight of you when you chanced to have your eyes uncovered. Besides, he has a rare talent for faces.'

'I wonder where you saw me. I try to wear them always.'

'Henrietta Street by Covent Garden, Your Honour,' Durrell said promptly. 'You was coming out of a house with a young lady.'

'Ah–you mean my daughter.' He felt his eyes fill with tears, which were perfectly genuine. 'I haven't seen my family since I went abroad. She came up to London to meet me. God bless her.'

'Amen,' said Mr Veal. 'Is she staying there?' He prodded Durrell with his finger. 'At the sign of the Rose, wasn't it?'

'No, sir. She stays with Mistress Dalton too. But she had a desire to see a friend of her youth, a Mistress Hakesby, and I escorted her to Henrietta Street.'

To his relief, the answer seemed to satisfy Veal. It might have complicated matters if Cromwell had been forced to admit that Mistress Hakesby was the daughter of the regicide Thomas Lovett, who had fallen to his death in mysterious circumstances in the ruins of St Paul's Cathedral, soon after the Great Fire.

They drove on, the coach's iron-shod wheels scraping and clattering over the stones and slithering in the mud. At Charing Cross the coach swung sharply to the right. It rattled on and turned into Pall Mall. It slowed and came to a halt.

'Where are we?' Cromwell said, alarmed. 'I thought you were taking me to the Duke.'

'So we are, sir, so we are.' Veal pushed aside the leather curtain to look out. 'But we don't want to announce your arrival to the world.'

They descended from the coach and passed through the gate into St James's Park. It was almost dark, but lanterns marked the lines of the principal paths. Veal and Durrell walked on either side of Cromwell. Their presence was ambiguous: on the face of it, they were protecting him from possible attackers, but they were also preventing him from escaping. They led him along the broad avenue lined with trees towards the garden wall of Wallingford House. There were gates set in it, wide and tall enough for a pair of horsemen riding side by side. A light burned above the archway.

'There, sir,' said Veal, pointing. 'A light to lighten our darkness.'

They were clearly expected. One leaf of the gates swung open as they approached. Two footmen with lanterns were waiting on the other side of the wall. Cromwell had a shadowy impression of a formal garden with the great house looming beyond. Veal and Durrell led him along a flagged walk, with a servant on either side to light their way, until they reached steps up to a broad terrace along the back of the mansion. They passed through a porch and into the house itself.

'This way, sir,' Veal said, gesturing towards a flight of stairs. 'His Grace gave orders that his private closet should be prepared for you.'

He escorted Cromwell up to the first floor and through a long chamber furnished as a library. The closet was at the end. It contained a desk, two chairs and an iron-bound chest. A coal fire burned in the grate, and candles were alight in sconces on the panelled walls. The room's simplicity was at variance with the lavishness of what he had glimpsed of the rest of the house.

'No one will disturb you here,' Veal said. 'His Grace won't be long. He will know you're here. Would you care for some wine? Or something to eat?'

Cromwell declined. He sat by the fire. Veal bowed and left him. Cromwell rarely felt nostalgic for his day as Lord Protector but in those days at least no one had kept him waiting, or at least not until the end when his power was slipping away from him. Despite the warmth of the room, he shivered.

I have done nothing wrong, he told himself, and the worst the King can do to me is have me thrown in jail for debt. But the words were hollow. In truth he could not pretend that he was as insignificant as he would have liked to have been. He was Oliver's son and himself the late Lord Protector of England: that gave him a political importance whether he wanted it or not. During the Commonwealth, there were people who thought longingly of the good old days when a king had ruled over them. Since the Restoration, there were people who thought longingly of the Protectorate.

There were hurried footsteps outside the door. Cromwell rose to his feet as Buckingham burst into the room.

'My dear sir,' the Duke cried. With great courtesy, he swept off his hat and bowed low. 'What a pleasure to see you here at last. A thousand pardons for keeping you waiting–I hope my servants have looked after you.' Buckingham was a big man in any case, but he seemed even larger than nature had made him. In this small room he radiated a vitality that was almost overwhelming. 'I beg you–let us sit and talk–but first I must thank you, sir, I must thank you from the bottom of my heart.'

'Thank me–why?'

'For freeing me. For granting me life and liberty, the greatest gifts of all. It grieves me greatly that your father and I were not friends. I must confess, when he sent me to the Tower I didn't think I would escape alive. But when you succeeded as Lord Protector, you allowed me to go free. Indeed, sir, it would not be too much to say that ten years ago you saved my life. I am for ever in your debt.'

Cromwell remembered the circumstances rather differently. Buckingham, having quarrelled with the King in exile, had come back to England and married Mary, the daughter and heir of General Fairfax. On her part it had been a love match; on his, however, it had clearly been a cynical attempt to win back a large part of his estates, since Parliament had confiscated these from Buckingham and bestowed them on Lord Fairfax. The Lord Protector had responded by placing the Duke under house arrest.

'He's a turncoat,' Oliver had said to Richard. 'I don't trust him. If a man changes allegiance once, he'll change it twice. The royal family treated him as one of their own since he was a fatherless child, and now he's turned his back on them. He's a rake and libertine, too. Poor Mary Fairfax will rue the day she married him.'

When Buckingham had broken the terms of his house arrest, he was taken up and sent to the Tower. But the following month, Oliver was dead. The Duke was kept in the Tower, however, though in very comfortable circumstances, all things considered, as befitted a duke who was also General Fairfax's son-in-law. He had stayed there for nearly six months more, until February 1659, when the Council had decided that he should be released with Fairfax standing bail for £20,000.

Richard himself had had nothing to do with the matter. During his short Protectorate, he had had far more pressing problems than the fate of a renegade duke who was safely lodged in the Tower. The question of Buckingham's freedom had been a matter for the Council, not him.

Then what was this show of gratitude for? Was it possible that Buckingham did not know that he, Richard, had done nothing to secure his release from the Tower? Perhaps the answer didn't matter. Whatever the truth, there was surely every reason to take advantage of the situation.

'Sir,' Cromwell said, 'when God set me briefly in such a high place, I acted as He directed me. I am delighted to find you in such a flourishing condition.'

'And I to see you back in your native country where you belong. We must celebrate this happy conjunction, must we not? We must drink to it, sir, I insist.'

Buckingham fetched wine, glasses and biscuits from the cupboard. He toasted Cromwell, and Cromwell could hardly decline to toast the Duke back.

'I know that you find it convenient at present to live on the Continent . . .' the Duke said, refilling their glasses.

'That's tactfully put, sir.'

'But here you are in London, neverthe-less, and not a stone's throw from

Whitehall.'

'I have slipped back to England for a week or two to see something of my family,' Cromwell said. 'After eight lonely years.'

'Aren't they living in the country?'

'My daughter Elizabeth has come up to London.'

'You must let me know if I can serve you or your family in any way. Perhaps–I would not mention this if I had not heard something of your circumstances–a trifling loan might smooth your way.'

Cromwell felt his cheeks grow warm. 'You're too kind, sir. But —'

'It would be a positive pleasure to assist you in any way I can,' Buckingham interrupted. 'Indeed, I'd invite you and your daughter to stay here for as long as you liked if I didn't think it might draw attention that both of us might find inconvenient.' He hesitated, drawing his hand across his forehead in a gesture so graceful it seemed rehearsed. 'And perhaps there are other reasons why you would not care for that.'

'I don't follow you, sir.'

'We live in sinful times, I'm afraid, and I myself am but human. *Errare humanum est,* as Seneca so wisely reminds us. You might not wish to associate with one such as me. Or for your daughter to do so.'

'That cannot be so, sir,' said Cromwell politely.

'But perhaps you do not know? There was a most unfortunate duel last month . . .'

Cromwell nodded. 'I heard something of it,' he said. 'And the circumstances. For a while, the town talked of little else.'

Buckingham, who had an actor's trick of amplifying his emotions, looked as if he were on the verge of being overwhelmed by grief. 'I have sinned, and I grieve for it from the bottom of my heart. In fact, I have invited certain worthy men to join me here tomorrow for a day of penitence and humiliation. My own penitence, first and foremost, and my own humiliation.'

'We all have to repent of something sir.'

'True, sir, very true. As I say, we live in sinful times–and the King's own court sets the worst example in the world to the Kingdom. But we must be charitable–as you say, we are all sinners, are we not? I cannot but hope that God may find our prayers tomorrow acceptable. I remember Our Lord's lesson of the widow's mite, and it gives me hope. Insignificant as we are, we must pray, we must strive to do good, we must repent our sins. So Dr Owen will preach to us tomorrow, and I'm sure it will be most edifying. You remember him? Your father had many dealings with him. Like poor Veal who brought you here, he was ejected from his places after the Restoration, but he is a most godly man.'

For a moment Cromwell was diverted: 'Mr Veal is a clergyman? The man who carried me here in the coach?'

'Yes, poor fellow, or so he was. He was an army chaplain after Cambridge, and then he had one of my livings in Yorkshire until he was turned out of it.'

'He wears a sword.'

'Indeed he does. And he knows how to use it in the service of the godly. But I am sure that when this country is a fit place for Christians again, he will beat his sword into a ploughshare, and I shall find him a living again as his reward. So will you come tomorrow, sir? It would mean a great deal to me.'

Cromwell hesitated. Why should his presence or absence matter to Buckingham one way or the other? There must be more to it, some underlying scheme. On the other hand, he could hardly afford to offend the Duke, who seemed so ready to offer him friendship and money. In the end, he temporized: 'Surely I would be a danger to you if I came? And I myself would not be safe. If Durrell recognized me, might not others?'

Buckingham seemed to swell still further. 'No harm will ever come to you in this house,' he said. 'My dear sir, I promise you that on my dear father's grave. Besides,' he went on in a more down-to-earth voice, 'if you wear those glasses, no one will recognize you from Adam. Indeed, I'm greatly surprised that Durrell knew you even when your eyes were uncovered. I hope you won't mind my saying that you are much changed from what you were, for your sorrows have marked you.'

'I . . . I'm not entirely convinced that —'

'Promise me you will come and hear Dr Owen. Veal will keep you safe. And afterwards'–the Duke smiled with great charm–'we shall arrange how I may best help you and yours.'

On Friday morning, I dressed in the glory of my Sunday suit. I left my lodging shortly after nine o'clock. I had not had an answer from Cat Hakesby. Stephen had taken my letter to the Drawing Office early yesterday morning. Presumably I could interpret her silence as meaning that she had seen nothing more of Roger or his master Veal. If I was right, it was good news. But I could not help feeling disappointed.

I walked along the Strand towards Wallingford House, which lay at the northern end of the Tiltyard between Whitehall and Charing Cross. I had passed its gilded gates thousands of times, but I had never been inside. It was a large building shaped like an E without its central projection and constructed of dark, soot-streaked bricks. The Duke of Buckingham owned several houses in London, including York House, a vast mansion on the river. But he and his father had both chosen to live at Wallingford House, old-fashioned though it was. It was nearer to Whitehall and the King.

Despite the earliness of the hour, there were already several private coaches in the court beyond the gates, and another was waiting to be admitted. I showed the pass that Williamson had given me. It bore Lord Arlington's signature. The porters let me through, directing me to the grand double doors in the centre of the building. The hall beyond was thronged by servants in Buckingham's livery. The Duke surrounded himself with dependants of all sorts, and he liked to make it clear that they belonged to him and no one else. I suspected that many in his household served little function but to project the illusion of their master's glory by sheer weight of numbers.

A clerk examined Arlington's pass, his

eyes flickering curiously over my face. Afterwards, two footmen conducted me up a broad staircase. Vast paintings hung on the walls, but their frames had been draped with black silk. Perhaps their subjects might be considered indecent by the pious company gathering here today.

On the first floor, the servants conducted me to a tall doorway, set in a richly ornamented frame and guarded by two footmen. One of them raised his finger to his lips, desiring me to be silent. He and his fellow threw open the two leaves of the door, releasing a sonorous voice on to the landing.

'Our worst earthly torments are no more than the merest fleabites compared to what awaits the sinners of this world who pass through the portal of hell.'

The room created an instant impression of size and muted splendour. The Duke, dressed in a magnificent black suit, sat in a high-backed oak armchair at the far end. He was upon a platform raised a foot above the floor. Sitting in lonely state, he was a king in all but name. Beneath his golden peruke, his florid face was still, the heavy features composed into a mask. There were bags under his eyes.

Everyone else in the room was standing.

The preacher, a clergyman with a pale face and tendency to spray spittle in his enthusiasm for his subject, was at one side of the platform, preaching his sermon with the aid of a thick pile of notes. I recognized him, for he was a man whom Williamson kept an eye on: his name was Owen; he was a prominent Independent minister and theologian who had been close to Cromwell under the Commonwealth and much favoured by many officers of the New Model Army. He was still influential, a man with many friends. He was one of those who had been calling for the Comprehension Bill, which must have brought him together with Buckingham.

Time passed tediously. Dr Owen was a scholar who believed it his duty to lay before us as many of the fruits of his erudition as he could. Moreover he would sometimes diverge from his notes and plunge into a digression, preaching extempore, waving his arms and striding about the stage. We might be here for hours.

'The devil works among us, invisible as yeast in the bread,' he was saying. 'Yea, take heed, lest ye consume him without knowing that ye do it.'

As for the rest, there must have been at least forty people, all men, in the room, though that was not enough to make it seem overly crowded. Many were clergymen. By their dress, and by their presence here, it was clear that most were inclined towards Presbyterianism, rather than the more traditional forms of worship favoured by the King's bishops, though some adhered to other forms of nonconformist belief. Other men were the Duke's more sober friends—among them Sir Robert Holmes, who had acted as his second at his duel with Lord Shrewsbury.

I stood near the door and listened to Dr Owen outlining the dreadful fate that awaited all of us miserable sinners who were not of the elect. His voice was harsh but monotonous, and I could not help feeling that listening to him was a form of hell in itself. He cast into outer darkness those who had fallen into Satan's great snare of papism. In particular, he condemned the sinfulness and luxury of the court, where such foul practices flourished. He did not go so far as openly to accuse the King of condoning and encouraging this vast cesspit of evil, but the implication was unavoidable.

'If the tree is rotten,' he thundered, 'so is the fruit thereof.'

I did not for a moment believe that Buckingham hoped this self-inflicted purgatory would bring him spiritual advantage. His motives were altogether more earthly. Much of his political support derived from the Presbyterians and their religious bedfellows. Now, as he attempted to get the King's business through Parliament and consolidate his power at Whitehall, he needed all the friends he could muster.

As the minutes crawled past, I stared about me. The Duke's father, or perhaps a previous owner, had designed the apartment as the Great Chamber, the room reserved for entertaining honoured guests. It was shaped like a double cube. Far above my head, the plaster ceiling was a riot of fruit and strap work, enriched with the occasional plump-bellied cherub. Two tall windows gave a glimpse of the leafless treetops of St James's Park, which lay to the rear of the house. Armorial bearings in stained glass filled their upper lights. A portrait of the present Duke filled the place of honour above the fireplace.

After a few minutes, I had the sensation that someone was looking at me. I glanced to the left. My old adversary, Mr Veal, prominent by his height, was standing in the corner beside a shabbily dressed gentleman. Veal's eyes locked with mine. His companion turned his head as well, perhaps curious to see what had attracted Veal's attention. He wore tinted glasses and an untidy grey beard that straggled down to his collar.

Veal was the first to look away, shifting his position as well, shielding his companion from my view. He scanned the room. A moment later, Durrell, Veal's servant, made his way through the crowd towards me from the other side of the room. He too was dressed in black. For once he looked almost respectable, though his great belly strained at the buttons of his coat. I watched him approach, as helpless as a rabbit before a fox.

'For ye are all sinners,' cried Dr Owen. 'Woe upon you all.'

When Durrell reached me, he took my elbow and swung me round to face the door through which I had come. The footmen stationed on either side sprang to life. Durrell propelled me on to the landing. Half a dozen servants were waiting there. They straightened up when they saw us.

The door closed, reducing the preacher's voice to a grating mumble, like the sound of distant sawing.

'I won't throw you down the stairs, you pox-ridden knave,' Durrell said in his gravelly voice. 'Not with the gentlemen at

186

their prayers.' He beckoned the nearest manservant. 'We're going to take this rogue down to the kitchen yard and beat him within an inch of his life. Half an inch, if we can.' He turned back to me, thrusting his face so close to mine that a wave of his foul breath swept into my nostrils. 'That's what we do to trespassers here.'

My legs were shaking. I put out a hand to the wall, to steady myself. Durrell terrified me. It wasn't just the man's strength. It was the ruthlessness I sensed in him. Unlike Veal, he was a man without boundaries.

Inside me, however, was a tiny flame of anger born of fear. 'I advise you to let me be, fellow,' I said. My voice was faint but at least it didn't tremble. 'I'm here at your master's invitation.'

'You whoreson liar. Come on. This way.'

'I'm here to represent my Lord Arlington. If you lay hands on me, you lay hands on him.'

That gave him pause. 'What folly is this?'

'The Duke invited my lord. To this–what does he call it? This day of humiliation. And my lord sent me in his place. I have his pass in my pocket. Why do you suppose the servants admitted me, you fool? You know they're checking everyone who comes in.'

Durrell held out his hand and I gave him

the pass. He stared at it for several seconds, though I was by no means certain that he was able to read.

'I've no mind to go back and hear the rest of the sermon,' I said. 'Not now, after this rude interruption. Pray have them show me out.'

He cleared his throat. His cheek muscles moved as if he were gathering phlegm before spitting. He came close to me. My stomach clenched. 'One day,' he murmured, 'you wait.' He drew back. 'Let him go,' he said to the footman. 'Make sure he leaves.'

Durrell turned away. Another servant opened the door of the Great Chamber for him. The preacher's voice rolled out on to the landing.

'Yea, I say unto you again, ye are all sinners.'

There was no reply from Cat when I returned to my house. By this time I had reminded myself that I had given her no reason to write to me again unless she saw Veal or Durrell. I'd written to her too much in haste, I thought—I should have asked her what she had wanted to discuss with me at Arundel House the other day.

The next day was Saturday, and I spent it working at Scotland Yard. I told Mr William-

son about Dr Owen's sermon at Wallingford House, and how two of the Duke's
people had recognized me, and turned me
out of the gathering.

'Did they offer violence?' he asked. It
might have suited him very well if they had
damaged me.

'One of them wanted to, sir, but I showed
my lord's pass, and that held him back.'

'If they'd mistreated you, we might have
made something of it.' Williamson shot me
a glance and added without much conviction, 'Though of course I'm glad for your
sake that you weren't inconvenienced.'

He sent me back to my work. One thing I
hadn't mentioned to him was the man I had
seen with Veal–the elderly gentleman in the
green spectacles and the shabby clothes and
the ill-kept beard. I hadn't mentioned it
because there was nothing of substance to
tell. Only the barest hint of something: Veal
had moved so swiftly when he saw me there;
whether he meant it or not, his change of
position had shielded the old man from me;
and he had wasted no time in sending Durrell to eject me from Wallingford House.

In the afternoon, Mr Williamson called
me back into his private office and, to my
alarm, told me that the King commanded
me to attend him this evening.

'He's heard about the Duke's day of penance yesterday, and he wants to hear what happened from somebody who was actually there.' My master frowned, possibly at me, possibly at the King. 'He finds the notion entertaining, I understand.'

'I'm surprised he doesn't ask the Duke about it directly, sir.'

'Perhaps he will.' Williamson rubbed his eyes, which were bloodshot with too much close work. 'The Duke will amuse him, the King knows that. But he won't necessarily tell him the truth. The King knows that too.'

When I waited on the King that evening, I was directed to Lady Castlemaine's lodgings. That was not a good omen. She was the King's principal mistress. By birth she was a Villiers, first cousin to the Duke of Buckingham and not unlike him in her vigorous appetite for intrigues of all sorts. Sometimes the cousins quarrelled with each other, and sometimes they were allies.

Last year, they had allied themselves in the party that strove to expel Lord Clarendon from the office of Lord Chancellor. When the news of Clarendon's downfall reached her, she danced for joy in her aviary, wearing only her shift and caring nothing if the whole world was watching her. At present she and Buckingham were still close friends, and I couldn't help wondering if she would report everything I told the King to the Duke.

Lady Castlemaine's lodgings were at the far end of the Privy Gallery in a large and lavishly furnished suite of apartments that ran westward above the Holbein Gate towards the Park. It was growing late–Mr Williamson had told me the King would find a moment for me after supper. I walked through the Privy Garden to her ladyship's recently built private staircase in the corner. Around me, the windows of the palace glowed with candlelight, and lanterns had been hung at intervals in the garden to light the paths. It was a cold night, but dry.

At the door of the staircase, the guards let me through when I gave them my name. A servant escorted me through the chambers over the gate and to the range of apartments beyond. The painted ceilings, the gilded cornices and the furnishings were as lavish as those in the royal apartments themselves.

The servant brought me to an anteroom. He told me to wait until I was called and whispered something in the ear of a page. The page went through an inner door, allowing a burst of music and laughter to escape.

I was left alone to kick my heels. Servants came and went, and occasionally ladies and gentlemen went through the same door. Time passed, measured by the chiming of clocks and the growing emptiness of my belly.

At last a gentleman emerged and told me I should follow him. To my surprise, he did not usher me into the chamber where the King was, but through another door and a passage to a closet. It was hung with tapestries that showed St Sebastian shot through with arrows. A prie-dieu stood in front of it. I wondered if my lady used the chamber as an oratory–she had converted to the Catholic faith a few years earlier, which did not make her more popular with the staunchly Protestant Londoners who already loathed her for her profligacy. A second door, opposite to the one by which we had entered, was ajar, and the sounds of the supper party poured through the gap.

My guide put a finger to his lips. 'You're to wait, sir,' he murmured. 'Someone will come for you.'

The closet was lit only by the broad stripe of light that came through the doorway from the other room. I took a pace to the right that enabled me to see directly through the gap. The music had stopped. I heard the sound of men's voices and then a great bray of laughter.

'Here's the gown and bands,' a man shouted. 'Show us, Bucks.'

'Let me help you robe, sir,' said another voice, a woman's.

'Aye, sir,' said another man. 'A carelessly dressed clergyman is an abomination in the eyes of God.'

There was more laughter and a shuffling of feet. I shifted my position again, which enabled me to see directly into the apartment, a drawing room furnished in the French style with the light of many candles sparkling on the gilding. At least a dozen men were there, and three women; some were sitting at a table, others stood in a knot near the fire.

One of the women was Lady Castlemaine. Over the years I had glimpsed her on several occasions, but I had never before seen her at such close quarters. She had grown plumper than she had been, though that did not diminish her allure; her charms had always been on the grand scale. She had black hair, vivid blue eyes and a reputation for greed.

Suddenly there was a cheer. 'A toast!' someone called. 'A toast to the reverend gentleman.'

'Faith, you look the part, Duke,' another man said. 'What a loss to the stage you are.'

'Yet more of a loss to the Church,' added Lady Castlemaine, which earned another burst of laughter. 'George, you must ask the King to make you a Bishop.' Her voice took on a caressing tone. 'You'll do it, sir, won't you?'

I heard the King's soft laughter and then the rumble of his voice, too low for me to distinguish the words.

'Yea, verily,' Buckingham declaimed in a loud nasal voice that was not unlike Dr Owen's, 'I say unto you, ye are all sinners, and the gates of hell yawn open before you.'

It was, in its way, a virtuoso performance. The Duke strode up and down the drawing room, in his black clerical gown and his white bands, declaiming upon his chosen text, 'A lewd woman is a sinful temptation, her eyes are the snares of Satan, and her flesh is the mousetrap of iniquity.' He captured perfectly Dr Owen's mannerisms. Even the content of his sermon was a wicked parody of the preacher's at Wallingford House. 'My text (beloved) I could divide into three and thirty parts, but for brevity's sake I shall confine myself to three only —'

At this point there was a cheer from some

of his audience. Others shouted 'More! More!' and hammered their glasses on the table. Buckingham ignored them, and continued his sermon.

'. . . I shall now explain at large what I mean by a lewd woman. I mean that unsanctified flesh which breaks through the confines of modesty and rambles through the brambles of impurity to graze on the loathsome commons of adultery and glut their insatiable appetites with the unsavoury fodder of fornication . . .'

'Oh, sir!' cried Lady Castlemaine. 'Should I cover my ears to spare my modesty?'

I moved a few inches to my left, which gave me a clearer view of her. Her ladyship was not the King's only mistress, or even the current favourite, but she was by far the longest established of them. She was also the one who most effectively exploited her influence over her royal lover–as much by force of personality, it was rumoured, as by the attractions of her body.

'. . . in the tents of the wicked,' Buckingham proclaimed, his voice rising to a stentorian whine, 'nobody will hear till they have glutted their souls with forbidden fruit and sowed their polluted seed amongst the thorns of abomination . . .'

Mr Williamson was particularly wary of

Lady Castlemaine, though he had not said as much to me. He was never at his ease with women. With her, it was more than that. I suspected that he feared her shadowy power over the King, and her habit of using it erratically in ways he could neither understand nor predict. She meddled with politics, and he did not think women should do that.

'. . . Thus ye are never satisfied till you are well pickled in the abominable souse-drink of corrupt filthiness and come out loath-some swine, fit for nothing but the company of that polluted herd which the devil drove . . .'

Her precise relationship with the King was the subject of much speculation at Court. She had been his mistress since the beginning of his reign, and she was the mother of several of his children. But it was said that he rarely lay with her now. In truth, he had plenty of alternatives available, and at this present time he was particularly taken up with an actress named Mary Davis. But he continued to shower wealth on Lady Castlemaine and her bastard children, not of all of whom, it was rumoured, were his. He still spent much time in her apartments, relaxing there with his intimate friends. He treated her almost as some men treat their wives of longstanding, with an offhand affection rather than desire.

'. . . This trap of Satan lies hid like a coney burrow in the warren of wickedness between the supporters of human frailness, covered over with the fuzzes of iniquity which (beloved) grow in the very *cleft* of abomination.'

The Duke paused here, because this latest sally earned an even louder and longer burst of applause and catcalls than the others. His audience was as drunk and as easy to please as Sam and his cronies in the alehouse.

Lady Castlemaine leaned forward in her chair, clapping her hands, her face alight with amusement. She was lovely enough for any man. Indeed, the likenesses of her that the print shops sold by the thousand did not do her justice. But I felt no desire for her. I had learned to be wary of beautiful women of high station, and it had been a hard lesson.

Buckingham reached his peroration at last. 'May Providence hedge you and ditch you with His mercy and send His dung-carts to fetch away the filthiness from among you. For–verily, verily, I say unto you–you are all sinners.'

Had the King forgotten I was here? Or

had he intended me to hear this blasphemous parody of yesterday's sermon? He kept us all in uncertainty. Sometimes I wondered whether he did so from carelessness or policy.

The whooping and clapping died down at last. The King said something, and the party reshuffled itself like a pack of cards. Two footmen appeared and set up a tall leather screen around the fire, shielding the King, Castlemaine and Buckingham from the rest.

Suddenly the door from the drawing room was pushed fully open. Mr Chiffinch, the Keeper of the King's Private Closet, appeared on the threshold. I blinked at him–I had grown used to the half-light, and the glare of the candles near blinded me.

'You're to attend the King now,' he said curtly. There was no love lost between us.

He turned without another word, leaving me to follow him. The King was sprawling in an armchair, his face flushed with wine, and his heavy eyelids half closed. Lady Castlemaine sat opposite on a sofa, and Buckingham stood beside him, with his back to me. The servants had herded the other revellers to the far end of the drawing room.

I wondered if Mr Williamson realized how close the friendship between the Villiers cousins had become. Given this private access to the King, an alliance between them could be a formidable counterweight to anything Lord Arlington and Mr Williamson could contrive.

The Duke's clerical gown was draped over the end of the table. His face was red and shiny with sweat. He tore the bands from his neck and tossed them into the fire.

'Faith, sir,' he said to the King, 'preaching is hard work. Labouring in the vineyards of the Lord ain't as easy as it looks.'

'You make everything look easy, George,' the King said, slurring his words a little. 'If you ever finish your play, you should act it on the public stage: you have a gift for it.'

'Your Majesty is too gracious. I feel shockingly virtuous. I must souse myself in sin to restore the balance of nature.' He laughed. 'When you give me leave to go, the dog shall go to sniffing after the bitch. Or rather bitches, if God vouchsafes me strength.'

'Ah.' There was a low chuckle from the shadows of the armchair. 'The dog and the bitch. I remember it well, pox on it.'

'Oh, sir!' said Lady Castlemaine, covering her face with her hands in mock horror. 'Pray spare my blushes!'

The dog and the bitch? The words resonated in my memory. In his fever, Lord

Shrewsbury had been rambling about the dog and the bitch when I had left him on his sickbed at Arundel House almost three weeks ago. And perhaps Buckingham had said them a day or two before, in those desperate moments after the duel. Now here they were again, in quite a different context.

Chiffinch stood aside and gestured that I should approach the King. No one spoke as I stepped forward and bowed low to him. The first person to break the silence was Buckingham.

'Good God, sir,' he drawled, turning his head to stare down at me from his greater height. 'I do believe it's the Marworm.'

The King glanced at him. 'I hear your people insulted Marwood yesterday morning, when he was representing Lord Arlington at your day . . .' his mouth twitched, 'your day of penitence.'

'Sir,' Buckingham said, bowing, 'it distressed me beyond measure when I heard of the indignity offered to my lord through his lowly proxy. If only I had known at the time, I should have moved heaven and earth to prevent it. The difficulty was that two of my people had reason to believe that Marworm—I mean Marwood; I do beg his pardon—was a nasty sneaking spy. So they acted as seemed best to them, believing they were anticipating my wishes. Of course they were quite wrong, and I've reprimanded them most sternly. But indeed, sir, their only fault was loyalty to me, and since my lord did not see fit to tell me he was sending me a deputy, let alone who it would be, it's hard to see how it could have been avoided. By the by, I wonder why Lord Arlington didn't come himself.' Buckingham cast his eyes towards the ceiling, as if expecting to find the answer there. 'I can only assume he felt he had repented enough already.'

The King burst out laughing. 'Perhaps you're right. But we mustn't keep you from your bitches any longer.' He beckoned Chiffinch in a sharper voice. 'Clear the room.'

It was hard to be sure by candlelight, but it seemed to me the Duke's face stiffened, as if this abrupt dismissal had taken him by surprise and he did not altogether like it. But in an instant he was smiling and bowing again, making his farewells to the King and my lady his cousin.

He withdrew. The rest of the party was shooed out of the room by Chiffinch. Finally, after glancing at his master, he left as well.

That left the three of us alone. The King, Lady Castlemaine and me. Her ladyship appeared to be asleep but she was most certainly awake. Everything I said to the King would probably be reported to her cousin.

'It's damnably stuffy.' The King rose to his feet and stretched his arms towards the ceiling. Lady Castlemaine's lashes fluttered. 'I shall take a little air in the garden.'

She opened her eyes and held out her hand to him. 'But it's freezing, sir. You'll catch your death of cold.'

'I believe I shall survive.'

She pouted like a frustrated child.

The King was already moving to the door to the passage. 'Marwood, attend me and light my way.'

At the head of the stairs to the Privy Garden, we paused while the servants brought our cloaks and a lantern for me to carry. We walked in silence down the broad staircase and into the garden.

It struck me that the King had taken the trouble to show Buckingham and Lady Castlemaine that he had confidence in me, and that the reverse was true as well. I was beginning to realize that he used this tactic in many of his dealings. He rationed the sunshine of his attention among us. He kept all of us vying for his favour with the result that none of us could feel sure of our place with him.

202

The temperature had dropped in the last hour or so. The paths and the bushes between them glinted with frost. Above us was a starlit sky only partly concealed by the smoke from the palace's chimneys. To the north and east, candlelight glittered softly in the windows of the long ranges overlooking the garden.

The King walked briskly. Our footsteps crunched on the gravel. His legs were longer than mine, and I had my work cut out to keep up. In the distance, male voices were singing in harmony behind one of those windows; a sad song, of lost love and blighted hopes. There was too much sadness in this place.

My eyes adjusted. The King did not speak, and it was not my place to speak first. He led me a zigzag course, constantly chopping and changing among the paths. My hand carrying the lantern grew uncomfortably cold.

The garden was laid out so the paths made a grid; within the enclosed squares were beds planted with low shrubs, and at the centre of each a statue glimmered palely in the half-light of the stars. At night, the Privy Garden was an enchanted place, made for the whispering of secrets.

We reached the line of trees along the line

of the garden's southern boundary. There were no buildings beyond, only the wall that divided the Privy Garden from the Bowling Green. The King stopped and turned to look across the garden to the Privy Gallery on the far side.

'Shield the light,' he said softly. He waited until I had set the lantern behind a tree. 'Well? What was it truly like, this day of penitence?'

'This evening, sir, the Duke made it sound as if the whole thing was an elaborate joke.'

'You mean yesterday he was serious? What happened?'

I was tempted to guard my tongue. If I answered fully, perhaps my frankness would reach Buckingham's ears and increase his hatred of me. But in the end a man must choose where his loyalties lie and, for better or worse, I had chosen the King. After all, at a moment's notice, he could strip me of my employment and my lodging and turn me into the streets to beg my bread. Or he could consign me to the Tower, as he had my father, to await his pleasure. On top of this, when all was said and done, he was our lawful sovereign, whatever his private shortcomings.

'Marwood?' he said. 'Cat got your tongue?'

So I told the King about the paintings

shrouded in black silk and the splendid setting of the Great Chamber of Wallingford House. I told him how Buckingham had sat enthroned like a king in mourning on the dais, and how the preacher had ranted at us. I told him of the audience, the clergy, the Presbyterian citizens and the Duke's political allies. I told him of the sermon, and how the preacher had pointed at Whitehall as a nest of papists and the great cesspit of evil–and therefore by implication to the King himself. I told him how I had been ejected as soon as Mr Veal had seen me, and how only Lord Arlington's letter had protected me from violence.

The darkness spurred me on, as perhaps the King had intended; it made the enormous barrier of rank between us seem less important. He listened in silence. When I came to an end, he stirred and lifted his heavy head. 'Leaving the play-acting aside, what construction do you place on all this?'

'I think the Duke feels himself vulnerable, sir. It's true that he enjoys your favour and he's one of your ministers. But–precisely because of that–he's in danger of losing the support of those he depended on before.'

'You mean his friends in Parliament.' It was not a question. 'And in the City–both the wealthy sort and the rabble of apprentices. Aye, and the Nonconformists and the Presbyterians. Those who hate the Catholics.' He paused. 'Those who hanker for the Protectorate.'

'His duel with my Lord Shrewsbury weakens his position with many of his supporters. He flaunted his adultery. He killed a man, too.'

The King sighed. 'Shrewsbury looks like to recover, so there's little harm done in the end.'

Little harm? What of the dead man at Barn Elms, poor Jenkins?

'Besides,' the King was saying, 'Buckingham had no choice but to fight. He's a nobleman, when all's said and done. He's bred to defend his honour.'

'Honour, sir?' The darkness made me bold. 'Perhaps it seems like honour in Whitehall, but it's not the name they give it in the City and among the Dissenters. He knows he needs to restore their confidence in him. That's what yesterday's mummery was for, to show them he was penitent. And now he comes here and mocks them for your amusement.'

I stopped abruptly. My dislike of Buckingham had made my voice sharper than I intended, and it had also made me say what had better been left unsaid.

Neither of us spoke. I listened to the King's slow breathing. The longer we stood here, the more a sense of strangeness crept over me. What would my father, that old Fifth Monarchist who had hated all kings except King Jesus, have thought of his son in private conference with Charles Stuart in the Privy Garden under the stars?

Without a word, the King moved away, leaving me to scurry after him with the lantern. The old fear returned: my outspokenness could cost me my employment and perhaps my liberty. I followed him back to the foot of Lady Castlemaine's staircase. He stopped some yards away, out of earshot of the guards.

'Go home, Marwood. I thank you for your honesty.'

In my relief, I was suddenly desperate to make sure he understood me before it was too late, I blurted out: 'His Grace can't run with the hare and hunt with the hounds. Not forever.'

The King was already moving towards the staircase that would take him back to his mistress. 'Perhaps,' he said over his shoulder. 'But that won't stop him trying.'

CHAPTER SEVEN

If the Protector Wishes
Wednesday, 5 February–Sunday, 15 March
  1668

Master was young once. Sometimes he smiled. Not at Ferrus, no, no, no. Master had men under him. Gave them orders in a loud voice like Windy barking.

Other men gone.

Long, long, long ago, Mistress Crummle smiled at Ferrus. The smile is for him, no one else. Hold out your hand, she says. She gives him a newly minted penny. It shines like a reddish-gold sun. It has the Protector's head on it.

'Protect it,' she says. 'For me.'

Ferrus protects the penny. He keeps it between two of the planks at the side of the kennel. No one goes in the kennel, no one dares, except Windy and Ferrus. Penny is brown and dull now, like dry shit.

But still his penny. The Protector's head is still there. The smile is still his too. Protect.

Cat's irritation with James Marwood lodged in her mind like a stone in her shoe. Small though it was, it grew with time and exercise into something more than irritation.

After all they had gone through together, after all she had done for him, his last note to her had been curt and unmannerly. Indeed, when she allowed herself to dwell on it, which was inevitable because she re-read it at least twice a day, she thought it positively churlish in both tone and content.

Cat had received the letter on the fifth of February. She discovered afterwards by enquiring of the porter that it had been brought round by the African boy whom Marwood had acquired a few months ago. 'He didn't want to wait for an answer,' Pheebs had told her. 'He said there was no need.'

She had not seen Veal or Durrell again, so she had had no reason to write to Marwood. The days passed into weeks. Cat decided that what had made her particularly angry was his postscript, the few words he had scrawled to the effect that if they chanced to meet again, they should pretend to be strangers for reasons of safety. It was a thin excuse, she considered. The truth of it was that he probably felt himself grown too grand for the Hakesbys.

In the past, they had certainly quarrelled. But they had also protected and helped each other. They had even saved each other's lives. But if he wanted them to be strangers, then so did she. He was an odious, ill-bred man.

On the fourteenth of February, St Valentine's Day, her husband woke in the early hours and thrust himself on Cat.

Mr Hakesby had difficulty sleeping since his ague had come upon him. He often rose from their bed in the middle of the night and spent an hour or two in praying, or reading the Bible, or sketching designs in his notebook. (These sketches, done by candlelight and with a shaking hand, were nameless forms, the images of disintegrating creatures rather than architectural designs.)

Occasionally, when he could not sleep, he turned to Cat for distraction instead. Not often, fortunately–the last time had been just after Christmas. He was of course entitled to insist on his conjugal rights at any time, so long as he did not offend public decency, and so long as the manner of it would not appear unseemly to the all-seeing eyes of God.

Nevertheless, Cat could not help feeling aggrieved when he pawed at her with his long, bony hands. Before their wedding, she had understood from him that their marriage would remain unconsummated; instead it was to be a matter of business, a contract between them by which he provided her with a name, a place in the world, an occupation and a future; and in return she gave him her assistance–a sharp eye, a steady hand, a quick understanding–in the Drawing Office; and also served as his housekeeper in the apartments below and, when necessary, as his nurse.

She was asleep, but she woke to the sound of her husband stirring restlessly beside her. Then came the rattle of curtain rings as he drew back the bed curtains, followed by his increasingly noisy attempts to find the tinderbox and the candle. When he knocked the tinderbox to the floor, she gave up the pretence of sleep, climbed shivering from the bed and lit the candle for him.

The wavering flame lit up his face, a pale arrangement of sharp edges and shadowy hollows topped by a nightcap that had slipped to a misleadingly jaunty angle. She hoped he would leave her to sleep and go to pray or draw in his closet. Instead —

'Come,' he said, beckoning her. 'Lie beside me.'

They lay on their backs for a moment, neither of them moving. By the light of the candle, Cat watched the shadows shifting on the walls and listened to the rasp of her husband's breathing. She heard a rustling and felt the bedclothes move. His hand tugged up her shift. Grunting with effort, he rolled his angular body on top of her.

What followed was a humiliation for them both, albeit in different ways, just as it had been last time. Desire outran performance. When at last he rolled off her, he was trembling.

'You are an unnatural wife,' he said to her. 'You blight a man's powers with your cursed coldness.'

She did not reply, knowing from experience that any word of hers would merely nourish his anger.

'Why can't you be like Mistress Cromwell?' he whispered. 'I warrant that when she finds a husband she will treat him as a husband deserves. There's a lady you should study to imitate. Though God knows you would be an imperfect copy whatever you did.'

The mazer scourer whom Hakesby had mentioned to Richard Cromwell was called Ezra Reeves. As luck would have it, it was not until the end of the month that Hakesby was able to meet him. They fixed on the back room of an alehouse near the Tower. The place was much used by the labourers clearing the ruins. It was three or four miles from Whitehall, so neither Hakesby nor Reeves was likely to be recognized.

The day appointed was Saturday, 29 February. It was cold and grey, with flurries of wind gusting round the corners of buildings and making men's cloaks bulge and writhe like living creatures. With the wind came bursts of rain, spattering and squalling.

In the late afternoon, Hakesby and Cat took a hackney from Henrietta Street. He had been reluctant to bring her, but the palsy was unpredictable in its manifestations. Though at present he was unusually vigorous, almost his old self, this happy state might vanish without warning. If the shaking grew worse when he was away from home, he would not be able to manage without help.

'I can hardly take Brennan to assist me on this business,' he said. 'Besides, you've quite a good head on your shoulders for a woman. You might think of something I've missed. But don't speak unless I say so.'

It was in its way a compliment, Cat thought, albeit a backhanded one. Compliments of any sort from her husband were rare since their marriage. Was it because they were married or was it because his illness had made him selfish? Whatever the reason, he had turned in on himself like an ingrown toenail.

Cat herself felt sullen and out of sorts. And she thought Hakesby worse than foolish for agreeing to help Richard Cromwell at his own expense of time and money, purely for the sake of old loyalties and Elizabeth Cromwell's smiles. She had tried to dissuade him time and again, but with an old man's obstinacy he would not be shifted. Perhaps the palsy was enflaming his brain as well as weakening his body. Hakesby had convinced himself that it was no more than his duty, and that there was no danger to either of them. But if the authorities got wind of this affair with the Cromwells, she shuddered to think of the consequences.

Reeves was already waiting. He was sitting in a booth by a window overlooking the yard at the back. Before she even saw him, Cat was aware of his smell. It surrounded him like a miasma. She was used to foul smells–London stank, from one end to the other–but this was something different.

He rose when he saw the Hakesbys approaching through the crowd. Their progress was slow because Hakesby shuffled along, supported by a stick on one side and Cat on the other.

Reeves made a clumsy attempt at a bow. He was a small, hunched man with shoulders that seemed too heavy for the rest of his body. 'Mr Hakesby, sir.' His eyes settled on Cat, and he looked disconcerted, if not suspicious. 'And . . . ?'

'My wife,' Hakesby said, lowering himself by degrees on to the bench. 'I allow her to assist me a little in my work. We ordered a jug of ale as we came in.'

Cat sat down on the other side of her husband and tried to mask her nostrils with the collar of her cloak. There was nothing visibly foul about Reeves. His face looked passably clean, and so was his shabby brown suit. Perhaps the smell clung to his hair. Or perhaps it had become so much part of him that it oozed through the pores of his skin.

'How have you been since we last met?' Hakesby asked.

'In truth I'm much changed, sir, and not for the better.' His mouth was small with thin lips that barely moved when he was speaking. 'Like this unhappy country of ours.'

'We are none of us what we were ten years ago.'

'No, no–that I can bear, as all men must.' Reeves paused as the waiting woman brought their ale. He watched greedily as she poured. He drank deep, then wiped his mouth on the trailing cuff of his shirt. 'I was the foreman when you knew me before, sir. Do you recall? All the palace sewers west of King Street were my responsibility, as well as most of those in Scotland Yard.'

Hakesby nodded. 'Yes–of course.'

Reeves ignored the answer. Like many people with a grievance, he wanted to tell the world everything about it, irrespective whether they already knew. The foreman's role, he said, included that of allocating men to the work gangs that cleaned the sewers of Whitehall and Scotland Yard, and advising on the necessary repairs and who should be employed to do them. A foreman could hire a man one day and discharge him the next, as the whim took him. A foreman could decide to clear one blockage before another. Naturally, therefore, a foreman received a steady diet of presents and services from those who wished to oblige him. As was right and proper and hallowed by the custom of the ages.

'And the cream of it was, sir, I had the pick of what the day's work turned up. My scourers always found something in the mazers.' He plucked at Hakesby's sleeve and lowered his voice as if communicating an important secret, 'It's beyond belief, what people let fall into their privy, whether they mean to or not. Why, sir, I've seen everything from diamond rings to dead babies.'

At the Restoration, Reeves had fallen on hard times. Royalists had been appointed to the principal positions of the palace. They had brought in their own subordinates, and favoured their own people over those who had served the Cromwells. The changes had filtered down through the various levels of the hierarchies of servants who depended on Whitehall for the bread they ate and the very clothes on their back. Reeves had seen a younger man appointed over his head to the post of foreman.

'Turned out like an old dog,' he said, still pawing at Hakesby's arm. 'After all those years of service. Ain't right.'

'Indeed, it's not right,' Hakesby said.

'A sewer is a most delicate thing,' Reeves

said. 'If it's to give you its best, it needs to be handled like a woman. Firmly. To understand it truly, you must know its particularities, sir. Somewhere like Whitehall, the buildings have changed so much over the years. So have the sewers. Why, a man could study them for a lifetime and they would not give up half their secrets. I tell you, sir, to see these fools and blockheads at work on my sewers makes me weep. And to have them giving me orders rubs salt in the wound.'

He was fortunate, Reeves said bitterly, to be allowed to work at Whitehall still, albeit at the beck and call of a foreman twenty years his junior. And the work itself had become harder than it had been: an old man of fifty lacks the vigour and suppleness of a young man of twenty.

'Any man,' Hakesby said, motioning Cat to refill Reeves' mug, 'can dig out night soil or clear a blockage. Any young fool.' He tapped his forehead. 'But what they lack is this. The experience you have. The knowledge. That's what interests me.'

Reeves set down his mug on the table with the elaborate care of the slightly drunk. His head swayed. 'And which particular knowledge would that be, sir?'

'The Cockpit lodging.'

Reeves pursed his lips in a silent whistle. 'You don't make it easy, do you?'

'How so?'

'It's a jumble underneath there, sir. Not the Cockpit itself, that's not too bad since they converted it to a theatre. It's the rest of the place, the lodgings and the tennis courts. Worse than anywhere at Whitehall, except maybe the old royal apartments.' His voice acquired a whine as it fell into the rhythm of a familiar complaint. 'First the Cromwells, then the Duke of Albemarle. Change this, change that, rebuild here, extend there. No rhyme or reason to it. No one gives a thought to what's underneath, where the waste goes. And when it all goes wrong, and when the neighbours complain, and when even the King notices the stink's got worse than ever–who do they turn round and blame?' He thumped his chest with the hand that wasn't holding his almost empty mug of ale. 'Us mazer scourers, that's who. Pox on them all, that's what I say.'

'But you're the ones who solve their problems, too. Without you, where would they be?'

'Up to their ears in their own shit, sir, that's where.'

Hakesby took a roll of paper from his coat and smoothed it out on the table. 'As it happens, I've a little problem of my own. Unlike them, I shall be properly grateful to you when you solve it.'

His hand began to tremble, and Cat finished the job for him, weighting one side of the paper with the jug. It was a copy she had made of his original sketch of the Cockpit lodgings before the Cromwells' alterations in the 1650s. He nodded to her, a signal for her to speak.

She angled the plan towards Reeves. 'There.' She traced the line with her finger. 'King Street. Here's the Cockpit, with the main buildings of the old lodgings to the south, with its garden.'

Frowning, Reeves leaned over the table to study the plan, bringing with him his smell. 'Phoo,' he said, addressing Hakesby and ignoring Cat. 'You wouldn't recognize it now, sir, indeed you wouldn't. They've put up a whole range on that side, into the Park. And the garden's smaller because they've built over the south of it.'

Hakesby pointed at the line showing the boundary of the kitchen garden. His finger was shaking so badly that it was impossible to tell what he was indicating.

Reeves looked askance at him. 'Faith, sir, what's wrong? The trembling?'

Hakesby drew back his hand. 'An ague,'

he snapped. 'This cold damp weather brings it on. It's nothing.'

Cat said, 'This enclosure here.' Her own finger tapped the area enclosed by the line. 'Do you mark it, Mr Reeves? It used to be a kitchen garden in the old days.'

'Ah—yes. Mainly service buildings down there now.'

Hakesby had moved his treacherous hands under the table. 'The dotted line,' he said. 'That was the run of the sewer. A stream ran through it.'

'No stream now, sir, or not above once or twice a year when the rain's bad.'

'It's still in use?'

'Yes. But there's another one now, much bigger. The new one runs south, too, but over towards the Tennis Court passage. It's wider than the old one.'

'Tell me about the old one.'

Reeves turned his head and spat on the floor. 'Not in good shape, last time I saw it. That old brickwork crumbles soon as look at it. Ventilation's bad, and it backs up in bad weather. We've had a couple of roof falls, too. What do they expect? It hasn't been looked after. I told you, a sewer's like a woman, sir. Gives you good service if it has a little attention from time to time, and regular rodding.'

221

Cat cleared her throat. Reeves met her eye. She scowled at him. He looked away.

Hakesby said, 'How do you get into the old one when it needs cleaning? There used to be a shaft in the kitchen garden.'

'Still there. It's in the cellars.' Reeves tapped the plan with a horny fingernail. 'But it's tricky even to get down there, because it's so narrow.'

'What are the cellars used for?'

Reeves peered into the empty jug. 'Thirsty work, sir, this talking. And before we go on, maybe you could tell me why you're so curious. I mean no impertinence, but a man has to watch out for himself. And you says you'd show your gratitude, but a token of that beforehand would have a mighty convincing effect.'

There was a delay while another jug of ale was ordered. Hakesby fumbled in his purse and drew out a handful of change. The coins slipped through his fingers and skittered across the table. Reeves swept them into his hand. Cat was quietly furious that Hakesby was willing to use their own money for the benefit of the Cromwells.

'Thank you kindly, master,' Reeves said, as he pocketed the money. 'These cellars. His Grace's servants keep a deal of stuff down there. A lot of it came out of the

Cockpit when it was refurbished. Rubbish they used in the theatre. Old costumes in boxes. Painted boards.'

'Suppose someone wanted to have a look at the old sewer privately,' Hakesby said. 'To study its construction, say.'

Reeves snorted. 'Someone who wasn't wanting to disturb the people of the house unnecessarily? That sort of study, sir?'

Hakesby compressed his lips, biting back a reproof. 'Perhaps.'

'It wouldn't be easy. You'd have to get into the Cockpit to begin with. Even when the Duke's not in residence, there'll be servants around.'

'Of course,' Hakesby said. 'But we might gain admittance as your friends, as country folk in town on a holiday, with a desire to see how the great people live at Whitehall?'

'You wouldn't want to see the sewers, though, would you?'

'Suppose,' Cat said, interested despite herself, 'suppose someone went in there as a mazer scourer?'

'To clear a reported blockage?' Reeves tilted his head to one shoulder and stared at Cat with bright little eyes. 'Aye, mistress, that might answer. You'd need a warrant for that, and the tools of the trade. And it'd be risky.' He raised his eyebrows. 'Which means expensive.'

'When the Duke's not in residence,' Hakesby said slowly, 'there must be fewer servants about.'

'Over Easter,' Reeves said. 'If His Grace ain't there, the place will be half empty.'

'Easter Monday then,' Cat said. 'If the Duke is away, that would be the time to choose. It's a holiday, so most of the servants wouldn't be there.'

'Yes,' Hakesby said. 'That would answer.'

Reeves looked at Cat, frowning. His hand lifted his mug and his eyes moved back to Hakesby. Cat could read his thoughts as if he had spoken them aloud: *How could an old fool in your condition play the part of a mazer scourer? How could you even get down a sewer?*

'We'll need help in the sewer,' she said after a pause, since this point seemed not to have occurred to Hakesby. He was nodding to himself and staring into his ale with a vacant expression on his face. 'Would you go down with us?'

'Better not me,' he said.

'Then how will we know where to go?'

'Don't fret about that, mistress. If you're willing to pay, I'll let you have Ferrus.'

'Ferrus?' said Hakesby, suddenly alert

again. He cupped his hand over his ear. 'What?'

'You'll need me too, obviously,' Reeves said, his eyes still on Cat. 'Ferrus is no use at all without me. He's like a dog, you might say. No good to man or beast without his master to tell him what to do.'

'Who is Ferrus?' Hakesby demanded.

'Look out the window, sir. See the corner by the necessary house? That's Ferrus.'

The diamond-shaped panes of glass were thick and distorted. A layer of grime and candle grease obscured them still further. Cat rubbed at a lozenge with her fingertip, clearing a spyhole. The glass was green. It gave a murky tinge to the wavering world outside.

'You don't have to worry about him blabbing, either. He won't say a word, I warrant you that. He don't say any words.'

The rain was falling steadily. The overhang of the roof of the privy extended a few feet into the yard. Two leather buckets were hanging underneath, a standard requirement for all houses in London to meet the danger of future fires.

A solitary figure crouched on his haunches between the buckets. Perhaps it was the distortion in the glass, but he looked unnaturally thin. He turned his head towards

225

Cat, as if sensing her gaze. His face was narrow, with the eyes seemingly quite separate from each other, like a fish's. He had a low, sloping forehead and a large, broad nose.

'There's Ferrus,' Reeves repeated with a certain pride in his voice. 'Faith, sir, you've never seen anything like him. I could show him at Bartholomew Fair if I had a mind to it. Why, I believe he'd squeeze himself through a keyhole if I told him to.'

One of the worse things about this business with the Cromwells was that nothing happened quickly. It dragged on, Cat thought, until it became woven into the fabric of everyday life. It gave her a constant sense of foreboding. It was like always being hungry or never being quite warm enough or having a toothache.

After the meeting with Reeves, Hakesby wrote to Richard Cromwell, under his assumed name of Cranmore. Or rather he dictated the letter to Cat. Not trusting the Post Office, whose clerks were rumoured to examine the contents of every letter that passed through their hands, he ordered the porter's boy to take it to Mistress Dalton's house.

Despite this precaution, Hakesby was guarded in what he said. He had made enquiries, he told Mr Cromwell, and he had learned that Easter Monday (despite its being a holiday) might be a convenient time to explore the matter further. However, he added, there were preliminaries to be settled first, and conditions to be met, and he begged the favour of a meeting with Mr Cranmore at his earliest convenience.

To Cat's surprise, her husband derived a childlike enjoyment from dictating this carefully phrased letter; the secrecy of the matter charmed him for its own sake, quite apart from the pleasure and the excitement he derived from his acquaintance with the former Lord Protector and his daughter.

In return, Mr Hakesby received a quick, uninformative reply, which did little more than acknowledge with thanks the receipt of his letter and say that Mr Cranmore would write more fully as soon as he was able. This left the matter in limbo, and Hakesby and Cat with it. As the days passed without a second letter, the more her husband's disappointment grew. He betrayed it by his increasing irritation with Cat, and even with Brennan.

Hakesby still seemed to have given no thought to the risks that this connection with Cromwell involved, nor to the practicalities of retrieving whatever the late Lady

Protectoress had concealed in the Cockpit. When Cat tried to raise such matters, he brushed the questions aside, flapping his hands as if pushing them physically away from him.

Hakesby's temper was always worse at night, when they retired to bed. When the fit was upon him, he cursed her for an interfering clumsy fool, a witch who had stolen away his manhood. Sometimes he lashed out at her with his fist as well, though he was too weak to do much harm.

She did not strike him back. Instead she retreated, sometimes locking herself in the closet and ignoring his shouting and banging. Once or twice she slept there, wrapped in two cloaks and lying on bare boards that smelled faintly of the lemon juice and vinegar that she and the maid had used to scrub them.

Neither Brennan nor the Hakesbys' maid seemed to notice anything amiss. Marriage was a private place. No one was fully aware of what went on within it except the parties involved.

In the house by Hatton Garden, there was a knocking on the gate, and the porter admitted the all too familiar figure of the Reverend Mr Veal.

Mistress Dalton summoned Mr Cromwell to the window to watch the thin figure striding across the courtyard. Veal's long, dun-coloured coat made him look even taller than he was. He paused to say something to Thomas, the manservant, who had come out to greet him.

'I wish he wouldn't come.' Mistress Dalton plucked a loose thread from her skirt. 'He's always here. It's every day now. Turning up again and again, like a bad penny.'

Cromwell smiled at her, trying to suppress his own unease. 'I'm surprised at you, mistress. Mr Veal's but a poor clergyman when all is said and done. I don't know what would have become of him if the Duke hadn't taken him in.'

The smile felt false, but he could hardly tell her the complete truth. Even Elizabeth didn't know that.

'That may be so,' his hostess said tartly. 'But I wish he didn't come to my house. He hovers so strangely about the place, like a great brown bird looking for something to peck. And he never says anything, or not to me.'

'It's true that Mr Veal is a man of few words. And you are most gracious to allow him to call on me in your own house.'

'But why does he come here so often?'

'The Duke and I have business to discuss; nothing that need trouble you, I promise. He may be able to help me with some of my difficulties. Mr Veal is his emissary.'

There were footsteps outside, and the servant showed Veal into the parlour. He bowed silently to Mistress Dalton, and then to Cromwell.

'I'll leave you to your conversation, sirs,' she said with a sour look.

After she had gone, Veal made sure that the door was latched. He turned back to Cromwell. 'His Grace commanded me to give you this, sir.' He took a small purse of kid leather from his pocket and placed it in Cromwell's palm, where it lay, soft and heavy. 'There will be more, of course,' he went on. 'Much more, when all's done.'

'At our last meeting, I gave you the schedule of my debts–my English debts, that is.'

Veal inclined his head. 'His Grace has seen it.'

'His Grace is most generous. Has he indicated whether he will be able to lend me something towards meeting them? This'–he glanced down at the purse in his hand, weighing it–'is very obliging, but it's no more than a drop in a bucket.'

Cromwell hated the wheedling tone in his voice. Poverty diminished a gentleman in his own eyes, as well as in the eyes of others.

'There will be no difficulty, sir. All in good time.' Veal lowered his voice. 'In return, though, His Grace asks for a small service from you. Not for his own sake, but for this unhappy kingdom's.'

'With all my heart, sir. What service?'

'To meet a few gentlemen. In private, naturally. But not incognito as you were last month at Wallingford House. The Duke says that it's time for you to appear in your proper character as the former Lord Protector and the son of the great Oliver.'

'That would be dangerous for both of us. Indeed, it would be folly.'

'You need not worry, sir. His Grace would choose the company with care. He desires to show himself a friend to reconciliation and true religion. You saw the proof of that last month, when Dr Owen preached so affectingly at Wallingford House. He wants to show by his actions that old quarrels can be forgotten.'

Cromwell sat down. He rubbed the arm of his chair with his thumb, avoiding Veal's eyes. 'I can't let it be known that I'm in England. It would be disastrous for me. It would not look well for the Duke, either, if he were seen consorting with me.'

'That depends on who was looking, sir. As I said, he would choose the company with care.' Veal drew closer. The light from the window fell on his face. The skin on his high, bony forehead was flaking. Abruptly he changed the subject: 'In ten days' time, it will be Easter Monday.'

'Easter Monday? That's not quite convenient to —'

'His Grace has something in mind, and he wishes to have your company then.'

Veal paused. Cromwell smiled, as he always did when he felt uneasy, and continued to rub the arm of his chair.

'He will arrange everything,' Veal went on. 'You need not disturb yourself in the least. But you will be here at Easter, won't you?'

Cromwell moistened his lips. 'I'm anxious to oblige the Duke in every way I can. But I cannot be absolutely certain that Providence won't take a hand in some way, and —'

'You need have no fear as long as you stay here,' Veal interrupted. 'At Mistress Dalton's.'

'What do you mean?'

'Precautions have been taken to ensure your safety, sir. My master told me only this morning that he would never forgive himself if any harm came to you. But if you leave this house, it becomes harder to protect you.'

There was a threat concealed in the words. 'You almost make it sound as if I'm His Grace's prisoner,' he said. 'That he has set guards about me.'

Mr Veal bared his teeth in what was perhaps intended as a smile. 'You're pleased to jest, sir.'

After dinner, Cromwell told his daughter that he wished to walk with her in the garden. The day was fine, with a foretaste of spring despite the chill in the air. The garden, which lay to one side of Mistress Dalton's house, was not large, but its high walls made it secluded. The hedges bordering the paths were evergreen. The rest of the garden was barely awake. It was holding its breath, waiting for something to happen, just as he was.

Elizabeth took his arm as they paced along. She looked up at him. 'Mr Veal was here again today, sir?'

He knew by her tone that she had sensed that something was amiss. He had not taken her fully into his confidence about the Duke. In some ways, the less she knew the better. But she was no fool, he knew; she was the most intelligent of his children, as well as his favourite.

He said, 'Mr Veal is our friend, so far as it goes, but the Duke is his master. You understand me? We should not trust Mr Veal entirely, any more than we should the Duke.'

Her face was bright with understanding. 'The Cockpit?'

'They mustn't know about that. It's quite separate, Betty. Something for us alone.'

He called her 'Betty', he realized, just as he had when she had been a little girl. He watched her rubbing her chin against the fur collar of her cloak as she considered what he had told her. It was a sensuous action, and it disquieted him. His father would not have approved of such a luxurious cloak for his granddaughter, nor of her taking such obvious pleasure in it. The trouble with having Oliver Cromwell as your grandfather, or indeed as your father, was that you could never live up to such a yardstick. Even after his death, you were condemned always to fall short.

'The Duke has ordered this house to be watched.' He saw alarm flare in his daughter's eyes. 'It's for our own protection.' He hesitated. 'Chiefly. But it means I can't communicate with Mr Hakesby without running the risk of his learning of it sooner or later. It's perfectly possible that someone here is in his pay. Thomas, perhaps–I saw him talking privately to Mr Veal this morning, on his way in.'

'Then has it all been in vain, sir? Our business with Mr Hakesby?'

'Is there a private way you could pass a letter to him through his wife? Two women meeting, seemingly by chance, just as you did before? It might not strike anyone as worthy of note. Women are always gossiping to one another, even if they are perfect strangers.'

Elizabeth's eyes narrowed to slits. She puffed out her cheeks, giving her father an unwanted glimpse of the heavy-jowled woman she might become, if God spared her for another twenty years.

Suddenly she smiled at him. 'Aren't some things better spoken than written?'

He nodded, accepting the point. 'There is another difficulty. The Duke wants me to meet some gentlemen in private.'

'Will they know who you are, sir?'

He nodded.

'But surely that would be too dangerous? The news that you were here would soon spread.'

'It's not just that. He's named Easter Monday for the meeting.'

Her eyes widened. 'But that's the day that you and Mr Hakesby fixed on for the Cockpit.'

On the morning of Palm Sunday, Mr and Mrs Hakesby walked arm-in-arm across Henrietta Street and joined the crowd of worshippers at the door of St Paul's, Covent Garden. As they waited to enter the church, her husband pinched the fleshy underside of Cat's forearm, making her wince.

'Look at this press of people,' he hissed. 'I told you we should have come earlier.'

'We'll soon be inside, sir.'

'The wind's bitter. I'll catch my death of cold beforehand.'

At last their turn came. A verger led them with stately deliberation to the pew they rented by the quarter. (When Cat had questioned the expense of having their own pew, Hakesby had told her it was essential for him to show the world that he could afford such respectable luxuries.)

The verger opened the door and stood aside. Her husband entered first, for he was convinced that the far end of the pew was less draughty than it was next to the aisle; and the draught set off both his ague and his rheumatism.

While she waited, Cat glanced over her shoulder at the people entering the church behind them, her eyes flicking idly from one to another. Suddenly she stared harder at a young lady who had just come in with her maid. Cat stiffened. The lady was Elizabeth Cromwell.

The verger coughed. 'Mistress?'

Elizabeth must have tipped her own verger well–he was leading her and her maid to one of the front pews on the north side of the church, an area that was not reserved for regular worshippers. Elizabeth kept her eyes cast down. She gave no sign that she had seen Cat.

'Mistress?' Cat's verger repeated, in a louder voice. He tapped his wand against the door of the pew.

She glanced up, irritated by this sign of impatience. 'Don't be impertinent,' she said.

He flinched from her anger. Without undue haste, she joined Hakesby in their pew. He was fussing over his cloak, wrapping it more tightly around him as a preliminary to slumber. It was a rare preacher who could keep him awake for longer than five minutes.

Cat did not tell him that Elizabeth Cromwell was here. She could not rely on him to be discreet. She hugged the uncomfortable knowledge to herself for the next hour and a half.

She could not have said what the sermon was about. After it was over, most of the congregation filed out of the church. Hakesby's limbs were stiff from inactivity; he and Cat were among the last. Elizabeth Cromwell had hung back, sending her maid to look for a handkerchief she claimed to have dropped. She contrived to time her departure to match theirs, and fell in beside them in the churchyard.

Hakesby started violently when he saw her.

'Pray be calm, sir,' Cat murmured.

Elizabeth drew them aside, out of sight from the street. 'Forgive me for surprising you, sir,' she said to Hakesby. 'I could not think how else to do it.'

'Is Mr . . . Mr Cranmore with you?' Hakesby asked.

'He thought it safer not. And he told me not to call at your house in case they've bribed your porter.'

'They?' Cat said sharply. 'What do you mean, "they"?'

'My father was recognized by one of the Duke of Buckingham's people. The Duke has been most obliging in every way. He assures us that he will keep it secret that my

238

father's here. But he's set a watch on us.'

'Why?' Cat demanded.

'For our own safety, I believe.' Elizabeth bit her lip. Her face was pale and drawn, older than her years. 'But . . . but my father can't be quite sure of that. And he wishes to keep our business—yours and ours, that is—entirely separate.' She tried to smile, but instead looked desperate; after all, for all her cunning she was very young. 'My father's condition is so precarious. I–I fear for him greatly.'

At that moment Cat came closer to liking Elizabeth than she had ever done. 'Why is the Duke kind to him?'

'That's what worries me. The Duke believes my father ordered his release from the Tower when he was Lord Protector. That's what he says. But my father tells me that in fact he had little to do with it. And I think, if the Duke's so grateful, why wait until now to show it, nearly ten years later, if that was really the case? God knows my father has had need of friends with deep pockets in these last few years.'

'I'm cold,' Hakesby said abruptly.

Cat glanced about her. She felt as if a thousand eyes were watching them. But, as far as she could see, only Elizabeth's maid was looking at them, and she was ten yards away, out of earshot. They couldn't go back to the sign of the Rose–the porter would see them. She thought it all too likely that if anyone had offered Pheebs a bribe, he would have taken it.

'A tavern,' she said. She looked at her husband. 'Should we not take a coach to the Lamb? They know us there and they will always find us a room.'

There was a hackney stand in Covent Garden and, as luck would have it, a coach was waiting for a fare. The driver grumbled at taking them so short a distance–the Lamb was in Wych Street, only a few hundred yards away–but Elizabeth surprised them all by snapping at him: 'What's it to you? You will have the whole shilling for it, will you not? Take us there directly or I'll complain to the Guildhall and have them take away your licence.'

The streets were quieter than usual because it was Sunday, and the coach took them there with barely a stop on the way. Wych Street lay north of the Strand. The Lamb itself was on the north side, set back in its own court and embracing three sides of it. It was a shabby, sagging building with mossy tiles on its roofs.

The landlord's boy was waiting in the doorway, and he rushed out to greet them as soon as he saw the coach. When he had helped them down, Elizabeth gave him the fare and told him to pay the driver. Afterwards Cat sent him scurrying upstairs to command a private room for them. They were given a little chamber overlooking the court, some distance from the din coming from the ordinary downstairs where men were gathering to dine at the host's table.

'Shall we dine?' Elizabeth asked.

'A glass of wine and a biscuit, perhaps,' Cat said.

'Perhaps you're right–we shouldn't linger.'

They ordered the wine. Elizabeth told her maid to wait outside on the landing and bring it in when it arrived. When she was alone with the Hakesbys, she spread out her hands in a gesture that was part apology and part a confession of helplessness.

'My father fears that one of Mistress Dalton's servants is in the Duke's pay,' she said, 'and that he also has someone outside the house to watch our comings and goings. Mr Veal comes every day, and —'

'Mr Veal?' Cat said.

'Yes.' Elizabeth glanced at her. 'You know of him?'

'Veal?' Hakesby said, his voice quavering. 'Who is this Veal?'

'I believe he's a clergyman, sir, who was

241

ejected from his living,' Elizabeth said. 'Though you would not think so to look at him. He has a servant with him sometimes, a ruffian built like a tub of lard.'

'This touches us,' Cat said. 'We must abandon the Cockpit business.'

'No, I beg you, Catty, pray let us discuss it before we decide anything. My father cannot live on air. He is determined to have what my grandmother left for him.'

'Consider: if the Duke's people are watching your every step, for whatever reason, how can you hope to move in the matter without their knowing? And then we must be known too.'

'But what if we're discreet about our meetings? As we are now. If we take precautions, we shall be perfectly safe.'

'But it isn't —'

'If the Protector wishes it,' Hakesby interrupted, slamming the palm of his hand on the table, 'it shall be done. Somehow we shall find a way.'

'But, sir, consider how rash it would be,' Cat said. 'Our fortunes are precarious. We cannot take the risk.'

Hakesby swept his hand from the table and pointed his forefinger towards her. He could not hold the finger steady. 'We shall assist His Grace the Protector as agreed.'

Elizabeth coughed and glanced at the door. 'Pray, sir, lower your voice. And my father does not care to be addressed by his former style–it's dangerous, quite apart from anything else. Perhaps you'd tell me what you learned from the man who cleans the sewers at the Cockpit.'

The maid brought their wine and biscuits while Hakesby was giving her a rambling but essentially accurate account of the meeting with the mazer scourer. Elizabeth coaxed him when his strength showed signs of flagging, placing her hand on his arm and bringing her face very close to his so he might whisper to her. Every now and then, he would shoot a glance at Cat, as if to make sure she was witnessing this intimacy, the consequences of the triumph of his will over hers.

She felt sick at heart, knowing that his illness must be at least part of the reason for this folly of his, that it made him unreasonable and subject to strange spurts of anger; and she also knew that she was powerless to stop him from doing what he wanted. She almost wished his ague would take a turn for the worse and confine him to bed. She could see no other way to avoid his leading them all into ruin.

When it was over, Elizabeth sat back, smiling. She filled Hakesby's glass and raised her own in a toast. 'To our enterprise, sir. God send it prosper.'

As an afterthought, she threw a smile at Cat, whom she had ignored completely while Hakesby was talking.

'So it is all set for Easter Monday, then,' Hakesby said. 'As we had hoped. The mazer scourers will be on holiday, and many of the other servants too.'

'Pray God the Duke of Albemarle is down in the country,' Elizabeth said, 'and not in the Cockpit lodgings. And this man Reeves will play his part?'

'Yes. There will be no difficulty.'

'I'm afraid there's one difficulty,' Elizabeth said. 'On Friday, Mr Veal told my father that the Duke wants him at Wallingford House on Easter Monday, to meet some friends. Which means he may not be able to come to the Cockpit with us.'

'Us?' Cat said. 'Us?'

'I'm sure we shall contrive it by ourselves.' Elizabeth turned back to Hakesby. 'By the way, I have some money. My father gave me it for you to defray the costs.' She glanced sideways at them through narrowed eyes. 'The Duke has given him a little. He has his uses, you see.'

It was the smugness of Elizabeth's tone

that did it. Cat's patience with them both vanished as abruptly as a crack of thunder. 'Listen to yourselves,' she said. 'You've both run stark mad.'

Her husband and Elizabeth Cromwell stared at her.

'By God, you will ruin us all,' Cat said.

It was past the dinner hour when the Hakesbys returned to the sign of the Rose. Their food, sent up from the cook shop, was tepid, the sauces congealing in their dishes. Hakesby blamed Jane for failing to keep it warm. He reduced the maid to tears and threw a plate at her. The plate fell short, but Jane scuttled out of the room, leaving her employers to serve themselves.

'I shall beat the girl after dinner,' Hakesby said.

He fell upon the food, eating rapidly as if his life depended on it. There was no conversation. Cat was furious with her husband for indulging in such folly with the Cromwells, and he was furious with her for crossing him so openly at the Lamb. Old men have their pride. She lacked the diplomatic art of persuading another to act as you wished, while believing the choice was theirs.

She ate mechanically. It seemed to her

that they were surrounded by a close-set hedge of thorns, and they ran the risk of impaling themselves if they moved in any direction. Perhaps she should go to Marwood. She did not want to see Marwood, and it galled her that she should even consider approaching him, given his churlish behaviour earlier. Besides, she could hardly tell him everything without running the risk of incriminating them all, the Hakesbys as well as the Cromwells. At best, she thought, he would tell her that her difficulties were none of his business.

But if she didn't go to Marwood for advice, who else was there?

It was raining when Cat left the sign of the Rose. Her husband was sleeping in the chair by the fire, having forgotten his threat to beat poor Jane.

She hurried east through Covent Garden and cut down Drury Lane to the Strand. She wore her old winter cloak, which had a hood. Hakesby did not like her to wear it in public, saying that its shabbiness demeaned him and it was a poor advertisement of their standing in the world. Her hand was in her pocket, gripping the handle of the little knife she always carried there.

She crossed the road and went directly

down to the Savoy. As she passed under the gateway, the smell of the river grew noticeably stronger, the watery stench of mud, salt and sewage. Infirmary Close was near the graveyard, where the plague victims lay uneasily. Changes in the weather made the few inches of earth that covered them ripple like a blanket over unquiet sleepers. How could Marwood bear to live in a place like this, with the dead as his nearest neighbours?

A narrow alley led down to the door of his lodging. She stopped outside to catch her breath. She almost hoped he would not be there. She raised her hand to knock. In the same moment there was a scrape of a bolt on the other side of the door, and it opened. There was Sam Witherdine, Marwood's manservant if you could call him that, leaning on his crutch and smiling at her.

'Mistress Hakesby, as I live! Margaret thought she saw you through the pantry window. Come inside and dry yourself by the fire, and I'll tell master you're here.'

The Witherdines, Sam and Margaret, had always liked Cat. She accepted this as she accepted the weather, as something that had little to do with her personally. They treated her with more respect than they did their own master, the man who had paid their debts, put a roof over their head and filled their bellies. The undeserved esteem dated from nearly a year earlier, when Cat had stayed in this house and helped to nurse Marwood after he had been so badly burned.

Sam showed her into the parlour. He set Stephen, the boy who helped in the kitchen, to breaking open the fire and raking the coals into flame. Margaret came up from the kitchen and removed Cat's cloak, saying she would hang it by the kitchen fire to dry. She told Stephen to look sharp and fetch the master; he was in his closet, writing letters, and had given orders not to be disturbed but that did not apply to Mistress Hakesby.

A few minutes later, Marwood himself appeared. He was wrapped in his gown and wearing the cap he wore about the house. The scarring on the left side of his face and neck was clearly visible. He had not troubled to make an effort for her. He was also, she sensed, in a foul temper.

He bowed. 'This is a surprise, madam.'

'I wish I could have avoided it,' Cat said. 'For my sake as well as yours.'

Their eyes met. She realized belatedly that her words must have sounded hostile rather

248

than a simple statement of fact.

'Then you'll want to be brief,' he said. 'Pray sit down.' He added, with cold formality, 'How may I serve you?'

She sat down in the elbow chair by the fireplace. 'The only thing I want,' she said, 'is a miracle.'

She felt her eyes filling with tears, shameful and unexpected, as the hopelessness of her predicament washed over her. She turned her head away and stared into the fire. She would not give way to tears in front of him or in front of any man if she could help it. But especially not in front of Marwood.

After a moment, he said, 'I can't help you there.'

There was something in his tone that made her wonder if he was laughing at her. She turned, ready to snap at him.

'What is it?' he said gently. 'I'll help you if I can. You know that. Even if I can't contrive a miracle.'

'Forgive me. I hardly know what I'm saying.'

He sat down opposite her, gathering the folds of his gown around him. She noticed that his fingers were as ink-stained as a schoolboy's. He looked different without a wig–leaner, younger and more vulnerable.

'It's those men you warned me about. The Bishop and his servant.' She rubbed her forehead, where the ghost of a headache was struggling to materialize. 'I can't remember their names.'

Marwood's features sharpened, as if an invisible hand had tightened the skin that covered them. 'Mr Veal and Roger Durrell. What of them? You said you saw Durrell in Henrietta Street when you came back from Arundel House. Have you seen him again?'

'No. This is different. Worse.'

She paused, her mind struggling to grasp the full implications of the choice before her. She could tell Marwood nothing important without betraying the presence of Richard Cromwell in London, and without revealing the extent of her husband's involvement with the former Protector. In the end, it came down to a question of trust. Would Marwood keep her confidence? Or would he pass on the intelligence she gave him to his masters, perhaps disguising his self-interest, even to himself, by arguing that he owed a higher duty to the King than he did to his friendship with Cat?

No. Friendship was the wrong word. Whatever bound Marwood and her together, she reminded herself, had nothing to do with partiality. It concerned the debt that each owed to the other. The trouble was, they had come through so many horrors together that it was no longer possible to strike a balance. The calculations had grown too mutually entangled for simple allocations of credit and debit, laid out in two neat columns, as she did in Mr Hakesby's account book. In fact, perhaps she and Marwood would never —

'Tell me,' he said.

'I can't.'

'Why not?'

She shook her head, not knowing what she would say if she tried to answer him in words.

Marwood leaned forward in his chair. 'We've kept each other's secrets before. If this is a secret, and if you decide to tell me it, then I will keep your confidence.' He hesitated. 'As you keep mine.'

It was the unexpected gentleness of his voice that tipped the balance. 'Richard Cromwell's in London.' She saw alarm transform his face. She rushed on. 'He wants my husband to help him retrieve some valuables, which are concealed somewhere in the Cockpit at Whitehall. Unfortunately Mr Veal and his servant have discovered that there is a connection between them, though not the reason for it–these valuables, I mean. And now the Duke of Buckingham has drawn the Protector–the late Protector, that is–into some scheme of his own, I know not what. Veal and Durrell visit him at the place where he stays in London.'

She ran out of breath and stopped. Marwood rose to his feet and fetched a bottle and two glasses from a cupboard. He poured the wine and handed her a glass.

'How long has the Protector been in England?' he asked.

'At least two months.'

'Can't Mr Hakesby understand the danger he's in? And you, as his wife? It's playing with fire. You must talk to him.'

'Do you think I haven't tried?' Cat said, feeling rage flaring inside her. 'What do you take me for? A fool?'

'No,' he said quickly. 'Never that. Drink your wine.'

The rage subsided as quickly as it had come. She drank her wine, as he did. It was madeira, sweet and strong, and it warmed her. He refilled their glasses and sat down again.

'I wish to God —' She broke off.

'What?'

'Nothing, sir. It doesn't matter.' It did matter: she wished to God that she hadn't married Hakesby, for all the security he brought her, for the price was higher than she had thought it would be. But she couldn't admit that to Marwood.

He said, 'Why is Mr Hakesby acting so unwisely?'

'Because he has a fondness for the old days.'

'He's not alone in that.'

'Meeting Richard Cromwell has brought it on, and perhaps my husband's sickness makes him less able to judge the folly of his actions. The worse his ague grows, the less I can reason with him. Perhaps age makes him foolish as well. He almost venerates Mr Cromwell for the sake of the name he bears.'

'They call him Tumbledown Dick,' Marwood said. 'Or Queen Dick. Richard is no Oliver.'

'Indeed, sir, they give him those names, but he doesn't altogether deserve them. He never sought to be Protector after Oliver died.' Cat glanced at Marwood. 'Mr Cromwell is not a bad man, I think, nor an ambitious one. But he is perhaps weak. I–I used to be acquainted with his daughter Elizabeth when I was a child, and I saw something of him then. I think his need for money clouds his judgement.'

'How did the Bishop find him out?'

'I'm not sure. But Cromwell visited my husband with his daughter last month. And if Durrell or someone was outside the house, they might have recognized him. He tries to disguise his appearance, but it might not fool one who knew him well.'

'What does he look like?'

'Like a country gentleman come to town. He has an old-fashioned beard in need of barbering and in public he wears coloured spectacles for a disguise.'

'Spectacles?' Marwood said sharply.

'Yes. Green ones.'

He looked away from her and toyed with his wine glass. After a moment he said: 'So they have linked you and Hakesby to me on the one hand, and to the Cromwells on the other? And the Duke of Buckingham knows all?'

'Yes. And I don't know what to do. I'm sorry–you're drawn into it, because of me.'

'If you wanted, I could let it be known privately–to Mr Williamson, say, or even Mr Chiffinch–that Richard Cromwell is in London, and where to find him.'

'How would that serve? If they take him up and question him, he will implicate us all. And if he doesn't, then his daughter will. And God knows what Buckingham and his creatures would do to us.'

'If the Duke cannot have what he wants through the King,' Marwood said slowly, 'perhaps he thinks he might have it through Cromwell.'

'What do you mean?'

He shrugged. 'I hardly know myself. It's merely that I caught a glimpse of something, a possibility . . .'

'Promise you won't tell anyone that he is here. On your oath. Promise me.'

'But it's the wisest thing to do. Let me tell Mr Williamson that you came to me, asking me to pass on a message to him; he would see it as the clearest proof of your loyalty to the King.'

'No. You mustn't do that. If you do it will drag us all down.'

Neither of them spoke for a full minute. I've ruined everything, she thought, to save myself and Hakesby.

'All right,' he said at last. Then he threw a question at her that took her entirely by surprise. 'Tell me, do the words dog and bitch mean anything to you?'

'What in God's name are you talking about?'

'I've heard the phrase once or twice. It's something to do with Buckingham.'

'They mean nothing,' she said. 'Apart from what they say. A dog and a bitch.'

Marwood shrugged. 'The Duke nurses grudges. I've already given him reason not to like me. He won't care for you either if he learns that it was you who betrayed whatever scheme he has.'

'And I —' She stopped.

'What?'

Their eyes met. 'I am always the regicide's daughter. You know that.'

Neither of them spoke. The regicides would never be forgotten or forgiven while there was a Stuart on the throne. And their children still shared by association some of their guilt. Suspicion clung to them like a bad smell.

The coals settled in the grate. The light from the window was beginning to fade. Nothing had been settled, and Cat's headache had grown worse. Marwood had failed to solve the difficulties that threatened them all. She felt comforted nonetheless. At least there were no secrets here. In its way, that was a modest miracle.

Half an hour later, Cat rose to go. 'Mr Hakesby will be worried,' she said. Or rather, she thought, he will say he has been inconvenienced by my absence, even if it is not true, and that will make him angry again.

'When will I see you?' Marwood said. 'I'd better not show myself at Henrietta Street.'

She blinked, surprised by the directness of his question. She answered him equally directly. 'I don't know. If they're watching me, it won't be safe to meet. Besides, my time's not my own.'

'It's your husband's.'

She bowed her head. She was aware that something had happened between them during this last hour, some shift in their relationship to one another that had nothing to do with words. She felt herself strangely reluctant even to think about it. There was nothing improper, of course, nothing to be ashamed of. It was merely that their interests marched together in this predicament, as their interests had marched together on other occasions.

'I will try to send word,' Cat said. 'Though God knows how.'

'There must be a way. Shall I send Stephen to you?'

'No. They probably know you have a blackamoor here.' She hesitated. 'But I go to the cook shop in Bedford Street on most mornings to command our dinner. It's next door to the Fleece.'

'Is there someone there who would hold a letter for us, if need be?'

'No one I could trust. I'm usually there around nine o'clock. Meeting there could be dangerous too. But I can't think of anywhere else.'

'If Buckingham's men are watching your house,' Marwood said, 'they might not follow you to the cook shop. Not if it's somewhere you go to every day.'

'Who knows?' She rubbed her forehead. 'I'm frightened of my own shadow these days.' She glanced out of the window, estimating the passage of time by the alteration in the light. 'I must go. The longer I leave it, the worse it will be.'

'I'll walk with you.'

'You will not. What are you thinking of? The less we're seen in company with one another the better.'

The rain had slackened, and she made good time. In Henrietta Street, near the gate to the churchyard, a knot of men surrounded the oyster stall that often stood there. She glanced towards them as she reached the door of the sign of the Rose. One of the men was Roger Durrell. He stared across the road, making no attempt to hide his interest in her.

Cat hammered on the door. Pheebs opened it at once, and she hurried into the house.

'There's a man outside by the oyster stall,' she said as he was about to close the door. 'That gross fellow with the sword. Can you see him?'

'Aye, mistress,' the porter said, his face as stolid as a pudding.

'Yes. Mark him well, then shut the door.' She waited until he had obeyed. 'Have you seen him before?'

'Not that I can call to mind.'

'Tell me at once if you see him again. Here or anywhere else. And never admit him to the house. Do you hear?'

'Yes, mistress.'

Pheebs accepted the shilling she gave him with a bow. She felt his eyes following her as she climbed the stairs.

On the floor below the Drawing Office, she hesitated at the parlour door. Her husband was speaking inside, his voice at a higher pitch than usual, as it often was when something excited him. She opened the door and went in. Hakesby was sitting at the table. He was looking much more cheerful than he had been earlier today.

A tall man rose from his chair. He bowed awkwardly to her. He was very thin, and he wore a long brown coat.

'Allow me to present my wife, sir,' Hakesby said. 'My dear, this is a bosom friend of Mr Cranmore. Pray welcome Mr Veal to our house.'

260

CHAPTER EIGHT

Dog and Bitch Yard
Sunday, 15–Wednesday, 18 March 1668

Bells. bang, bing, bang. They hurt inside. Sunday bells, Sunday bells.

Peace, says Ferrus, peace, and bells are quiet. He waits. I am flat as a shadow, he thinks. I bend like a shadow.

After servants' dinner, servants sleep. Cook bars the door from the scullery to the kitchen. But there's a hatch above the stone sink. It is covered with a wooden shutter with no bolt. The opening is small. Windy's head would not pass through it, even if the head could be cut from the body.

But Ferrus is clever. He bends like a shadow. His long, long arms reach the pans waiting on the other side. Pans to be licked and scraped and sucked.

Ferrus likes Sundays.

After Cat had left me, I sat for an hour or

more in the parlour, huddled beside the fire while picking over the bones of our conversation. It had unsettled me at the time, and it unsettled me even more in retrospect. I had never seen Cat looking so worried. I had come to take her strength of character for granted, but this afternoon I had glimpsed another side. It made me strangely fearful for her. Poor, deluded Hakesby was no use to her. She would find no help from that quarter.

In all probability, Richard Cromwell had been the man I had seen beside Veal during Buckingham's day of penitence at Wallingford House. The green spectacles and the unkempt beard made it a near certainty. That explained Veal's determination to get rid of me as soon as possible. The day of penitence had been the seventh of February, more than five weeks ago. Cromwell must have come within Buckingham's orbit before then.

I had given Cat my word that her secrets would be safe with me. But the more I thought about her situation—and perhaps mine—the more hopeless it seemed. What could either of us hope to achieve in such an affair, which touched on matters of state, and indeed on the safety of the kingdom itself?

Richard Cromwell was little trouble to the government as long as he was living obscurely in another country, without money or friends. Mr Williamson kept a file on him and his movements, though I had never seen it. I heard from a friend in Lord Arlington's office that the former Protector had moved from the Low Countries to Switzerland, and then to Italy, before settling for the last year or so in France. I doubted that he was considered dangerous enough to require a permanent watch to be kept on him, so long as he did nothing to attract attention to himself. His debts kept him out of England, where his creditors were.

Once on this side of the Channel, however, Cromwell could not so easily be discounted. As a lodestone draws nails towards it by no desire of its own, so might Richard Cromwell attract the discontented men of this kingdom to unite around him.

As Mr Williamson's clerk, I was privy to much of the intelligence that came across his desk, both from his network of spies and informers and from the private newsletters he received from the provinces. The King and his government were increasingly unpopular. The Restoration of the monarchy eight years earlier had been met with widespread joy, but that had been dissipated.

The murmurs of dissent were growing ever louder.

Add to that our humiliating defeat by the Dutch last year, and the government's perennial lack of money. Parliament held the purse strings but, despite Buckingham's promises, the Lords and Commons seemed incapable of agreeing among themselves, let alone with each other, or with the King and his ministers. The ministers were also squabbling among themselves, as I knew to my cost from Arlington's manoeuvres against the Duke of Buckingham. The licentiousness and extravagance of Whitehall caused ill feeling in the City and throughout the entire country.

If Richard Cromwell were in England, and secure under Buckingham's protection, the effects would be unpredictable. He might even prove to be the single trump card in this pack of fools and rogues. Men called him Tumbledown Dick and sneered at his weakness. But no one had ever accused him of corruption; and even his weakness had been the fault of his circumstances, not of himself.

Above all, he was a Cromwell. His father had been a godly man, whose armies had made England feared and respected across Europe. There were those who remembered only that, and forgot that Oliver had also been a tyrant, more ruthless and more absolute in his rule than the king he had replaced.

Buckingham had the money and the desire for power and glory. He had influence in the country and the court. He had many supporters in the City and among the Protestants who hated the papists that flourished at Whitehall. With Cromwell as his ally–even as his titular leader–Buckingham's vaulting ambition could dangle the promise of a renewed Commonwealth before the people of England. A few knaves, a pocketful of gold and a slogan or two could overturn the kingdom.

And bring the certainty of another civil war.

On Monday, there was a strange atmosphere in the office. People whispered in corners, and little work was done.

Mr Williamson seemed particularly pre-occupied. He sent me over to Arundel House in the morning, to enquire how my Lord Shrewsbury was doing. This was a matter of form, I suspected–it was common knowledge that the Earl was much better–but Mr Williamson clearly thought it politic to show his concern for Lord Arlington's ally.

The day was dry, with bursts of sunshine bringing a foretaste of spring. If Buckingham's people were still watching Arundel House, I saw no sign of them. The porter admitted me. I crossed the court to the doorway of my lord's apartments, where I sent up my name, together with Mr Williamson's compliments to my lord.

Usually this would bring down a servant with a note. This time, however, Mr Weld appeared, the gentleman I had met here once or twice before. Like his patron the Earl, he was a papist. For all that, I found him a man with a cultivated mind and a dry, straight-faced wit that was much to my taste.

'God save you, Mr Marwood,' he said, bowing. 'Have you come to inspect the invalid?'

'He continues to improve, I hope?'

'You shall see for yourself, sir.'

He led me to the nearest window that looked over that part of the garden between the house and the river. Three men were walking slowly abreast along one of the gravel walks. As I watched, they paused to examine one of old Lord Arundel's Roman statues that were such a feature of the place.

I recognized the slight, stooping figure in the middle of the three.

'That's my lord, isn't it?' I said, surprised.

'It is indeed.'

Shrewsbury was leaning on the arm of a manservant. He wore a heavily furred gown and a beaver hat, but no periwig. The third man was dressed in a physician's robes. Shrewsbury turned his head to speak to him, and I glimpsed my lord's sharp-featured face. He looked clean-shaven and much as I had seen him before, at Barn Elms before the duel.

'He is so much improved.'

'He grows stronger every day. Against all expectation, they must have worked.'

I groped for an instant, and then took his meaning: 'Ah. The pigeons.'

'Precisely.' Weld's face was as grave as ever, but something in his tone—the merest inflection—suggested that he had come as near to a smile as he was ever likely to. 'Freshly killed, cut open and applied to my lord's feet and also, just in case, to the wound in his side itself.'

'A tribute to the skill of our doctors, sir. And perhaps to my lord's constitution.'

Weld nodded. 'His improvement has been slow, though. But he and his physicians are quite convinced that it dates from when the pigeons were applied. I believe there is talk of a paper for the Royal Society.'

'Ah–it will be interesting to discover the physiological mechanisms involved.'

'I understand there's still some uncertainty as to their precise nature.'

'Are pigeons essential to the healing art?' I asked, a bubble of mirth threatening to erupt. 'Or would any bird be equally efficacious? A sparrow, perhaps?'

'No doubt the natural philosophers will soon enlighten us.' Weld shrugged and then added, 'In truth, I thought we would lose my lord, that day you saw him. He was so sorely wounded, and his fever ran so high.'

His words took me back to my first visit to Arundel House, the only time that I had had the opportunity to talk to the Earl. I said, 'He was rambling, poor man.' I hesitated, only for a fraction. Weld glanced at me, narrowing his eyes slightly. I went on: 'He talked a great deal about the dog and the bitch. Dog and bitch. Over and over again.'

'We know what that means.' Weld's lips compressed themselves into a line. 'My lady and her gallant lover.'

'I wonder.' I remembered my eavesdropping at the duel, and the King's words to the Duke when I had seen him at Whitehall that evening. *The dog and the bitch. I remember it well, pox on it.*

Weld shrugged. 'What else could he have meant? Dog and Bitch Yard? I hardly think so.'

'Where's that?'

'Somewhere off Drury Lane, I believe. The bawdy house.'

'Ah yes,' I said, adding hastily, 'I know it only by repute.'

'I've never been there myself,' Weld said, 'naturally.' I sensed his distaste for the subject; some of these papists are as prim as a Puritan on Sunday. 'And,' he went on, 'I wager my lord has never gone there either.' He looked down his long, well-bred nose at me. 'But a man like Buckingham probably knows every last hole and corner of the place.'

Dog and Bitch Yard. Knowing Buckingham's habits, I should have thought of this possibility long before. I suppose it was a tribute to my innocence that I had not.

After I had said goodbye to Mr Weld and left Arundel House, I crossed the Strand and turned up Drury Lane. It was approaching midday, and the air was full of cooking smells. People were walking briskly into Bear Yard with dinner on their mind.

Why, I wondered, in those desperate moments immediately after the duel, had Buckingham mentioned dog and bitch to Veal? Had he meant Dog and Bitch Yard? At that point in the afternoon, with one man dead and another perhaps dying, even the Duke would hardly have desired the services of a whore.

Outside the King's Theatre, I paused, pretending to examine a playbill fixed to a post. It was said that on occasion the King himself visited London's bawdy houses incognito. I had never entered one of these stews, though God knew that my imagination had sometimes roved in that direction. In my younger days, the cost deterred me. Fear of catching the pox was now the stronger argument, regularly reinforced by the sight of those poor, broken-down drabs whose looks were gone; once pox-ridden, they were reduced to fumbling in dark doorways for sixpence a time, or less if their customers were prepared to haggle.

In some part of me there also lingered the effects of my upbringing; for our parents never leave us entirely, whether we wish it or not; and my poor father had beaten a sense of shame into me that I could never quite root out. 'We are all sinners,' he would say, and then grunt as he brought down his stick on my back.

I walked on. Cat was only a few hundred yards away on the other side of Covent Garden. I wished I could lay this affair before her and enquire her opinion. She had a way of cutting through to whatever was essential in a matter.

Though I knew that the Dog and Bitch Yard was off Drury Lane, I did not know its precise location. In the end I was forced to ask one of the cookboys hurrying past with someone's dinner on a tray.

'Up there, master,' he said with a toss of his head up the street. 'Just before Long Acre.'

A beggar nearby burst into lewd laughter and rubbed his privates. 'Get it out, your worship! Stick it in!' He was drawing unwanted attention to me, so rather than give him a blow with my stick, I walked quickly on.

Despite the boy's directions, it took me several minutes to find the entry that led into the yard. The alley was straight, and wide enough for a horse. I hurried along it into the yard beyond. It was less squalid than I had expected, being properly paved. The houses on either side were old, built before the Fire, but they looked sound enough. The one at the back of the court

271

was larger, with a modern frontage built of brick, though the house behind was older. The woodwork of the doors and window frames had been freshly painted. For all the world, the place looked as if a respectable citizen lived there.

The oddest feature of all was that Dog and Bitch Yard was empty. It seemed to be holding its breath and waiting for something to happen. There was no sign of life whatsoever, even a cat. I stared up at the windows, wondering if someone was watching me. It was not a warm day but I was sweating.

A sense of my own folly swept over me. What had I expected to find here? A clue that would unravel the mystery of the name's significance? But what if there were no significance to unravel? Perhaps I had misheard what Buckingham said after the duel; perhaps the feverish Shrewsbury had meant his bitch of a wife; and perhaps the King had been merely invoking the memory of some past debauch that he and the Duke had shared in one of these prim-looking houses.

I turned to go. And at once I stopped. It felt as though my heart had stopped too. The alley stretched ahead of me to the street beyond. At its far end was Roger Durrell.

His reactions were faster than mine. He

tugged out his sword and advanced down the alley. As I had noticed after the duel, he was surprisingly nimble for a man of his size.

Blind panic took me over. I ran to the back of the court. The brick house had a single door, at the top of a short flight of steps. But there was also a small gate at the left-hand side. I lifted the latch and pushed. By the grace of God the gate wasn't barred.

Another, narrower alley lay beyond, winding between this house and its less substantial neighbour. It was much gloomier than the yard. The upper storeys of both buildings were jettied out until they nearly met each other, making a tunnel of the passageway. The jagged rooflines admitted only a ribbon of sky.

I slammed the gate behind me, glancing wildly at the back of it in the hope of finding a bolt or bar. But there was no time: Durrell's footsteps sounded very close. I fled down the alley.

Behind me, the latch rattled and the gate clattered against the wall. Durrell's footsteps were louder, amplified by the walls on either side. I turned another corner. There was the exit from the passage not twenty yards away. But it was completely blocked by a cart carrying a load of hay.

In a moment I would be trapped. A couple of paces ahead, there was a doorway recessed into the wall of the house on the right. I backed into it, raising my stick. I had no choice but to fight. With luck I would have at least an element of surprise.

My shoulders nudged against the door behind me. It opened suddenly. I almost fell backwards into the house.

'God save you, master, you're in a hurry,' a man said behind me.

I felt a hand drawing me inside. The porter bolted the door and scowled at me. He was a large man with a flattened nose and pockmarked face.

'Thank you,' I said, panting.

'Shouldn't have been left open,' he muttered. 'I'll flay the damned boy alive when I find him.'

'Here,' I said, finding a shilling in my purse. 'I–I'm much obliged to you.'

The shilling improved his mood, if only by a fraction. 'You should come in by the front door, sir, not this one. That's the one for the gentlemen. Anyway, we're not receiving callers yet.'

I adjusted my hat and peruke. 'Yes.' I took a deep breath, trying to steady my breathing. 'I must have mistook the hour.'

'You'll have to come back later.'

'Or perhaps wait?' I suggested, mindful of who was on the other side of the door.

The shilling was doing its work. 'You're desperate for it, sir, I can see that. Tell you what, come with me, and I'll see what I can do. No promises, mind.'

I gave him another shilling to ram home the good work of the first. He led me into a broad hall at the front of the house. There was a flight of stairs at the back of it. As we reached it, a woman's voice floated down from above our heads.

'Who is it?'

'Gentleman, madam.'

'Why did you let him in?'

'I didn't. Tom left the side door unbarred. But he seems a very open-handed gentleman, madam, and willing to be generous. Shall I tell him to wait?'

There was no answer. I heard her footsteps pattering away.

The porter nodded familiarly to me. 'You're in with a chance, I'd say. She trusts my judgement, you see.'

Shortly afterwards, another man in livery came downstairs. But there was nothing of the servant in his manner. His movements were catlike, with a calculating grace about them. He carried a staff which had an iron ball at its head, and an iron spike at its foot.

He ran his eyes over me as he approached. 'Madam says you can come up, even though you're early,' he said. 'As long as you look the right sort. Madam is most particular.'

It cost me yet another shilling to look the right sort. He led me upstairs and opened a door. He stood aside to allow me to enter a large, high-ceilinged drawing room. The door closed behind me.

I was alone. Though it was the middle of the day, the curtains were partly closed. The air smelled of perfume, tallow and yesterday's tobacco. Paintings of naked and almost life-size figures, mainly female and billowing with pink flesh, adorned the walls. There were several sofas, which were piled high with cushions and arranged against the walls and before the fireplace.

I moved towards the window, hoping that it might be a means of escape. A table for writing stood before it. A broad stripe of sunlight ran over a disorderly pile of papers, with an inkpot and pen discarded beside it. The window looked out into Dog and Bitch Yard, which was no longer empty. Two gentlemen were down there, staring up at the house, one of them pointing it out to the other with his stick.

The sunlit papers on the desk caught my eye as I drew back into the room. The top sheet had only two words on it, scrawled in large capital letters a third of the way down the paper, and centrally placed, like a title: *THE REHEARSAL*. It was marked by the ring of a wine glass, and a few drops of candlewax.

I pushed the page aside. Beneath it was another, partly filled by a passage written in a fluent scrawl. My eyes skimmed over the heading:

Petition to the most Splendid, Illustrious, Lady of Pleasure, the Countess of Castlemayne &c: The Humble Petition of the Undone Company of poore distressed Whores, Bawds, Pimps, and Panders . . .

And at the foot of the page:

Signed by us, Madam Cresswell and Damaris Page, in the behalf of our Fellow-Sufferers in Dog and Bitch Yard, Lukenor's Lane, Saffron Hill, Moorfields, Chiswell Street, Rosemary Lane, Nightingale Lane, Ratcliffe Highway, Well Close, East Smithfield . . .

A hinge creaked.
'Well, sir, fortune smiles on you today.'

It was her voice I had heard earlier. I spun round. There was a second doorway in the room, partly concealed by a painted screen. A small woman was standing by the end of the screen. She was in her forties or even fifties, but the remains of beauty clung to her face. She was well dressed, but in a quiet, genteel way; she might have been the wife of a prosperous merchant welcoming a guest to her house.

'Madam,' I said, bowing, 'I'm so very much obliged to you, I'm sure.'

'We open at three o'clock in the afternoon. But, since you have somehow found yourself here, I suppose we must quench your ardour.'

I bowed again. 'You are kindness itself.'

She came towards me. Her movements were graceful, and her carriage could have been a court lady's. 'Let us have a little more light.'

She stopped by the window and pulled the curtains open. She tidied the notes on the desk into a pile and placed the inkpot on top to act as a paperweight.

'I think one or two of our misses may be ready to receive a gentlemen visitor. Indeed, they are so fond of the society of gentlemen that they are always beforehand in preparing themselves. But I fear that you are so early that some of them may still be in their shifts.'

I could think of nothing to say, so I bowed again.

'But first a glass of wine to sharpen your appetite and deepen the pleasure to come. You mustn't be bashful, sir–the young ladies like a man with fire in his belly. Would you ring the bell? The rope's by the fireplace.'

No sooner did I ring than the catlike manservant reappeared with a tray containing wine and biscuits.

'It's the custom of the house for a visiting gentleman to pay for a bottle of wine. Shall we say a pound? Pray give it to Merton.'

There was no help for it. I took out my purse and placed a little heap of silver on the tray that Merton held out to me.

'Let us sit and be cosy together,' Madam Cresswell said, waving me to one of the sofas. 'Have you visited one of my houses before?'

'No, madam. I–I haven't had the pleasure.'

She sat near me but on another sofa. I took a mouthful of wine. All the while, I was listening for sounds downstairs.

'What's your pleasure?' she asked. 'Are you a man of valour who likes to make a direct assault on the main gate of the citadel, and carry all before you with the impetus of your gallant charge? Or are you a subtler warrior, a cunning Odysseus perhaps, who slips in by the postern gate at the rear?'

'I-I scarcely know, madam.'

She smiled at me, chidingly, like a mother amused by her child's bashfulness. 'Or do you like to chastise a pretty rogue in order to urge her towards the path of virtue? No? Perhaps you yourself are more of a scholar? You prefer to go to school and be taught. And sometimes birched if you do not learn your letters fast enough?'

'No,' I said firmly. 'I believe I have been schooled enough.'

'At the school of love, sir, there is always something new to learn. What of the language of love? Some of my gentlemen like their miss to talk bawdy to them. For my most discerning visitors, I recommend the indescribably sweet company of a pair of fricatrices. That indeed is a rare pleasure, both to behold and to partake in. Sometimes they need a gentleman's rod to help them in their naughty play and to chastise them when they grow overbold.'

I finished my glass of wine. Merton was still hovering.

I cleared my throat. 'I'm a plain fellow, madam.'

'I understand. Like a wise man, no doubt, you prefer to see the goods before you buy. And so you shall.' She glanced at the servant. 'The bell.'

Merton tugged the rope twice. Less than a minute later, three young women filed into the room. They lined up in front of me.

'My dears,' said Madam Cresswell, 'allow me to present you to this gentleman. First, sir, from the left, we have Amaryllis. Turn round, you pretty little thing, and don't be shy. Let our guest admire your charms.'

Amaryllis was a plump, dark-haired girl with a snub nose. She wore a shift that was loose at the neck. As she rotated for my pleasure, she encouraged her breasts to swing before my eyes, giving me a glimpse of nipples along with a whiff of perfume and sweat. She was followed by Dorinda, a thin girl with a frightened face and blue eyes; she looked no more than twelve years old, and her forearms were smudged with bruises fading from purple to a delicate blue.

Finally, there came Chloris in a bedgown of silk trimmed with fur at the neck and cuffs. She stared directly at me, with no attempt at coquetry. God help me, she reminded me of Cat, though the latter's complexion was fairer, in both senses of the

281

word. She let the gown fall open. Underneath she was naked. Without haste, she drew the gown tightly around her.

There was a heavy double-knock downstairs. Someone was at the hall door.

'This one pleases me,' I said, indicating Chloris.

There was another, more prolonged burst of knocking.

'Ah,' said Madam Cresswell, ignoring the knocking. 'You have an eye for quality, sir. Chloris was brought up in Paris. She lived in a very good family indeed, and was much at court. The French have a peculiar talent for the art of love. But is it only Chloris you would like? Wouldn't you like her to entertain you with a friend?'

'Just Chloris, if I may,' I said.

Merton appeared at my elbow, holding out the tray.

'I have always remarked,' Madam Cresswell said, 'that a generous heart responds generously when beauty offers herself so sweetly. The usual present is a pound for the first half hour.'

There were voices below—two men engaged in what sounded like an argument. I stood up suddenly. I scattered money on Merton's tray and pushed aside his arm. Desperation inspired me.

'Madam, I beg you,' I said, giving Chloris what I hoped looked like a lascivious glance, 'pray let there be no delay. I burn! I'm in torment! My passion threatens to unman me.'

'That would never do.' There was a hint of amusement in Madam Cresswell's voice. 'Quick, child, take your admirer away.'

Chloris seized my wrist and drew me on to the landing. I heard Durrell talking below, and other male voices. The porter had clearly called for reinforcements.

'This way, sir.'

She drew me down the landing to a small but gloomy chamber furnished with a truckle bed, a table, a pot and a washstand. She closed the door and turned to face me. As she did so, she allowed her gown to fall open again.

'How do you want me, sir?' she said briskly in a voice that was closer to Bristol than Paris. 'What's your pleasure?'

I crossed the room to the window. The casement was closed. It faced the blank wall of the neighbouring building.

'On my back?' she was saying. 'Or on all fours? Some gentlemen prefer it that way, especially the quality. The Duke does, for one.'

The voices below were growing louder.

Among them was Madam Cresswell's.

I glanced back at her. 'The Duke?' I said. 'Which Duke?'

She grinned. 'Bucks. Right name for him. He's hung like a poxy stag, I can tell you, and it's always rutting season for him.'

'Is he often here?'

'When he has the humour for it, he spends more time in Dog and Bitch Yard than at Wallingford House and Whitehall put together. But if you please, sir, I ain't got all day and you've only got half an hour. I'll do whatever I can to oblige. Within reason, that is.' Chloris paused, her expression changing. 'I thought you were so hot for it you couldn't wait.'

I opened the casement and craned out. The alley was directly below me. This chamber must be more or less directly above the side door by which I had entered this house. Above me, the upper storeys of the two houses on either side were so close I could almost touch them.

'What are you about?' she said in a sharper voice. 'What do you want?'

'Your help,' I said.

'A little encouragement beforehand, sir? A lot of gentlemen like that. No shame in it.'

'No. Help me get out of the window.'

Chloris backed away, towards a bell rope

at the head of the bed. 'I knew you was a strange one. If it was me, I wouldn't have let you in.'

'Please,' I said, spreading my hands wide. 'I wish you no harm. I'm pursued. That's why I came here. It was by accident.'

Her eyes were bright with intelligence. 'Debt, is it?'

'Yes. The damned dice. It's my creditors making that racket below.'

As I was speaking, I was feeling for yet more money in my pocket. I scattered a handful of silver on top of the washstand. 'That's for you, just for you. Help me out of the window. You can say I pushed you aside and jumped out.'

She smiled, looking genuinely amused. 'You're a surprise, ain't you? Go on then.'

She tore the sheet from the bed and followed me to the window. I wriggled out, legs first, holding on to the mullion. When only my head and shoulders were left inside, she wrapped one end of the sheet around the mullion and gave me the other end.

'It'll make it less of a drop,' she said. 'Go!'

I let go of the bar and clambered hand over hand down the length of the sheet. The alley seemed to be empty. I looked up at Chloris. The gown had fallen open again. I jumped. Pain shot through my right leg,

285

from ankle to thigh. I sprawled on the path.

She pulled up the sheet. There was a clatter as she dropped my stick after me. I seized it and scrambled to my feet, ignoring the pain. I glanced up the alley. The cart of hay was no longer blocking the far end. People were moving in the street beyond.

I looked up at Chloris's face. She was laughing silently at me.

'Quick,' she said, glancing over her shoulder, and then back to me. 'Run, you fool.'

I ran.

It was a relief to be in the safety of Whitehall. By the time I passed through the King Street Gate towards Westminster, the pain in my leg had subsided and I was scarcely limping at all. A moment later I turned into Axe Yard, where there was a tavern, the Axe. The landlord knew me well, for I had spent many shillings there since I had first come to Whitehall.

I found a seat on the end of a bench in a gloomy corner near the door to the privy. My hands were trembling so much that I had to use both of them to lift the first mug of ale to my mouth.

After half a pot of ale, my breathing had returned to normal, and the haze of fear had thinned. I tried to bring some sort of order to what I knew. I had resolved the matter of the dog and the bitch that had so niggled at my mind since the duel. As he lay on his sickbed, Lord Shrewsbury might well have had more than one meaning for the dog and the bitch in his feverish mind: one was that Buckingham was the dog and my Lady Shrewsbury the bitch; the other, at the same time, was Dog and Bitch Yard, the location of a brothel that the Duke frequented, and perhaps the place where he had taken refuge after the duel, when there had been a warrant out for his arrest. If I was right, the house in Dog and Bitch Yard was more than a brothel as far as Buckingham was concerned: it was a bolthole.

'Marwood?'

I looked up with a start. I would have jumped at the sight of my own shadow. To my relief it was only Richard Abbott coming through the crowd towards me. He was a clerk at Scotland Yard–junior to me; a pudding-faced man with worried eyes and lips that permanently pouted.

'Where've you been, Marwood?' he said. 'Williamson's asked for you twice since dinner.'

'Faith,' I said. 'That's good to know.'

'You were expected before midday.'

'I'm engaged in other business,' I snapped.

'And what are you doing here?'

'Mr Williamson sent me to enquire at the Cockpit if the Duke of Albemarle's expected.'

'Is he?'

'No. He's in the country until May. Pray, have you noticed your coat's muddy?'

'I'm not blind,' I said. 'I'm glad to see you aren't, either.'

Abbott coloured. He was eyeing my grazed knuckles, probably wondering whether to comment on them, and deciding it might be wiser not to.

I sent him away. It would be foolish to linger much longer, but for pride's sake I waited for ten minutes. It would damage my position among the other clerks if I allowed Abbott to think he had frightened me into rushing back to Mr Williamson.

His mention of the Cockpit reminded me of what Cat had told me yesterday: Tumbledown Dick's claim that there were valuables of his concealed somewhere in the Cockpit. While I dawdled over the last of the ale, I turned it over in my mind. Perhaps there was some truth in the story. Something must have brought Richard Cromwell back to England, within reach of his debtors.

I knew old Oliver had lodged in the Cockpit before they proclaimed him Lord

Protector of England. After the Restoration, Oliver's wife–another Elizabeth, like Richard's daughter–had been accused of stealing royal possessions and smuggling them from Whitehall. No one had produced evidence of this, and the government had wisely let the matter drop; they had thought it better to push the surviving Cromwells away from the public view rather than run the risk of turning them into martyrs.

Oliver might have been as incorruptible as everyone claimed. But perhaps his wife had been another matter.

Despite Abbott's dark hints, Williamson was quite amiable, for him, when we met. I had returned to the office and was looking over the proofs for the *Gazette* when he sent for me. In his private room, he told me to close the door and gave me a sealed packet.

'This is for my Lord Arlington,' he said. 'He should be in his office now. I want you to wait while he reads it over. He may send a message back by you.'

I bowed in acknowledgement, and said nothing. As Secretary and Undersecretary of State, Arlington and Williamson were bound to work closely together, but there was something almost clandestine about Williamson's manner on this occasion.

Judging by the thickness of the packet, it held at least a dozen sheets. I noticed that lying on his desk was a file of reports from his informers. It was the London file, not the one that covered the rest of the country.

'The contents of this packet are confidential. I prefer to trust it to you, not to one of the others. Put it into my lord's hands yourself. Don't talk of it to anyone–apart from my lord, if he should condescend to address you on the subject.'

I bowed again.

'That's enough bowing and scraping for now,' Williamson said tartly, reverting to type. 'What have you been doing to yourself? You're filthy.'

'I fell in the street, sir.'

'I can't have you looking like that in public. Get the boy to brush you down before you go out.'

When I was fit to be seen, I left Scotland Yard and walked over to the Privy Gallery, where Arlington had his office as Secretary of State. It was, I thought, a compliment that Williamson had singled me out. If it had been my other master, the wily Chiffinch, I would have suspected some ulterior motive, some devious manoeuvre that might not be to my advantage.

Arlington received me in his private room

with as much lofty condescension as if I had been a lowly curate and he an archbishop. His face was unsmiling and pale. The black plaster across the bridge of his nose gave him an incongruously clownish appearance. I gave him the packet. He frowned at it and then at me.

'Wait next door while I read this,' he ordered.

I bowed and went to idle away my time in the outer office. I knew a clerk there, a man named Dudley Gorvin, with whom I occasionally dined. He was older than I. He had the reputation of being quiet and industrious, to match his master's unbending seriousness, but in private he could be as witty as any man I knew, and he was as sharp as a needle as well. When I came in, he was standing at his desk, pen in hand, and looking out of the window. He glanced over his shoulder.

'Good day to you, sir,' he said. 'What are you doing here?'

'Mr Williamson sent me with some papers for my lord to look over. I'm to wait.'

I crossed the room to him and we looked down at three of the Queen's ladies in waiting who were walking slowly along one of the paths with their heads close together. One of Arlington's letter files lay open on the desk.

'Are they gossiping, do you think?' Gorvin said, closing the file for he was a discreet man. 'Plotting? Both? It's something like that, Marwood, as God's in his heaven. It's all we ever do in this poxy place: intrigue about this or intrigue about that.'

'You're turning philosopher,' I said.

Gorvin jerked his head towards my lord's private room. He lowered his voice still further. 'He's at it, too, you mark my words. With your Mr Williamson.'

'Do you know what this one's about?'

'The Duke, I think. Bucks, I mean, not Albemarle or York.'

I raised my eyebrows. 'Something in the air?'

'My lord's convinced that Bucks has some great scheme afoot, but he doesn't know what it is. Or when he'll set it in motion.'

'Williamson's been studying our London informers' file.' I hesitated, aware of the need to reciprocate, for information is like any other valuable commodity: it is trans-ferred through trade, not gift. 'Sunday is Easter Day. Easter Monday's a holiday, of course.'

'You think there may be trouble then?'

I shrugged. 'Perhaps. There's a danger of trouble on any public holiday. Give the apprentices a little licence and they make the most of it.'

'I wonder. You may be right.' Gorvin leafed back through the letter file on his desk. 'Here it is, a note in the Duke's own hand. My lord had proposed a meeting with him on Easter Monday, but the Duke wrote to say he would be out of town.'

He passed the letter to me. It was only a few lines long, and I read it in an instant. But suddenly it wasn't the meaning of the words that mattered to me, but the handwriting that conveyed it. Buckingham wrote a firm, flowing hand, with few scratchings-out. It sloped markedly to the right and was easy to read.

I had seen a handwriting very similar to that only a few hours ago, on Madam Cresswell's desk in Dog and Bitch Yard. That hadn't been a letter, but a strange sort of petition concerning a list of brothels.

'What is it?' Gorvin said sharply. 'Have you seen something?'

'Nothing,' I said. 'I–I wonder where the Duke is going on Monday.'

I knew by Gorvin's face that he had sensed my evasion. Luckily the office's page boy chose that moment to rush over to me. His face was pink with urgency and self-importance.

'Your pardon, sir,' he gabbled. 'It's Mr Marwood from Scotland Yard, isn't it?'

'Yes. Why?'

'This, sir.' He held out a letter. 'Handed in downstairs.'

I took the letter. My name was written on the outside, but without any direction: this was from someone who had known that I was at my Lord Arlington's office. Murmuring an apology to Gorvin, I turned away, broke the seal and unfolded the paper.

Nothing was written inside. There was only a sketch in ink, crudely executed by someone with little talent for drawing. But the artist's intentions were clear enough for all that.

The picture showed a gallows on which was hanging a man with his feet dancing in the air and the letter M on his chest.

'Bad news, sir?' Gorvin asked. 'Why, you look quite pale.'

Mr Veal called unannounced at Mistress Dalton's on the Tuesday before Easter. Richard Cromwell received him in the hall because his hostess and Elizabeth were in the parlour. Cromwell loved his daughter and he wanted to spare her what he could.

Veal suggested they take a turn up and down the courtyard. His tall, austere figure

towered over Cromwell. Without any pream-
ble, he came directly to the point.

'You remember that His Grace requests
your presence on Easter Monday? To meet
certain friends of his.'

Cromwell cleared his throat. 'On that
subject —'

'He will send a coach for you early in the
morning, or even the previous evening.'

'Is my presence absolutely necessary, do
you know?'

'Indeed it is, sir.' Veal was looking grim,
but then he almost always did. 'All the arrangements have been made.'

'I see.' Cromwell felt a spurt of anger, and
for once did not trouble to suppress it. 'So I
have no choice?'

'We always have a choice.'

'Don't chop logic with me, if you please.
My daughter and I are your prisoners to all
intents and purposes. Isn't that the truth?'

Veal shrugged his thin shoulders. 'I
wouldn't choose to put it like that. For your
own safety, we —'

'What it comes down to is this. Either I
do what your master wishes, in every particular, or he will ensure the government
knows where to find me.'

'The Duke has no desire to do that.'

'What if I say that I have other plans for

Easter Monday, and that I regret I cannot meet his friends?'

Veal laid long fingers on Cromwell's arm, tightening his grip. They stopped and looked at each other.

'That cannot be, sir,' Veal said. 'His Grace has set his heart on your being there.'

'I may be otherwise engaged.'

'As it happens, he knows you had previously had other plans in mind for that day.'

'What do you mean?'

'On Sunday, I called at Henrietta Street and had a conversation with Mr Hakesby, the surveyor.' Veal paused.

Cromwell swallowed. He looked away.

'And his young wife,' Veal went on. 'We are all friends here, all supporters of the good old cause. There need be no secrets between us.'

'You've been following us,' Cromwell said.

'For your own safety, sir. His Grace is most solicitous on your behalf. In fact, we have already been aware of the Hakesbys at the sign of the Rose, about quite a different matter. But, leaving that aside, I understand from him that you wish to retrieve some family possessions from Whitehall. From the Cockpit lodging, to be precise. Is that correct?'

Cromwell nodded. 'But it's a private matter, of no interest to anyone other than myself and the Hakesbys.'

Veal went on as if Cromwell had not spoken. 'Mr Hakesby says that he's making the arrangements on your behalf, and by chance he had chosen Easter Monday for your commission. As it's a holiday, it's the best time—fewer servants will be about. Is that the truth of it?'

'I see I have no secrets from you,' Cromwell said as calmly as he could.

'Hakesby tells me that these valuables are concealed in a sewer beneath the Cockpit lodgings. He has enlisted the help of a malcontented mazer scourer who will act as a guide.'

Cromwell pulled himself from Veal's grip. A wave of bitterness threatened to overwhelm him. Hakesby had blabbed the whole affair to Veal. All this expense, all this danger, had come to nothing. Indeed, worse than nothing, because it had entangled him in the schemes of the Duke of Buckingham. He was caught, like a fly in a spider's web: and the more he struggled, the more he was entangled.

'I understand your not wishing to confide in His Grace or myself about the Cockpit. It's a private matter, is it not?' The words were conciliatory but Veal's voice was as hard as ever, and his face was as grim as a gravestone. 'Nevertheless it explains something that has puzzled me from the start: why you were prepared to run the risk of coming to London.'

'As you say, sir, it's a private matter. Or at least it was. It's scarcely private now. And I am ruined.'

'No.'

'What do you mean?'

'The Duke commands me to say there is no need to disturb yourself.'

'Speak plain, for God's sake.'

'He will do all he can to accommodate you with your private matter, sir. You're his friend. His ally.'

Again, the words were soft and obliging, but Veal's voice was abrasive, as if he were chiding a naughty child. The two men walked up and down the courtyard in silence.

'Perhaps,' Cromwell said when he could bear it no longer, 'you would tell me what His Grace has in mind.'

'Why, it's perfectly simple: he expects you to spend Easter Monday with him, as arranged, and to meet his friends. In return, he will undertake to provide any assistance that Mr Hakesby needs on your behalf at the Cockpit. It's to everyone's advantage.

You would hardly wish to crawl about in sewers yourself. And your personal safety must concern us all.'

'That's most obliging of him,' Cromwell said. 'You're aware that Mr Hakesby himself is not —'

'In the best of health? Yes. But everything is in hand. We ourselves can provide any other assistance Mr Hakesby requires on the day. We shall need full directions about where to find these valuables of yours.'

'Of course,' Cromwell reluctantly agreed.

'I rejoice this is settled. The Duke assured me there would be no difficulty. He knows that there is a perfect understanding between you and him. Either I or my servant Durrell will accompany Mr Hakesby on the day, and I'll confer with him about the details beforehand.'

Veal paused. He waited, like a parent who had granted his child a favour and expected a seemly gratitude. Cromwell said nothing.

'There's one other matter to discuss before I go,' Veal said after a moment. 'Mistress Hakesby.'

'Mistress — ?'

'Come, sir.' Veal's voice had lost its veneer of respect. 'Let's be plain with one another, you know perfectly well who I mean. The pretty young wife of the old man. I under-

299

stand that she was the bosom friend of your daughter when they were barely out of leading strings.' His tone had become openly sarcastic. 'Pray correct me if I'm wrong, but did you not approach Hakesby through her?'

'Yes. She's of no significance apart from that.'

'Really? She was your daughter's friend when they were children, in the days when this country had a godly government. When there was a Cromwell in Whitehall. Why then, sir, you must know who Mistress Hakesby really is.'

Cromwell shrugged. 'I do. But we have all changed since then. She is merely the wife of —'

'Catherine Lovett,' Veal said. 'That's who she is, and she always will be. She's the regicide's daughter, sir. And His Grace has a powerful desire to meet her.'

On the Wednesday before Easter, I rose early. Margaret and Stephen had already been up for several hours. Stephen brought my breakfast, and then Sam hobbled in with a letter.

'When did this come?'

'Pushed under the door, master.'

'This morning?'

'It wasn't there last night.'

I broke the seal. Inside was what looked like a poem. It was written in a clerkly hand that I didn't recognize.

My First is to ruin, which my Whole
   always Doth
Whate'er it touches, from North to the
   South.
My second's a Serpent that crawls i' the
   mire
And draws Careless Mortals down to Hell
   Fire.
My Parts once united, tho' my Visage
   much scarred,
I Squat like a Turd in old Scotland Yard.

'What's this?' Sam said, peering over my shoulder. 'A poem of love?'

'No,' I said, glad for once that he couldn't read much more than his own name. 'It's a riddle of sorts.'

'I like a riddle, master. Will you read it to me? See if I can guess the answer?'

'Go away,' I said. 'Leave me in peace, for God's sake.'

Sam chuckled in a way he fondly imagined would sound lewd and knowing. He retreated before I could find something to throw at him.

I pushed aside the newly baked roll. This

301

was the second warning. Or insult. Or threat.

Fear rose like bile in my belly. First, on Monday afternoon at Whitehall, had come the picture of a man with the letter M on his chest dangling from a gibbet. And then this: a riddle that even a child could solve. Ruin signified 'mar', and the serpent signified 'worm': and the whole was Marworm, as the Duke called me, Marworm with his scarred face and his place in Williamson's office at Scotland Yard.

The cook shop that Cat had mentioned was easy to find. It was on the east side of Bedford Street and advertised itself as much by the smells as by any outward display of what was on sale within. Next door, the newly gilded sign of the Fleece creaked over the heads of the passers-by.

It wanted a few minutes to nine o'clock. The shop was full of housewives and maids, who were set on ordering their dinners and exchanging gossip while they waited. A man in a peruke, idling away the time in such a place, would stand out like a thistle in a bed of roses.

There was a bookshop over the road, with its flap open to display some of its wares. I waited there, turning over the pages of a

302

damp-stained sexto-decimo copy of Raleigh's *History of the World.* A hackney was standing by a row of posts outside the shop, and it offered me some concealment.

I waited long enough for the bookseller to start throwing me suspicious glances. He would have done more than this if my clothes had not been so obviously respectable. As I turned away, I saw Cat approaching from the direction of Henrietta Street. The Hakesbys' little maid was scurrying beside her with a basket on her arm. They went into the cook shop.

I beckoned the bookseller's boy. 'A lady wearing a blue cloak has just gone into the cook shop over there. She has her maid with her.' I dropped three pennies into the boy's waiting palm. 'Tell her that the gentleman she saw on Sunday would speak to her.'

The boy leered up at me; he could not have been more than eight or nine, but he considered himself wise in the ways of the world. He darted across the road and went into the cook shop. A moment later, he returned and gave me a wink. I learned nothing more from him because his employer chose that moment to emerge from behind his counter. He clouted the boy around the head and dragged him by the ear into the shop.

I waited. A few minutes later, Cat emerged alone from the cook shop. She glanced over the road and saw me. She crossed the road and pretended to examine another book on the shelf.

'I had to see you,' I said.

'Why?'

'I found out about the dog and the bitch. It signifies Dog and Bitch Yard, by Drury Lane. I went to a bawdy house there —'

'You did *what*?'

'Not for that reason. By accident. Durrell was chasing me. But it seems that Buckingham goes there regularly. Perhaps he even owns the place. I saw some papers written in his handwriting.' My words tumbled out, falling over one another in my haste. 'Since then he's sent me two anonymous letters . . . one's a drawing, in fact, the other's a riddle. He's trying to frighten me.' I turned my head to avoid looking at Cat's face. 'To speak truth, he's succeeded.'

'We were frightened of him before,' she said quietly. 'Nothing's changed.'

'This is different.'

I wanted to say that there was now something personal about Buckingham's dislike of me: I had become more than a minor obstacle in his path, more than a man he despised and disliked because of the masters

I served: he hated me now; not what I stood for, but myself. But I held back. The intimacy that we had shared on Sunday seemed to have evaporated.

'Interested in the *History,* sir?'

It was that damned bookseller.

'No,' I snarled. 'That is, perhaps. I am considering.'

'Very fine copy, sir. Said to have belonged to Sir Walter's poor wife. And the contents, sir–why, no one has written better of this world and its history, or knew more of it by his own experience. The volume's so convenient as well–you can slip it in your pocket and take it anywhere.'

'How much?'

'Eighteen shillings. Bearing in mind the associations. I could get more in Paul's Churchyard, if I had a mind.'

'Nonsense,' Cat said. 'It's worth six: no more than that.'

The bookseller hadn't expected an attack from this quarter. 'Twelve,' he said, recoiling from her.

'Six.'

'Very well, mistress, I can't deny you, though it's bread from my poor family's mouths. Eight if you must.'

'Seven shillings, and no more. Take it away and wrap it for the gentleman.'

He bowed low to her, and retreated with the book.

'Cheap at the price,' I said drily. 'As it was once my Lady Raleigh's.'

To my surprise she laughed. I smiled at her. Then both of us grew serious.

'Buck's planning something for Easter Monday. Dog and Bitch Yard has something to do with it, though I don't know what. It must involve Cromwell, too. I'm sorry, but I must tell Williamson.'

'No,' she said.

'Yes,' I said. 'I must.'

'You don't understand. We're part of it. Veal and my husband are the best of friends.'

'Veal? *Veal?*'

'He's convinced poor Hakesby that Buckingham will be the nation's saviour, with Cromwell at his side. The Duke has arranged a private meeting on Easter Monday, with gentlemen of like mind. No doubt they will discuss how they will do away with tyrannical bishops, and for all I know the King too, and how all men will worship as they please, except the papists of course. England will become an earthly paradise. That's what my husband believes. He says we must all work to help the Duke.'

'We? Not you, surely? Whatever folly Hakesby commits himself to, you needn't be part of it. Let me tell Williamson that you came to me of your own accord, and —'

'But I am part of it, Marwood, whether I will or no. They want me for who I am. Have you forgotten? I'm the regicide's daughter.'

'No,' I said. 'No.'

Cat stared up at me. Her face white with anger or perhaps fear. Or both. She wheeled round and left me standing alone and even more scared than I had been before. Not just for me. For her.

'Seven shillings then, sir,' said the bookseller.

His boy was beside him, with my overpriced *History* wrapped in a paper parcel tied with string.

I walked to Scotland Yard, with the *History* in my pocket.

I couldn't make up my mind. Should I talk to Williamson? Should I tell him the whole of what I knew about Buckingham's plans, while somehow trying to minimize the part that Cat and Hakesby were playing? Or should I listen to Cat, and hold my peace? But if I did that, what would happen to the country on Easter Monday? Nearer home, what would Buckingham do to me?

Williamson was with my Lord Arlington in his Privy Gallery apartments, and they remained secluded there for most of the morning. My desk in Scotland Yard was near the window. I did little work that day. I watched the court below while my thoughts went first one way then the other.

Then suddenly, there was Mr Williamson. But not alone: Mr Weld of all people was with him, Mr Weld from Arundel House, and they were talking as they walked, their heads close together. I stood up when I heard their feet on the stairs and went to the door of the outer office, to greet them when they came in.

'Sir,' I said, without any other greeting when Williamson entered, 'May I —'

'Marwood, there you are,' he interrupted. 'In my room. Now.'

Weld merely gave me a nod as he passed me, though usually he was as punctilious as a Spaniard in his greetings and farewells. He looked as if he hadn't slept for a week. His eyes were swollen and red.

I followed them into the private office.

'Shut the door,' Williamson snapped.

Weld sank into a chair without being invited.

'This will set the cat among the doves,' Williamson said quietly. 'My Lord Shrews-

308

bury died today.'

I looked from one grave face to the other. 'But I saw him myself the other day. My lord was walking in the garden–he seemed all but himself again.'

Weld cleared his throat. 'A sudden fever took him. There was nothing we could do. Nothing anyone could do.'

'And, because of this, Buckingham has disappeared again,' Williamson said. 'Because he fears a charge of murder.'

CHAPTER NINE

The Good Old Days
Thursday, 19–Easter Monday, 23 March 1668
Ferrus stinks.

Master sent him into the old, old sewer. The shit and the piss pours in. For years and years and years. And everything else they put down their privies.

You go down there, Master says, scour it well or I throw you in the river. Make you drown.

Ferrus here before in this old sewer. Long long ago, in that other time.

He digs and wriggles. Shovels and crawls. Scrapes and scratches. Ratty runs over his feet, over his arm.

The roof down. Ferrus stuck. Master pulls him free.

Poxy wretch, says Master. Clear that tomorrow, or I bury you there for the rats to have for dinner.

Master puts Ferrus under the pump. Water

makes him shiver. Ferrus squeals.

Ferrus weeps cold tears.

Pheebs watched Mistress Hakesby descending the last flight of stairs and admired the tantalizing glimpses of ankle and calf. Wasted on a dotard like her husband. Shocking. The thought of that trembling old man pawing at those pert bubbies made him feel ill. It was against nature.

'Pheebs!' she snapped, as she reached the hallway. 'A word if you please.'

He bowed, rubbing his hands together. 'How may I serve you, mistress?'

'Who brought that letter you sent up?'

She was in a passion, he reckoned, which had brought a fetching colour to her cheeks. 'The one that came this morning?'

'Of course. What else could I mean?'

Her tone angered him. He cuffed the boy, venting a little of his irritation, driving him back to the shadows by the stairs. He was tempted to lie to her. The fat man had paid him well when he gave Pheebs the letter on the understanding that he would say a strange servant had brought it. The trouble was, the boy had been there as an unwanted witness, and also the boy knew that the fat man and Pheebs had encountered each other on more than one occasion over the last few weeks, to their mutual profit. The boy was the next best thing to an idiot, which was useful in one way. But it also meant that he could not be trusted to keep his mouth shut.

'He was a big fellow, mistress.' Pheebs sketched a great belly in front of him. 'I seen him about in the street a few times. Shall I send the lad out to look for him?'

'No.'

She wheeled around and ran up the stairs, giving him another glimpse of ankle and calf, though she was gone so quickly it was almost as if he had imagined it.

Hakesby was in his closet, with the lid of his chest thrown open. He glanced wild-eyed over his shoulder at Cat. This morning's letter had thrown him into a panic.

'Where are they?' he demanded. 'Have you hidden them somewhere?'

'Hidden what, sir?'

'The Cockpit plans. You're always taking my things away and hiding them somewhere. I believe you do it to mock me.'

'You left the plans upstairs in the Drawing Office,' she said. 'Shall I fetch them?'

'What o'clock is it? We'll be late if we don't hurry.'

'There is plenty of time, sir. Mr Cromwell

sends the coach for us at three.'

'I'm sure he sends it at two. Give me his letter, and I will make sure.'

'At once, sir.'

Cat left him delving in the chest to no purpose. She went upstairs. The portfolio with the plans was where Hakesby had left it, on the shelf by his chair. The letter that Durrell had brought was on his desk. She glanced through it. Cromwell had named three o'clock for the coach. It was important that they meet before Easter Monday, he had written, to discuss how they would proceed at the Cockpit. Now, thanks to Pheebs, she knew that Durrell was somehow involved as well.

Until the letter arrived, she had hoped against hope that the expedition might be cancelled. My Lord Shrewsbury's death and the new warrant for Buckingham's arrest might have affected Cromwell's plans. Apparently not. Buckingham's involvement could only make the business more dangerous than it was already.

Brennan, hunched over his slope and hard at work, looked up. 'Trouble, mistress?'

'Trouble enough,' she said, turning away, not wanting to encourage a conversation.

She went downstairs to the parlour. It took her most of the next hour to calm her husband and make him look presentable. He insisted they keep the parlour door open so they would be able to hear the knock on the street door below.

They waited past three o'clock, and then past the half hour, with Hakesby growing increasingly anxious. 'Perhaps there's been an accident.' He wrung his hands. 'Perhaps Mr Cromwell's enemies have tracked him down.'

'There's nothing we can do, sir,' she said, not once but many times. 'Except wait.'

It was nearly four o'clock when they heard the sound of men's voices below, followed by slow footsteps on the stairs. No one had knocked at the street door–Pheebs must have seen the visitor in the street and admitted him without ceremony.

Hakesby went out on to the landing. 'Oh,' Cat heard him say in a flat voice. 'Oh . . .'

Cat heard the heavy breathing of the man outside and she knew who it was before he opened his mouth.

'Are you ready, Mr Hakesby?' said Roger Durrell in the thick voice that he seemed to dredge up from a muddy pond deep within. 'It wouldn't do to keep them waiting.'

The coach was plain and shabby, hired from a livery stable. It was drawn by a single horse with a dull coat and long scab where it had been whipped too hard, too long. Roger Durrell's bulk filled much of the space within. Hakesby and Cat squeezed together, with the sheath of Durrell's sword resting on the floor between them.

Hakesby clutched his portfolio to his chest. 'Where are you taking us?'

Durrell said, 'You'll find out, sir. No hurry.'

After that, there was no conversation. Cat listened to the breathing of Durrell and her husband, the one low and viscous, the other high and quavering. They mingled with the discordant sounds of London beyond the coach: hooves, wheels grinding on the roadway, cries and shouts of passers-by.

The leather curtains at the side of the coach swayed to and fro. Sometimes, especially at corners, they moved more, giving Cat glimpses of the world outside. They were travelling east, she thought, and perhaps north. As they slowed, the sloping roadway and a glimpse of blackened ruins confirmed it: the driver had brought them to Snow Hill, between Holborn and the City at Newgate.

The coach lurched through a gateway and jolted over cobbles into a yard. Durrell sat unmoving, staring at the Hakesbys with small, half-closed eyes. His jaw moved as if he were chewing.

'Well?' Hakesby leaned forward and pulled aside the curtain. The coach had been brought to a halt within a foot of a chimney stack built of soot-stained bricks. 'I can't get out this side. Where are we? Where's Mr Cromwell?'

'On his way, sir. We're to wait in the coach.'

Hakesby subsided into the seat, hugging his portfolio more tightly. They sat in silence for a few moments. No one came.

By accident or design, Durrell had extended a leg across the side of the coach opposite the chimney. It blocked the Hakesbys' exit from the coach as effectively as a tree trunk.

Cat shifted on the seat, feeling for the knife in her pocket. Durrell's eyes flicked towards her. She wondered if this was a trap. Could Durrell and Veal have turned their coats and betrayed Cromwell and the Hakesbys to the authorities?

A sense of futility swept over her. Even if she distracted Durrell for a moment by stabbing him in the leg, the easiest target he offered, his very bulk would still block their escape. Her husband would be a hindrance, not a help. Then there would be the coachman to deal with. Perhaps others as well.

Somewhere outside, a door closed with a bang. Hakesby sat up. Durrell continued to chew. There were unhurried footsteps. The leather curtain was drawn aside.

Light flooded into the coach. A tall man in a plain black cloak looked down on them. His face was red, bisected by a nose like a blade and framed by golden curls. He wore a sword.

He looked faintly amused by what he saw. He flicked a gloved finger at Durrell, who scrambled inelegantly out of the coach.

'Your servant, Mistress Hakesby,' the man said with a bow. He glanced at Hakesby. 'And yours, sir.'

His voice was mocking, for he clearly did not intend them to think he was anyone's servant, and his condescension was more to entertain himself for some obscure reason than to show respect to the Hakesbys.

'Your Grace,' Hakesby said, stumbling over the words and bobbing his head in an attempt to bow while seated. 'Forgive me, I had no idea.'

Buckingham's eyes were on Cat. 'You must pardon these surroundings, and my subterfuge in bringing you here.'

'Not at all, Your Grace,' said Hakesby. 'It's an —'

'At present my movements are more circumscribed than I should like.'

'Because of my Lord Shrewsbury's death,' Cat said.

'Indeed, madam.' The Duke smiled at her. 'I see there's no concealing anything from you. I like a woman who doesn't beat about the bush; it makes life so much more agreeable for all parties. I stand accused of my lord's death. I regret to say that there's a warrant out for my arrest. The accusation is quite unjust, of course, but my enemies have conspired against me to mislead the King.'

Hakesby cleared his throat. 'Mr Cromwell tells me that you've taken an interest in his affairs.'

Buckingham ignored him. 'I met your father once,' he said to Cat. 'When I came back to England during the Commonwealth. The Lord Protector sent him down to Yorkshire to examine me on my motives. A godly man, Mr Lovett, a true Christian and a friend to this country.'

Cat stared at him. In some quarters, heaping such praise on a regicide could be construed as the next best thing to treason.

The Duke must have sensed he was making little headway with her, for he abruptly switched tack. 'This business with the Cockpit and our late Protector–the son I mean, rather than great Oliver himself. It's a private matter, I know, but I mean to help my friend Mr Cromwell in his undertaking. And he has kindly agreed to lend me his assistance in one of mine.' He smiled at Cat, creating the illusion that he was confiding in her, and only her. 'As you know, our poor kingdom is sorely divided. Sin stalks abroad, and God will not let us go unpunished if we don't change our ways. Mark my words, if our reckless courses go unchecked, we shall have another civil war before the year is out. We must draw together if we are to prevent more bloodshed–all of us: Anglican and Presbyterian, high and low, and even'–here he smiled again–'those who wish for the return of the good old days. And there are far more of those than the government is aware of.'

More hints of treason. She said, with studied ambiguity, 'I'm sure Mr Hakesby and I wish you all the success you deserve.'

'Yes, to be sure,' Hakesby put in, failing to register the ambiguity, and smiling and frowning at the same time. 'You're in the right of it, Your Grace, and all good men must agree with you. As to this matter of the Cockpit —'

The Duke waved him aside. 'Not now, sir, if you please. Durrell will take you to Mr

Cromwell in a moment, and you can arrange all that with him.'

'The good old days are gone,' Cat said. 'And best forgotten.'

'Gone, madam, but not forgotten. Which is the reason I want you to attend a private meeting I have arranged.'

'Why?'

'Mr Cromwell will be there as well. Your very presence will add immeasurable glory to the occasion.'

'That's nonsense, sir,' she said.

If he was shocked at her rudeness, he didn't show it. 'You needn't say anything. It would not be fitting for a lady in such company. It's merely that seeing you there, your father's daughter, would please me— and please many of the other gentlemen there. Your father was Oliver's friend.'

'No,' Cat said.

'Your father would have wished —'

'My father and I were estranged. And now he is dead. His possible wishes have nothing to do with me.'

Hakesby said in a tremulous voice that was meant to be a whisper, 'My dear, I really can't see the harm in it. Indeed, it's a great honour that the Duke should wish you to join him and Mr Cromwell at this meeting. And who knows where it might lead in the way of business for us?'

'I will not.'

'You will.' Hakesby's voice grew shrill. 'You're my wife. I order you.'

The Duke stepped back. There were more footsteps in the yard. The tall figure of Mr Veal appeared. He put his hand to his mouth and whispered in his master's ear.

Buckingham sighed. He stooped and put his head inside the coach. He was so close that Cat felt his breath on her cheek.

'I'm sorry, madam, but I fear I must leave you. The King's sergeant-at-arms and his men are at Holborn Bridge, and they are coming this way.' He withdrew his head, swept off his hat and bowed. 'We shall meet again soon.' He kissed his fingertips to Cat. 'Until then.'

'Dearest Catty!' Elizabeth said, scarcely half an hour later. 'You don't know what it is to see a friendly face.'

When the Duke had gone, Durrell had brought the Hakesbys to a tavern on the Oxford Road. Here, in a private room, they had found the Cromwells and Mr Veal waiting for them.

Elizabeth folded Cat into an embrace. 'See, I have brought you a present.'

She held out a package that proved to

contain a pair of grey gloves–plain, but of fine leather, and a good fit too. Cat was ready to be suspicious of anything Elizabeth did or said. On this occasion, though, there was a hint of sincerity, even relief, in her behaviour. Whatever else Elizabeth might be, she wasn't a fool. Perhaps her father's involvement with Buckingham and his servants was not to his daughter's taste.

Richard Cromwell greeted the Hakesbys courteously. He was wearing his thick green glasses again, and his beard had grown noticeably longer and bushier since Cat had last seen him.

On the surface, at least, the meeting could not have run more smoothly. Veal produced a purse containing ten pounds in gold, which he presented to Hakesby for his expenses at the Cockpit, and in particular with Reeves, the mazer scourer. That resolved the immediate financial difficulty.

Cromwell, it seemed, had agreed to attend the Duke's Easter Monday meeting. 'But,' he said to Veal, 'what if His Grace is–ah–well, I understand his liberty may be curtailed at present. Perhaps the meeting will be cancelled.'

'Don't worry about that, sir,' Veal said. 'The Duke has it all in hand.'

'But surely if — ?'

322

'Take my word for it. Now–Mr Hakesby? This affair at the Cockpit.'

Hakesby had already arranged to meet Reeves on Saturday. It was settled that Mr Veal would be present, and that he would also accompany them on Easter Monday. If all went well, at one o'clock on Monday afternoon, they would assemble at the western end of the canal in St James's Park. The Park would be particularly busy on the holiday. They would enter the Cockpit lodging by the private door into the garden. Reeves had made arrangements with a servant to let them in.

'And then what?' Veal asked.

'Reeves has a worker under him who will retrieve the property. It's hidden in a sewer that runs from the lodging under the garden.' Hakesby glanced at Cromwell. 'Can you tell us where to find it exactly?'

'Forgive me, sir, but I prefer to keep that close for the moment.'

'Then how will Reeves know — ?'

'I shall send my daughter to you on Monday,' Cromwell said. 'She will meet you in the Park at the appointed hour, and she will bring you the information.'

'Do you trust this Reeves?' Veal said to Hakesby.

'He prospered under the Protector, sir.

Now he is unhappy.'

Cat said, simultaneously, 'No.'

Veal frowned. 'Why not, mistress?'

'He helps us for money, sir, not for old loyalties. He knows the–the property was hidden under the Commonwealth, but not by whom, or precisely where it is. If he learns that Mr Cromwell is a principal, I wouldn't trust him to keep his mouth shut. He might calculate that there was more money to be made, and more safely, by selling the information than by helping us.'

Cromwell rubbed the table with his finger. Without looking up, he said, 'Mistress Hakesby talks sense.'

There was a gurgling sound as Durrell cleared his throat. 'You want me to talk to this Reeves, master? Make him understand who his friends really are?'

Veal shook his head. 'Better not. If necessary I will speak to him on the day.'

Before the party broke up, Elizabeth drew Cat to the window at the far end of the room and pretended to show her the silk lining of the gloves. 'I don't trust these men,' she whispered.

'I don't think they wish you or Mr Cromwell harm.'

'But they plan to use my father for their own ends. And they leave him no choice in the matter.' There was nothing sly about her now. She looked scared. 'Catherine, Buckingham will only protect him while it suits him. What can we do? Will you help us?'

The Hakesbys were already helping the Cromwells, Cat thought, and much against her own will. She said, as soothingly as she could, 'We must hope that all goes well on Monday. Then they will let your father go back to France, and leave the rest of us alone.'

Elizabeth made an almost inaudible mewing sound. There were tears in the small blue eyes. She began to say something. Cat laid her hand on her arm to stop her.

Durrell was approaching with their cloaks. He lingered in their company, helping Elizabeth put on her cloak, and looming over her like a bear with his prey. When it came to Cat's turn, she snatched the cloak from him.

'I'll manage this myself,' she said.

His eyes flickered. 'As you wish, mistress.'

He turned away, and the sheath of his sword brushed her skirts, forcing her to step back against the wall.

On the afternoon of Easter Saturday, Mr Hakesby met Reeves at Fulton's, a barber's shop in Long Acre. The choice of meeting place showed a low cunning on his part because it excluded Cat. Fulton's was an all-male establishment; there was not even a maid, only a boy to sweep the floor and heat the water, and a manservant to stand at the door.

Before Hakesby left, he quarrelled with her. 'You treat me as a child,' he said to Cat. 'You forget you're my wife. You forget I raised you up from the gutter.'

'Sometimes I wish you'd left me there,' she said.

'Have a care I don't throw you back.'

He stormed off, an old and fragile man. She sent the porter's boy after him so he would have someone to lean on, someone to bring him safely home.

Despite this, as time passed, Cat grew anxious. She considered sending someone to enquire at Fulton's but in the end she called for her cloak and went herself. The barber's shop was busy because of the forthcoming holiday. The porter's boy was outside, hugging himself against the cold of the afternoon.

'Your master's still there?'

'Yes, mistress. He's talking to a man at the back.'

'What's he like?'

'Didn't see his face.' The boy's eyes slid

past her. 'He came along with him.'

Cat turned. Hunched against the wall at the end of the shop was the thin figure who had accompanied Reeves before. Then she had seen him only briefly, and through the distortion of glass. He had been squatting in the rain by the privy in the yard of the alehouse near the Tower.

'He's bleeding,' she said. There was a cut on his forehead, and what looked like a fresh bruise on his cheek.

'Some apprentices threw stones at him. He looks cursed, don't he?'

Cat approached him warily. There were streaks of grey in the dark, matted hair and among the stubble on the chin. The man covered his face with his hands as she approached.

'You work for Reeves,' she said.

She had never seen someone so thin and wraithlike. He seemed barely to have shoulders worth the name. Like a spider, he gave the impression that he consisted mainly of limbs rather than body.

'Ferrus,' she said, his name coming back to her.

His hands, which were narrow and with very long fingers, fell slowly away from his face, with its unsettling resemblance to the head of a fish. The eyes were not only far apart from each other but they seemed to operate independently, which gave Cat the unsettling sensation that two people were looking at her, not one. Trembling, he stared dumbly up at her. A drop of mucus shone like a diamond on the end of his nose.

'There's nothing to fear,' she said. 'Are you all right?'

Ferrus wriggled away. Suddenly, so quickly it took her breath away, he was on his feet and running down the street.

'He don't like it when people talk to him,' the porter's boy said. 'Scared of his own shadow.'

Cat returned to Henrietta Street. She tried to find solace in work. She settled at her slope and continued to ink in the design for the southern elevation of the Royal Society's proposed Solomon House in my Lord Arundel's garden.

The work needed concentration, but her thoughts strayed to tomorrow and the Cockpit. Fear had become a physical pain in her stomach. Perhaps she had been wrong and Marwood had been right: taken all in all, it might have been better to tell Mr Williamson that Richard Cromwell was in London, and reveal what they knew of Buckingham's intrigue. Despite the fact that she was a regicide's daughter, it might be better to throw themselves on the King's mercy than face what might lie ahead to-morrow.

Hakesby was gone for nearly three hours. When at last she heard him slowly climbing the stairs, her anxiety turned to irritation. Swearing at the porter's boy, he stumbled into the parlour and sank into his chair without even removing his cloak. He brought with him only a smell of wine and tobacco smoke. At least he had managed to have himself shaved, and his peruke was newly combed.

'It's all arranged,' he said without looking at her. 'You weren't needed.'

'What's arranged?'

'Reeves has done it all. A footman will let us in. We are to go to the Cockpit at one o'clock in the afternoon.'

'We? Sir, is this wise? Perhaps —'

'Peace, woman. There's news. Though whether it's good news for us I don't know. At Fulton's, everyone's saying that the doctors have opened up my Lord Shrewsbury to see how he died.'

'Because of his wound from the duel?'

'No. They say he died of natural causes. And so the King has given the Duke of Buckingham a royal pardon.'

CHAPTER TEN

Three Ships of Gold
Easter Monday, 23 March 1668
Crow, crow, cockle-de-crow, cock crow,
crow crow.

Ferrus shuts eyes tight. Sees stars. Windy
stirs. Whimpers. Farts. Ferrus wriggles close
as close as can be to Windy. Draws blanket
over his shoulders.

The woman fills his head. Saw her yesterday. And he ran away.

Master comes early. Here, Ferrus, he says
and throws him a roll. White roll. Scraps of
bread that Ferrus gets are almost always
brown, coarse stuff. Hard bits hurt teeth
and gums.

White roll tastes of heaven. Food of
angels. Food of God.

From my Lady Castlemaine's kitchen,
master says. Her very own fingers might
have touched it. Think of it. Ah, Ferrus,
think where them fingers have been. Master

scratches himself between the legs. Oh, just think of it.

The sun comes out like a blessing. Master stands in the doorway to the kitchen. Watches Ferrus eat. Smokes pipe.

Holiday, today, says master. Blows out smoke. Grey feathers, grey sky. But not for us, lad, not for us.

Mr Williamson had made it clear that his clerks should attend the office on Monday, despite its being a holiday. I walked down to Scotland Yard. I was in an ill humour.

Easter Monday at last. It was still early, and there was no sign of the rumoured unrest. But London in a holiday mood was liable to be unpredictable. The usual rules were suspended. The City became drunk on its brief liberty. I had a disagreeable sense that this was the lull before the storm–for all of us: me and Cat, for Buckingham and the Cromwells, and even for the country as a whole.

At Scotland Yard, I went up to the office. The door to Williamson's room was open and he saw me come in. I hadn't seen him since Saturday morning. He beckoned me inside and told me to shut the door. I had come to dislike these private conferences. They usually meant bad news.

'You've heard, I take it?'

'About the examination of Lord Shrewsbury's corpse?'

'Aye. It's the most cursed luck imaginable. My Lord Arlington is furious.'

'Are the physicians sure?'

'Of course they're sure. Do you think we'd let Buckingham and his party draw the wool over our eyes? No, one physician was chosen by Lord Shrewsbury's own kin, and another by me. It was a putrid fever that killed him. Believe me, if they could have found a way to blame Buckingham for my lord's death, they would have done so.'

Williamson ran out of words and stared angrily at me instead.

I stared back. 'And the Duke, sir?'

'He's as free as air.' He rubbed his forehead, dislodging a shower of flaking skin on to the letter he had been reading when I came in. 'He's up to mischief, I know he is. If you hear anything–the slightest whisper–I must know at once.'

Williamson dismissed me and I went about my duties. A little before midday, he decided in a rare moment of self-indulgence that he had had enough of work for one day. He went off to dine, saying he would not be back, and the rest of us should continue in our allotted tasks.

That suited me well enough. I had an appointment with our printer, Mr Newcomb, whose shop was close by my lodgings. I saw him and then dined at an ordinary in the Strand. I propped open Raleigh's *History* in front of me to discourage casual conversation.

Rather than return to Scotland Yard in the afternoon, I decided I might more conveniently work at home. I walked back to Infirmary Close. I gave orders that I should not be disturbed and had my papers brought to the parlour. Work was a distraction, albeit a tedious one that was only partially successful. I checked the proofs for the next *Gazette*, and afterwards sent them by my boy Stephen to Mr Newcomb. I then set to making notes of suitable items for Mr Williamson's next newsletter.

The only sound was the scratching of my pen. While I worked, part of my mind was fruitlessly revolving my difficulties. Gradually, I became aware of a knocking downstairs, and of voices in the kitchen. Then came footsteps, which approached the parlour door, followed by a gentle tapping on the door.

'Come in,' I shouted, not best pleased to be disturbed.

My servant Margaret entered, her face red

from the kitchen fire. 'Your pardon, master, but I thought you should hear this. But if I've done wrong, I'm sure I —'

'Hear what?'

'It's Dorcas, sir.'

'Who?'

'She delivers the *Gazette*. You remember–Mistress Hakesby lodged with her for a week or so last year.'

I remembered her then. I'd even seen the woman once–small and brown, like a dusty sparrow; she had looked seventy but was probably no more than forty.

'Her son's home on leave, master, her son that's a sailor. He told her there's trouble brewing down Poplar way.'

I laid down the pen. 'What sort of trouble?'

'Crowds gathering, and apprentices coming down from the City. And strong ale. There was a lot of talk last night.' She paused. 'About the bawdy houses by the river.'

'They mean to attack them?'

'Yes, sir–and Dorcas's son heard they go to Moorfields next.'

There was nothing more. I sent Margaret away with sixpence for Dorcas in return for her trouble. Suddenly restless, I stood up and walked about the room.

A little violence, according to Mr Williamson, even a little riot, was not necessarily a bad thing. It was like applying leeches, he said–letting blood was an infallible way to bring down a fever and cleanse the toxic humours from the body. The official response was usually to contain such outbreaks rather than crush them, and afterwards to treat the unrest as public disorder, a matter that could be resolved with fines and short terms of imprisonment for one or two ringleaders.

But this story, if it was true, was unusual, and for several reasons. Poplar was not in the City or even in the immediate suburbs–it was a straggling hamlet on the Thames downstream from the Tower, a good five miles away from the Savoy. Why would the trouble start there, and why so early in the day?

Then there was the mention of the bawdy houses. In the old days, before the Great Rebellion, there had been a tradition in the City that on Shrove Tuesday the apprentices would band together and attack the brothels. I remembered my father telling me about this with evident nostalgia; he portrayed such riots as occasions for smiting sin in the persons of these fallen women, but even then I had sensed that his nostalgia drew its force from other sources as well. For young and lusty apprentices, the opportunity to do God's work by abusing the whores and tearing down their houses must have had a particular appeal.

But Shrove Tuesday was at the very start of Lent. Easter Monday was six weeks later, so on the face of it this attack could not be an attempt to revive the tradition.

I glanced out of the window. The day was fine, and I was tired of being cooped up. Perhaps here was an opportunity to give myself a holiday. I suspected that this unrest was a tale that had grown in the telling. Perhaps a handful of disgruntled sailors and drunken apprentices had been making much ado about nothing. But there would be no harm in going down to Poplar and finding out.

If Williamson later questioned me about how I had spent the day, I would justify the excursion by reminding him of the rumours of trouble that we had heard. In the circumstances, I would say, it had seemed prudent to assess the situation myself. After all, I could not refer the matter to him, as he himself was away from Scotland Yard.

I called for my cloak. The tide was on the ebb. It would be good to put the fumes of the city behind me for an hour or two. On my return I might even look in at a theatre.

An excursion, I thought, even a mild adventure, followed by an evening of pleasure. The whole world was on holiday. Why not I?

I went by water to Old Swan stairs in the shadow of London Bridge. The tide was churning so violently under the arches that I refused to let Wanswell take me through. There were the usual holidaymakers pouring over the London Bridge from the Southwark side. People seemed cheerful, looking for amusement rather than riot.

On the downstream side of the bridge, I took another boat past the grey bulk of the Tower, and had myself rowed to Limehouse, where I landed. The sun was out, and it was growing warmer. I went on by foot towards Poplar, with the marshy lands near the river on my right.

I grew content as I walked, breathing the fresh, salty air blowing off the river. Long stretches of rope were drying by the road and, even on a holiday the sailmakers were at work. In this place, everything had to do with the sea and the Thames. Before the Great Rebellion, the East India Company's docks at Blackwall had begun its transformation, which was now proceeding apace.

But, for all that, it was still quite distinct from London and in places quite rural.

I came almost imperceptibly into Poplar itself. It was hardly a town, yet barely a village–a long, single street with lanes running off it, especially to the south, where they sloped down to the river and to the pastures of the Isle of Dogs. The houses were chiefly of wood, many of them single-storey hovels with weather-boarded walls. Scattered among them, however, especially on the north side of the street, were more substantial buildings, including an almshouse and a chapel. Their new red bricks made a brave show in the sunshine.

The taverns and alehouses were packed with sailors, apprentices and artisans up from Blackwall, which lay beyond Poplar. Further along the street, a crowd was moving eastwards, by fits and starts. As I drew nearer, the mood of the day changed. There were fewer families here. Men lingered in knots of three or four, talking among themselves. Some carried staffs and staves.

As I passed one group, I heard the name 'Damaris'. One youth detached himself from the others and walked ahead towards another group of apprentices.

'A poxy bawd,' he said to them. 'That's what she is. Lying doxy. Cheated our boys of their money, didn't she? Then she sold them like slaves.'

He gave me a sharp glance and fell silent. I had heard enough. Most of London knew who Damaris was: Mistress Damaris Page, who had grown steadily richer from the profits of her bawdy houses since before the Civil War. Like her colleague, Madam Cresswell, she had invested her earnings in property. The heart of her empire was east of the Tower and along the river, an area that attracted a shifting, constantly refreshed population of sailors, desperate for the company of women after weeks or months at sea. There were rumours that she not only cheated some of her customers but sold them to the press gang, making a handsome double profit. The navy was always hungry for men, especially those who already knew one end of a rope from another.

The further east I went, the more sullen the crowds became. I stood out in this part of Poplar, and I attracted hostile looks. Dressed as I was, as one of the prosperous middling sort who could afford a peruke and a respectable suit of clothes, I did not belong here on a holiday, let alone a holiday that was assuming the character that this one was.

Men had gathered outside a large house

which stood gable end to the road. They spilled across the street, blocking the traffic. As I watched, reinforcements swelled the crowd, including a party of middle-aged men who came striding up from the direction of the river with an almost military sense of purpose.

Two of these were wheeling a barrow containing a long canvas bundle. Another was carrying a staff that was quite ten feet long. He lowered it, and his friends clustered around him. A moment later, they raised the staff again. Attached to the end was a piece of green cloth, a makeshift flag. The men gave a ragged cheer, which spread like sparks from a fire to the apprentices and sailors outside the house.

Dear God, I thought, here's trouble. These men and their flag were evidence that this riot had gone beyond the usual mischief that apprentices made on a holiday. The green flag was the emblem of the Levellers, those dangerous radicals who had flourished during the Rebellion. They believed such nonsense that the franchise should be extended to everyone (apart from servants and women), and that all men should enjoy liberty as a natural right. The Levellers had gathered substantial support in the New Model Army and in London before Cromwell and his allies had tightened their grip on the country and put an end to their folly.

The doors of the house were closed, and the windows were shuttered. Someone must have warned the people within that trouble was on the way. The building looked solid, but only the chimney stacks were of brick, and the walls were merely weather-boarded.

One of the newcomers approached the apprentices. He gestured towards the house. A youth picked up a stone and threw it at the nearest door. A cheer went up.

As if this had been a signal, the attack began in earnest. Two men unfolded the canvas bundle on the barrow. They handed out crowbars and two heavy mauls. Another man came out of a nearby yard with a pitch-soaked torch sputtering and sparking in either hand.

'Come on, boys,' bellowed a deep voice behind me. 'Reformation and liberty!'

There was a burst of cheering. I swung round, looking for the source of that deep, thick voice. But the people behind me blocked my view. Someone shouldered me aside so violently I almost fell in the gutter.

A red-headed giant of a man lifted one of the mauls and carried it across the road to the house. He swung the maul above his head with an easy grace and brought it down with a crash on the centre of the door. The wood split with a crack like gunfire.

For a second the crowd was silent. Then the cheering began again.

A burly apprentice set to levering off a ground-floor shutter with a crowbar. The giant tugged the head of the maul free from the remains of the door and raised it above his head. I turned aside and retreated as discreetly as I could.

Behind me, the maul smashed into the door for a second time.

'Down with the Red Coats!' shouted the same voice. It had a liquid quality, as though the man was shouting through a mouthful of phlegm. I turned towards the sound. Roger Durrell was standing half-hidden in a shallow porch on the other side of the road, his body obscuring the door behind him.

He pointed at me. Two of the men peeled away from the group near the barrow and moved towards me. I had left my departure too late. In the last few minutes, the immediate neighbourhood had emptied of everyone except the rioters and myself. I was alone and, apart from my stick, unarmed.

I broke into a run. Footsteps pounded behind me. I dared not look over my shoulder for fear of losing ground. The almshouse was ahead of me on the right-hand side, looking reassuringly respectable. I ran towards it–someone would help me there; it was my only hope. My heart and lungs felt as if they would burst.

To my horror, the gates of the almshouse were closed. I had no time to knock and wait. The railings on either side were too formidable a barrier to climb. I ran on, for I had no other choice. An alley opened up on my right, following the blank western wall of the almshouse. I turned into it, my shoes slipping and sliding on the paving.

There might be a side gate. Or someone of sufficient authority to —

The footsteps were still pursuing me. Two or three men, by the sound of it. They were nearer now. The sobbing of their breath mingled with my own.

The alley led to a chapel surrounded by freshly made graves among green turf. There was an orchard beyond.

I saw no way out of the enclosure so I made for the chapel itself. It was a plain modern building with a belfry at one end. The path brought me to a door at the south-west corner. It was ajar. I burst inside, praying there would be a congregation, or anyone who might protect me from my pursuers.

But the chapel was empty. It was a white-washed place with a flattened vault held up by pillars. I tried to shut the door behind me, but I was too late. I ran down the nave. The men behind me entered the chapel. Their footsteps slowed to a walk. I stopped, for there was no longer any purpose in running.

Before I could turn to face them, something hit my back immediately below the shoulders. The blow landed with such force that it flung me forward on to the ground. The impact drove the breath from my body. My hat and peruke fell off.

I rolled on to my side and drew up my legs to protect myself as far as I could. Two men stared down at me: not apprentices: they looked some years older than myself; they were dressed as working men in plain, serviceable clothes.

'Sirs,' I gabbled, 'pray consider what you do, and who I am. Let me stand your friend and —'

One of them kicked my shoulder. I cried out with the pain. The force of the kick pushed me on to my back.

I lay there, feeling the hard stones beneath me. My limbs throbbed with pain, and I panted for breath like an overheated dog. Strangely, I felt almost peaceful. I was powerless to do anything. I stared up at the white ceiling. Directly above me was a splash of vivid colour: a painted boss at the centre of the vault.

The two men stood on either side of me, looking down. The door creaked on its hinges. It slammed shut. A third set of footsteps walked slowly down the nave.

The roof boss bore the arms of the East India Company. Two red roses and, between them, the quartered lions and lilies, the old royal arms of the Tudors. And below, at the bottom of the shield, three golden ships sailed serenely from left to right: bearing cargoes from the East Indies, I thought, my mind desperate for any distraction whatsoever, cargoes that would line the pockets of the Company's investors with gold. I wondered whether they would be the last things I saw in this world.

The footsteps stopped. 'Devil take you.' The words bubbled like hot tar from Roger Durrell's throat. 'It would have to be you, wouldn't it?'

I dragged my eyes away from the three golden ships and looked at him. I couldn't see his face. His belly was in the way. He pulled back his leg. From this angle, it looked as thick as one of those pillars holding up the roof. He kicked me in the side of the head, and the world stopped.

CHAPTER ELEVEN

Jollyboy, Flurry and Dido
Easter Monday, 23 March 1668

No words.

She comes across the Park. Young lady at Fulton's on Saturday. Lady who spoke to him. In very God's own truth she spoke to him. And what did Ferrus do? He ran and ran.

Master gave Ferrus a beating later for doing wrong, though he is not quite sure which wrong.

Here she is again. A wonder greater than my lady's white bread roll. Truly, this is a day of wonders. She's with the old man who met Master at Fulton's. Old man clings to her arm. Her grandsire. Ferrus doesn't know, doesn't care.

Another walks by her other side, towering over her. He wears a long brown coat (colour of old shit left to dry, Ferrus knows shit if nothing else). He has a stern, narrow face, and a long sword swinging by his side in an old sheath.

Good day, Reeves, grandpa says.

Master looks at the shit man. Who's this, sir?

A friend. As he speaks, grandpa trembles like a leaf in the wind. He'll help us.

No need for names among friends, says shit man.

Don't look like he has any friends, nor wants them neither.

No matter.

All that matters is her. No words for her.

Ferrus breathes faster and faster. He can't suck in enough air when she's there. He drowns in her. There's a chill in the air but he's hot and sweaty. Something inside is about to burst from his mouth and explode into a flock of doves. Joy hurts.

No words, but Ferrus can't stop staring. She drags his eyes towards her.

Her face is full of wonders. His eyes want to eat her up. He swallows a great lump in his throat.

Pox take you. Master cuffs Ferrus's ear, so hard that his head almost snaps off his shoulders. Stop mooning. Then–in the slithery voice he uses for his own masters, he says, Ferrus here is like the proverb, sirs. A woman, a dog and walnut tree. The more

348

you beat him the better he be.

Only Master laughs. He cuffs Ferrus again, but more gently this time, and this time Ferrus is ready for the blow, ready to fall without hurting himself.

He looks up at the lady, upwards and slantwise through his lashes. Joy blazes like a bonfire. Oh, there are no words for her. Or for this thing inside him.

Ferrus. the unnaturally thin, fish-faced man, was lying where he had fallen on the wet grass and staring at Cat. His eyes made her feel uncomfortable. There was a long, bloody scab on his forehead, perhaps the result of one of the stones that had hit him outside Fulton's last week. His cap had fallen off, exposing a mass of dark, tangled hair streaked with grey. His twisted length lay still until Reeves kicked him back to life.

That unsettled her in a different way. Pity was a dangerous emotion. Irritation was safer.

'Enough of this foolery,' Mr Veal said in his hard, grinding voice. 'People are looking at us.'

The Park was busier than it usually was in the early afternoon, partly because of the fine weather, and partly because of the holiday.

'Well, Reeves,' Mr Veal said, wrenching them back to the matter in hand. 'How are matters at the Cockpit?'

'The Duke of Albemarle's in the country, sir, and half his servants are with him, and the other half are in town.' He chuckled, and produced another proverb. 'You know what they say, master–when the cat's away, the mice will play.'

Veal stared stonily at Reeves and said nothing in reply. Reeves looked away, the grin fading from his face.

'You can get us inside without difficulty?' Hakesby said.

'Easiest thing in the world. But the servant will need something more in his palm, and maybe one or two of the gardeners.'

'And if we're challenged?' Veal said.

'I said you're cousins up from the country, sir, if you pardon the liberty. It's usual enough to show people the Great Garden and even the state apartments when the Duke's not in residence. But not something you talk about, if you get my meaning.'

'But most visitors don't poke about in the sewers.'

'Aye, sir, but it's all taken care of.' Reeves glanced down at a canvas bundle on the grass. 'That's my tools. I've said we've had reports of a blockage further down the run

350

of the old sewer, so I need to send Ferrus down while I'm there with you.'

Hakesby looked at Ferrus and wrinkled his nose. 'Can you trust the fellow? Seeing him here, I have my doubts.'

Ferrus wilted visibly in the face of the attention. He was taller and younger than Reeves, and with a far longer reach. Reeves was built like a badger, with great strength in his upper body and short, thick arms.

'He won't say a word, master, I told you that.' Reeves prodded Ferrus, who recoiled. 'In truth, you're as dumb as a post, aren't you?'

Cat said, 'Look. They're here.'

Elizabeth Cromwell was walking towards them along the ornamental water. She was arm in arm with Mistress Dalton. An elderly manservant trailed behind them.

When Elizabeth saw Cat, she broke away from Mistress Dalton and ran towards her with hands outstretched. 'Oh God be thanked,' she said. 'I feared you wouldn't come.'

Cat allowed herself to be embraced by Elizabeth's soft, scented arms. I wouldn't be here at all, she thought, but for my husband's blind folly.

'My father's with Buckingham,' Elizabeth whispered. She seized Cat's hands and squeezed them. 'They came for him in a coach yesterday evening and took him away. I'm so afraid that someone will betray him.'

Hakesby bowed so low to Elizabeth that he almost fell forward. 'Your servant, mistress. Did your father give you the directions? We can do nothing without them.'

Elizabeth glanced at him and then back at Cat. 'I'll tell *you*. Privately.'

She drew Cat aside. Mistress Dalton and her servant had stopped about fifty paces away from them and were staring at the ducks on the water.

'You're the only one I trust,' Elizabeth said. 'How can we be sure that those men won't steal what they find?'

'They won't if I have anything to do with it.' Cat glanced at the four men. 'My husband would never cheat you or your father, I can vouch for that. The mazer scourer's man will do as he's told by his master. I don't think there's any malice in him. As for the mazer scourer, he's greedy enough, but he's being well paid already, and Veal will make him cautious. Veal's a clergyman of sorts and he serves God and Buckingham. He may be a fanatic but I doubt he's a thief.'

Elizabeth looked over her shoulder at them. 'I'll tell you, and then I'll leave you to decide how and when you tell them.'

'And afterwards?'

'It will be best if we come to you, I think, or send word to Henrietta Street about where to meet. This place is too public for us to linger. May God speed us all. I'll go back to Mistress Dalton's to wait, and pray. Come closer, Catty. Let me whisper in your ear.'

The Duke of Albemarle's footman allowed them to pass through the garden gate. He showed a studious lack of curiosity in their movements, turning aside to slip the coins Reeves had given him into his purse. If he thought that Reeves had a strange set of cousins from the country, he gave no sign. Nor did he seem surprised that Reeves intended to combine unblocking a sewer with showing visitors the Great Garden of the Cockpit. Once he had bolted the gate, he entered the lodging by a side door. He had not once looked at their faces.

Hakesby peered about him. 'It's much changed. I barely recognize the place.' Bewilderment spread across his face. 'The garden was larger when I was last here. It was laid out quite differently.'

Reeves walked quickly down a gravel path between hedges planted with box. Ferrus trailed behind, close as a shadow. Cat took her husband's arm and drew him after them. Last of all came the slow, deliberate footsteps of Mr Veal.

It was unexpectedly warm, for the garden was sheltered and faced south. The Duke of Albemarle's lodging was a sprawling place dominated by the octagonal bulk of the Cockpit itself to the north. Most of the apartments that faced the garden were newly built, or at least equipped with modern facades to match the new work. The big windows reflected back the sun. It was all too easy to imagine there might be watchers on the other side of the glass.

Reeves reached the range of buildings along the south side of the garden. These were lower pitched than the rest, and partially screened by trees and a high hedge.

'Where's he going?' Hakesby asked in a voice that was almost a wail.

'Hush,' Cat said, pointing to the right-hand end of the range. 'I think the old kitchen garden must have been over there. Near that door.'

Reeves glanced furtively over his shoulder and raised the latch of the door. The others followed him down a short flight of steps into a long, poorly lit chamber. Apart from two small and heavily barred openings near the ceiling, the only light came from the doorway. Hakesby stumbled over a roll of canvas on the floor. He would have fallen if Cat had not caught his arm and steadied him.

Veal was the last to enter. The ceiling was so low that he could not stand to his full height.

'Leave the door ajar, sir,' Reeves said. 'We need the light to see.'

'What's all this rubbish?' Veal said.

A bust of a man wearing a laurel wreath glimmered in the gloom, next to a column made of wood that had at some point in the past been painted to resemble stone. A pair of faded cherubs floated in the centre of a sky-blue screen pockmarked with holes; it looked as if someone had stabbed it frequently but unsystematically with a sword.

Reeves glanced over his shoulder. 'It came from the old theatre, sir.'

'What theatre?'

'They used the Cockpit for plays. Back in the old king's time.'

'Works of the devil,' Veal said. 'Where's this sewer?'

'Over here.' Reeves tugged at the screen. 'Ferrus? Take the other end. Not like that. Push, you poxy dolt.'

Between them they manoeuvred the

screen to one side, exposing a dusty wooden hatch set in the floor. In its centre was an iron ring. Without waiting for orders, Ferrus unstrapped the bundle he had carried down with him, took out a crowbar and pushed it through the ring. He levered up the hatch, grunting with effort, and slid it to one side across the floor. A waft of foul air drifted upwards.

'Smells better than I expected.' Reeves sniffed, as if to prove the point. 'Almost sweet.' He glanced at Hakesby. 'I told you, sir–the new mazer takes most of it from here. Just as well for us, eh?'

Hakesby squeezed Cat's arm. 'Tell him then, tell Reeves where to find what we're here for.' His voice sharpened. 'And hurry.'

'I won't go down myself, sir, if you don't mind. Not if it ain't necessary, and me in my holiday clothes and all.' Reeves nudged his assistant. 'Ferrus can follow instructions, can't you?' He nudged him again. 'And you can go places I can't, eh?'

Ferrus shrank away.

'He's not as stupid as he looks,' Reeves said. 'He understands a good deal, especially about sewers and what's in them, as long as you speak clearly and don't take any nonsense.'

Cat removed Hakesby's fingers from her

arm. She moved closer to Ferrus, closer to the smell of him, and the competing smell that rose from the dark square among the flagstones. 'It's all right,' she said, as if soothing a dog or a child.

For the first time he looked directly at her, with his left eye at least, for the other stared somewhere over her shoulder.

'Down in the mazer, you must go that way.' She pointed south, away from the Cockpit and the main apartments of the lodging attached to it. 'For about twenty paces. As you go, look at the brick courses on the left-hand side at the height of about two feet.' Again she used her hand, this time her left, to show her meaning, measuring the height against her body. 'Look for a brick with a mark like this.' She crouched and drew with her forefinger in the dust on the hatch: xXx. 'Three crosses, and mark this: the one in the middle is much bigger than the others. They're not scratched, either–they are cut into the brick with a chisel. You understand?'

Ferrus nodded. Meanwhile Reeves crouched to unroll the bundle. There was a scrape of flint on steel. He cupped his hands and blew on the tinder. The spark caught almost at once, and a wavering flame glowed behind his fingers.

'When you find the brick,' Cat went on, 'Count three bricks further on'–she held up three fingers–'and then two up from there'– she held up two more fingers–'and scrape out the mortar from around that brick and the one above. It should come out easily. Take out the bricks. And bring us what you find in the hole behind them.'

She repeated the instructions slowly. She watched the muscles twitching in his cheeks. It was as if he were chewing the meaning of what she was saying, as a preliminary to digesting it.

'Do you understand?' she said.

He smiled at her, his face splitting in two, and nodded.

Reeves lit a candle from the flame, nursed it for a moment and set it within a small iron-framed lantern. He handed it to Ferrus, along with an iron spike. 'Dig out the mortar with that. Off you go.' He put his face very near the other man's. 'Don't fail us, will you? You know what that means.' He gave him a push. 'Go.'

Ferrus slipped away and slithered into the shaft leading to the sewer. Cat stepped closer and watched. He was letting himself down slowly, feeling for the footholds cut into the brick, and holding on to a vertical iron rail fixed into the wall of the shaft. The floor of the sewer was six or seven feet below the level of the flagstones above. The light from the lantern glinted on moisture. Ferrus glanced up at her. For an instant she thought he was still smiling, but that seemed so improbable that she dismissed it as a trick of the light.

Crouching, he moved slowly out of sight. She straightened up. Below them, Ferrus's dragging footsteps grew fainter.

No one spoke. Reeves glanced towards the door. Frowning, Hakesby picked at something invisible on his sleeve. Veal stood apart from them, his face expressionless. Cat wondered why he—or his master Buckingham—had thought it necessary for him to be here at all. It was Richard Cromwell that mattered to Buckingham, not whatever valuables that old Mistress Cromwell might have concealed before they ejected her from the Cockpit nearly nine years ago.

Veal cocked his head. 'Someone's coming.'

Even as he spoke, Cat heard the crunch of running footsteps on the gravel. Veal's hand fell to the hilt of his sword and he drew back behind the screen. Hakesby began to tremble violently. Reeves swore under his breath.

The footman appeared in the doorway. 'Get out. Now.'

'What?' Reeves took a step towards him. 'Why?'

'Castlemaine's coming to walk in the Duke's garden. She doesn't like to be overlooked, not when she has a mind to be private. You must go. Quick.'

Veal emerged from behind the screen. 'Very well.'

He took Hakesby by the arm and urged him towards the door. Reeves followed. The footman was already outside.

'But Ferrus?' Cat said.

'Leave him be,' Reeves said as he left. 'He probably won't show himself, and if he does, he won't say a thing.'

'Run,' the footman called. 'I can hear my lady at the gate.'

Cat turned and crouched over the hatchway. 'Ferrus? Can you hear me? You're to stay down there for a while, and keep very quiet, until Mr Reeves comes back and calls you.'

She heard faint, moist scuffling somewhere down in the darkness. She stood up and walked quickly towards the cellar door, which was still open. She stopped abruptly on the step below the threshold. A woman was talking angrily outside.

The doorway of the cellar could be seen from much of the garden. Cat's escape was cut off. She assumed the others had had time to escape into the Park, but if she went outside now, she would probably be seen. She dared not run the risk. Besides, the gate to the Park might have been bolted again.

Even closing the cellar door was out of the question, because Lady Castlemaine might hear the sound of the latch or see the door moving. Cat retreated into the cellar. She had no other choice. She skirted the open hatchway and slipped behind the screen.

If she peered through one of the holes in the screen, she had a view of the doorway. Her pulse was beating rapidly but she told herself there was no need to panic if she kept quiet. After all, there was no reason why Lady Castlemaine or her companions would come in here. Even if someone came to the doorway and looked in, Cat was hidden from sight.

The woman's voice was becoming louder and, by the sound of it, angrier. 'How can you treat me so?'

A man answered, his voice low and soothing. Cat could not make out his words but the couple could not be far from the door.

'It's abominable!' the woman screeched. 'Such a small thing to ask.'

The voices continued, lower in volume,

first hers then his. Cat's mouth was dry. They must move away in a moment, she thought, for this end of the garden was in shadow; they would grow chilly if they lingered.

Suddenly there was a new sound, or rather a multitude of them: something came running into the cellar; claws scrabbled on stone and brick; then barking, high and excited, and snuffling; and the creak of the hinges, the clatter of the door against the wall and a man's voice shouting, 'Devil take you—come here, you little rascals.'

She saw the man then, through the hole in the screen, a tall, ugly gentleman with a thin moustache and a black peruke. He was dressed in a long shabby coat.

If the woman is my Lady Castlemaine, then this man — ?

Cat saw one of the dogs, too, a fluffy spaniel wreathing around his master's legs, and still barking frantically. As she watched, it ran down the steps into the cellar, where the other dogs were scurrying about.

'Pray be quiet, Barbara, you've excited these poor dogs beyond all reason with your chatter. Now I'm obliged to hunt for them down here.'

Cat wriggled across the floor and dangled her legs into the shaft of the sewer. She found the handrail and swung herself on to her belly, feeling for a foothold. With luck, the noise of the dogs would cover the sounds she was making.

'Here, damn you,' the man shouted, though he sounded more amused than angry. 'Jollyboy! Dido! Flurry! By God, it stinks like a cesspool in here.'

The hatch was too heavy for her to move back in place, over her head, even if she could have done it without making a noise. She would have to leave the shaft open.

With a clatter of claws, a spaniel trotted round the end of the screen and saw Cat. It barked, shrill and excited, and poked its nose into her face. Its collar was made of velvet, decorated by what looked like semi-precious stones.

'Go away,' she hissed.

'They've found a rat or something. We'll never get them out at this rate. Call a servant.'

The spaniel sniffed at her and licked her cheek with enthusiasm. Cat climbed lower. Her head was still above the floor of the cellar. The dog whined softly and rested its front paws on her shoulders so it could continue to nuzzle her face. She heard footsteps on the far side of the screen and the yapping of the other dogs, who appeared to have found something else to interest them.

'Here, Jollyboy!' roared the man. His voice switched abruptly and became caressing. 'Good dog, good dog.' It hardened again. 'Now you, sir—come, Flurry, come—come to your master.'

'At last, sir, a servant,' the woman called, sounding distinctly pettish.

'Damn it, I might have known it would be Dido.' The man raised his voice. 'Dido, you naughty little minx. Come here at once.'

There were running footsteps and another male voice, the footman's: 'Your Majesty. Forgive me, I had —'

'Quick, man—there's a dog somewhere in this rubbish. She could have hurt herself.'

Cat swore under her breath and climbed down to the floor of the sewer. Dido came too, tumbling the length of Cat's body, her paws scrabbling for purchase. Cat's shoes sank into something moist and yielding, and liquid lapped at her ankles. The dog yelped with surprise as it landed.

The stench was suddenly much worse. Cat covered her nose with her cloak. She felt the walls of the sewer with her free hand. They were about two feet apart, rising to a barrel vault, also of brick, about four feet high. The bricks felt old and damp.

She crouched down into the sewer, bringing her head below the level of the vault.

'Hush,' Cat whispered. 'Hush now.'

To her surprise, Dido fell silent. She nuzzled at Cat's hand. Further down the run of the sewer was a faint glow of light, which must come from Ferrus's lantern. Voices filtered down from the cellar above, but she could no longer distinguish the words. In a moment, someone would find the opening of the shaft.

Cat turned awkwardly in the confined space and, crouching, moved as fast as she could towards the light in the distance. The further away from the shaft she was, the less likely she would be seen. The surface beneath her feet was firm, and fortunately the sewage seemed not to be more than an inch or two deep.

The light ahead vanished. 'Ferrus,' she whispered, not daring to raise her voice. 'Ferrus.'

Something brushed her ankles. She prayed it was Dido. There must be legions of rats down here, she thought, but perhaps the dog would scare them away. Thank God for small mercies. The trouble was, they were looking for Dido, and Dido could lead them to Cat: so Dido was a curse as well as a mercy.

'God's fish, man, there's a sewer here.' The King's voice was muffled but still audible. 'Some booby's left the hatch off.' The voice was suddenly louder. 'Dido! Come here, you wretch! Come here at once.'

It was unfortunate that the dog caught sight of something, probably a rat, and shot off into the gloom ahead of them, barking frantically. Cat stayed still, in case her movements betrayed her.

'Damnation, she's down there. I can hear her. You there. Fetch a mazer scourer.' There was a pause. 'A holiday? There must be somebody here who knows the sewers. Find them.'

The King was still talking, but Cat could no longer make out the words. After a moment or two, she couldn't hear him at all. The dog had fallen silent. She must be somewhere ahead.

Cat edged forward again. 'Ferrus?' she said, more loudly than before. 'Ferrus? Are you there?'

The light glimmered again. It was nearer than she had expected. Dido whined. It sounded as if the dog was close to the light, which must mean close to Ferrus.

Suddenly a glistening eye appeared in the darkness. For an instant, Cat's stomach lurched with fear. Then: 'Ferrus,' she said.

'Thank God it's you.'

The eye vanished as Ferrus lowered the lantern. She hobbled closer until they were within touching distance of each other. Ferrus was crouching in an alcove in the right-hand wall, with his knees at the level of his chin. He was framed in the bricks, like a sinister saint in a papist chapel. Dido had squeezed herself between him and the brickwork; she pressed herself against his side.

'We have to get out,' Cat whispered. 'They'll send people down to look for the dog.'

The lantern dipped, and its glow revealed the dim outlines of a rat lying between Dido's paws. Ferrus raised the lantern up to the level of his shoulder, so its faint radiance shone on what was behind him. It was more than an alcove. Another sewer ran upwards, on a slight slope, from the one in which Cat stood. It was of a similar pattern, but it looked narrower and lower.

The lantern swayed. Ferrus wriggled, turning 180 degrees. Dido gave a protesting yelp. Ferrus began to crawl up the branch sewer, placing the lantern in front of him and moving it further ahead every foot or so. The dog followed. Cat glanced up and down the main sewer. There was no sign of light in either direction. Not yet, apart from the faint radiance that marked where the shaft came down from the cellar.

To go forward meant, if she was lucky, crawling for hundreds of yards underground and, if the run of the main sewer were clear enough, and if the rats or bad air didn't kill her first, she would find herself staring through one of the gratings that belched out Whitehall's sewage on to the foreshore of the Thames. But to go back the way she had come meant certain capture.

She closed her eyes and tried to visualize Hakesby's survey of the Cockpit and its sewers. After a hundred and fifty years of rebuilding and extensions, the palace of Whitehall was a warren below the ground as well as a warren above it. She could not remember seeing this side passage marked on the old plan. Could it have been dug after the survey had been made? She ran her fingers over the bricks. These weren't the crumbling Tudor bricks of the main sewer. These were larger and smoother, and the mortar between them was hard. This was new work.

She touched the floor of the sewer. It was dry.

It was this that decided her. Anything with a dry floor was better than being ankle-deep in shit and piss in the main sewer. Cat wriggled into the side passage and followed Ferrus and Dido.

She heard them scrabbling ahead of her, but could not see them. Dido whined, and then fell silent. Apart from the noises that the three of them were making, it was very quiet, and increasingly warm. The sewer ran straight. She calculated that they were probably moving west, more or less, which meant away from the river and towards the Park.

As she crawled, she realized that the air was growing steadily less foetid. It was cooler, too, and once she felt it moving against her skin. There must be at least one ventilation shaft.

But darkness still blanketed everything. If the candle in the lantern was still alight, its flame must be completely shielded by Ferrus's body.

The scrabbling ahead stopped. There were quiet, irregular noises instead. A scratching. A scraping, followed by iron clanging on stone, the sound sudden and shocking, painfully loud in the confined and silent space of the sewer. More shocking still was the narrow column of white light that poured into the sewer twenty yards ahead. Ferrus was crouching in the light, transfigured by its radiance into a bright, unearthly being.

Dido barked, high and excited. Cat crawled towards the light.

Ferrus was looking at her. A few feet away from him, she stopped. She saw him smile—a flicker of the lips; a glimpse of brown, rotten teeth.

'Where are we?' she said. 'Can we get out this way?'

The smile vanished. He tilted his head, so the daylight shone directly on his upturned face. Dido licked his left hand, which was dangling by his side. He beckoned to her with his right hand, urging her closer.

He opened his mouth as widely as he could. He pointed into the pink cavern within. She looked inside. He had no tongue.

'And who the devil is this?'

Reeves, still on his knees, looked up at the King, who was standing in a doorway that lacked a door. 'No one, Majesty. Just poor Ferrus.' He tapped his own head. 'He's dumb, sir, and a simpleton. I gave him a job as a labourer out of pure charity.'

Ferrus was kneeling next to his master, his head and shoulders drooping as if his slender body was unable to bear their weight any longer.

'I'm like a father to him,' Reeves said.

Dido barked, reminding her master of her presence. The King stooped and caressed her ears.

'You stink, my love,' he said, and scratched the top of her head. He glanced over his shoulder at the Duke of Albemarle's servant, the man Reeves had bribed to let them into the garden. 'You. Take Dido away. Give her a bath in the fountain. The other two are tied up outside. Keep her away from them. Mind you be gentle. Bring her back to me at once.'

The footman, pale and sweating, stepped warily around the King and took hold of the spaniel's jewelled collar. Dido barked at him.

'Hush now, dearest,' said the King. 'We'll soon have you smelling sweet again.'

The servant dragged the spaniel away. Somewhere out of sight, Jollyboy and Flurry burst into a volley of barking.

A few minutes earlier, the service shaft from the new sewer had brought Cat and Ferrus into a building site. They were in a room intended as a scullery or a kitchen, if the drain in the corner was any guide. It belonged to a half-built range of apartments between the Great Garden and the Park,

yet another of the seemingly endless alterations required by the Duke of Albemarle.

There was nothing above them apart from
a blue and cloudless sky. The brick walls
had reached about eight feet in height. The
tops of scaffolding poles rose above the
bricks. Cat had pressed herself against the
back wall of a recess; a future fireplace,
perhaps, or the site of an oven.

There was no sign of Lady Castlemaine,
or of Hakesby and Veal. Everything had
happened so quickly that Cat was still trying to untangle it. When they had come out
of the sewer, Cat had sent Ferrus to look
for Reeves or the footman who had admitted them, in the hope they would let her
out into the Park without anyone's being
the wiser. In the meantime, she held on to
Dido by her collar and tried to stop her
barking.

Ferrus had stumbled out of the scullery,
through the unpaved yard beyond and into
the Great Garden. He had found Reeves
and the footman, but unfortunately the
King had been with them; he had been on
the verge of sending them, both in their
holiday finery, down the sewer to search for
Dido. Ferrus had brought all three of them
back with him. If Cat hadn't had the presence of mind to release Dido before they

entered the scullery, she would have been discovered.

The King was now talking to Reeves. 'Are you telling me that you'd lifted the hatch to the old sewer to check for a blockage?'

'Yes, Majesty. There was a report of one earlier. So I sent Ferrus down to have a look, and I went off to change into my working clothes and get some tools. The poor dog must have rushed in and fallen down the shaft somehow. Luckily Ferrus found him down there, and managed to get him out by the sewer they laid for this building here. We'll have to check for the blockage. That's probably where the poor dog got stuck.'

It was a good performance, in its way. Cat would not have believed that Reeves could speak so humbly and with such an oily air of sincerity. If only they could keep the King in the doorway: if he came into the scullery, he could hardly help seeing her. Perhaps that was the reason Reeves and Ferrus were still on their knees: they formed a human wall, protecting themselves by protecting her from discovery.

There was a stir behind them, and Dido shot between her master's legs into the scullery. She shook herself vigorously, throwing drops of water over the King, Ferrus and Reeves.

'Your pardon, Your Majesty,' the footman said, sounding out of breath, 'she wriggled out of my arms, I couldn't hold her, I —'

'Peace, fellow,' the King said. 'Be off with you. Dido, come here.' His voice changed, becoming softer, the sort of voice a man uses to woo a woman. 'What shall I give your rescuers as a token of my gratitude?' The voice sharpened abruptly. 'You there. What's your name?'

'Reeves, Majesty.'

'Go to the Back Stairs and ask for Mr Chiffinch. He'll give you something for your trouble, and you can share it with your labourer.'

Cat heard the King's footsteps walking away. Reeves and Ferrus stayed where they were, silent and on their knees.

'Come, Flurry!' called the King. 'Come, Jollyboy! Here's Dido again.'

In St James's Park, everything was the same and everything had changed.

The crowds were still there: the strollers, gentlemen arm-in-arm, swaying after a good dinner; the ladies parading their charms with varying degrees of discretion; the ducks on the canal pursuing their own mysterious lives; and the people, ebbing and flowing in choppy, brightly coloured currents of movement.

Behind Cat, the private gate to Cockpit's Great Garden closed with a clatter. She heard the bolts being driven home.

'Tell Mr Hakesby,' Reeves had said to her as she left the garden, 'that enough's enough. If it had gone much worse today, I'd have had a rope around my neck.'

Cat walked away, skirting the end of the canal and making for the gate beyond Wallingford House, which would bring her to Charing Cross. People stared at her. She was respectably dressed, but the sewers had left her damp, stained and evil-smelling.

The wet material of her skirt and shift slapped against her calves at every step. The hem of her skirt, the bottom of her cloak, her shoes and stockings were still soaked. It seemed to her that the filth of the sewers had saturated the very pores of her skin. She wanted to be at home. Above all, she wanted desperately to be clean again.

She would have nothing more to do with this foolish and dangerous business. It was more than likely that Reeves would go in search of whatever old Mistress Cromwell had hidden down there. What did it matter if he did? The Cromwells could fend for themselves in future.

'Fell in your pisspot, did you?'

She glanced to her left. Two page boys were pointing at her, their faces twisted with derision.

'Nah,' said the other. 'Couldn't find the pot in time, more like.'

'It's Mistress Shit! Mistress Shit!'

Cat hurried on, but they kept pace, enjoying the sport of jeering at her, but careful not to come within range of her arm. After a moment, though, they sheered away, their faces alarmed. They separated as they went and darted for cover into the crowds.

There were running footsteps. Ferrus appeared beside her. She stopped in surprise. He was carrying a stick, which he shook in the direction of the fleeing boys.

'What are you doing?' she said.

He thrust his hand into the front of his filthy smock and drew out a blackened package about nine inches long. He held it out to her.

She stared at it.

With his mouth closed, Ferrus gave a high wordless cry, like the mewing of a cat or a bird or a small child. He thrust the package at her again.

In a rush, Cat understood. She took it from him and weighed it in her hands. It was filthy and heavy. She looked from it to his face.

'Thank you.' She felt in her pocket. 'Here. This is for you.'

She held out a penny to him. She wished she had a crown piece to give him. Ferrus did not take the coin. He smiled again. He looks happy, Cat thought, if a fish can look happy, and–this next thought ambushed her–made almost beautiful by joy.

'Take it,' she said. 'It's for you.'

The expression vanished, as if wiped by a sponge. He snatched the penny from her fingers. Turning, he stumbled away, lurching at once into a clumsy, hobbling run and waving his stick from side to side. People scattered before him as though he were mad.

Perhaps he was. Perhaps they all were.

Chapter Twelve

As Sure as the Coat on Your Back
Easter Monday, 23 March 1668

Master don't get no reward. Man says he don't know who Master is. Tells Master go away and not come back if he knows what's good for him.

Ferrus hears Master telling the servant about it, the one who let them in the garden. Him and Master drink and smoke and curse. Ferrus lies quiet as any mouse next to Windy in his kennel.

Anyway Master didn't save little dog. Lady did. Ferrus did.

By God, says Master, I'll drown his poxy carcase in a cesspit.

He says more, much more, but Ferrus wraps himself in memories warm as a blanket and shuts him out.

Ferrus has reward on this day of wonders and joy.

Inside his head she smiles at him. She says

thank you. She gives him his reward. She gives him his penny.

Again and again and again.

After the attack, I don't know how long I lay in a faint. Not long, I think, half an hour at most, judging by the glimpses of the sun.

Consciousness had returned gradually, by fits and starts. I was aware first of a pain in my shoulder. Then, I thought someone was jolting and shaking me. I moaned that he should stop. A little later, I discovered that I had a severe headache. I was also thirsty. The gag in my mouth had something to do with that.

The sounds of many hooves and the grating of many wheels filled my head. I was in a moving vehicle. I opened my eyes. Above me was a sheet of canvas. The sun sent splinters of light through the patched and coarsely woven fabric.

I was lying upon planks of crudely planed wood that smelled unpleasantly of fish. My wrists and ankles were tied with rope drawn so tight it chafed the skin. After a few minutes I worked out that my arms and legs were also attached to something, perhaps the side of the cart, which limited my range of movement.

Two men were talking nearby in the

leisurely, laconic way of old acquaintances. I couldn't make out what they were saying, but they sounded calm. I closed my eyes.

The pain in my head fused with the pain in my shoulder and the pains in my limbs. The nausea receded. I tried to empty my mind of everything, especially the pain and the fear. The sounds around me eventually twisted themselves together and made a harsh music, a dark lullaby that sent me drifting back to unconsciousness.

The attic was a long, thin chamber with a sloping ceiling. Something was tapping erratically above my head. The sound was constantly in motion, zigzagging across the slope of the roof. There must be a bird up there, I realized, and what I was hearing was its feet as it scurried about the tiles.

My headache had receded. I was no longer gagged, which presumably meant that no one who mattered was in earshot. I was still tied up, however, and I was still thirsty. My shoulder was so sore I could hardly move it. I needed to piss.

There was a small window in the wall at the far end of the room. The light had a muted quality, as if the afternoon were already shading into evening. There was a film of dust, grey and gritty, on the floorboards. Apart from myself, the room was empty.

It was very quiet. I had been dumped in a corner of the room. I had fallen to one side, dragged down by my own inert weight. My hat, my wig and my shoes were gone. I had a dreamlike memory of being carried up many flights of stairs, my head and my legs occasionally colliding with the walls on either side.

A bolt slid back. I struggled into an upright position. The door opened. A young woman entered. She was plainly dressed– she looked like a servant in a moderately respectable family. But her feet were bare. And there was something teasingly familiar about her face.

'Hush,' she whispered. 'Old Cresswell's got long ears. I brought you something to drink.'

I recognized her then: Chloris, Madam Cresswell's whore, the one who had helped me to escape from her window when Durrell had found me in Dog and Bitch Yard. She hitched up her skirts and knelt beside me. She held a wooden mug to my lips. It was half full of watery milk. It tasted sour but I was so thirsty I would have drunk anything.

'Where am I?' I said at last in a voice that

sounded strained and rusty.

'Where do you think? Dog and Bitch Yard.'

'Why did they bring me here?'

'How do I know? It was Mr Durrell's orders, which means it's for the Duke, and that means old Cresswell's happy to oblige.'

I was puzzled by her attire. 'Why are you dressed like that?'

'We ain't open for business. Haven't you heard? The apprentices are attacking the bawdy houses. They started in Poplar and now they're in Moorfields. Ma Cresswell must have known something was in the wind.'

'I need a pot.'

'What?'

'To piss in.'

She grinned. 'You're easily satisfied.'

'It's no joke.'

Chloris left the room, leaving the door open. In a moment she returned with a chamber pot in her hand.

'Would you untie my hands?' I said.

'Ah–I see your game.' She looked mockingly at me. 'Trying to fool an innocent girl into letting you escape.'

'Truly,' I said, growing desperate. 'I give you my word that I will let you tie me up again. I can hardly contrive it if my hands aren't free.'

'You don't have to worry, sir. I'll do it for you.'

'I cannot–you must see —'

She snorted with laughter. 'You can trust me not to be affrighted. In this house, we've seen everything a man has to offer. I won't be rough, I promise. Gentle as a nurse with a suckling.'

'Very well then. But–but pray be quick.'

I closed my eyes. I felt her fingers unlace me and delve into my breeches. I heard the blessed hiss of water rushing into the pot. Afterwards, when she had made me respectable, I opened my eyes.

'Thank you,' I said. 'My purse is in my coat, the left-hand pocket, if —'

Chloris was already patting my sides. 'No it ain't.' She sounded resigned. 'Of course not. Just a poxy book. They wouldn't leave you with your purse, would they?'

'I'm sorry.'

'I know,' she said. 'You wanted to make me a present for helping you. And not just now, with the pot. To get you out of here as well.'

'You read me like a book. If you help me, I give you my word of honour that I will pay you handsomely. In gold, if you wish.'

'I've heard that before.'

'There must be something I can offer you.

Anything.'

Chloris crouched down, bringing her head level with mine. Her dark eyes considered me. There was a sprinkling of freckles across the bridge of her nose.

She opened her mouth to speak but then stopped. I had turned my head to look at her, and for the first time she had a clear view of the left side of my head. In the absence of my wig and hat, there was nothing to conceal the scarring, the discoloured skin and the remains of my ear.

'I was in a fire last year,' I said. 'Have you seen enough?'

She coloured. Frowning slightly, she searched my clothes, patting me and stroking me quite impersonally, as though I were a horse or a cow and she a potential purchaser. Before long her fingers found the concealed pocket inside my coat where I kept such papers that I would prefer not to lose to a pickpocket.

My warrants were there. Mr Chiffinch had arranged to have one signed for me last year for the better discharge of my private duties for the King. There was another one too, signed by my Lord Arlington, that Mr Williamson had given me.

Chloris unfolded Chiffinch's paper and peered at it, lifting it near her eyes.

'J–James Mar . . . wood.'

'Yes. James Marwood'.

Her eyes travelled to the bottom of the paper. 'This is . . . ?'

'The King's signature.'

'You work for the King?'

'Yes,' I said. I added, gambling on the probability that reading did not come easily to her, 'I am here on his business. As I was before. The warrant explains all, and the importance of your helping me.'

'You have influence?'

'In my way. I have the King's ear.'

'Perhaps there is something you can do for me,' she said.

'Anything. Anything in the world.'

She thrust both warrants into her bodice. 'I'll keep these. If I help you escape, you must take me with you. You must take me back to your house and under your protection. You must keep me safe from the Duke and Cresswell, Merton and Durrell. And give me . . .' She took a deep breath. 'Let's say twenty pounds in gold . . . and you'll give me your Bible oath you'll help me leave London and Dog and Bitch Yard for ever.'

'Where do you want to go?' I asked.

'I want to go home.'

Even then, in the depths of my own danger, I realized that Chloris must be desperate indeed to help me, trusting only to my word and to the doubtful power of my warrant.

'Home? Where's that?'

'Near Bristol. A village, not five miles away.' She swallowed. 'There's–there's someone there. Who's waiting for me.'

I saw her eyes were moistening. I said, 'Where is everyone?'

'The bawds are in the kitchen when we're closed. It's warmer. The men are downstairs in case of trouble.'

'The men who brought me?'

'No–they went away. Our three–Merton, the porter and the outdoor man. As for Cresswell, she's in her chamber doing her accounts. She says the Duke will keep us free from harm, the crowds won't trouble us.'

'You don't think — ?'

'What?'

'Nothing.'

She stared at me but let it go. 'Stay there. I'll be back in a moment.' She left the room, and I heard her moving about in a neighbouring attic.

It wasn't nothing. It sounded to me as if someone had given Madam Cresswell forewarning of the riots, and had also advised her that Dog and Bitch Yard would be safe from attack. I remembered those curious papers I had glimpsed on the desk in her drawing room during my last visit here.

Chloris returned with a cloak, a small bundle wrapped in a shawl, and a pair of shoes. She took a knife from her pocket and sawed at the ropes that bound me. I struggled to my feet. I leaned against the wall, groaning as I rubbed and stretched my aching limbs.

'Hush, sir–you'll bring the whole pack of them about our ears. Come on. We ain't got all day.'

The attic window was just large enough for us to squeeze through, first Chloris, then me. My sore shoulder gave me great pain. We slid down the tiles to a lead gutter between two roofs and followed this to the back of the house. It butted against two outbuildings whose roofs were lower than those of the house. We dropped down to these, crawled crabwise across the slope of their roofs. From there, we clambered on to the wall along the side of the yard–no easy matter, since it was topped with a row of rusty spikes. I lowered myself into the alley beside the house and stretched up my arms to help Chloris down.

Afterwards Chloris took my arm to support me. I staggered beside her as fast as I could to the street at the end. There were plenty of people about, and almost at once I earned curious glances. No wonder–my clothes were dishevelled, and I lacked both hat and shoes.

'Where are we going?' she said.

'My house. As you wanted.' My feet were bruised, and it was only a matter of time before they started bleeding. 'It's not far–off the Strand.'

'Are you going to walk there? It'll take us about a week if you go at this rate.'

'We'll find a hackney,' I said. 'Isn't there a stand in Long Acre?'

'What you going to pay the coachman with?' Chloris demanded. 'Promises?'

'I've money at my house.'

'He'll want it in his hand, not in your house.'

'Have you any money?' I said. She gave a quick nod. 'Then pray lend me a shilling or two, and you shall have it back and double within the hour.'

She stared at me. 'Faith,' she said at last. 'I must be moonstruck.'

She turned aside into a doorway. While I stood guard, she felt in her pocket for her money. She gave me a shilling in silver and coppers, dropping them coin by coin in my hand.

'A shilling,' she said. 'Mark it well. No more. No less.'

'Thank you, Chloris.'

'My name's not Chloris.'

I frowned but then I understood. Chloris was a name for a whore, albeit one in an establishment that catered for gentlemen, rather than a whore in a doorway who did what men wanted for pennies. 'What shall I call you then?'

'It doesn't matter.' She sniffed, and for an instant I thought she might start weeping.

'You can trust me.'

'Can I?' She shrugged, and walked on, leaving me to follow. 'You all say that,' she said.

At my house in Infirmary Close, a new trouble arose. Hands on hips, Margaret confronted me in the hall.

'We were worried, master,' she said, and if she had been worried that meant she was angry. 'We thought you'd be back hours ago.'

'I was set upon by footpads,' I said.

She ran her eyes over me, taking in the absence of my hat and wig, my torn clothes and my bare and filthy feet. She also took in the fact that I was leaning on the arm of a young woman.

'And who's this?'

'You may call her Chloris. She helped me back after I was attacked. From the kindness of her heart.'

'Very kind, I'm sure.' It was clear that Margaret was prepared to put the worst construction on my relationship with Chloris. Her name didn't help.

'Faith, mistress,' said Sam, who was in the back of the hall and eyeing Chloris with interest. 'That was very Christian of you.'

Chloris ignored him. Some of the assurance she had shown in the street had dropped away from her.

'She'll stay with us for a day or two,' I said, 'before going back to her family in the country.'

'Staying here?' said Margaret. 'Here? You mean in this house?'

'Yes, here.' I raised my voice, for I was growing angry too. 'Take her down to the kitchen, give her some food. Treat her as you would your own sister–she's done me a service. No doubt she will make herself useful while she's here–help you about the house and so on.'

'Very well, sir. As you wish.' Margaret jerked her head at Chloris. 'You better come with me.'

'One moment. Send Stephen up to my

bedchamber with some hot water. Stay, make it two bowls—I want him to wash my feet. And I want something to eat, as well, and at once. Sam—make sure the doors are barred, and the windows secured, and then come up to my chamber.'

'Trouble, master?'

'Perhaps.'

I began to climb the stairs. Chloris put her hand on my sleeve to stop me. I saw Margaret's eyes widen at the impertinence.

'Hey,' Chloris said. 'Where's my money then?'

Half an hour later, my life had improved. I was clean, for a start, and warm in gown, cap and slippers. I was sitting by the fire in my bedchamber and eating the cold venison pasty that Margaret had sent up. My shoulder was still painful but the headache had lessened.

Sam came up to report that he had secured the house and to ask if he should look out the few weapons we had about the place.

'Yes. Though I hope we won't need them. This is merely a precaution.'

He cocked an eyebrow. 'Against what, sir?'

I decided to take him at least partly into my confidence. 'You remember those men I sent you to look for a couple of months ago?'

'By Arundel House? At the sign of the Silver Crescent.'

'Yes–the tall thin clergyman called Veal, and his servant, one Durrell.'

'Oh aye–they were with that doctor. Except he wasn't a doctor, young Stephen said. The Duke of Buckingham?'

'Yes. Veal and Durrell are in his employ.' I hesitated and added primly, 'I'm afraid that all three of them have taken a dislike to me.'

'And has this something to do with the attacks on the bawdy houses, master?'

'Perhaps.'

His voice changed, became confidential. 'And the girl?'

'You'll treat her with kindness,' I said, my voice suddenly sharp. 'And respect. So will Margaret. Whatever she is, or has been, she acted as my friend today.'

He bobbed his head.

'Send her up now.'

He bobbed his head again but wisely resisted the temptation to say anything.

While I waited, I unlocked my smaller strongbox, for I had two now; a sign of my growing prosperity. One box was for my immediate expenses, and the other contained what I had managed to save, together with a few pieces of plate. Gradually, as I began to accumulate a little money, I had discovered the unexpected problems that came with it. The greatest of these was how to keep it safe. The security of my boxes was a matter of considerable worry to me. They might so easily fall prey to thieves or be destroyed by fire. Some people trusted their valuables to the care of a goldsmith's strong-room, but goldsmiths did not always prove worthy of trust. Others lent out or invested their wealth to make it grow, but debtors could default and investments could fail.

The smaller box contained almost thirty pounds in gold and silver. I counted out twenty pounds. The coins made a shining heap on the table. After a moment's thought, I took out another shilling and placed it apart from the rest.

There was a knock at the door.

'One moment,' I called.

I relocked the box and put it away in the closet. I opened the door of the bedcham-ber. Chloris was on the landing, picking at her teeth with a fingernail. I beckoned her into the room. Her eyes widened when she saw the money. She moved towards it, her hand outstretched.

'One moment. Give me back my warrants.'

She tore her eyes away from the gold and reached into her bosom with an absence of modesty as complete as a child's. She handed me the papers. Her eyes strayed to the table.

'It's yours,' I said. 'Count it.'

She rushed forward, her face bright with excitement. She hunched over the money, her fingers pushing the coins to and fro, heaping them into piles. She looked back at me, tapping the shilling on the table. Her face was flushed.

'It's all there,' she said. 'I didn't think you would. I thought you'd . . .'

Her voice trailed away. I knew what she had thought: that I would turn out to be like the other men who had offered her money for a service and then cheated her of it afterwards.

She took out a kerchief and scooped the coins into it. She tied the ends in a double knot and pushed the little bundle through her skirt and into the pocket beneath. The weight of all that money must have been considerable.

'Tell me,' I said. 'Did you often see the Duke at Madam Cresswell's?'

Chloris nodded. 'He's always there, two or three times a week. Not just for us girls. Sometimes he scribbles away in Ma Cresswell's sitting room. There's a desk by the window, and he's the only one with the keys for it. He meets people there sometimes.

There's a big bedchamber kept for him, too.'

I filed this away in my mind for later. 'Will you do something for me?'

She looked at me and smiled. 'Maybe I'd do just about anything for you, master.'

'I'm going to write two letters. I'd like you to deliver them for me.'

She blinked. 'Where to?'

'One to Whitehall or rather to Scotland Yard. Do you know where that is?'

She nodded.

'And the other to Henrietta Street by Covent Garden.'

She frowned. 'Covent Garden's but a hop and a jump from Dog and Bitch Yard.'

'Henrietta Street is on the other side of Covent Garden. Wear a shawl over your head–tell Margaret to lend you one of hers.'

'She don't like me.'

'You must both make the best of it.'

'And what's this about helping her in the house?'

'You're meant to be a maidservant,' I said. 'Would you rather I told her you were a whore?'

She shrugged. 'That's what she thinks, in any case.'

I ignored this, though I knew she was right. 'Keep your wits about you when you go out. The house is at the sign of the Rose, on the south side. As for Scotland Yard, you can leave the letter with the porter at the main gate. There will be no danger if you're careful. And I promise you won't regret it.'

I was reluctant to send one of my own people with the letters, in case they were seen. Both Sam and Stephen were conspicuous, each for his own reason, and I needed Margaret here. Using Chloris was a risk, but a calculated one.

She shrugged. 'All right.'

'Go down to the kitchen. I'll send for you when I'm ready.'

She was still looking at me. I took a deep breath and turned away. I took off my cap and scratched my scalp, partly because it was itching, and partly to avoid her eyes.

'Do you want me to comb your hair first, sir?'

'What?'

'I reckon you got lice, the way you was scratching. And there will be eggs, as well. As sure as the coat on your back.'

My face grew warm. It was true that my head had been itching lately. Now that I wore a wig in public, I had my head shaved occasionally. But I had not had it done for several months, and my own hair was growing back. Usually I had Stephen comb me for lice but I hadn't for some weeks; the lice were less troublesome in winter.

'Where's your comb?'

'In the drawer of the dressing table. There's a bowl of water over there.' My voice sounded thicker than usual, as though I had a cold.

I heard her footsteps cross the room and the sound of the drawer opening. I stared at my hands on my lap. Her footsteps returned. I did not look up at her face. Her hands, I noticed, were long-fingered and unexpectedly delicate. The nails were clean.

She stood very close to me, her thigh touching my arm. I felt the comb, moving across my scalp, and the touch of her fingers, which seemed to tap and probe the very bone beneath the skin. It was a long time since a woman had touched my head so gently, so intimately. Every now and then, she would deposit the lice and their eggs in the water, and wipe the comb on her sleeve. I was conscious of everything she did. I could not think of anything else.

'You'll be glad I did this, sir.'

Her very voice, it seemed to me, was an invitation. I sensed her willingness, her desire to please. I stared at my hands, willing them not to move from my lap, and willing myself not to look at her.

'That's enough.' I spoke curtly. 'Leave me.'

'Sure, sir?' She had a low voice and it sounded somehow warmer than before, like a caress.

'Leave me,' I repeated, my voice louder than before. 'I must write those letters.'

I went down to the parlour. I wrote the letters at the table, sealed them and sent for Chloris. It was still light when she went out, but she had no fears for her safety, despite the holiday crowds.

'It's not what happens outside that scares me,' she said when I asked if she was sure. 'It's what happens inside.'

'Do you want me to look after your gold for you? It's a great deal to carry around with you.'

'No, sir.' She grinned at me. 'What do you take me for?'

I told her to go to Scotland Yard first, and then to Henrietta Street. I gave her the names of the recipients in case she wasn't able to read them herself.

The Scotland Yard letter was for Mr Williamson. I had no idea where he was this evening. He would probably not receive the letter until the morning. But in case I was prevented from seeing him in person, it seemed wise to let him know what had happened. I had found evidence that the attacks on the bawdy houses were politically inspired, I wrote, that they were designed to undermine the government and the authority of the King. I judged it wiser not to mention that Buckingham was orchestrating the riots. The letter might fall into the wrong hands. I said I had been seized by some of the Poplar rioters and confined in the bawdy house in Dog and Bitch Yard. I had escaped from there and was now at my house.

My letter to Cat was short and, I hoped, would not upset Hakesby if it chanced to fall into his hands. I begged her pardon if I had offended her by accident the other day, and asked her to send word how she and her husband did.

While I waited for Chloris, I tried to distract myself with Raleigh's *History,* perhaps taking in one word in ten. The light faded, and I ordered more candles. Margaret brought them into the room.

'What's that Chloris doing?' she demanded. 'It's getting dark.'

'I don't know. I was expecting her back by now.'

'Maybe she's run off. You can't trust a girl like that.'

'Peace, woman,' I said.

Margaret sniffed. 'Did you mark the quality of her cloak? The silk lining? That's no servant's cloak.'

I kept my eyes fixed on the open book. 'I expect her mistress had no further use for it and gave it to her.'

There was a silence. But Margaret didn't leave.

'That will be all,' I said when the silence had become unbearable.

'Sam's sharpened his sword twice, and now he's started on yours. And all at the kitchen table, and me trying to prepare your supper. He'll drive me to Bedlam one day. I tell you fair, master, I don't like this.'

'Nor do I.' I looked up at her worried face. 'I don't have any choice in the matter. And nor do you.'

She scowled at me. I scowled back.

Half an hour later, to my great relief, Chloris returned. She came through the gate to the yard–which was barred, of course, but she and Sam had arranged a signal for him to let her in. He brought her up from the kitchen, slowly because of his lameness, and quite unnecessarily since she knew the way. I could hear him talking to her on the stairs. He flung open the parlour door.

'Here she is, master,' he announced. 'Safe and sound, just as I said.'

Chloris came into the room, blinking in the candlelight. She was still wearing Margaret's old shawl and her shoulders were hunched; I would not have recognized her if I had passed her in the street.

'All well?' I asked. 'Why were you so long?'

'The streets are crowded, you can't hurry.'

'And the letters?'

'I left the one at Scotland Yard, as you said.'

Chloris took out the letter for Cat and dropped it on the table. The seal was unbroken. I frowned.

'I tried to leave it with the porter at the sign of the Rose.' She unwrapped the shawl. 'But he said she wasn't there, Mistress Hakesby, I mean. He said a man had just that moment called for her, and she'd gone with him, and I could catch her if I ran. He pointed her out, at the end of the street. Couldn't miss them, he said, because he's such a tall fellow. So I went after her.'

I felt a sudden chill.

'I caught up with them in St Martin's Lane,' Chloris said. 'But I didn't give the lady the letter.'

'Why not?'

'Because I seen the man before, sir, that's why. At Dog and Bitch Yard.'

'Was he a . . . a patron?'

'No. And I only saw him once. But a man that tall, that thin, you don't forget.'

I said, suddenly suspicious, 'But surely it was dark when you saw him just now?'

'Not quite, not then. Anyway, it was outside a tavern, and I could see his face quite plain by the light from the window.'

'What was he doing at Dog and Bitch Yard? Was he there recently?'

'Last week. He came up to the drawing room. I was in there, with Ma and one of the other girls, but he wasn't interested in us. He said, where's Durrell, he should be here, and Ma Cresswell said he was not quite at leisure yet.' She shot me a sly glance to make sure I understood her meaning. 'He was with Dorinda, in fact–you remember her?'

I nodded. She was the whore who looked no more than a child, whose arms were covered in bruises, old and new.

'This man, he knew what Ma meant too, and he looked down his nose, all disapproving. Then he started reading some papers . . . . He didn't even glance at me and Amaryllis. There's not many men you find like that at Ma Cresswell's. I didn't hear his name, though.'

'He's a clergyman called Veal,' I said. A thought struck me. 'Which way were they going just now? Up towards St Giles' or down to Charing Cross?'

'Charing Cross.'

I could guess where Veal might be taking Cat. I hoped to God I was wrong.

'I followed them.' Chloris's face was sharp and intelligent. It had a reddish tinge, from the candlelight. She looked like a vixen. Then she confirmed my guess. 'The parson took her into Wallingford House. Why would he want to do that?'

I ignored the question. I said, 'Did she seem willing?'

Chloris's mouth twisted and for a moment she looked much older than she was. 'She wasn't putting up a fight, if that's what you mean.'

CHAPTER THIRTEEN

A Wife's Duty to Her Husband
Easter Monday, 23 March 1668

The evening of the holiday. Night comes. Master gone to drink.

Ferrus lies by Windy in the kennel. Ferrus weary but cannot sleep. Kindness turns with a click in the memory. Like a key.

Maybe it was the lady this afternoon. Who gave him the penny. There are no words for her.

The penny is shiny and new. The head on it is different from the head on Mistress Crummle's. He has put the new penny next to the old penny. Now both pennies are hidden in the kennel between the planks with Windy to keep them safe. If he stretches a hand over the dog's sleeping body, he can touch their cold, curved edges.

It's the mazer, Ferrus thinks, the mazer makes the kindness happen. All those years ago, when Mistress Crummle lived at the

Cockpit, the sewer's roof fell down and blocked the whole run. They had to dig the whole thing up, which made Master curse and swear and kick Ferrus. Mistress Crummle came down to see the sewer open to the air, before they rebuilt the roof and put the earth back on top.

Only Ferrus was there.

Mistress Crummle saw the stone with the mark on it: xXx, cut with a chisel into the brick, said what's that? And Ferrus said (he had the words then) maybe the maker's mark, mistress, from olden days. Look, he said, see the hideyhole behind this brick.

She put her finger to her lips. Our secret, says she, yours and mine. And she smiles at him.

Three bricks along, she says, counting, then two up from there. That's where the secret place is.

Put this in the place, she says, and she gives him the thing to put there. Let it stay there until I send for it. What's your name?

Ferrus, he says.

She puts her finger to her lips. Protect our little secret, Ferrus, she says. Tell no one. Here, take this penny. One day there will be more.

The next day the soldiers come and Mistress Crummle and her people go away for ever and ever.

That is the day everyone gets mad with drink because the King is coming back soon. When Master and his friends want Ferrus to tell them what Mistress Crummle wanted with him. What he was doing for her.

Ferrus won't tell them. No, no, no. Mistress Crummle is kind and gave him a penny. She said protect her secret, and he will protect. Tell no one.

Master grows angrier and drunker, and redder and drunker. And if you don't tell me, he says, by God's blood you'll never tell anyone anything again.

Master calls for his tools and more wine. Give me my pliers and my knife, he says. Five men hold Ferrus down on the ground and laugh and spit at him.

And then Master cuts out Ferrus's tongue.

And Ferrus has no words. Ever again.

The evening of Easter Monday dragged by. Pheebs sent out the boy for a jug of ale to help time pass. When there was a knock, he thought it must be the boy returning. But when he opened the door, he found Mistress Hakesby shivering outside. He stared at her and blinked.

'God's name, mistress. What's happened to you?'

There's a pleasure in seeing a pretty woman looking like a drowned rat, especially one you can't have, not in a million years, because the bitch would spit in your face soon as look at you.

'I slipped and fell in the gutter,' she said, hurrying past him towards the stairs.

'God save us all,' Pheebs said. Christ, he thought, she stinks. 'Anything I can do to help, mistress?'

Like undress you, he thought, though not until I've put you under the pump in the yard to wash off all that shit. Shit all over you.

She glanced back. 'Is anyone upstairs?'

'No. Mr Brennan's not in the way, and your maid went off to see her mother in Bow.'

'What about Mr Hakesby?'

'Not back yet.'

Strange, thought Pheebs, the old fool usually keeps her close, especially when he goes out. Scared she'll find herself a lover, no doubt.

She hesitated, frowning, hand on the newel post. 'He'll be back at any moment, I expect. Tell the boy to bring me some water at once. Cold will do, I can't wait for them

407

to heat it. Two buckets.'

Off she went, climbing the stairs two at a time and giving Pheebs an agreeable view of ankles and calves.

Upstairs, Cat broke open the parlour fire and set a pan of water to warm. Only then did she take out the package that Ferrus had given her. She probed it with her fingers. It was filthy, but then so was she.

The outer covering was made of some sort of oiled skin and encrusted with dirt. There was something soft within, perhaps an inner wrapping, and then, underneath that, what felt like a narrow container eight or nine inches long.

A line of stitching ran the length of it. The ends had been tucked under and sewn even more securely than the rest. Someone had known what she—or just possibly he—was doing with a needle.

Was this really what all the fuss had been about? Or was it instead something irrelevant and probably worthless that the poor man had picked up down there rather than come back empty-handed? His wits were obviously wandering far and wide. But it was obvious that someone had wrapped the package with great care. Best assume it was valuable.

She heard the boy coming up the stairs with the water. She tucked the package behind the fire irons on the hearth. The boy knocked and stared wide-eyed when he saw the state of her.

'Leave the buckets here,' Cat told him. 'And go away.'

She locked herself in the closet by the bedchamber, took off her clothes and scrubbed herself clean. First, she knelt by one of the buckets and plunged her head under the water, scraping her fingers through her hair. When the hair was as clean as she could make it, she dried it quickly and bound it in a towel. Shivering violently, she stood between the buckets and used the brush mercilessly on her skin. One bucket for the brush and the filth; the other for rinsing herself clean. Then the cloths to dry herself. Her skin tingled.

Afterwards, Cat pulled on the old clothes she used about the house. The water on the fire was now warm, and she used it to wash her face and her hands and feet again. The clothes she had worn lay in a foul heap on the floor. She bundled them into the bag for soiled linen, wrinkling her nose as she did so. Thank God someone else would have to deal with them.

All this took time, and darkness was falling. She lit a candle, set more water to warm on the fire and sat down to wait–for the water, and for her husband. She was increasingly worried. She couldn't understand why Reeves and Veal hadn't yet brought him back to Henrietta Street. He was no longer of any possible use to them. He could only be a hindrance.

The time dragged. It was unnatural to be doing nothing but worry, and her eyes were drawn again and again to the carefully wrapped packet on the hearth, half concealed by the fire irons. It wasn't hers to open. Besides, she did not want to touch it.

She would give it to the Cromwells intact. That, God willing, would be the end of it. She didn't want anything more to do with that cursed family.

Tiredness overwhelmed her. She slipped into an uneasy trance-like state, half awake, half asleep. The day's events chased through her mind. So that, she thought, was the King. He had seemed so ordinary. She could not equate her image of the sovereign, with his power of life and death over them, with the shabby, hen-pecked gentleman she had seen at the Cockpit, who had seemed far more interested in his missing spaniel than his harridan of a mistress.

She woke with a start, snatched back to

consciousness by the sound, faint and far below, of someone knocking on the street door. She sat up and straightened her clothes. She waited, praying that it would be Hakesby.

The usual rule was that, if a stranger called, Pheebs would send his boy to enquire if the lodger wished to receive him. That was the point of having a porter. But not in this case. The footsteps mounting the stairs were steady and deliberate. Not a stranger, then, and not Hakesby either, because his footsteps were slow and halting.

She panicked. A visitor might see the package on the hearth. There was no time to think how best to hide it. She seized the shovel, scooped the roll into it, and dropped it into the scuttle. She piled lumps of coal on top of it.

The steps mounted higher. The caller was coming to call on the Hakesbys. Cat flung herself back into her chair. She wished she had not dressed herself in such old clothes. The parlour was untidy, and it probably smelled like a sewer, but there was nothing she could do about that.

Perhaps, she thought with a leap of hope as irrational as it was unexpected, it's Marwood.

There was a single knock on the parlour

door. She had forgotten to bolt it after the boy had left. She rose, but the door opened before she could reach it. The light was poor on this side of the room. She made out the outline of a tall, lean man on the threshold.

'Mistress Hakesby,' said Mr Veal, 'I'm glad to find you safely home. Your husband needs you. I'm afraid he's had a seizure.'

Her hand flew to her throat. 'What? Where?'

'He was taken ill as we were crossing the Park. We must hurry. Where's your cloak?'

'Where is he?'

'Wallingford House.'

Halfway across the room, she stopped. 'Does the Duke of Buckingham know my husband's under his roof?'

'Most unlikely, I should think. Though I'm sure he would have no objection in the world. He has a generous heart. But pray make haste, mistress.'

Suspicions crowded into her mind. But if Hakesby was ill, she couldn't abandon him, wherever he was. She allowed herself to be hurried downstairs. Pheebs was in the hall.

'Mr Hakesby has been taken ill,' she said, glad to tell someone where she was going.

The porter bowed and said he was sorry to hear it. 'God send him good health, mistress.'

412

'He lies at Wallingford House, and this gentleman's taking me there. Tell Mr Brennan when he comes, if I'm not back. I'll send word when I know more.'

'Very sensible,' said Mr Veal as they went down the steps to the street. 'One can't tell how long this will take.' He took her arm and urged her down the road. 'Everywhere's so busy, madam, it will be quicker for us to walk, if you don't object.'

They turned into St Martin's Lane. 'But why didn't you bring him back to Henrietta Street?' she asked.

Veal glanced at her. 'For the same reason as we are walking now: the crowds. It would have taken an age to get a coach through from the Park, even if I could have found one. Besides, Wallingford House was so much nearer. We could go there directly, by the Park gate into the Duke's garden.'

'But what about his servants. Will they — ?'

'They know me well there,' he said. 'You mustn't concern yourself. His Grace is my patron. I assure you that his servants will give Mr Hakesby every attention.'

They walked on in silence. It was much noisier than before. There were many more drunks about, and London seemed to seethe with excitement. Cat was glad of Veal by

413

her side. His tall, forbidding figure, and the sword he wore, protected her from unwanted attentions.

'A seizure?' she said, raising her voice to make herself heard. 'Did he fall?'

'No, but he grew faint. He would have collapsed, I think, if Reeves and I had not supported him.'

'Have you called a doctor?'

'Not yet. I thought he seemed a little better when I left to fetch you.'

'Can he speak?'

'Oh yes–he was asking for you.'

She looked away, fearing her face might betray what she was feeling. She had spent too much time lately being irritated beyond measure by her husband. She had forgotten his kindness to her.

'Have you heard?' Veal said. 'There's rioting in Moorfields. The apprentices are attacking the bawdy houses. Once that sort of thing starts, it spreads like the plague. That's why the streets are so busy.'

They passed St Martin's in the Fields and came down to the Royal Mews and Charing Cross. Wallingford House lay before them in all its old-fashioned grandeur, with the lights and smoking chimneys of Whitehall beyond. Mr Veal took her to the Spring Gardens side of the mansion, where there was a gate in the wall surrounding the grounds. It was closed, but he knocked on the wicket and spoke in an undertone to the man who slid back the shutter.

They were admitted to a spacious service courtyard, lit by lanterns above the doors of the offices around it. Despite the hour, there were lights in most of the windows, and servants were milling about.

'Is the Duke entertaining?' Cat asked.

'The Duke is always entertaining,' Veal said. 'He conceives it to be his duty as a nobleman to be hospitable to those less fortunate than he.'

Something in Veal's air of calm certainty reminded Cat of her father and his friends. Perhaps, like them, he lived in a world of absolutes which he could not understand that others did not share. He led her through a door to a lobby. A footman was sitting on a chair at the foot of the stairs. He sprang to his feet when he saw them.

'Light this lady to the White Parlour,' Veal told him. He turned back to Cat. 'Mr Hakesby is there. I'll join you presently.'

Taken by surprise, Cat could only nod. Veal opened a door and disappeared.

The footman bowed to her and took up a candle. 'Pray follow me, madam.'

He led her up to the first floor, opened a

door and stood back for her to enter. There was a burst of laughter. Cat paused on the threshold, disconcerted by the laughter and blinking in the light of many candles.

She was in a large, square room that glittered in white and gold, with a carpet of deep reds and blues on the floor. Her husband was sitting in an armchair by the fire, a glass at his elbow. Richard Cromwell stood before him, and Elizabeth was on a sofa beside him, facing Mr Hakesby. The remains of a substantial supper were on a table by the window.

The three of them turned their heads to stare at Cat, the smiles fading from their faces. She had the disagreeable sense that her arrival had broken up a pleasant party.

'My dear,' said her husband, beaming foolishly. 'Come and warm yourself by the fire.'

'But sir,' she said, advancing into the room, 'Mr Veal told me you had been taken faint in the Park.'

'Faint with hunger, perhaps,' he said. 'You must have misunderstood him. No, he said Mr Cromwell was here, and had a particular desire to see me, to have news of our expedition. Naturally I was glad to oblige him.'

Cromwell himself came forward and

bowed to her. 'Indeed, I'm sorry it's been such a fruitless business for all of us, but I'm more glad than I can say to see you safe and well. Mr Hakesby told me that you were nearly discovered in the Cockpit, he was forced to leave without you.'

'Oh Catty!' Elizabeth stretched out her hands. 'I must ask. Did you find it?'

Cat ignored her. She went up to her husband and stood over him. 'Mr Veal told me you were ill. Why would he do that?'

For a moment he cowered from her anger. Then: 'My dear, calm yourself. We are not alone.'

'He should not have lied.'

'Hush. That's unbecoming. No doubt Mr Veal wished to be discreet.' His eyes indicated Mr Cromwell. 'He wouldn't wish to risk mentioning certain names in public.'

Cromwell cleared his throat. 'Forgive me, madam. You must blame me. The truth of the matter is, I shouldn't have involved you and Mr Hakesby in my private concerns.'

'But you don't mind helping us, do you, Catty?' Elizabeth rose to her feet. 'Come, let us all kiss and make up.'

'I don't understand,' Cat said, pushing Elizabeth away. 'A few hours ago, the only thing you wanted was whatever Mistress Cromwell hid in the Cockpit. And you distrusted the Duke of Buckingham, and you feared what he might drag you into. But now you're having a supper party in his house. You don't seem at all cast down that you haven't found what you've been looking for.'

'Catherine!' said Hakesby. 'This is unseemly behaviour. Do you put your judgement above mine? Above Mr Cromwell's?'

She ignored him. 'The Duke's put a spell on you all.'

'I understand your confusion,' Cromwell said, his voice as sweet and meretricious as medlar jelly. 'It's most natural.'

She turned, ready to snap at him too.

'Let me explain. I still hope to retrieve my mother's legacy, but it's less urgent now than it was.' He smiled at her, and she saw relief in his face. 'The Duke has very kindly given me a substantial loan, very substantial indeed–he calls it a present but I cannot accept it as such–which relieves my immediate wants. And he's also undertaken to intercede on my behalf with the King.'

'Why?'

'Partly in gratitude for my services to him many years ago, such as they were. And partly for my support today, and in future. Though why he should think I'm of much use to —'

'Oh sir,' Elizabeth interrupted. 'You must not undervalue yourself. The gentlemen you met this afternoon made much of you, did they not, and so did the Duke. Your value to their cause is inestimable. And the very fact they trust Buckingham's good faith is all the more reason for you to do so as well.'

Cat stared from one to other–Elizabeth, Cromwell and her own husband. They were all smiling at her, willing her to share their good cheer. Why, she thought, do people so easily believe what they want to believe? Whatever was happening in this house was dangerously close to treason, and Buckingham was no more trustworthy than the weather.

'There you have it,' Cromwell was saying, smiling at her. 'Pray let me help you to a glass of wine. Are you hungry?'

'No,' she said, and immediately realized that was not true. She glanced at Hakesby, who was draining his glass. 'My husband and I must go home now.'

'There's no hurry,' he said, stretching out his legs towards the fire. 'None in the world.'

That was when a footman flung open the door, and the Duke entered the room. He was splendidly dressed, as if for a ball, and he glittered in the reflected light of the candles.

'What a delightful party!' he said. 'And I'm so pleased that Mistress Hakesby has joined us.'

He bowed low to her as if she were a great lady. She curtsied automatically in return.

'There are some gentlemen waiting to meet you nearby. I'm sure you will recognize some of them from your childhood.' He smiled at her. 'Friends of your father's, anxious to renew their acquaintance with you.'

'No,' Cat said, looking up at the Duke's florid face. 'I have already told you, sir: I will not.'

'That was last Thursday. This is now. Circumstances alter. Now the time has come. And now you have no choice in the matter.'

'My dear . . .' quavered Mr Hakesby behind her. 'Such a small thing to oblige His Grace, so harmless. And he will stand our friend, Mr Veal assures me, in the matter of future commissions. Just . . . just think of where it might lead. There's talk of a mansion in Yorkshire, another Cliveden.'

Cat was still looking at Buckingham. His lips were fleshy and petulant, she decided, taking refuge in cold observation to reduce this great man to manageable size; he had the air of an ill-schooled infant, unused to contradiction and liable to throw tantrums if thwarted.

'No,' she said again, this time more loudly. 'I'm sorry, but I hate my father's memory and I despise what he stood for.'

The room fell silent. Buckingham cocked his head, still staring at her. He bent down, bringing himself within a few inches of her. She forced herself not to recoil.

'In that case, my little one–and much against my will–you leave me no choice,' he murmured in a voice that only she could hear. His eyes were large and slightly blood-shot. His face seemed to pulsate with anger. 'If you don't do as I wish, I shall have to give your husband to Durrell. He will take the old man down the cellars and set to work on him. Until you change your mind.'

'That is barbarous, sir.'

'You may watch, if you wish,' he went on as if she had not spoken. 'But if you can't stomach witnessing the consequences of what you've done, I'll have someone bring you word of how he does. Meanwhile, Durrell will continue in his work of persuasion until you find it possible to oblige me.'

With two footmen lighting their way, a middle-aged maid conducted Cat and Elizabeth to a bedchamber on the second floor.

The footmen were guards as well. They took up their station on the broad landing outside the chamber door.

Inside, a maid curtsied to the space between the two young women. She had a flat face and dark, deep-set eyes like chips of obsidian.

'There's hot water in the jugs, my ladies. I can dress your hair if you wish, tidy your clothes. Cosmetics, too, on the dressing table. A touch of Venetian ceruse, perhaps?' She glanced at Cat, whose skin, even in this light, lacked the fashionable pallor of a well-bred lady and was in need of whitening. 'And there are clothes, too, in the closet. Perhaps I could find something more suitable for you to wear, mistress?'

'I shall do perfectly well as I am,' Cat said.

The maid shied away. Cat was still wearing the clothes she changed into at Henrietta Street a few hours earlier. In truth, she looked little better than a servant herself. What did that matter? She wasn't prepared to wear finery borrowed from Buckingham. She would not give him that satisfaction.

If she could safely have killed the Duke at that moment, she would have done so without a qualm. The threat he had made against Hakesby had been so crudely violent, the sort of tactic that a swaggering ruffian from Alsatia might use, that it had put him outside the pale. For all his wit, his court civility and his wealth, the great nobleman was nothing but a bully underneath. Perhaps they all were, these noblemen, bankrupting their hapless creditors, stealing other men's wives and settling their disputes with the violence of cold steel. They felt themselves by birth and breeding to be above the law, both God's and man's.

Elizabeth submitted herself happily to the maid's attentions, even agreeing to accept the loan of a discreet gold necklace with a sapphire pendant set in a frame of small diamonds. 'Nothing too ostentatious, though,' she said, staring approvingly at her reflection. 'I would not want His Grace's friends to take me for a court bawd.'

Cat allowed the maid to brush the mud from her clothes and dress her hair, but accepted nothing else.

When they were done, the maid went to the door and held a whispered conference with the servants on the landing. She turned back to Elizabeth and Cat.

'His Grace is ready for you. I'm to take you down to the Great Chamber.'

Again the little procession formed: the two footmen and the maid escorting Elizabeth and Cat. The five of them descended the broad staircase, with the maid in advance and the menservants behind.

'Can you hear me?' Cat said in a whisper.

Elizabeth glanced at her. But as she was opening her mouth, Cat went on in an even softer voice than before:

'Look ahead and say nothing.'

They went down a step, then a second, then a third.

'I've something in my house that may belong to your father.'

Elizabeth stumbled. She would have fallen if Cat hadn't steadied her. She smiled her thanks, and they continued their descent of the stairs.

Two more footmen stood sentry outside the Great Chamber. There was a rumble of voices inside. The footmen flung open the doors.

Cat and Elizabeth paused on the threshold. The voices faltered, and diminished into silence. The high, wide chamber stretched down to two windows, curtained against the dark. Dark, distorted reflections swam in the tall mirrors. The walls and ceiling shimmered with a faint, golden glitter, for every possible surface, it seemed to Cat, had been gilded.

The splendour diminished the room's inhabitants. There were about a score of them, all men, mostly in sober clothes, many in black, and they were unfitted for the magnificence that surrounded them. The one exception was the Duke himself, who came hurrying down the room towards the two women like a gorgeous golden bee towards two particularly tempting flowers.

'Such an honour,' he murmured as he bowed to Elizabeth, who blushed becomingly and fluttered her eyelashes. To Cat, his words were: 'If only your dear father could be with us, madam. He would indeed be proud of you.'

Buckingham offered his right hand to Elizabeth and his left to Cat. Holding their hands high as if they were his partners in a stately dance, he led them down the room, introducing them to each man as they passed.

'Mistress Elizabeth Cromwell–yes indeed, the late Protector's eldest daughter, but the whole family joins us here in spirit, sir–yes, and here is Mistress Hakesby–you knew her father, Thomas Lovett well, I know, and he was great Oliver's confidential friend; what a loss to our cause his death has been–but at least she and her husband are with us today, and his memory will inspire us.'

Some of the faces Cat recognized from her childhood; others had a teasing, dreamlike familiarity. But how elderly they looked, how ineffectual. In memory they had been austere, remote figures endowed with extraordinary powers: now most of them were old men like her husband, faded and infirm.

'United,' the Duke was saying to one of them in a carrying voice designed to be overheard, 'we are stronger than we know. Men and women, rich and poor, we serve God first, and the country second–but all within the law, sir, and under the King.'

It was in its way an impressive performance, Cat thought, carefully staged and designed to dazzle. Buckingham had the courtier's skill of moving effortlessly from man to man, from group to group, with a confidential word here and a touch of the arm there. All the while, he displayed Elizabeth and Cat to his guests like the trophies they were. Unlike Elizabeth, Cat refused to be drawn into conversation, keeping her eyes downcast.

'Very good, madam,' the Duke murmured to her. 'Very demure. They like that in a woman, you know. Personally I prefer a little more fire but one must not be selfish when one's doing God's work.'

They came at last to the fireplace, where Dr Owen, the clergyman, was talking with Richard Cromwell. The latter, perhaps hoping for relief, looked up as Buckingham appeared with his captives in tow. But Owen merely seized the opportunity to expand his audience.

'I was informing Mr Cromwell how admired he is, throughout the country.' Owen's voice, which had something of the quality of a saw, was increasing steadily in volume and acquiring a preacher's rhythms. 'Consider, I say to members of my congregation, and consider this well: here is Richard Cromwell. Once he held supreme authority in this country. He did not seek it. He accepted it for the common good, and he relinquished it for the same reason, with his honour unstained. Does not his life show that he walks the paths of righteousness in private and in public, unlike some rulers I might mention?'

'You're too good, sir,' Cromwell said, shifting his weight from one foot to the other and clearly embarrassed by the encomium.

'Dr Owen speaks only the truth, sir,' Buckingham said. 'Now and always. By the way, is Mr Hakesby with you?'

'He felt weary and retired to lie down.' Cromwell turned to Cat. 'No need for concern, madam.'

'Of course not.' The Duke's fingers tightened on Cat's hand, and he turned his head towards her. His grip was growing painful. 'It's perfectly natural at his age and in his state of health.' Briefly, his face twisted into a lascivious mask, and again his voice dropped to a murmur that only she could hear. 'One cannot expect the thrusting vigour of a younger man, can one? How you must yearn for that.'

She tore her hand away. 'Forgive me, sir, I must attend my husband.'

She curtsied to the three men and nodded to Elizabeth, who smiled uncertainly at her.

'Very proper,' she heard Dr Owen say as she walked away. 'A wife's duty to her husband is second only to her duty to God.'

She did not have an opportunity to speak privately to Elizabeth before they left Wallingford House. It was almost midnight by the time the Duke allowed them to leave.

The streets were rowdier than before and Veal sent them back to Henrietta Street in sedan chairs, with six of the Duke's manservants as an escort. There was no trouble. Buckingham was popular with Londoners, and men in his livery were usually allowed to pass without hindrance.

By this time, Hakesby was both drunk and tired. He was trembling badly too. At the

428

sign of the Rose, two of the servants helped him up the stairs, while Pheebs watched and listened in the hall. Once in their apartments, her husband retired to his closet, leaving Cat to listen to his paying a prolonged and noisy price for the evening's excitement and the evening's wine.

They were alone. The maid had been given permission to spend the night at her mother's lodging. The parlour fire was out. There was no kindling left and it wasn't worth trying to light it. The bedchamber felt even colder than the parlour. Cat bolted the door to the landing and went to bed. Lying there in the curtained darkness, she let the events of the day pour through her mind like storm water down a drain.

Figures rose up in her memory: the King in his dun-coloured coat and his scuffed shoes; the richly dressed and far more regal-looking Buckingham; the barely human Ferrus; the dog Dido, soft and excited; the clergyman at Wallingford House with his slug-like face and his unctuous certainties; Richard Cromwell, blandly uncaring that he was the cause of so much trouble and relying on good manners to placate everyone; and his daughter Elizabeth, more worried than sly despite the pleasure that wearing a sapphire pendant gave her.

And Hakesby himself, a shambling, wine-sodden wreck of a fine man. But still her husband, she reminded herself, for better or worse. Who had saved her from penury. Who had taught her more than she could ever have hoped to learn about the design of buildings and about the practicalities of bringing those designs to fruition. And who was now making strange, unnatural sounds on the other side of the closet door.

The worst of it, it seemed to her, was her loneliness. She had no one to talk to, no one she could confide in. Even Marwood had abandoned her. It was her own fault, after she had torn into him so savagely at the bookseller's. When all was said and done, he had been trying to help her.

Later, much later, as she was dropping into an uneasy doze, she remembered the packet that Ferrus had given her. It was still in the coal scuttle in the parlour. For all she cared it could stay there for ever. It was the cause of all their troubles.

CHAPTER FOURTEEN

The Undone Company of Poor Whores
Tuesday, 24 March 1668

The light creeps red and watery into the sky.

Ferrus listens to Windy's breathing. He touches the curved edges of his pennies.

He waits and waits. Master does not come. Master drunk and stupid last night. Master fell asleep and three of my lord's servants dragged him away on his back with his clothes unlaced. His belly gaped to the world and his mouth was open.

Ferrus could have put his fingers inside and tugged Master's tongue out of his mouth.

Light glints on streaky puddles among the cobbles. Ferrus wriggles past Windy, who stirs, snorts but does not wake. He crawls from the kennel into the morning. Stands and stretches. Sniffs.

Fresh-baked bread in the air. Oh, for my

lady's soft white roll. Hunger lives in his belly like Windy lives in his kennel. Master says to his friends, I keeps Ferrus thin. You don't feed up your ferret before you put him in a rabbit warren, do you?

Cat's away, so micey plays.

Ferrus slips out of the yard and down the long passage by the kitchen to the servants' door to the Park. He's hungry for white rolls, oh yes, but also for wonders.

Dew lies heavy on sodden grass. Mist clings to the treetops along the Mall. Lords and ladies lie fast asleep. Ducks draw lines on the long water of the canal. Grooms and horses go clip-clop, clip-clop. Thin boys and thin maids take fat dogs for walks. Dogs cock legs against the stone man who stands for ever and ever at the end of the canal. Dogs shit wherever and whenever they want.

No mazers for them, oh no.

Ferrus goes round the outside of the park. He shakes his stick and makes his noises if people come close. Men chase him. But Ferrus runs faster, faster than the wind.

Lady is nowhere. No wonders this morning. But here's the tall thin man, the one in the shit-coloured coat, with the long sword. Man with lady, and with shaking grandpa. Man comes out of the gate in the wall at the end of the Park. He carries a sheet of paper, which he waves as he walks.

Shit-coloured man doesn't see Ferrus. Ferrus hides behind a tree and watches, in case the lady follows him out. No lady. Only man like a barrel. His head turns from side to side. They go into the passage that leads to Whitehall.

No wonders. No lady. No food. No words.

Mistress Dalton's welcome was wearing thin. Nothing was said, but Elizabeth sensed it in the tone of her voice, in the dishes she ordered for her guests, and in her absences from the parlour. In the past she and her father had often found it hard to find privacy, for Mistress Dalton had always been with them if she could be. Now it was the other way round.

On Tuesday, the Cromwells walked arm in arm in the garden after breakfast, as they did every morning when it wasn't raining. It was their first opportunity to talk confidentially. Her father was in good spirits after yesterday evening's visit to Wallingford House. He looked younger too. Happiness, or at least relief, had smoothed away some of the lines from his face.

Her father swept aside her fears about Mistress Dalton. 'You imagine things, my dear. I've known Meg Dalton since I was a child. My father was her godfather. She would let us live here for ever if we had a mind to it.'

'But did you not mark how she served us nothing but a piece of bread and dry cheese for supper?'

'Perhaps that was all she had in the house. She knows that old friends need not stand on ceremony in the way of food, as in other matters. In fact, I've a mind to stay a little longer. A month, perhaps. Or even more.'

Elizabeth stopped and wrenched her arm from his. 'But, sir, I thought you meant to go back to France in a few days.'

'Well, yes. That was my plan. But our enterprise at the Cockpit failed, and I have a mind to try again if we can find a way.'

'Why? Thanks to the Duke's kindness, you no longer need it.'

He shrugged, frowning. 'Yesterday he gave me a purse with a hundred pounds in gold. That's something, I grant you. A great deal. But —'

'And he also gave you a bill for another four hundred on his man of business in Paris. Isn't that enough?'

'My dear, the money would barely last me a year, even with the utmost economy. I have creditors to satisfy in Paris as well as here. Buckingham told me last night–indeed

434

he promised me–that if I would but stay in London and help him for a few weeks, he would get me a pension of seven hundred a year from the King, and all my debts discharged. And if by chance he failed in that, he said he'd pay it all himself, including the pension, out of his own pocket.'

'You believe him?'

'Why not? He's a man of honour, and I believe he's sincere. And it's in his interest to keep his word.'

'Why?'

'Many reasons. Because my name and reputation still mean something to his supporters. Indeed, if it's known that I stand with him in this, he may well gain more. The money aside, I think his cause is just. This country will never be united under God unless we have toleration for all. Apart from Sectarians and Catholics, naturally. It's no more than the King himself promised at the Restoration. And . . . well, if I am honest with myself, it is agreeable to feel I am of some use again. Idleness does not become a man.'

'That's well and good, sir. But not if you lose your liberty because of it. You must look to your own interests.' Elizabeth bit her lip. 'And those of your family.'

'But I do look to my own interest. If I go

back to Paris now, I lose the pension–and perhaps the chance of another attempt at the Cockpit. Perhaps the Duke would cancel the bill as well.'

It was growing chilly, and Elizabeth started walking again. 'Catherine told me last night that they were successful yesterday, after all.'

He stopped abruptly. 'You mean they found it?'

'I think so. Though we don't even know what my grandmother hid there.'

'It'll be worth the having, whatever it is.' Her father fell into step beside her. 'She wouldn't have written to me from her deathbed if that were not so. My mother was a prudent housekeeper. She knew the value of money as well as anyone.'

'Then will you leave England once you have it? I beg you, sir, consider it.'

He smiled at her but did not answer. Father and daughter walked in silence to the end of the garden. There were buds on the espaliered apple trees that lined the wall. Green spikes poked from the earth beneath.

Cromwell stopped. He touched one of the buds with a fingertip. 'I want to see this blossom. It won't be long, if this mild weather continues.' He turned back to her. 'I miss this.' He waved at the wall, at the fruit trees and the shoots in the earth. 'I miss my garden at Hursley. I miss England. That's the true reason I want to stay longer.'

Elizabeth took his arm again. 'I know,' she said in a softer voice. 'And one day they will surely let you come back home. But to stay here for longer now would be to risk all.'

'The Duke will protect me,' her father said. 'He gave me his word.'

On Tuesday, I was at Scotland Yard in good time. My shoulder was stiff and badly bruised, but the damage was less serious than I had feared. I wore an old hat and a scratchy, ill-fitting periwig, hired until I had the leisure to buy a new one.

'You look as if you've been in the wars,' Abbott said, putting his head on one side. 'I haven't seen you in that peruke before, have I?'

'Probably not.'

'Williamson's been asking for you,' he went on, pursing his little mouth as if he was going to kiss someone. 'Trouble? He's not in a good humour.'

'No,' I said. 'I don't suppose he is. Is he in his room?'

'He had to go out—my lord sent for him.'

Mr Williamson had come in about twenty minutes before me, I learned, and so at least

437

he must have seen the letter I had sent him by Chloris yesterday evening. With some difficulty, I forced myself to concentrate on drawing up draft copy for the next *Gazette.* Abbott tried to start a conversation about yesterday's disturbances but I gave no encouragement to his chatter and he fell to sucking his teeth and scratching away with his pen. The distant tolling of the guard-house clock marked the passage of time, and still Williamson did not come.

However, three of his informers put in an appearance at the office. They came one by one, and each brought more news of the rioting. The unrest was spreading. The reports said that hundreds of active rioters were on the street today, many of them armed and arrayed. Disturbances like this always attracted bystanders, and there were estimates of crowds in the thousands on the fringes of the violence, eager to see the spectacle and perhaps not unwilling to join in. Even allowing for the probability that such numbers were exaggerated, the news was alarming.

The apprentices and their allies were tearing down brothels in Moorfields again, and the attacks had also reached East Smithfield, Shoreditch, and the area around St Andrew's in Holborn. I heard a rumour that whores who had not escaped in time had run shrieking through the streets pursued by the mob.

The man who told me of the Holborn attacks was the last of the three informers. As I was paying him, I said, 'By the by, did you pass by Long Acre on your way?'

'Aye, sir. Not much going on there.'

'What about Dog and Bitch Yard?'

'Quiet as the grave. I poked my nose in, in case. No one there except a couple of bravos. They told me to move along.'

So far, at least, Madam Cresswell's establishment had not been troubled. It looked as if Chloris had been right about Buckingham's protection.

By midday, Williamson had still not returned. I left the office and walked across to Axe Yard, where I ate my dinner at the common table of the Axe. While I was there, I heard the steady beating of a drum.

My neighbour at table, a clerk from the Lord Chamberlain's Department, cocked his head. 'They're beating to arms at the Horse Guards. I knew they would.'

I looked up from Raleigh's *History*. 'They are taking it seriously, then?'

The man nodded. 'Aye. Those cursed apprentices. I'd flog the lot of them. I blame the masters too. They give them too much liberty.'

On my way back to the office, I heard someone shout my name as I was walking across the Great Court. I turned. Chiffinch was coming out of the passage leading to the chapel and the public stairs. He waved me over and fixed me with his watery eyes.

'I heard something today that might interest you.' His lips curled into a smile like the sparkle of sunlight on a freshly sharpened mantrap. 'In fact, I wager it will. I seem to remember that you're acquainted with Mistress Hakesby.'

'Yes, sir.'

'Not well, I hope?'

I shrugged. 'As you know, I've had dealings with her on the King's behalf.'

He raised his eyebrows. 'Nothing more?'

I shook my head.

'No? Then you're a wise man.' He gave me another of those smiles. 'Good day to you.'

Chiffinch strolled away in the direction of the Stone Gallery. I stared after him. I wished I could ask him what he meant, but that would have been to fall into his trap and allow him to bait me further. Suddenly he turned and caught me watching him.

'Is that a new peruke, Marwood?' He had

raised his voice, so his words must have been audible to at least a dozen people in the court. 'It doesn't become you, you know. Makes you look as if you've got a pair of dead squirrels on your head.'

Someone laughed. Chiffinch walked off, and so did I.

Williamson returned to Scotland Yard half an hour after I did. He glanced about the outer room, where the clerks were at work with suddenly renewed industry. He crooked his finger at me, and I followed him into his private room.

'A bad business. You escaped unharmed yesterday?'

'I lost my purse and my shoes and my wig, sir. Otherwise it could have been worse.'

'The effrontery of these rogues is beyond belief. But I can't understand it, Marwood: why should the men who attacked you in Poplar have you taken to Dog and Bitch Yard? If they were set on tearing down the bawdy houses, why send you to be kept in one? And why choose a house quite on the other side of town from Poplar?'

'Because the house in Dog and Bitch Yard is the Duke of Buckingham's.'

'What?' Williamson's eyebrows shot up. 'How so?'

'Madam Cresswell's name may be on the lease or even on the deeds themselves. But I believe the money behind her comes from the Duke.'

'How do you know?'

'I bribed one of her whores to help me escape. She tells me that all things are done in the house as the Duke desires. And that he often visits himself, and not just to use the whores. He meets people there too. He writes there. He even sleeps in the house on occasion.'

'Your whore told you a good deal. Do you believe her?'

'She had no reason to lie, sir. She also said that her mistress was forewarned about the riots, and assured that her own house would not be attacked.'

Williamson let out his breath in a silent whistle. 'You tell me that she was warned by the Duke?'

'Or by one of his men.'

'Which is tantamount to saying that . . .'

His voice trailed away. We looked at each other in silence. I didn't want to be the first to put it into words and nor did he. It was tantamount to saying that the riots were not a spontaneous affair bred by the licence of a holiday. They had been planned beforehand. And if Buckingham had not organized

442

them himself, he had at the very least known about them, kept his mouth shut and arranged for his own particular bawdy house to be left untouched. All of which meant that —

'This rioting is different,' Williamson said. 'I knew it. My Lord Arlington was saying just now that it was similar to the old Shrove Tuesday attacks on the brothels, and nothing more. The apprentices used to attack the bawdy houses every year before the war. But this isn't like that at all.'

'No, sir,' I said.

'Which therefore throws quite a different light on this.'

He unlocked a drawer of his desk and took out a single sheet of paper. It had a brown stain covering near half of it, but the printed words on it were perfectly legible. 'Someone went about Whitehall this morning and left it outside the royal apartments and the Duke of York's lodging. The ink was still a little damp, I understand, so it was probably run off the press this morning. This particular copy was pinned to my Lady Castlemaine's door.' He tapped it. 'See that mark? She was so angry she threw her cup of chocolate at it. Then she took it straight to the King.' He handed the paper to me. 'A pound to a penny there will be copies all over town by tomorrow.'

The sheet took the form of a petition. The first thing I realized was that I had seen a version of some of it before: the fragmentary draft, written in Buckingham's hand, in the drawing room at Dog and Bitch Yard on my first visit there.

The second thing I noted, as my father's son, was that the petition was clearly set out and decently printed, which was not, I knew from bitter experience as a printer's apprentice, something that could be done in a hurry. I skimmed the text:

The Poor-Whores Petition to the most Splendid, Illustrious and Eminent Lady of Pleasure, the Countess of Castlemayne etc. The Humble Petition of the Undone Company of poor distressed Whores, Bawds, Pimps, and Panders, etc.

Humbly sheweth,
That your petitioners having been for a long time connived at and countenanced in the practice of our venereal pleasures (a trade wherein your ladyship hath great experience, and for your diligence therein have arrived to high and eminent advancement for these late years), but

now we, through the rage and malice of a company of London apprentices and other malicious and very bad persons, being mechanic, rude and ill-bred boys, have sustained the loss of our habitations, trades and employments . . .

'The impudence,' Williamson said. 'To address it to my lady, and in such terms. And with those sly insinuations.'

I quickly read the rest of the petition, which continued in the same satirical vein. It was neatly done. It purported to be written by Madam Cresswell and Damaris Page on behalf of their 'Sisters and Fellow Sufferers'. The writers begged for her ladyship's help in bringing a stop to this 'before they come to Your Honour's palace and bring contempt upon your worshiping of Venus, the great goddess whom we all adore.'

'It's not madams Cresswell and Page who wrote it, of course,' Williamson said. 'Everyone knows that. Those whore-mistresses may be bound for damnation in the next world, but they know how to prosper in this one.'

The petition was implying that Lady Castlemaine was the greatest whore in England; and, moreover, that, if unchecked, the crowds would march on Whitehall it-self–her palace, rather than the King's. In other words, the writer was threatening that this disorder would turn into something close to rebellion against the Crown.

I ran my finger down the page. Near the bottom were two lines that I read for a second time. In return for Lady Castle-maine's protection, the writers of the petition pledged that 'we shall oblige ourselves by as many oaths as you please, to contribute to your ladyship (as our sisters do at Rome and Venice to His Holiness the Pope).'

'Ah,' Williamson said. 'You mark the part in parentheses. About paying her for protection. That struck me too.'

'My lady is a Roman Catholic,' I said. 'The writer is reminding us of that —'

'In case we'd forgotten,' put in Williamson.

'— and he links it to the corruption of the papacy to boot. It connects the Court with the papists.'

'Indeed.'

Neither of us reminded the other that the Queen was a papist, and both the King and his brother were widely believed to favour them. Nor was it a secret that both men delighted in bawds. This so-called petition would be widely interpreted as an attack on

446

the King.

Not just on the King. There was something else here.

I said cautiously, 'Is it possible, sir, that this foolish squib is somehow concerned with the failure of the Comprehension Bill to pass through Parliament?'

'Yes?' Williamson gestured for me to continue.

'The bill would have granted toleration to all but the Catholics and a few sectarians. But the bishops and their supporters fought it tooth and nail. They don't want to yield an inch of toleration even to the Presbyterians and their kin, because it would undermine their authority, their power. And accordingly half of London, not just the apprentices, hates the bishops and their allies. Because of their opposition, the bill wasn't even presented to Parliament. And of course the bill's sponsor at Court was . . .'

Williamson held up his hand, and my voice trailed into silence. We both knew that the bill's principal supporter had been the Duke of Buckingham, and that its failure to pass had helped to destroy his claim that he could manage Parliament for the King.

Thanks to Cat, I knew more than Williamson. I knew that Buckingham's allies included Richard Cromwell. I knew that the

Duke was actively cultivating the Presbyterians and other Dissenters as well and putting himself forward as their champion. He was playing on the widespread dissatisfaction with the King, his court and the bishops. He had planned this outbreak of rioting for some time. This petition formed part of his scheme.

Since Buckingham could not control the government by the King's favour, I guessed, he was trying to do it another way: with the support of the King's disaffected subjects. There was a sort of genius about it, I conceded, and a boldness too. A lesser man might have felt such intrigues were both dishonourable and dangerous. A lesser man might have been reluctant to show himself to all the world as so inconsistent in his loyalties and so devious in his scheming. But Buckingham had always felt that the world should be his for the asking, and if he could not have it by one way, he was quite entitled to have it by another.

Mr Williamson and I looked at each other in silence. My master had his own secrets no doubt; we all did in this place. Mine was Cat and this dangerous business with the Cromwells. I wished I could tell it all to Williamson. But Chiffinch had clearly heard something that affected Cat, and for her sake I dared not make a move before knowing what it was. Moreover, if I told Williamson what I knew about Richard Cromwell and his connection to the Duke, he would demand to know how I had come by the knowledge.

That would put Cat in danger of a charge of treason. The King's Council would be automatically suspicious of a regicide's child, and no court would be inclined to show mercy to her.

Prudence, my own safety and the welfare of the kingdom itself urged me to speak out, to betray her to Williamson. I own I was tempted.

For all that I held my peace.

The King ordered the City to double the watch and call up two of its militia companies. The army was under arms, waiting for orders. Lord Craven led a troop of the Life Guard out of Whitehall in the afternoon.

As the hours passed, we received a steady trickle of intelligence about the riots. The City authorities arrested some of the rioters and threw them into the New Prison at Clerkenwell. Their comrades thought they had been taken to Finsbury, and they besieged the gaol there. They found none of their friends but freed four common criminals. It spoke volumes for their boldness that the apprentices promptly marched over to Clerkenwell and attacked the New Prison, where they released their captured friends.

One of Williamson's people reported to me, in a voice not much more than a whisper, 'I heard they put the Clerkenwell gaoler in fear of his life. And they told him–mark this, sir–they said to him: we have been servants, but we will be masters now.'

I made a note of it and passed it on to Williamson immediately.

'We have been servants,' he repeated, 'but we will be masters now. It's Leveller cant, Marwood. It's but a short step to saying that all men are equal. I thought Oliver had stamped out that impious nonsense once and for all.'

For the rest of the afternoon, the other clerks and I pretended to work but none of us achieved much. This unrest in the streets was worse than any yet since the King's Restoration. A faint, unsettling smell of treason hung in the air, like the taint of bad meat.

Lord Craven sent Mr Williamson an express which said, in a few scribbled words, that some of his men had been attacked by rioters solely because they were believed to be led by the Duke of York. Here was yet another hint of the political motives behind the disturbances: the Duke was not only the King's heir: he was also rumoured to be on the verge of going over to Rome.

Dusk was gathering, and the candles were lit in the office. Most of the clerks left but I stayed, and so did Williamson. Shortly after six, a palace messenger arrived with a letter for him. A few minutes later, he rang his bell for me.

I went into the private room and, without waiting to be told, closed the door behind me. Williamson passed me the letter.

'They are calling for a revolution,' he said. 'Or the next best thing. And there's something here that touches you.'

I glanced first at the signature. It was from William Chiffinch. I ran my eyes over the contents.

Chiffinch said that one of his own informants had claimed to hear the mob in Clerkenwell chanting 'Down with the Red Coats'. Moreover, some rioters were saying that if the King did not give them liberty of conscience, there would be worse, much bloodier riots on May Day, the next big public holiday. They also threatened that before long, they would march on Whitehall and tear it down. Presumably, I thought, on the grounds that it was the biggest bawdy house of them all.

Then I reached the last few lines of the letter. Suddenly I found it hard to breathe.

I have also received information that a number of Dissenters gathered at Wallingford House yesterday evening. You may already be aware of this but not perhaps of this more recent intelligence I received from my informer. Two people arrived there later than the others. One was a disaffected clergyman named Veal, a member of the Duke's household. He was escorting a woman, Mistress Hakesby, the wife of an architect and surveyor who thrived under the Commonwealth.

It is not widely known that this woman is the daughter of Lovett the regicide, that most fanatical rogue who fell to his death in the ruins of St Paul's a year or two ago. The daughter herself lay under suspicion of murder last year, and we were also obliged to arrest Hakesby himself and bring him in for questioning. The King has an interest in her activities, as your clerk Marwood will confirm, and His Majesty will probably command you to question both Hakesbys about this present matter.

'Hakesby,' Williamson said. 'The name's familiar–didn't you have a cousin of his working as your maid last year?'

I kept my eyes on the letter. 'Yes. It was while I was ill, sir, if you recall, and half out of my mind on opium. My cook took her on. I don't think the girl stayed long–she didn't suit.'

'It grows worse and worse. Buckingham is plotting with a regicide's close kin–and God knows who else. We shall need to talk to Mistress Hakesby. And to her husband. I'll ask my Lord Arlington to sign the warrant.'

'Might it be wiser to hold our hand, sir?' My voice sounded as artificial as an actor's in my ears. 'To set a watch on them, but not bring them in.'

He scowled. 'Why?'

'Because . . .' desperately, I cast about for plausible reasons to leave the Hakesbys alone '. . . because seizing them now would send a warning to the Duke that we were uncovering his intrigue. Would it not be better to gather more evidence, and then bring them all in?'

Williamson considered. 'Whatever we do, this must be nipped in the bud. If you're right that Buckingham is behind it all, that

453

he encouraged the unrest and plans to profit by it–why then, I must have certain proof. Something that Lord Arlington can take to the King. Otherwise our hands are tied. The Hakesby woman may give us that proof if we question her thoroughly.'

'Perhaps, sir. But she's not important in herself, only because of her father. I doubt she would be privy to the Duke's schemes.'

'Can you suggest a better way to proceed?' His voice was rougher than usual, with the hard Cumbrian vowels more in evidence. 'Well?'

I hesitated. 'Documentary proof cannot be ignored, it cannot be disputed. It would be much more valuable than testimony from a tainted source. Even supposing we could extract such testimony and it proved worth the having.'

'True. But what documentary proof? The Duke's people would hardly give you free run of Wallingford House if you had a mind to search his papers.'

'The whore I mentioned, sir. She said the Duke often sits and writes in the drawing room at the house in Dog and Bitch Yard. He keeps the keys of a desk there, and probably locks away his papers in it.' I watched Williamson's face, trying to interpret his expression. 'The Duke lives in public at

Wallingford House, sir. But in Dog and Bitch Yard, he is private. He meets his trusted servants there, men like Veal and Durrell who forward his intrigues.'

'It would be hard to get a warrant for raiding a bawdy house at present. Unwise, too, with the people so inflamed and disordered. Besides, the Duke might hear of it. He has his people everywhere.'

'Better if it could be done privately,' I said. 'Without the need of a warrant. And there's a chance it could. Why not try that first? If it fails, we bring in the Hakesbys, and nothing will be lost by it but a few hours.'

'How could it be managed?' Williamson said.

I cleared my throat. 'Through the good offices of the whore who helped me escape yesterday.'

'You'd trust a whore?' He almost shouted the words, throwing them at me one by one like stones. 'Is your brain between your legs?'

I let the words hang in the air. Williamson was usually careful with me, and even prudish in general conversation; a rarity in Whitehall. I could count on the fingers of one hand the occasions that he had flown into a passion and spoken without calculation.

'She's greedy for money, sir,' I said.

'They all are.'

'She wants to leave London and settle down. I wouldn't let her cheat us.' I paused. 'But I would need money for her.'

'Money?' Williamson repeated, frowning. His meanness with money, both his own and the Crown's, was ingrained.

'The men who took me yesterday stole my purse. And I had to spend another twenty pounds to secure my release from Dog and Bitch Yard. And one shilling.'

Williamson stared at me, raising the candle on his desk to see me better. He shrugged, and I knew the battle was won.

'I'll give you a warrant for twenty pounds from the Private Fund. But remember this, Marwood, I don't look on this as a repayment for what you lost. I look on it as an investment in what you will achieve. Don't fail me.'

It was dark by the time I left Scotland Yard. The streets were still crowded. It would have been faster to walk but I shared a coach with Abbott. He lodged further to the east than I, in Fleet Street near the Devil Tavern. His chatter irritated me, but I judged it safer to travel in company.

As we passed Charing Cross I wondered

456

when Cat had left Wallingford House. She might still be there. The very thought of her coloured my mind with the familiar mix of irritation, tenderness and worry. Now that she had been seen at Wallingford House, she was in serious danger.

If I could but talk to the obstinate woman, I thought, perhaps I could persuade her to come to an arrangement about Richard Cromwell. Or even if she would let me talk directly to the man himself, with her acting as the broker. That would wipe her slate clean with Williamson and indeed the King. But I feared that she would never consent to give me information that might endanger Cromwell and her husband.

Husband. Even now, the word left a sour taste. Catherine Lovett's *husband.*

At Infirmary Close, Sam opened the door to me.

'Any news?' I said as he took my cloak.

'You've heard the latest about the bawdy houses? They're tearing them down in Holborn now.'

'I know. What about here?'

He grinned at me. He would have winked at me if he had dared. 'The new maid has been making herself useful. You'll keep her on, sir? A girl of many talents. Could do worse, I'd say. Brightens up the place.'

I ignored the question. 'Tell Margaret to bring supper in fifteen minutes.' He was about to go but I stopped him. 'Stay–tell her that I want Chloris to bring it.'

'Aye aye, master,' Sam said.

I went to my bedchamber and threw off the cursed, itching periwig. I put on my cap, gown and slippers. I went down to the parlour. Chloris came in with a tray to lay the table. Though her dress was modest enough and befitting her station, her colour was high and she avoided my eye. She looked, I thought, remarkably pretty by candlelight. At the moment I recalled the touch of her fingers on my scalp last night, and how she had assisted me so intimately in my hour of need in the attic at Dog and Bitch Yard, I felt my own colour rising.

She poured my wine, went away and returned with the food. 'Shall I stay to serve you, sir?'

'Yes.'

For a few minutes I ate and drank. I was aware of her behind me. I even fancied I heard the sound of her breathing. I beckoned her to refill my glass and she came forward to stand at my shoulder.

'Tell me,' I said as she was pouring the wine, 'do you have friends at Madam Cresswell's? Not among the gentlemen, I mean.

Among those that work there. Someone you trust.'

'I don't trust anyone overmuch, sir.' She snorted. 'Even myself.'

'There are degrees in all things.'

'None of the men, for a start. They want it for free, and they'd sell their mothers for tuppence, especially that Merton.'

'The tall man who takes the money?'

'Aye. And who has strange tastes. He's the one who scares me.'

'What about the women?'

'Us bawds, you mean.' Her voice was flat, purged of emotion. 'We're all bawds there, you know. Even the kitchen maid's at it. Everyone's out for themselves. There's no room for a friend.' She hesitated. 'Nearest thing I got to a friend is Meg.'

'Who?'

'We have to call her Amaryllis in company. You remember?'

I nodded. I had a memory of plump flesh, inadequately covered, and a snub nose.

'We look out for each other, she and I,' Chloris said. 'But I wouldn't call her a friend.'

'Could you get a message to her?'

She frowned. 'Why? You don't want her, do you? I thought you didn't care for what we can give you.'

459

I ignored that and turned away to take another mouthful of food. A moment later I said, 'You saw my warrants. You know I work for the King. He has need of certain papers which are in Madam Cresswell's house.'

Her hand flew to her throat. 'I don't know nothing about that, sir, I —'

'When I was there the first time,' I said, 'there was a desk in the drawing room.'

'Yes, I told you,' she said, suddenly loquacious. 'That's where His Grace sits. He likes to see who comes and goes in the yard below. He says it's as good as a play sometimes, to see how they hesitate before they dare knock on the door, and how they count their money and how they spew in the gutter, and how their friends urge them on.'

'And his papers?'

'How would I know? He has the keys to the drawers of the desk. No one else has. Maybe he locks them in there. Maybe he takes them when he goes.' Chloris paused and then added casually, 'He fucked me over that desk once. The window was open. I had my head outside.'

I turned aside to take another mouthful. Then, 'I want the contents of the drawers. Any papers, that is. How can I get them?'

'Meg won't get them for you. She

wouldn't dare. If you want them, you'll have to get them yourself.'

I set down my knife. I had lost my appetite. 'Suppose–just suppose–I did get them myself. How would I go about it?'

Chloris hesitated. 'The best time would be early morning. We're busy most of the night so we all rise late, including the men.'

'Are you sure Meg wouldn't fetch them for me?'

'Why should she run the risk? She ain't foolish like me. And she ain't got twenty pounds off you already. Besides, they'd kill her if they found her at it. She knows that.'

After a while, I said, 'If a window could be left open . . .'

She burst out laughing. 'You like going in and out of windows, don't you?' She clapped her hand over her mouth. 'Forgive me, sir, it just slipped out.' Then she frowned and the hand dropped away from her face. 'But there might be a way, sir. It would cost you.'

It always does, I thought. One way or another.

When Chloris had cleared away my supper and left me, I took pen and ink and wrote a letter. The words did not come easily, but they had to be written. I finished at last,

461

sanded the ink dry, folded the letter and wrote *Mistress Hakesby* on the outside.

I sealed it, feeling like a gambler who had just cast a pair of dice but does not yet know how they will fall. Had she gone willingly to Wallingford House yesterday evening? Or had Veal forced her to accompany him?

I shouted for Sam, who was lounging in the hall. Late though it was, I told him to send Margaret to me. He looked puzzled but he obeyed without a word. When Margaret appeared, she was wearing the shapeless gown she put on when she retired.

'Tomorrow,' I said, 'I want you to take this letter to the sign of the Rose at about ten o'clock.'

'Me?' She rubbed her eyes. 'But morning's my busy time, master. Couldn't Stephen go? Or Sam?'

'No. It's possible that the house is being watched by Mistress Hakesby's enemies. And mine. They know Stephen is my servant, and Sam too. But they don't know you.'

'Could you send a boy? Sam could bring you the one from the alehouse.'

'No,' I said. 'I want you. Someone I can trust. And someone she can trust.'

I waited but Margaret didn't speak. She stood there, quite still, her eyes fixed on me,

462

and her lower lip thrust out. Her very passivity was a wordless, red-faced objection.

'It's for Mistress Hakesby's sake,' I said at last. I felt a twinge of envy for the loyalty that Cat inspired so effortlessly in my servants. 'Do it for her, Margaret, if not for me.'

CHAPTER FIFTEEN

The Rehearsal
Wednesday, 25 March 1668

The kennel shakes and bangs. Windy's scratching.

Ferrus crawls out to piss in the corner by the coal shed. So cold. Only piss is warm.

A clock strikes five. Clang clang. Others join in. Devil's fire irons. Clang clang.

He thinks of the lady.

In the street that time, when Master was in Fulton's and talking secrets to the grandpa man. Lady spoke kindly, but he was full of fear and ran away and hid. But he saw her later on his way back to Fulton's and Master. Lady was walking through the big square full of people. Covent Garden, though nothing grows there. She went into a house in a street beyond.

Where lady lives?

Bolts rattle behind him. He turns. Master in the doorway to the passage. In his hand, a dogwhip. Face all blotchy. Body swaying. He swings the three knotted cords of the whip to and fro, to and fro.

Usually, when Master drinks hard, he falls asleep. But sometimes he drinks hard and does not sleep. Oh no, no, no.

'Poxy idle bufflehead,' Master says, nodding his head to agree with himself. 'You cost me the King's reward on Monday. You poxy pricklouse. You disgusted him, you disgust everyone, and that cost me a purse of gold. I'll thrash your poxy hide to jelly. Teach you manners.'

Windy comes out of his kennel. He growls. Master veers away from him. He raises the whip and staggers towards Ferrus.

'Come here,' he says, 'come here, you whoreson knave.'

Ferrus screams as the cords wrap themselves around his head in stripes of pain.

Windy's chain rattles. He lunges at Master. But the chain isn't long enough and it tugs him back.

This time the whip catches Ferrus on the neck and the arm. He tries to move away. But the wall stops him. Windy snarls and snaps.

Master laughs in the dog's face. 'Think you're fierce? Why, I could tear you limb from limb.'

He brings down the whip on Windy, who cries out.

Oh Windy. Ferrus makes a wordless noise. He springs. Snatches whip from Master. Master stumbles. His mouth falls open.

Blood on Windy's face. Oh, poor, poor Windy.

Ferrus brings down the whip on Master. Master stumbles again. Trips and falls. Windy seizes him by the ankle. Oh, Master screams and screams and screams.

The world in front of Ferrus is red. Master lies on the ground, curling up like a cat by the fire. Ferrus beats him with the whip about the head and body. Windy bites his leg.

Up goes the whip. Down goes the whip. Master shrieks. Master cries. Master screams.

Someone's shouting from the scullery window. A bolt scrapes on the door.

Ferrus drops the whip. It falls on Master. Master whimpers. Master whines. Windy growls.

The shouting's louder. Ferrus runs. Through the open door to the passage. With long strides he lopes through the gloom of early morning. His arms turn like windmill sails, pushing him along. At the servants' door to the Park, he pulls back the bolts.

Into another world. Where the air holds its breath.

His face is wet. Wipes it with his hands. Red hands. He wipes them on his breeches. He runs, following the line of the canal.

A grey light fills the world. Slowly it becomes silvery.

I couldn't have found the house without Chloris. The mouth of the alley that led to it was almost invisible.

The entry was on Long Acre, tucked in the shadow of a candlemaker's establishment. It was not yet fully light, and the walls on either side were high. The path wound its way among a maze of buildings and yards.

Chloris took my arm. I was carrying a bundle of tools under my cloak as well as a stick. The plan had seemed rational yesterday evening, the only possible way out of our difficulties. Now it showed itself in its true colours as the wildest and most foolish scheme imaginable.

'We're nearly there,' she said, squeezing my arm, as if I were a child in need of reassurance.

The entrance of the house was at the top of a flight of steps. There was a workshop underneath, its heavy double doors chained

467

up. We climbed the steps. The sky growing lighter: above us was a grey day, streaked with smoke from scores of newly-lit fires. Chloris had stayed a few nights in this house when she was cast off by her master, before Ma Cresswell had found her and transformed her from a servant to a whore.

'Best if I do the talking.' She squeezed my arm again. 'On account of my knowing the way of things here.' There was a flash of teeth as she grinned. 'We'll need your purse again, sir.'

She knocked on the door. No one came. She knocked again. I heard someone shouting. She tried a third time. A shutter on the door slid back.

'What's the racket?' The voice was sharp and hard as a nail. 'Oh, it's you. Ain't you with Ma Cresswell now?'

'I left.'

'She put you out, more like.'

'I got a person of quality with me that's mortal weary, mistress. Needs a bed to lay himself down on. And a chamber to himself, and me to look after him there. He likes it private.'

'How long?'

'To midday, let's say.'

'Five shillings.'

'Five? What's this? Somerset House?'

468

'You want a room all to yourself, don't you? That means someone's got to go, don't it? So: five shillings, take it or leave it.'

'He's got a fancy to have that little one at the top of the house. Right at the top.'

'Why?'

'Closer to heaven.'

'Eight shillings then.' There was a noise that might have been laughter or a creaking hinge. 'If he wants heaven, he has to pay for it.'

Chloris prodded my side. 'If you'd be so kind, sir. Cheap at the price, eh? We can't wait, can we?'

She winked at me and slipped her arm around my waist. Her head was cooler than mine. I counted out the coins with difficulty, partly because of the gloom and partly because my fingers were trembling. Chloris scooped the money from my palm and handed it through the shutter. The shutter closed and we waited, shivering in the cold.

'Are you sure she won't take the money and leave us on the doorstep?'

'Don't worry, sir. You paid her eight shillings without a murmur. We don't look like trouble, we spoke her fair. She'll be hoping to get more from us before we're done.'

A few minutes later, bolts slid back and the door opened. Inside was a narrow passage. In the gloom, a tall, stooping woman dressed in black stood with her back to the wall to let us by. She looked like an old crow. She held out a rushlight to Chloris.

'Up the stairs as far as you can go. There's a ladder to the attic.' She ran her eyes over me. 'Not too much in liquor, is he? If he is, you'll have to get him up there yourself. And clean up if he spews.'

'I'll manage, mistress.' Chloris took my hand. 'Come, sir, let me lead you up to paradise.'

Crooked, slanting stairs climbed through the heart of the house, a wooden building grown crazy with age. The air stank like an alehouse privy. We passed closed doors and heard the sounds of other occupants, some sleeping, some not.

On the top landing, a man and a woman lay huddled together for warmth. Beside them was the ladder. The man muttered a curse as we passed, and I guessed we had caused their eviction.

Chloris climbed the ladder first and scrambled into the attic. I followed her into a narrow space. It was almost entirely filled by a low truckle bed covered with a stained and crumpled sheet. The atmosphere was fetid, as though all the smells below had risen over the years and concentrated their essence up here.

After the darkness of the stairs, the attic was unexpectedly light. The room was squeezed into the top of one of the house's gables. On either side of the bed, the roof sloped down to the boarded floor. Of the two triangular vertical walls at either end, the inner one behind the bed consisted of a plank partition. The outer wall, however, was largely filled by a tall casement that looked if it might have been reused from another building.

I set down my bundle and stick, and threw open the window. Fresh, cold air flooded into the room, together with the smell of burning coal. Immediately in front of me, no more than a yard away, was another window. A piece of cloth made a makeshift curtain which obscured what lay within.

The upper storeys of both houses were jettied out to the point that the attics came close to touching one another. I looked down and then wished I hadn't. Directly below was the alley that ran along the side of Madam Cresswell's house in Dog and Bitch Yard. It was a long drop.

'Meg sleeps in there, and me too.' Chloris was standing at my shoulder, her breath warm on my cheek. 'Unless a man pays to lie with us all night.'

I took my stick, poked it over the alley and tapped on the glass. I did it gently at first and then more vigorously. A dog barked in the distance.

'Gently,' Chloris whispered. 'You'll wake the house.'

There was a flutter of movement in the cloth over the window. I tapped once more, and withdrew the stick. The cloth vanished. A white-faced child was staring at me.

'By your leave.' Chloris pushed me aside and leaned out of the window. 'Mary,' she said, and mimed to her that she should open her window.

The child obeyed. As the casement swung open, I saw her clearly for the first time. I recognized her face.

'Dorinda,' I said, remembering the bruised arms of the third of the three whores whom Madam Cresswell had paraded before me.

'Mary,' Chloris corrected me. 'That's her true name.' She looked at the girl. 'Where's Meg?'

'Downstairs with Mr Durrell.'

That was a blow. Chloris had thought that Meg would be a useful ally. I had even wondered if I could bribe her to break into the desk while I waited here in relative safety.

'Where have you been?' Mary was saying.

'What's —'

'What ails you, child?' Chloris whispered. 'You're like a ghost. Why are you up in the attic?'

The white face trembled and crumpled. 'I can't keep anything down. I spewed over a gent yesterday. Ma Cresswell put me up here to keep me out of the way.'

'Oh devil take her. Are you with child?'

Mary nodded. 'She's so angry. I never seen her like that. She told Merton to beat me. But it didn't make it go away. It just made me puke over his shoes.'

'God have mercy,' I muttered, startled into something like prayer.

Chloris swore. 'Listen,' she said. 'Open your window as wide as you can.'

'But I didn't think I was old enough yet,' the girl wailed. 'It's not fair.'

'Hush. I'm coming over to you. And this man is coming, too. But don't worry, he won't touch you. Is anyone out of bed yet?'

'No–last night was late for everyone. Ma opened up for a private party. No one's even gone down to light the kitchen fire.'

Chloris removed her shawl and tossed it on the unmade bed. She unclasped her cloak and dropped it on top. She scrambled on to the windowsill.

'Stand back and give me room.'

With surprising grace, she wriggled out of the window. Clinging to the frame, she straightened herself. Then she stepped without hesitation on to the windowsill of the neighbouring attic. She ducked her head and clambered inside. She turned to me.

I passed her the bundle of tools.

'Come on,' she whispered.

I dropped my cloak and hat on the bed. I had not bothered with a peruke this morning. I climbed on to the windowsill. Clutching the mullion, I crouched there for a moment. A yard is nothing, the length of a man's step. We lift our feet from one end of a yard to the other. It is an easy thing, and we do it thousands of times a day without a second thought. But it is different when you are twenty-five feet or more above the ground. A yard is a chasm. A yard is the mouth of a pit that sucks you into it. And I am a coward.

Mary was standing out of my sight, but I heard her thin, hopeless wail. I leaned across the gap and gripped Chloris's outstretched arm by the wrist. Staring into her eyes as if I hoped to find salvation there, I stepped without a downward glance into Madam Cresswell's house.

I found myself in another attic, slightly larger than the one I had left. I unwrapped the bundle. I picked out a pair of chisels, a hammer and a small crow, which I had taken from Sam's box of tools. Unfortunately I had never acquired the art of picking a lock.

Mary's eyes widened. 'What are you about, sir?'

Chloris said, 'Don't worry, my love. We'll be gone before you know it, and no one the wiser.'

Mary lunged at her and gripped her arm. 'Take me with you,' she whispered. 'Please. Please.'

'All right.' Chloris's eyes met mine over Mary's head. 'But me and the gentleman need to go downstairs for a moment first. Stay here. Get dressed.'

The house was larger than I had realized. Chloris took me past the attic where I had been confined and down a narrow flight of stairs. We came to a long passage with many doors opening into it. The next set of stairs was wider and with shallower treads. It brought us to the landing I had seen on my first visit to Dog and Bitch Yard. She tried the latch of the drawing-room door. It lifted, but the door was locked.

Putting her finger to her lips, she tiptoed to the neighbouring door. She stood on tiptoe and took a key from the ledge above the lintel. Slowly and stealthily, she inserted it in the lock and turned it. She gave me the sort of smile that is halfway to being a grimace. She raised the latch and the door opened.

We found ourselves in a shabby closet furnished with a table and a chair. The table was laden with trays of bottles and dirty glasses. From the closet, a communicating door led into the drawing room. I peered round the tall screen on the other side. The room was empty. The air was stuffy and smelled of sweat, candles and stale alcohol. There were more dirty glasses and empty bottles, including a smashed wine glass in the hearth. A pack of cards had been dropped on the carpet, where it lay in a ragged arc of pasteboard.

I crossed the floor to the desk by the window. I opened the curtains to give me light. The rattle of the rings was loud in the silence.

The desk was plain, with no ornamentation in the way of carving or inlays. It was flat-topped with two drawers beneath and a space for a man's legs between them. I remembered with sudden distaste that Chloris had lain over it for the Duke's pleasure with her head poking out of the window.

I set down the tools and tried the drawers. Both were locked. They fitted closely into the frame of the desk. I took up the smaller chisel and pushed it between the top of the left-hand drawer and the desk. I eased it from side to side, scarring the wood above and below, gradually enlarging the gap. It would have been faster to use the hammer to force the chisel deeper into the crack, but I couldn't risk the noise it would make.

But the chisel did its work in the end. When the gap was large enough, I pushed the wedge-shaped end of the crow into the hole. I glanced over my shoulder. Chloris was by the door to the landing, listening for sounds on the landing. She grimaced at me. I pushed the crow down. The wood cracked and split. I levered harder and wrenched the drawer open.

My spirits sank as I picked over the contents. There were blank sheets of paper, ink, pens, sealing wax, a small knife and a shaker of sand. That was all.

I attacked the other drawer. It was harder work than the first had been. I was tiring. Perhaps the gap was narrower.

The chisel slipped in my sweating hand, and gouged a jagged groove down the front of the desk. I swore softly. It took me at least a minute more to enlarge the hole sufficiently to take the end of the crow.

This time the noise was louder. The lock split the wood. The front of the drawer parted company with the rest of it and fell with a clatter to the floor.

'God's death, sir . . .' Chloris hissed.

I ignored her. My hands were shaking. I took out the remains of the drawer and laid it on the desk beside the other one. There was nothing but a loose pile of papers inside. The top sheet was covered with Buckingham's rapid, sloping writing. I snatched up the whole stack.

'Hush . . .'

I turned. Chloris was looking at me, her eyes huge with fear, with her finger to her mouth. Silently her lips moved: 'Someone's outside.'

I stuffed the papers into my coat pocket. I had left my stick in the attic of the house next door. I took up the crow in one hand and the hammer in the other.

We stood still, listening. All I could hear was distant barking. Chloris was frowning. Then she shrugged and beckoned me to follow her to the closet door behind the screen.

It was at that moment, as we both began to move towards the door, that without warning the screen lurched forward and fell with a clatter on the floor in front of us.

Chloris gave a scream, instantly hushed.

Merton was standing where the screen had been. He was almost as tall as the doorway behind him. He wore nothing but his shirt and nightcap but he was holding a raised sword. Its blade dropped and pointed at me. The tip swung towards Chloris.

'No, sir,' she wheedled, 'no, Mr Merton. Don't be unkind to poor Chloris. Not after all the pleasure we've given each other. See what I got for you . . .'

There was no conviction in her voice. But she held out her hand, which was empty. For an instant the movement distracted his attention from me. I flung the crow at him.

The iron bar caught him on the side of the head. Surprise as much as the force of the blow made him take a step back. Hammer in hand, I rushed towards him. I had no other choice. But he had already recovered and, with the speed of a trained swordsman, he riposted. The blade leapt towards my chest. It was too late for me to attempt a parry. Indeed the impetus of my own advance increased the force of his thrust.

The tip of his sword hammered into my chest with a force that drove the air from my lungs. The impact flung me backwards. But the sword's tip did not penetrate my skin. The blade recoiled.

I glimpsed the astonishment in Merton's eyes. Chloris seized a chair and hit him with it. He tripped on the corner of the hearth and staggered against the wall. Again he recovered, and jabbed at her with the sword. She screamed. I ran towards them. She dropped the chair and fell back. I swung the hammer down on Merton's head.

There was a dull thud, followed by a gasp. The force of the blow made him crumple. His head was now resting against the wall. I hit him again, harder this time and with the wall behind him. The head of the hammer sank into his skull. Something broke. The sword fell from his hand.

I stood like one paralysed. Chloris stared at me, her face white, and her hand over her mouth. I could not believe the evidence of my eyes. I could not believe what I had done.

Someone shouted down below. The spell broke. I left the hammer where it was, for I could not bear to wrench it out. I snatched up Merton's sword. 'Quick.'

Chloris stumbled through the door, and I followed her into the closet and out on to the landing. There were voices somewhere, both men's and women's, shouting and shrieking. I pulled her towards the stairs.

It was only when we reached the next

landing that I saw the drops of blood on the bare boards behind us. Chloris had her other hand pressed tightly against her side to staunch the flow. But the blood was trickling between her fingers.

'I need . . . I need to . . .'

'We can't stop.'

I dragged her up the last flight of stairs. Mary took one look at us and she screamed. I put down the sword and let go of Chloris, who propped herself against the wall. I pulled the bed in front of the door. There was so little space I contrived to wedge it against the opposite wall.

'I'm going through the window,' I said to the girl. 'Bring her over to me, and I'll haul her across.'

A greater fear drives out a lesser. I crossed from one window to the other as easily as if I had been doing it twice a day for years. Mary helped Chloris to the window. I gripped her wrists. I leaned across and, with Mary's help, transferred her from one attic to the other. For a moment, as I dragged her through the window, her eyes met mine. Her eyelids fluttered. She slumped on to the floor and groaned.

I turned back to the window.

'What about me, sir?' Mary said. 'They'll kill me.'

481

I heard the hammering on the door.

'They won't. Tell them I held the sword to your throat.'

'Take me with you. I beg you, master. She said you would.'

I looked at the pale, unhappy child, barefoot and pregnant in her shift. 'Oh, for God's sake.'

I held out my hands to her and drew her over the alley into the attic. Compared to Chloris, she had no weight at all. I shut the window and latched it.

There was a sharp cry behind me. Chloris had rolled on to her side and curled up her legs. The blood was pooling under her, spreading across the floor. Her face was white. She was trying to say something, but the words were inaudible.

I knelt beside her. Her hand plucked at my sleeve. 'Leave me,' she said. 'Take Mary, take her away.' She released me and pawed at herself. 'Give her my cloak. She —'

Her hand fell to the floor. Her head slumped. Her eyes were still open. Mary cried out, a high wail.

I heard the sound of splitting wood from the house over the way. They would be through the attic door in an instant.

I snatched the cloaks from the bed.

'Quick,' I said to Mary. 'Take her shoes and shawl.'

'Who the devil are you?' Pheebs said.

The woman was standing in the street, and her head barely reached his waist. She looked up at him. She had a broad, high-coloured face. She said, 'Margaret, sir. For Mistress Hakesby.'

'What's Mistress Hakesby want with the likes of you?'

As Pheebs spoke, he ran his eyes up and down the woman. A plump partridge, he thought, not as young as he liked them. But big enough in the right places and probably soft if you squeezed her hard to make her squeal. Nothing wrong with a bundletail.

'I take in washing,' the woman said. Her dark eyes stared at him. 'I do mending too, if needed.'

'Touting for work. I see. Be off with you.'

'But she asked me to come.'

The woman looked past him at the boy, who was leaning against the wall, as the idle rogue always did when Pheebs wasn't looking. He was carrying the kindling basket.

'If you don't believe me, send your lad up with my name. You'll see. Margaret Wither-dine. She asked for me most particular.'

Pheebs shrugged. He said over his shoulder. 'Hear that, boy? Margaret Withers for Mistress Hakesby.'

'Witherdine,' the woman said.

Pheebs ignored her. 'Hop up and find out if this one's lying or not.'

The boy abandoned the basket and ran for the stairs.

'Stop,' Pheebs shouted. The boy obeyed. 'Take their kindling up with you, you numskull. Why haven't you done it already?'

One of the drawbacks of being a married woman was that it was difficult to be alone. But it could be done. This morning Cat had sent the maid to collect a pair of shoes from the cobbler and order their dinner. Her husband was upstairs in the Drawing Office with Brennan.

Early yesterday morning, Cat had retrieved the package from the coal scuttle. Later, she had rinsed the worst of the filth from it with a rag soaked in the water the maid brought her to wash in. Yet again she had been struck by the fine stitching. She hid the package in the press where she kept the bed hangings and curtains for the summer months.

The unwanted responsibility lay heavily on her. She had hoped that Elizabeth would call on her yesterday and remove the problem. But she hadn't come. Why not? If Buckingham was still having the Drawing Office watched, he could hardly object to Elizabeth coming to see Cat, though he might think it an unnecessary risk.

Cat was tempted to take the cursed package downstairs and let the night soil men take it away. On the other hand, though, the horrid thing had an unhealthy fascination for her, as did a guilty secret.

She went into the bedchamber and opened the press. In a moment, she had the parcel in her hands. She carried it to the window and felt it carefully. A long box or case, she thought; in cross section it was rectangular but not square. A slight protrusion halfway down one side was probably made by a catch securing the lid of a box.

If she opened the packet, at least she would know what she was dealing with. Was she not entitled to do so, since she was running the risk of keeping it? She felt in her pocket for her knife. The blade was thin with much sharpening, and it tapered to a fine point.

She pushed the tip into one of those perfect loops of thread. The stitch sprang apart. She paused. Dear God, there were scores of stitches, if not hundreds, double- and treble-stitched as if the seamstress–it had to be a woman–had found it hard to surrender the package.

Footsteps were coming up the stairs. Cat swore under her breath and pushed the bundle under the curtains at the bottom of the press. She straightened, brushing a fragment of thread from her skirt.

There was a knocking. She went through to the parlour and opened the door. The porter's boy almost fell into the room.

'What is it?' she said. 'Oh the kindling. At last. There was barely enough this morning. Put it by the fire.'

He obeyed, saying over his shoulder, 'Mr Pheebs says there's a woman asking for you. A washerwoman. Name of Margaret.'

'We've already got a washerwoman,' Cat said. 'No–not by the scuttle. On the other side.'

He set down the basket, took out the kindling and stacked it neatly on the hearth. 'She said most particular that you'd asked her to call on you.'

'I didn't. I want you to chop some more kindling this afternoon. There's never enough. Chop some of it smaller this time, would you? And we need more shavings, too.'

He ducked his head, acknowledging the order. 'Her name's Wither . . . Witherdine.'

'What did you say?'

'Margaret Witherdine, mistress.'

For a moment Cat said nothing. Then: 'Yes, of course. That one.' She hesitated. 'Yes, I did ask for her. She takes in fine laundry. You'd better send her up. Off you go.'

The boy clattered down the stairs. Cat waited. The parlour door was still ajar. She heard Margaret's footsteps approaching, slow and deliberate. She came in, breathing heavily from the exertion, and curtsied.

'Close the door,' Cat said. 'What are you doing here?'

'Master sent me.' Margaret sniffed. 'In the middle of the morning, mark you, and me with a list of tasks to do that would fill a week.' She took a letter, much creased, from her pocket. 'For you.'

Cat broke the seal. There was neither date nor salutation. It was unsigned. But she recognized the handwriting.

It has been reported that you went to WH yesterday evening in company with a certain clergyman. They will soon bring you and H in for questioning. Send word by the bearer if you will talk to me first, and as soon as possible. It is most urgent, for your sake. I must know where you stand, and whether you might alter your mind. Pray destroy this.

Conscious of Margaret's eyes on her, Cat read the letter twice. Afterwards, she crumpled it into a ball and threw it on the fire. Pale flames flickered along the edges. When the paper was ablaze, she turned back to Margaret.

'Did he bid you tell me anything as well?'

Margaret shook her head. 'No. Just to wait for an answer.'

'How are you all?'

'Truth is, mistress, the house is topsy turvy.' Margaret's face blazed, not with exertion but with anger. 'It's that cursed woman.'

Cat stared at her. 'A woman? What woman?'

'Some doxy he brought back. Oh yes, she looks demure as you please, I grant her that. You'd think she goes to chapel thrice every Sunday. Master says she's to help me in the kitchen for a day or two before she goes back to the country. Says she's a maidservant. Oh no she ain't, not in any way. I can tell a bawd when I see one. Sam doesn't know what to do with himself, the poor fool. Master has her up in his bedchamber, all by themselves when he's in his gown, and she gives him sly looks when she thinks I'm not looking. And besides'–Margaret paused, squeezing her lips before launching her most damning argument–'she calls herself Chloris, and if that's not a punk's name, I don't know what is.'

'How long has this been going on?' Cat was suddenly furious, and her voice was louder than she intended. 'How did he find her?'

'He came back with her Monday evening. He said he'd been set upon by footpads, and —'

'Footpads? What happened?'

'I only know what they told me, and that ain't much. He'd lost his purse, and his wig and his shoes too. That's true enough. He says she found him lying in the gutter and helped him back out of the kindness of her heart.' Margaret inflated her cheeks and let out her breath in a rush of outrage. 'If you believe that, you'd believe the fairies fill the pot under your bed with gold coins every night.'

'Footpads . . .' Cat repeated. 'Do you know any more than that?'

'Sam says he's a sly dog, master is, didn't think he had it in him. I give him a clout for that.'

'Your master wants to talk to me.'

'Oh please do, mistress. Talk some sense into him. If anyone can, it's you. He went out with the whore at break of day–God knows where they are, but I can guess what they're —'

Cat held up her hand, and Margaret stopped. They heard the tap of a stick and slow, dragging footsteps in the room above their heads.

'My husband's on his way down.' Cat had made up her mind. 'I can't come to Infirmary Lane. Mr Hakesby wouldn't care for it.' She hesitated. 'Besides, if I leave the house, I may be followed.'

Alarm flared in Margaret's face. 'Someone's watching you?'

The footsteps were already on the stairs.

'It's possible. For that reason, Mr Marwood can't come to me here. Or not by the street door.'

'What's going on, mistress?'

'But if he wants, he could come by Maiden Lane,' Cat said, ignoring the question. 'Do you know it? It runs behind Henrietta Street, and the back gates of our houses are on the left-hand side. Ours is the eighth one along. Tell your master to come at seven this evening. I doubt they're watching the back as well. I'll be in the garden, and the gate to the lane will be unbarred.'

Margaret repeated the message, first aloud in a whisper, and then to herself, her lips moving silently as she framed each word.

The parlour door opened. Hakesby shuffled into the room, leaning on his stick. His face was drawn with pain or anxiety; perhaps both.

He frowned. 'Who's this?'

'A laundry woman, sir–she takes lace and fine needlework, and she will do some mending for us.' Cat turned back to Margaret. 'Leave us. I'll send for you when I need you. A trial piece first, I think, to see if I like your work.'

Eyes downcast, Margaret curtsied low with uncharacteristic humility. 'Yes, mistress. And thank you, mistress, thank you, master. God bless you.'

She left the room. Hakesby continued his slow progress towards the privacy of his closet.

Cat waited until she heard him bolting the closet door to ensure that no one could disturb him. Then, with a sudden spurt of fury, she made a fist of her right hand and hammered it on the table with all her strength. The pain made her gasp. It was all she could do not to shout.

How dared Marwood indulge in such folly? To sport with a whore in his own house. She shouldn't be surprised, she supposed. Now he had money, there was nothing to stop him in these dissolute times. All men were the same under the skin. Old or young, rich or poor, puritan or libertine–it made no difference. If you peeled away their outer seeming, you found that they all carried inside them the same muddle of lusts and failings. They cared only for themselves and for the satisfaction of their brutish needs.

Not that it mattered. Not a jot. Not a tittle. She would see him as much for her husband's sake as her own. She owed a wife's duty to her husband, though in truth she cared nothing for any man. Especially not for James Marwood.

With a last glance at Chloris's body at the foot of the bed, I clambered down the ladder from the attic. Mary followed. We ran down the stairs as fast as we could. The old crow emerged from the rear of the house as we reached the ground floor.

It was fully light now, and the old woman could see that I was no longer with Chloris. She started swearing at me. Then she saw the naked sword in my hand. She backed away but I rested the tip of the blade on her chest.

'Open the door, mistress, and no harm will come to you.'

She obeyed. I pushed Mary outside and backed over the threshold behind her, with the sword still raised. The door slammed in my face.

I took Mary's arm and urged her down the steps. Her face was as pale as Chloris's had been just before she died. We walked along the alley. I realized that I was still carrying Merton's sword. I could hardly saunter unnoticed down Long Acre with such a weapon in my hand, so I let it fall.

We came out of the alley and into the street. It was busy now, and the shops were open. Mary stumbled, and I knew that she was close to collapse.

We weren't out of danger. Madam Cresswell's people would soon find Chloris, if they hadn't already. They knew she had helped me to escape on Monday, so they might well suspect that I had been her companion this morning. The old crow had seen my face. Buckingham's men knew where I lived.

I steered Mary to the right and then to the left up Drury Lane. We were going north, away from the Savoy. I saw a sign for an alehouse and I drew Mary inside. It was a mean place, crowded with labourers and artisans taking their morning draught. There were a few women, too, though not of the respectable sort, and a handful of shabbily dressed tradesmen. In the clothes we were wearing, neither Mary nor I looked out of place.

I found a place for us on a bench to one side. I grabbed the arm of a passing potboy and ordered a jug of small beer. I glanced at Mary, who was leaning against the wall with her eyes closed, and ordered the lad to bring us milk and rolls as well.

'We don't have them, master.'

'Yes, you do. Go and buy some.' I dropped a shilling in his hand. 'There'll be two more of those when you bring them. As long as you don't make us wait.'

When we were alone, I looked at her again. The shift she had worn in bed was decently covered with Chloris's cloak, and her head with Margaret's shawl. She wore Chloris's shoes on her feet. They were too big for her. She was like a girl trying on her mother's shoes.

We sat in silence. I stared straight in front of me. My thoughts and my feelings were as frozen as a pond in winter. I was vaguely aware that our neighbours were talking about the riots yesterday. Early though it was, the apprentices and their allies were already on the streets. So were the militia and the King's guards. It did not interest me. Nothing interested me.

The food and drink came within minutes. Mary opened her eyes. She snatched one of the rolls. She tore fragments from it and stuffed them in her mouth. She was chewing and trying to swallow at the same time.

'There's no hurry, girl,' I said. 'Calm yourself.'

She ignored me. She took a draught of milk and then seized another roll. Even as her fingers were ripping it apart, her face changed. She raised her eyes to me, and they were full of fear.

Then she bent forward and puked up her breakfast over my shoes.

'I shall go to Henrietta Street today,' Elizabeth Cromwell said as she and her father took their morning walk in Mistress Dalton's garden.

'Is that wise?'

'I believe so. At any rate, I'm quite decided.'

Her father sighed. 'If Catherine has truly found what my mother hid, there's no hurry to get it back. I trust her entirely. And Hakesby. Don't you?'

Elizabeth said nothing. When her father

had left England, all those years ago, she had been little more than a child, and she had never questioned his authority over her. But now she was a grown woman and these last few weeks had modified her opinion of him. She still owed him her duty and her love but, to tell truth, he often irritated her. Her father lived far away and he could not even provide for his family. Sometimes it seemed to her that time had reversed their roles: that she had become the wise, sober parent, and he the reckless child.

'My mother's legacy can wait,' he said. 'I have more important things to do. I promised the Duke that I would write something for him to show our friends, a public statement to make clear my support. It's for the good of the country. And if–when–matters move forward as we hope they will, he will have it printed and distributed: in the provinces as well as London.'

'Sir,' she said, losing patience at last, 'these are castles in the air.'

'No, no. The Duke is not only a good man at bottom, he's a man of great parts and a shrewd leader.'

Elizabeth bit her lip. Her father had a foolish tendency to see only the best in others and to believe what he was told. Perhaps that was why he had let them make him

Lord Protector when Oliver died. Perhaps that was why he was now a penniless exile from the country he had ruled.

She reined in her vexation. 'With your permission, sir, I shall go to Henrietta Street.'

'But it's too dangerous,' he said.

She shook her head. She thought it worth the risk. If her grandmother's legacy was worth the having, it could make her father financially independent of Buckingham.

'If I go this evening–at six or seven, perhaps–I can manage it discreetly.' She smiled at him, trying to coax him. 'It would be better to relieve the Hakesbys of the responsibility. There's no need for you to come if you are occupied with business. In fact it would be safer if you didn't.'

He shrugged and looked away. She knew she had won.

'My dear,' he said, 'I suppose you must do as you think best.'

It was the middle of the morning before I hailed a hackney for us in High Holborn. Mary sat opposite me, her eyes squeezed shut. We travelled by fits and starts through the streets to the Strand.

The coach dropped us at the main gate of the Savoy. As we passed under the arch I glanced about me, but I saw no one who might be watching out for me, only the usual beggars who clustered there as much out of habit as in expectation of receiving alms. I hurried Mary into Infirmary Close.

'Where are we, sir?' she asked.

'My house. You'll be safe here.'

Her face showed her disbelief. She began to cry.

Sam opened the door to us. His eyes widened when he saw Mary beside me. I pushed the girl inside and followed.

'Where's the other one?' he said.

'Bar the doors.'

'Trouble again, master?'

'Just do it. Any visitors?' I pushed open the parlour door. 'Anything suspicious?'

'Not a thing. But —'

'Look to your arms, just in case. Send Margaret to me at once.'

I drew Mary into the room and told her to sit on the bench along one side of the table. She sat down and, without removing the cloak or the shawl, rested her head on her arms, and her arms on the table.

I threw down my hat and cloak. A great weariness welled up inside me. My stomach hurt through my clenching the muscles there so tightly for so long. I slumped into the elbow chair by the unlit fire. With my mind's eye I saw Chloris lying curled in the pool of blood, the pool that grew larger every second. I saw the hammer embedded in Merton's head. I saw Merton's face.

I had caused the poor girl's death with my foolish, fantastical scheme. I had killed a man. I had snuffed a man's life for ever. True, he had attacked me. But my first blow with the hammer would have been enough to disable him. I had not needed to hit him again. I had not needed to hit him so hard. I had not needed to make sure he was dead.

Running footsteps crossed the hall. Margaret burst into the parlour without knocking. She stood looking at us for a moment. I raised my head and looked back.

'Master,' she said, 'master . . . what is this? Who's this? And where's that other woman?'

'She won't be coming back.' I gestured towards the huddled figure on the bench. She was shivering as if she would never stop. 'This child is called Mary. She has been much abused in her past employment. Take her down and warm her by the kitchen fire. She will stay with us for a day or two.'

'Master . . .' Margaret repeated. 'I went out this morning, as you commanded. I —'

I waved a hand, cutting her short. 'Later.'

She and I stared at each other for a moment. She went over to Mary and put an arm around her shoulders. 'Come, my dear,' she said. 'Master's right. We must warm you by the fire.'

They left me. I sat alone in the parlour. I thought about Chloris. I would never know her real name now. She had told me she wanted to go home, to the village near Bristol where someone was waiting for her. Or so she had believed.

I sat undisturbed in that chair for the better part of an hour. Guilt and distress made me torpid. My chest was hurting on the left side, in the region where I assumed my heart lay. I pressed it and felt a twinge of discomfort. I also discovered that Raleigh's *History of the World* was still in the pocket. I removed it and stared at the flaking leather cover.

A book had saved my life.

There was a wound in the cover, almost exactly in the middle. The *History* had taken the full force of Merton's thrust. The tip of the sword had gouged a ragged hole into the leather and penetrated the board beneath. I flipped the book open. The blade had pierced only the first few pages inside. A book printed in sexto-decimo, as this one was, is only about four inches wide and seven inches high. But this one had many pages. A child can poke a finger through a single sheet of paper. But several hundred sheets are a different matter. They make a barrier quite sufficient to stop a sword.

I took out the papers I had taken from Buckingham's desk, the whole purpose of my sorry expedition which had led to two deaths. I smoothed out the papers and laid them on the table. They were certainly in the Duke's hand. I picked up a sheet and angled it to the light from the window:

THE REHEARSAL
ACTUS I. SCÆNA I.

A Street near the Theatre Royal \ Drury Lane \ Johnson and Smith

JOHNS: Honest Frank, I'm glad to see thee with all my heart: how long hast thou been in Town?

SMI: Faith, not above an hour: and, if I had not met you here, I had gone to look you out; for I long to talk with you freely, of all the strange new things we have heard in the Country.

JOHNS: And, by my troth, I have long'd as much to laugh with you, at all the impertinent, dull, fantastical things, we are tir'd out with here.

SMI: Dull, and fantastical! that's an

excellent composition. Pray, what are our men of business doing?

I muttered an oath. It was nothing but a fragment of a cursed play. So Buckingham desired to be a playwright. It was typical of him that he must try his hand at drama, as well as everything else. It was clearly not enough for him to plot to take over the government, to fill London with rioters, to cuckold and then kill a brother peer, and to indulge himself in a bawdy house of his very own. The Duke had too many advantages, I thought sourly, and too many talents, for any one man, and he seemed incapable of using any of them well. With a sweep of my arm, I sent the sheets of paper fluttering to the floor, along with Raleigh's *History* for good measure.

I instantly regretted my petulance and stooped to pick them up. Most of the sheets of paper were blank on one side, for Buckingham of all people was not a man to practise economy. But one sheet was different. It had writing on both sides: the first contained more dialogue from the play, but the other, though scored through diagonally and heavily annotated, was instantly familiar to me:

. . . these ill home-bred slaves ~~and apprentices~~ That threaten your destruction as well as ours that so your ladyship may escape our present calamity. Else we know not how soon it may be your honour's own case: for should your ~~ladyship~~ eminency but once fall into these ~~rude~~ rough hands, you may expect ~~to be thrown on your back and roughly ravished by the grimy multitude~~ no more favour than they have shown unto us poor inferior whores . . .

Against all expectation I had achieved my aim. Here was a fragment from an early draft of the whores' petition to Lady Castlemaine. And it was in Buckingham's own hand.

CHAPTER SIXTEEN

A Bird in the Night
Wednesday, 25 March 1668

In covent garden where nothing grows, the boys bait him. Whooping and screeching, they chase him.

Like before, when Master went to Fulton's. When Ferrus saw the lady.

Ferrus waves his arms up and down, and he runs. He runs up and down Henrietta Street, around and around the Piazza, in and out of the arcades. He trips. The stones are hard-hearted. Blood pours from his nose. A woman screams. Up again, quick as a wink, and running and running, faster than the wind.

I fly. Breath hissing and gasping, sucking in oaths and cries. A bird without no master. I fly.

I fly to Henrietta Street again. Down the road, round the corner and into a smaller street. Oh. The end is blocked with a high wall.

But an alley winds away from the street. There's a doorway tucked in the wall. Withered weeds half choke it.

Ferrus stands in the doorway. Like a redcoat in a sentry box outside the Great Gate of Whitehall. Doorway smells of urine, quite fresh.

Out of the wind here, out of the rain. Boys can't see him.

Someone's whistling in the street. He peers out. It's a boy, but not one like the others. This one strolls along and kicks pebbles.

Oh . . .

It's the boy who was waiting outside Fulton's when grandpa man was talking to master inside. When lady talked to Ferrus and Ferrus ran away. Boy is lady's servant.

The boy, in a world of his own, raises the latch of the gate almost opposite the alley. He goes inside. The gate closes behind him. Click-clack.

Light bursts inside Ferrus's head. This gate is the way to the lady's house.

I sent for Margaret and said I would dine at home. It was already two o'clock.

'There's nothing ready, master—we weren't

505

expecting you. Shall I send out?'

'No. I'm pressed for time–I go to Whitehall this afternoon. Anything will do. Bread, cheese. But first–how did you fare at the sign of the Rose?'

'I saw Mistress Hakesby, sir, gave her your letter privately.' Margaret was looking anxious, as she so often did these days. 'She says it's best you don't come to the street door. Go round to Maiden Lane at the back at seven o'clock tonight. Theirs is the eighth gate along. She'll make sure it isn't barred, and she'll meet you in the garden.'

I sent her away. But she stopped at the door.

'What happened, sir? Where's that woman gone? Chloris.'

'She . . . she's gone away. That's all you need to know.'

'What about her bundle, sir? It's in the kitchen.'

I remembered the twenty pounds in gold. 'Send Stephen up with it. I'll deal with it.'

'And the other one? The little maid? She's in a bad way. She sits and cries by the fire with a bowl on her lap.'

'She's suffered much. Has she told you she's with child?'

'I guessed as much. You can tell by looking at her. That and the puking. She's half starved, as well as all the bruises on her.'

'I don't know what we'll do with her.'

'We won't turn her out,' Margaret said, and the way she said the words placed them halfway between a statement and a question.

'No,' I said, thinking of poor dead Chloris. 'We won't turn her out.'

There was no sign of the gold in Chloris's bundle. She must have had it concealed about the clothes she was wearing. Madam Cresswell had probably seized it, or perhaps the old crow next door.

After I had eaten, Wanswell rowed me up to Whitehall. I had the papers I had stolen from Buckingham in my pocket, and also Raleigh's *History of the World.* Cat had made me buy the book, and this morning it had saved my life. Perhaps it would act as a charm and protect me now.

It wasn't raining, but it was bitterly cold on the water. I huddled into my cloak and closed my eyes. I wanted to hide myself away and sleep for ever.

I had played a part in two deaths this morning. The knowledge weighed heavily on me, and I feared it always would. True, Merton would have killed me without a second thought. But I was not a man like

Merton, I hoped, yet I had killed him when there had been no need to do so. As for Chloris, Merton's sword had run her through, but the responsibility for her death lay squarely with me. Guilt lingered like an overeager actor in the wings of my mind, ready to rush on stage whenever it could.

Nor were my troubles over. The last thing I wanted to do this evening was to have a whispered argument with Cat Hakesby at her garden gate. True, I had written evidence against Buckingham in my pocket. If nothing else, that should lessen the danger of Williamson's bringing in the Hakesbys for questioning. But it didn't make me easier in my mind about her intrigues with the Cromwells.

Wanswell was bringing the boat towards the shore, deftly negotiating the cluster of craft near to the riverside frontage of the palace. He landed me at the public stairs. I walked through the courts to Williamson's office in Scotland Yard. I was wary. I didn't know whether Buckingham's men were on the alert for me, but it was safer to assume that they were.

In the office, I knew at once that Williamson was not in his private room by the lively hum of conversation. Abbott was playing dice on the windowsill with one of the juniors. The noise slackened as I came in, for I was more senior than most, but it did not cease.

'Where is he?' I said. 'At my lord's?'

'No.' Abbott grinned. 'Called away on business. He won't be back till tomorrow morning. Lord Arlington's away too.'

'Pox on it,' I muttered, my hand on the door.

'Cheer up, Marwood. Heard the news?'

'What news?'

'They say there are tens of thousands out in Moorfields today. The apprentices have been throwing stones at the red coats then running away like the devil. Then they come together and start again. They've been attacking the New Prison again too. And there's a petition doing the rounds. It'll crack your sides. It's a satire, it's meant to be from the whores to —'

'I know all about it,' I said, cutting him off.

Abbott looked hurt but only for a moment. He was not a man to nurse a grudge. Waving towards the dice, he said: 'Would you care to —'

I didn't hear the end of his sentence. I left the room and slammed the door.

It was after five o'clock when Elizabeth

Cromwell left Mistress Dalton's house in a hackney coach, leaving her father at work on his papers in the parlour. For decency's sake, she was accompanied by two of her hostess's household–the elderly manservant who had escorted her to St James's Park on Monday, and one of the maids, a plump child terrified of her mistress and indeed of almost everyone else.

'Make sure the girl attends you at all times,' her father said as they were leaving. 'I would not have you lay yourself open to malicious gossip. And Giles will keep you from harm if you should chance to encounter the rioters.'

The risk of malicious gossip, Elizabeth thought, was the least of their problems. And Giles, who was sixty if he was a day, was unlikely to be able to deal with a recalcitrant child, let alone with a crowd of drunken apprentices.

During the journey, she heard the church clocks striking the half hour. She wished the coachman would drive faster. Her fingers were tightly knotted together on her lap. So much depended on the consequence of this visit. Her father was increasingly infatuated with Buckingham and his intrigues. If her grandmother's legacy were sufficiently substantial, Elizabeth would stand a far better chance of persuading her father to go back to the relative safety of Paris. Perhaps there would even be money left over for the rest of them.

The coach turned off Holborn into Drury Lane. Not far now.

It was fortunate that Catherine Hakesby was honest. She was also foolish. Why on earth had she married that terrible old husband of hers, who quaked like an aspen, and forced Catherine to work for their living? Her hands were red and chapped; not like a lady's hands any more. Even with a regicide father, she could have done much better for herself.

The three of them swayed as the coachman took the corner into James Street too fast. The maid gave a squeal, instantly suppressed.

Everything depended on what Catherine had found in the Cockpit. On the principle that no source of assistance should be overlooked in a time of crisis, Elizabeth closed her eyes and prayed briefly and fervently that Grandmama's legacy would consist of a vast quantity of gold or jewels, if not both.

Bless my father, she added as an afterthought as they turned into Covent Garden, and teach him to be wise. Through Christ Our Lord, Amen.

When Cat heard the knock, she was sitting at the table in the parlour and trying to restore the accounts to a semblance of order. Mr Hakesby had gone through a pile of invoices and receipts this afternoon. During his examination of them, they had somehow fallen on the floor and were now in a state of confusion.

'Come in,' she called, thinking it was Brennan or the maid.

The door opened, and there was Elizabeth Cromwell on the threshold. 'Catty,' she cried, advancing into the room with her hands outstretched and bringing with her a waft of expensively perfumed air. 'My love—how do you do?'

Cat rose to greet her. 'Thank you, I'm well. And you? And Mr Cromwell?'

'Oh well enough. My poor father has a maggot in his brain at present and will not see sense, but I mustn't trouble you with my woes. How did you enjoy the Duke's party the other night? Isn't Wallingford House fine? But some of the company was so dreary. I should have died of boredom if you'd not been there.'

'Have you come here quite alone?' Cat

512

said, wishing that Elizabeth had chosen some other time to come. 'Is your father with you?'

'No–but pray don't concern yourself–you are always so solicitous of others, are you not?–I've a maid below in the coach, and Mistress Dalton's Giles as well. He brought me safely to the door, and your porter let me up unannounced. He remembered my face, and he knew I was a friend. You train your servants well.'

The devil could take Pheebs and welcome, Cat thought. She would have to speak to him about sending up people without warning. Elizabeth's visit could hardly have been worse timed.

'Pray sit down. Can I offer you —'

'No, nothing, thank you.' Elizabeth dropped her cloak on a chair and sat down. 'Only–oh Catty, you must guess why I'm here. What you said to me on the stairs at Wallingford House. I've been thinking about it ever since. Have you–have you found something?'

'I wasn't the one who found it. Ferrus did.'

Elizabeth looked blankly at her. 'Who?'

'The very tall thin man. Do you remember? The mazer scourer's labourer, or whatever he was.'

Elizabeth gave a little shiver. 'Oh yes. That one.'

'It's a package. He gave it to me on Monday afternoon, as I was leaving. I don't know what's in it. I assume it's what you're looking for, but I can't even be sure of that. You see, Ferrus couldn't tell me where he'd found it. He's dumb, you know.'

The tip of Elizabeth's tongue moistened her lips. 'Is it . . . is it here?'

'I'll fetch it.'

'Stay–where's Mr Hakesby?'

'It's all right. He's working upstairs. The maid's out. No one should disturb us.'

Cat rose and went into the bedchamber, closing the door behind her, shutting out Elizabeth's avid gaze. The package was where she had left it, in the press with the summer bed hangings and curtains. She retrieved it and, for a moment, weighed it in her hand.

On the other side of the road, St Paul's clock struck the third quarter. She had not realized the time was so advanced. She had to get rid of Elizabeth and her cursed package as soon as possible. She was due to meet Marwood at seven. He would come, and he would be on time. She knew that without examining the reason for her certainty. She had already bribed the porter's boy to leave open the garden gate.

She went back into the parlour, where Elizabeth was drumming her fingers softly on the table. Cat laid the parcel on the table before her.

Elizabeth touched it. She turned down the corners of her mouth. 'Is this all?'

'It's all that Ferrus gave me.'

Elizabeth weighed the package in her hand. There was still dirt on it and she glanced automatically at her fingertips, frowning when she saw the dark smudges on them. Now that she had it within her grasp, she seemed in no hurry to open it. She examined the stitching.

'I can believe my grandmother made these stitches,' she said slowly. 'She always sewed more than was needed when she mended something. She . . . she liked sewing, you know.'

'Forgive me, but I'm pressed for time. Could you not take it away and open it later?'

'But I must open it. Immediately.'

'Then shall I cut the stitches for you?'

Elizabeth glanced at her, her eyes wide and dazed. She put the parcel on the table and pushed it towards Cat. 'It can't be gold, can it? Wouldn't gold be heavier?'

Cat took the knife from her pocket and

sliced through the stitches. She worked with deliberation, conscious of Elizabeth's eyes on her, and conscious too of the other woman's swift, shallow breathing. When the last stitch parted, the package remained wrapped. After all these years, the oiled canvas was reluctant to release its contents.

'Pray let me,' Elizabeth said, and stretched out her hand.

She unwrapped the package, peeling the canvas away. There was another covering beneath, this one made of thick paper, which she tore off with greedy fingers. Then came a layer of thick black broadcloth. She pushed it aside.

'Oh,' she said, and her lips made a perfect O.

Elizabeth lifted out a case covered with dark green leather and secured by a golden clasp. It had rounded corners and a lid that was slightly domed. In the centre of the lid was a small shield, made like the clasp of gold, for it was untarnished. She breathed on it, and the condensation threw the design into relief.

'I don't know the arms,' she said in an undertone, to herself. 'Five roundels . . . and at the top another, larger one. With something inside it?'

Her fingers shook like Hakesby's when she

released the catch. Despite herself, Cat craned her head to see what was inside. First was a folded sheet of paper, which Elizabeth brushed aside. And then —

'Pearls,' Elizabeth said. 'And oh–what pearls.'

She held up the necklace. It hung from her fingers in a lustrous cascade. The pearls were large, perhaps half an inch in diameter or even more. They looked symmetrical and perfectly matched.

'Oh,' Elizabeth repeated. 'Oh, Catty. This was worth the trouble indeed. My aunt Fauconberg once showed me a string of pearls she said was worth nigh on twenty thousand pounds. And they were not half so fine as this.'

'And the paper?'

Elizabeth laid the pearls gently into their case. She unfolded the paper. 'It's my grandmother's hand. "A gift to the Lady Protectoress, Mistress Cromwell, from the Grand Duke of Tuscany, April 1655." There. That settles it, does it not? A personal gift to my grandmother. It belongs to her heirs, therefore, and to no one else.'

Cat doubted that the King or his ministers would agree. She stretched out her hand and, almost against her will, laid a finger on one of the pearls. It felt cold and unloved.

'No, pray don't touch.' Elizabeth drew the case away from her and fastened the lid. 'I thank you from the bottom of my heart for all you've done.' She smiled without warmth. 'But I mustn't trespass any more on your time.' Her face changed. 'That is–I hardly like to say this–do you think it possible there might be more?'

Cat frowned. 'What do you mean?'

'Well perhaps this man–what was his name?'

'Ferrus?' Cat's anger was rising steadily.

'Yes, Ferrus–perhaps he took this, but left other things. Who knows? Did the fellow strike you as trustworthy? Do you think he might —'

'No.' Cat said. 'No. Pray leave it. Enough is enough.'

'But my love —' There were heavy footsteps on the stairs. 'Is that Mr Hakesby?'

'No. Someone's coming up, not down.'

Elizabeth tried to push the case into her pocket, but there wasn't room. She placed it on the chair beside her and covered it with her cloak.

The footsteps reached the landing. They paused. They did not continue up the stairs that led to the Drawing Office. Instead the parlour door flew open.

Roger Durrell's large figure filled the

doorframe. He stared at them. 'Well, well. Your servant, ladies.'

He advanced slowly into the room, eyes roving from side to side. The sheath of his sword collided with a chair leg. The smell of beer and tobacco mingled with Elizabeth's perfume.

'Well, ain't this a blessed thing?' Durrell said. 'The Lord be praised in all His glory. Two little birds with one big fat stone.' He cast his eyes up to heaven. 'But in fact I only want one of them.'

That evening I went alone. I had toyed with the idea of bringing Sam—he was a useful man in a difficult situation, and he could have kept watch for me. But his stump made him both slow and noticeable. Besides, this matter had nothing to do with him. It concerned Cat and me. After what had happened to Chloris this morning, I did not want to throw another innocent person in the way of danger.

Maiden Lane was no distance. I left the Savoy by one of the side gates. I carried a weighted stick but I was not otherwise armed. After this morning, I was weary of bloodshed.

It was raining, the moisture drifting invisibly and unkindly from heaven. Perhaps the weather would dampen the enthusiasm of the rioters. I crossed the Strand by the Black Bull Tavern and went up Half Moon Passage. Within a few yards, the alley widened and became Bedford Street. At this point, Maiden Lane went off on the right-hand side, leading east. The lane was blind, for the far end was closed off by the high garden wall of Bedford House.

It was growing dark, and I walked cautiously along the street to avoid both the gutter and the gathering shadows. To the right, or south side, was an irregular line of houses of the middling sort, whose residents would be neither wealthy nor fashionable. Among them were the entries of one or two narrow paths winding down to the Strand; they were best avoided after nightfall. To my left were outbuildings and gates. These belonged to the more substantial houses of Henrietta Street to the north, from which they were separated by their gardens and yards.

I counted as I went: the eighth gate along, Cat had said, and at seven o'clock. I found it about halfway along. It was more substantial than I had expected, and with an inset wicket. Beside it was an outhouse that might have been a coach house or stable with a loft above. From the lane, I could see only the top storey of the house, which was where the Drawing Office was. Its large windows glowed faintly with light.

I should not have long to wait. I raised the latch of the wicket and pulled it gently towards me. The gate opened. I stepped into the garden beyond. Something rustled behind me.

A cat, I thought, or a rat.

Ferrus watches the man open the lady's gate. In he goes. He closes the gate behind him.

No dog barks.

All the time he has been standing in this piss-scented doorway, Ferrus hasn't heard a dog bark behind that gate. He misses Windy. A sense of loss threatens to overwhelm him. He can't recall a time when he slept without Windy's warmth beside him.

Ferrus go through the gate? No Windy, but no dog to bark at him either. Perhaps he could find a place to sleep.

Near the lady.

Elizabeth Cromwell rose to her feet, gathering her cloak into her arms. 'I shall leave you to your business, Catherine.' Her eyes flickered towards Durrell. 'The coach is waiting below, and my father will be wondering where I am.'

Durrell remained where he was, his body blocking the door. He glanced at Cat. 'His Grace commanded me to bring you to him.'

'Pray give His Grace my compliments. Tell him I'm engaged.'

'No, mistress. He wants you now.'

'Why?'

'I don't know. Maybe he'll tell you when you get there.'

'It's not convenient for me. Tell him that instead.'

Elizabeth cleared her throat. 'Move aside, my man,' she said to Durrell in a voice that was not quite steady.

He ignored her. 'I got a coach outside too,' he said to Cat. 'At least you won't get wet and mucky.'

'Leave this house.' Cat's anger was rising but her fear was rising faster. 'You should not have been allowed in.'

'Mistress.' Durrell's thick voice lingered on the word. 'Either you come along with me, and everything's pleasant and you're back here in an hour or so. Or the old man comes too.'

'My husband's not at leisure to go anywhere. He's working.'

'He'll come if he's made to come.'

Cat stared at him. 'Go away.'

'I've a couple of men waiting in the coach. If the young lady's obstinate, the Duke says, bring the old fool as well. It's not right to allow a wife to have such shrewish ways. He said to remind you that he talked to you about that at Wallingford House the other evening.' Durrell shook his heavy head in mock disapproval. 'When you was being obstinate again.'

'Catty,' Elizabeth said, trying to edge round Durrell. 'Catty, dear–what harm can there be, after all? The Duke's a gentleman, and he honours your father's memory. I'm sure he wants you for something important.'

Durrell still did not move. 'Which is it to be?'

Cat said nothing for a moment. She stood perfectly still. The bully at Wallingford House thought himself above the law, as in practice indeed he was.

'Catherine!' Elizabeth said, her voice sharpening. 'Remember where your interests lie. The Duke is our friend. Your husband's patron, if you but let him.'

'Hold your clack, you foolish woman,' Cat snarled.

She watched the shock grow in Elizabeth's face, as plain speaking did its work as swiftly as an earthquake. In that moment, the fragile edifice of their friendship, if that was the right word for it, trembled and fell.

'Well, mistress?' Durrell said, as implacable as fate but more partial and far less patient.

A church clock struck seven.

After I came through the wicket I crossed a cobbled yard to another gate, also unbarred. I startled a cat, which hissed at me and slid away into the darkness.

Beyond the second gate was a small garden, screened by a fence from another, smaller yard. God be praised, there was no sign of a guard dog.

There was no sign of Cat, either.

I stood in the shadow of a bush for a few minutes. My cloak grew wetter. I tilted my head to look up at the house. Water streamed from the brim of my hat, and some of it trickled down my neck.

There was a sound behind me, and my heart missed a beat. I thought for a moment that someone might be standing there, just inside the gate to the yard. But I could see or hear no one.

Lights shone in at least some of the windows on all the floors. I knew that the building had been let to a handful of lodgers, who shared the use of the garden, the outbuildings and the services of the porter and his boy. The Hakesbys had the top two storeys and were the major tenants. I guessed there were two back doors from the house—one to the yard at the side, where the cesspit would be, and the other directly into the garden. If Cat were coming at all, she would probably use the garden door.

Time passed slowly. The rain fell and the air cooled. After the day I had had, I was weary and unhappy. As I waited, I grew increasingly disgruntled. I was trying to do Cat a favour, but she hadn't even honoured the arrangement that she herself had made.

At that moment, as I was cultivating my irritation as assiduously as wiser men culti-vate their gardens, two things happened.

The sudden, shocking noise of breaking glass.

And a woman screamed.

The stairs were wide enough for three.

Durrell walked between them, gripping both Cat's arm and Elizabeth's. Elizabeth had her cloak draped over her arm in such a way that the hand clutching the case of pearls was hidden. They went slowly, for Durrell was short of breath and a little unsteady, but Cat was aware of his bulk. Neither woman came up to his shoulders. His arm felt like the branch of a tree.

525

As luck would have it, he had taken her right arm, which meant she could not reach the slit in her skirt where the pocket containing her knife was. Even if she could, what use would a small knife be? It would not protect her husband from Buckingham.

Only the King could do that. It struck her that Marwood had been right all along: that she should have traded information about Buckingham and Cromwell in return for her own safety and her husband's.

Hakesby had no idea of what was happening. Durrell had refused to allow Cat to speak to him. 'Best to come with me directly, mistress,' he had said, 'and get it out of the way. If the old gentleman misses you, the porter will tell him where you are. You'll only fluster him if you tell him now.'

There was truth of a sort in that, but in any case Durrell had given her no choice. He wouldn't even let her fetch her cloak and hat.

'Warm enough in the coach, you'll find. And if it's not, you can have one of our cloaks.'

But on the next floor down, she heard the door of the Drawing Office open, and familiar footsteps shuffle out.

'Sir,' she cried, twisting her head and

shouting up the stairs. 'Durrell's taking me to —'

He released her arm and clamped a large hand over her mouth. 'No, no, no,' he said. 'You're a wayward bitch, aren't you?'

They descended the last flight to the first-floor landing. Cat tried to find the slit into her pocket, but Durrell had her squeezed against him. The hilt of his sword dug into her waist.

She peered into the hall passage below. There was no sign of Pheebs.

There were rapid movements above. It must be Brennan, Cat thought, and he was coming downstairs. At least he might be in time to see what was happening.

Durrell paused on the first-floor landing. He was breathing hard, but whether that was from exertion or irritation wasn't clear. He turned his head to face Brennan.

But it wasn't Brennan.

Hakesby appeared around the half turn of the stairs from the floor above. 'What are you doing?' he said, his voice that of a younger man. He was carrying his inkwell in his hand and he shook it at Durrell, scattering a trail of ink down the stairs. 'Where are you taking these ladies?'

'I ain't taking this one anywhere.' Durrell nodded his head at Elizabeth who, strangely, smiled at him as if he had done her a service. 'Just offering her my arm downstairs. But the Duke wants to talk to your lady, and that's where we're going.'

'Then His Grace should have asked leave of me,' Hakesby said, stumbling down the last of the stairs and advancing across the landing. 'And if he's a man of honour, he should have done it himself rather than send a servant. And I would have refused him. Am I not her husband? Release her, you rogue. At once, do you hear? Or by God I'll make you.'

Durrell obeyed. He stretched out his hand and snatched the inkwell from Hakesby. He threw it through the window at the end of the landing.

Hakesby was now white and trembling, the unnatural burst of energy gone. 'You– you —'

Durrell seized him by the collar with one hand, and by his belt with the other. He heaved Hakesby down the last flight of stairs to the hall.

Elizabeth screamed. Cat ran down the stairs to her husband.

'Looks like the poor old gentleman slipped,' Durrell said.

The noises penetrated the walls of the airless closet under the stairs. Pheebs kept his possessions here, including the straw mattress he slept on. Now he was sitting on a stool and cleaning his teeth with the ivory toothpick he had stolen from the young man who used to lodge in the first floor back.

The noises grew worse. The shouting. The screaming. The running footsteps. Something falling.

It wasn't right. This wasn't part of the bargain. Durrell had paid him ten shillings. In return, Pheebs had let Durrell into the house and allowed him to go directly upstairs. He had come to fetch Mistress Hakesby, Durrell had said–nothing to worry about, but probably better for everyone if it was managed discreetly. Send your boy out on an errand, Durrell added. Bid him not to come back for a couple of hours.

Pheebs had told him that Mistress Cromwell was up there in the Hakesbys' parlour. Durrell had poked Pheebs in the ribs and said she didn't matter, she was a friend, but thanks for the warning all the same. I can let myself out with the ladies, he said with a leer, I like it when there's two of them. You can bar the door after we've gone.

But the racket in the hall was beyond bearing, even for ten shillings. Someone was going to ask: Where was the porter when all that was going on? Perhaps he could say he'd had an urgent need to empty his bowels and had been in the necessary house at the back.

Pheebs cautiously opened the closet door and looked out. Oh, God's death. Old Hakesby was lying on his face in the hall. And his wife was kneeling over him. And Durrell was thumping down the stairs with a face like a pickled walnut, dark with anger. He was dragging the other wench behind him, the one with the nice tits, and she was red-cheeked as any drunken slut and screeching like a baby and she didn't look so well-favoured now.

More footsteps above. Someone shouting down the stairs.

Then, behind him, the scrape of the garden door opening.

Devil take them all. Pheebs retreated into the closet and pulled the door shut. He slid home the inner bolt as quietly as possible and covered his ears.

Cat?

Like a fool, I rushed towards the garden door. My shoes crunched over pieces of glass from the broken window above. The door wasn't barred. I pushed it open. I hesitated on the step.

Two candles were burning near the street door at the far end of the hall, and a couple of rushlights in the intervening passage. I couldn't see anyone, but I could hear them.

There was another scream, followed by the rumble of a man's voice.

Like an even greater fool, I raised my stick and advanced up the hall. There was Cat. I felt a rush of relief that she was alive. She was kneeling by Hakesby, who was lying on his side at the foot of the stairs. The gown he wore about the house had come loose and it floated around him on the floor. His slippers had fallen off. I opened my mouth to say something, but by then it was too late.

Cat raised her head. She was staring at something or someone I couldn't see. A moment later she was on her feet. She had her little knife in her hand.

Durrell came into view. His arm lunged towards her. She ducked under it and stabbed him in the side, just above the waist. He bellowed with pain and rage. He gave her a backhanded blow that swept her aside.

Falling back, she tripped over something on the floor. There was a chink of metal. She lost control of the movement and fell heavily. The back of her head collided with the side wall of the passage. She cried out and dropped the knife.

Another woman appeared. She ran past Durrell towards the door. He snatched at the cloak she carried and hauled her back. She screamed like a mad thing and batted his arm with the flat of her free hand, like an infant in the grip of a tantrum. He slapped her into silence. She crouched down, covering her head with her hands, and wailed. Durrell turned his head to look at Cat, who was struggling to her feet. He lumbered towards her.

I was in the shadows to his side. As he passed me, I ran forward and hit him over the head with my stick. His hat took some of the impact, but the blow was hard enough to stop him in his tracks. I gripped the stick with both hands and hit him again, this time full in the face. I heard the crack of his nose breaking.

Durrell slumped sideways, against the wall, and fell to the floor. He raised his left arm to shield himself from another blow. His right hand stretched towards Cat.

Someone rushed past me and flung himself on top of Durrell. Durrell grunted and writhed, trying to throw off his new attacker. He was a stranger to me—a tall man, twitching like a great spider on top of Durrell; he seemed all legs and arms; and with him he brought a foul smell.

There was a small axe on the floor. I could see it quite clearly by the light of the candles. It didn't occur to me to wonder what it was doing there. By this time I was beyond surprise, beyond thought.

The tall man snatched the axe and brought it down with precision and great force on Durrell's right wrist.

Durrell screamed.

One moment the arm had a hand at the end of it, a hand that was only inches away from Cat. The next moment, the hand was quite separate from the arm. It was resting beside Cat's foot. And the arm was spurting blood towards her. In this light the liquid was as black as ink.

The tall man let the axe fall to the floor.

The other woman had stopped screaming for the time being. She had contrived to scramble to her feet. She was at the door, struggling with the bars and bolts. She got the door open, and the noise of the street rolled into the hall. She glanced back, frowning.

Elizabeth Cromwell, I thought. It must be.

'Give me it, Catty,' she said, her voice hard and imperious. 'It's mine.'

She was pointing at something that lay beside Hakesby's motionless head. A small leather case.

'No, it isn't,' Cat said. 'Get out.'

The tall man made a high, chirruping noise, pure and birdlike. He flapped long fingers at Cat, as if pushing the case towards her, and the fingers said as clearly as any tongue could speak: 'Yes, I give it to you, it's yours, it's a present.'

Elizabeth lunged towards the case and scooped it up. She turned and fled. But in the doorway, the tall man seized her arm and snatched the case from her. She clawed at him with her hands. He shouldered her out of his way and ran into the street.

Cat crouched by her husband. She said, 'He's dead.' She found there were tears rolling down her cheeks.

She glanced at Marwood, who was kneeling beside Durrell. He didn't look at her. Durrell was lying on his belly like a stranded whale and moaning quietly and monotonously. Marwood was squeezing the end of his right arm with both hands, trying to stem the flow of blood. The severed hand was a few inches from its former owner. It did not lie flat on the floor. The fingers were at an angle to the palm. It looked as if the

534

hand was still trying to crawl towards where Cat had been.

'A belt,' Marwood said loudly, without looking up. 'Give me a belt, someone. Or rope.'

Brennan thundered down the last flight of stairs. He stopped, staring at the scene in the hall.

'Quickly,' Marwood shouted.

Cat tugged at the cord that hung from Hakesby's gown. He rarely tied it unless he was particularly cold, preferring to wear the gown loose. She handed it to Brennan.

'Give it to him,' she said, and went back to looking at Hakesby's face.

'Shut the street door,' Marwood said as he took it. 'Bar it.'

Hakesby's face in profile. His mouth was open. So was the visible eye. Presumably, Cat thought, the other eye was open too. She placed her fingers on the eyelid and drew it down. When she released the pressure, the lid immediately retracted, but only a little, as if her husband wanted to peep at the world he had left behind. To peep at her.

Someone was hammering on the street door.

'I need something for a lever,' Marwood said. 'The axe will do.'

Brennan picked it up and gave it to him. Marwood made him squeeze the end of Durrell's arm while he wound the cord around the stump and used the handle of the axe to draw it tighter and tighter.

Cat thought, Let the fat devil bleed to death.

Some time later, Marwood touched her shoulder. 'We must get Durrell out of the house.'

'There's a coach outside.' She looked up. 'He said there are two men in it. It's probably them knocking on the door. They can take him down to hell and leave him there. If they leave him here much longer, I swear I'll kill him.'

They chase him like the hounds chase the deer in the Park. But Ferrus runs faster than any deer.

In his right hand is the case. His gift to her. He will find the lady. She will smile at him when he gives it to her again, and perhaps there will be another shining penny, and another smile.

'Oh what sport!'

The boys are here, and apprentices too, and screeching hags, and barking dogs. They bar the streets that lead away from Covent Garden and force him to run round and

536

round the piazza.

Whoop, whoop, they cry, huzzah, huzzah. Stop thief.

He runs like the wind up the steps of the church and behind the pillars of its porch. He follows the line of the long wall on one side of the piazza and dodges through the arcades and dives between coaches. If his arms flail fast enough, they will lift him from the ground and he will fly over the rooftops to the Cockpit where Windy, the kennel and his two pennies are waiting for him.

'Pull him down, boys! Pull him down!'

Lanterns and torches light the arcades. Braziers glow beneath. The smell of food is in the air. The ladies and gentlemen of the night warm their hands as they watch. In the middle of the piazza is an open rectangle enclosed by chains across low white posts. Ferrus jumps over the chain and runs among the knots of people. They scatter before him. They poke their sticks at him.

'Good as a play,' a man says, and he snorts and snuffles with laughter.

A horseman joins in the fun. He rides straight at Ferrus, who swerves to avoid going under the hooves. One of the chains catches his shin. He stumbles over it and staggers across the roadway to the arcade on the other side.

The kerbstone beneath an arch is his undoing. He trips. He falls. The case flies from his hand. It hits the side of the arch and it bursts open. A line of marbles falls out.

Ferrus hits the flagstones under the arcade. He rolls over and springs to his feet. The marbles shimmer red and orange in the glow. They scatter as they fall. There are marbles everywhere, underfoot, in the gutter, under the wheels of a passing coach. Some fall into the brazier. Someone shouts and tries to hook the marbles out.

He picks up the case. It's the lady's.

'Thief!' a man shouts. 'Stop thief! Take him!'

A boy stamps his heel on a marble and laughs. A man cuffs him.

Ferrus runs. Arms flailing. Faster and faster he goes, faster and faster.

I fly like a bird in the night.

CHAPTER SEVENTEEN

The Far End of the Park
Thursday, 26 March 1668

The following morning I was at Henrietta Street shortly after nine o'clock. Pheebs opened the door for me, his face as doleful as a bereaved son's. There was a strong smell of vinegar. His boy was on his hands and knees scrubbing the floor. He had been doing that yesterday evening when I left the house. He had probably been doing it all night. There had been a great deal of blood.

'A most doleful day, sir.'

'Is Mistress Hakesby within?'

We were playing a game, Pheebs and I. Yesterday evening, I had discovered where he had hidden himself under the stairs. I knew he had let Durrell into the house. He knew I knew, and we both pretended I didn't. When the excitement was over, he had emerged blinking from his hole, pretending surprise and claiming to have been asleep, to hear the news of Hakesby's fatal fall. He had even helped Brennan and myself carry the body upstairs and lay it on the Hakesbys' bed.

As part of the game, I had given Pheebs a pound in gold, in theory for his service to the Hakesbys, both alive and dead, but really to keep his mouth shut about anything that suggested the old man's death might not have been an ordinary domestic accident or that other strangers might have been in the house that evening. I also gave him a sight of my warrant and made him understand that if he gave me trouble I would see him committed for trial as an accessory to murder.

'I'll send the boy up to see if mistress can receive you, sir.' Pheebs lowered his voice. 'The midwife came early to lay out the poor gentleman.'

A moment later, I went up to the Hakesbys' parlour. The maid with the frightened face opened the door. I told her to wait outside on the landing.

Cat was at the table. She was staring at the wall. I bowed and she nodded her head. I sat down opposite her. There was a mattress on the floor with a pile of blankets beside it. She wouldn't have wanted to spend the night with her dead husband in the bedchamber. I doubted she had slept much.

'I hope they let me bury him properly,' she said suddenly, as if we had been talking together for some time. 'St Paul's church-yard, I thought, here in Covent Garden. He would want that. Did you know he worked on the church as a young man? Under Inigo Jones.'

I shook my head.

'He had a great admiration for Mr Jones. Have your masters sent you to bring me in?'

'What? No. I haven't been to Whitehall yet. I don't know what they will want.'

'Either Buckingham will fetch me or they will. But I hope they will let me bury my husband first.'

Rage or anger or blame would have been easier to deal with than this unnatural resignation. It surprised me that Hakesby's death had dealt her such a blow. But Cat always had a genius for the unexpected.

'I was not a good wife,' she said. 'I know that. I should have been kinder.'

'There's no point in thinking about that now,' I said. 'Think about the funeral instead, and the other arrangements. You've given out that the light was poor and he slipped and fell downstairs.' I wanted to make sure that we all had the story straight.

'As we agreed, and as Pheebs and Brennan will confirm. Everyone knows Mr Hakesby's ague was growing much worse. There's no reason why he shouldn't be buried directly.'

'Yes, you're right,' she said. Then: 'Brennan's dealing with all that.'

'Good. Margaret's coming here later today, and she'll do whatever you want to help. Do you have money?'

'Enough for the time being. After the funeral, it doesn't much matter.'

'Of course it matters. Where do the Cromwells lodge?'

'Mistress Dalton's, by Hatton Garden.' She paused. 'You were right, by the way. I should have betrayed them to the King. They cared nothing for me, after all. And it's because of them that my husband is dead.'

I walked from Henrietta Street to Charing Cross. I was lightheaded from lack of sleep. My skin felt grubby and my eyes were full of grit.

I had been up half the night writing letters. I had dozed for an hour or so, until I woke with a start from a dream about Durrell's severed hand crawling like a monstrous insect across my pillow and leaving a red

542

smear behind it. After that, it had not been worth trying to sleep.

It was a fine morning. The streets glistened after yesterday's rain. The sky was a cloudless blue, apart from the streaks of smoke. Sam had been out early to gather news. The unrest had continued into the night, but the troubles were past their peak. The authorities had tightened their grip on the town and the ringleaders of the rioters had been arrested.

At the golden gates of Wallingford House, the porter declined to admit me. I asked for Mr Veal. The man was reluctant even to allow the possibility that Mr Veal might exist, either at Wallingford House or anywhere else. I showed him my royal warrant and said that he himself might not exist much longer if he didn't stop obstructing an officer of the Crown and send for Mr Veal at once.

A boy hared off to the house. The porter retreated into his box. I stood outside the gates with the little crowd of beggars who were always there, waiting for the Duke to come out and throw them a handful of silver. I was coming to hate these palaces of the rich: Wallingford House, Arundel House in the Strand, Clarendon House in Piccadilly and even Whitehall itself. I had seen

543

too much of what went on inside them.

The tall, upright figure of Mr Veal came round the corner of the house's west wing. He walked slowly across the forecourt towards me. He wore his old brown coat, as unfashionable as a ruff, and his heavy sword swung by his side. He didn't look much like a clergyman. His life had led him to unexpected places, as mine had, and I felt an unexpected twinge of sympathy for him. He stopped a yard away from the gates and stared at me. By the look of him, he hadn't had much sleep either.

'Well?'

I gestured at the beggars that flanked me, and the porter beside him.

He shrugged. 'I've nothing to say to you.'

'I've nothing to say to you either. I want to talk to the Duke.'

He shrugged again and began to turn away.

'Tell him it's about a whore called Chloris, a bully called Merton, and a desk in Madam Cresswell's house in Dog and Bitch Yard.' I had the attention of my audience now, all of it, including the porter and the beggars. 'Tell him —'

Veal held up his hand. 'Enough. I will pass on your message.'

'And tell your master I shall be at Whitehall this afternoon. After that it will be too late.'

I was about to walk away when he called me back. He waved the porter and the beggars to stand aside for us.

'He's alive still,' he said in a low voice through the bars of the gate.

'Durrell?'

'Who took off his hand?'

'I don't know.'

He frowned. He examined my face. 'Truly?'

'A man rushed in from the garden. He attacked Durrell in the hall, and then fled by the street door. I've never seen him before.'

There was a silence as we both considered this.

'He'll probably live unless the wound gets infected,' Veal said at last. 'I suppose you saved his life.'

On Thursday, the weather was so sunny and warm that Richard Cromwell spent longer than usual in the garden after breakfast. He and Elizabeth walked up and down the paths. He studied what was growing there with great attention.

'Why, if this weather continues, we shall have a most glorious spring. Hampshire will be a veritable paradise. I wonder whether I might be able to slip down and join you there for a few days.'

'Sir,' Elizabeth said, 'you grow reckless. A man died last night, and another wounded, perhaps mortally. You can't run yourself even deeper into danger for the sake of a few flowers.'

'Who knows? If the Duke's plan works, I shall be able to spend the whole year round there.'

'But it isn't working.' She kept her voice low but she would have liked to scream at him. 'There's a lot of talk at Wallingford House but that's all. Just talk. The Duke will do nothing more for us unless it helps him in some way.'

'But he gave me his word. He's a man of honour.'

Her father stooped to examine the new shoots appearing on a rose. Poor Tumbledown Dick. Elizabeth was eighteen years old, and her father more than twice that. Yet she felt as though their ages had reversed themselves in the last few weeks. He still had the foolish optimism of youth, whereas she felt half as old as time.

Last night she had not slept. What had happened in Henrietta Street was as vivid in her mind as if it were still in front of her. There had been all that blood. In those few terrible minutes at the foot of the stairs, she and her father had lost everything: the strange creature from the sewers had snatched the pearls and run into the night with them. This morning, to make matters worse, Mistress Dalton had told them that it was no longer convenient for them to remain with her. But still her father would not face up to the truth.

He glanced at her. 'You're very like your grandfather, my dear.'

'What?'

Her father seemed to have forgotten their troubles for the moment. 'Your face seen in profile. You have quite a look of him.' He smiled, belatedly remembering to be tactful. 'But in a way that's becoming to a woman, I mean.'

The side door of the house opened. She looked up, expecting to see Mistress Dalton or her steward. But it was a stranger.

'Who's that?' her father said.

'I've seen him somewhere . . .' The memory hit her like a blow. 'I think he was at the Hakesbys' last night. I didn't see him properly and the light was poor, but —'

She broke off. The man was almost upon them.

'Mr Cromwell, I believe.' The stranger bowed. 'Mistress Cromwell, your servant.'

547

Her father drew himself up. 'Who are you, sir?'

'My name's Marwood, sir. Pray have a sight of my warrant.'

He handed her father a creased piece of paper. He knows who we are, Elizabeth thought, which means he must also have known about us last night. He was not an imposing man–his clothes were on the shabby side of respectable, his wig was a disgrace. She glimpsed scarring on the left side of his face and neck.

'The King sent you?'

'As you see, sir. The King knows of your connection with the Duke of Buckingham and others, and he knows of the intrigues you have lately been engaged in. The breaches of the peace we have seen this week, the destruction of property in various quarters of the City–why, that's only a small part of it. A conspiracy by the late Protector, a judge would call it, a conspiracy against the Crown.'

'No–no, my dear sir, that is a complete misunderstanding, a misinterpretation. Allow me to —'

'Or to use another name for it, sir,' Marwood interrupted, 'treason.'

He held out his hand for the warrant. Wordlessly, Cromwell returned it.

'There's also the matter of the pearls.' Marwood glanced at Elizabeth. 'Theft from the Crown. Another charge, if one were needed, along with trespass: bribing persons to enter a royal residence by stealth in order to commit a felony on your behalf. Oh, and you have also laid yourself open to a charge of accessory to murder.'

'Murder?' Cromwell's face had lost its colour. 'Murder? That's nonsense. It's . . .'

Elizabeth took her father's arm and led him to a bench against the wall. He was trembling. She looked up at Marwood. 'Whose murder?'

He stared back at her. 'The Duke's servants have committed at least two murders in the last few days in order to further this conspiracy. As an active member of that conspiracy, madam, your father has aided and abetted those murders. You yourself were a witness to one of them last night. When the Duke's hired bully threw an old man down the stairs. He was a distinguished architect and surveyor named Mr Hakesby. He was murdered in his own house.'

Cromwell put his head in his hands. 'I'm innocent, sir. I wish no one harm, least of all the King. True, I'm in pressing need of money, but there's no crime in that. The Duke was kind enough to offer me a pension. I —'

'The King's not a vengeful man.' Marwood stood over Cromwell, blocking the sun from him. 'But those around him are not so forgiving.'

There was silence. Cromwell looked at his daughter, who stared stonily at him, barely able to contain her anger. He turned back to Marwood.

'What does the King want me to do?'

'To sign this letter I've brought with me. Both you and your daughter will need to sign. In it, you confess that Buckingham lured you back to England and forced you to lend your name and presence to his efforts to build an independent party in opposition to the King and Parliament. You received money from him, and you attended meetings with disaffected men at Wallingford House. We shall be merciful and forget this matter of the Cockpit entirely.'

'Who will see this letter?' Elizabeth said.

'No one but the King, if all goes well. He himself has no malice towards your father, unless he threatens the peace of the realm. The letter will keep Buckingham on a tight leash if the King has need of it.' Marwood turned back to Richard Cromwell. 'Sign it now. Then you must leave London. At once. Today, not tomorrow. Take a coach to Harwich or Dover as quickly and discreetly as you can, go abroad and stay there. Otherwise I can't guarantee your safety, and your life will be forfeit.'

Richard Cromwell rubbed his finger on the seat of the bench. He glanced at Elizabeth, who thought her father looked like a confused sheep. 'But if I sign, I could be putting my head in a noose,' he said.

'You've done that anyway, sir,' Elizabeth said. 'You have no choice. You must sign.'

Tumbledown Dick, she thought. My father.

By the time I reached Whitehall it was midday, and I was exhausted. It occurred to me that lack of food might have something to do with it. I dined at the Angel in King Street. I had not been to Whitehall for two days; nor had I sent word to explain my absence. There would be a reckoning with Williamson but it would have to wait.

Even now, it was within my power to change all this: to do myself much good with both Williamson and Lord Arlington. I was tempted. But there would be a price to pay for advancement on those terms. I wouldn't be the only one who had to pay it.

I had almost finished my meal when I heard someone clearing their throat behind me, very close to my ear. I turned my head. A man I had never seen before was at my shoulder. I ran my eyes over him. He was soberly dressed in black, but the cloth was good and the stockings below his breeches were of silk.

'Have I the honour of addressing Mr Marwood?' he asked.

'Yes.'

'I have a message for you, sir.' He bent forward as if bowing, which brought his mouth closer to my ear. 'Mr Veal says two o'clock at the Chelsea Gate end of the canal. Near the deer houses. Thank you, sir.'

He straightened himself, cleared his throat again and disappeared into the crowd by the door.

Part of me wanted to hurry, for old habits die hard, to avoid the risk of making so important a man as the Duke wait for me. Then I remembered that even great noble-men are made of the same clay as the rest of us, and they are just as capable of acts of folly. I owed him nothing, certainly not re-spect.

I passed under the King Street Gate and turned into the Cockpit passage that led to St James's Park. I emerged blinking into the sunshine. Laying out the canal had been one of the King's first projects after the Restoration. It stretched from the Cockpit and the Tiltyard in the east towards the Chelsea Gate and Goring House in the west. The deer houses were at the western end because, being further from Whitehall, it was the quietest area of the park.

A statue of a gladiator stood at this end of the canal. Suddenly superstitious, I touched its base for luck as I passed. I sauntered down the path, with the water on my right.

As I walked, I glanced from side to side. There was no sign of Buckingham yet. Half a dozen guardsmen were acting the fool with a maidservant near the Chelsea Gate. Two little boys tumbled like puppies on the grass under the eye of their nursemaid. A gardener wheeled a barrowload of cuttings along the avenue of young trees on the other side of the canal. A group of courtiers was playing bowls in the sunshine. Further away, three young men exercised their horses and showed off to each other. A servant was walking a pair of mastiffs, tight-leashed and muzzled. The roofs of Goring House, Lord Arlington's London residence, were visible beyond its garden wall and a belt of trees. I hoped that my lord and Williamson weren't staring down at me from an upper window.

I stopped at the end of the canal and

looked about me. It was an innocent spring afternoon, fresh and green. If a man didn't know better, he might almost believe that all was right with the world.

'If it please Your Honour.'

The gardener was standing between two of the young trees on the other side of the canal. He was leaning on his barrow and looking at me over the water. He was a tall man with a red face. He wore a stiff leather apron to protect his clothes and a broad-brimmed hat.

'What is it?' I said. Then, in a sharper voice: 'Oh, devil take it.'

Buckingham laughed. He abandoned his barrow and walked round the end of the canal towards me. The Duke made a sport out of everything, even a crisis.

'Did I fool you?' he said.

'I had forgotten Your Grace's taste for the theatrical.'

'Come now, Marworm, you must admit it was well done. The stance–the clothes–the complexion: why, I had the part to a nicety. Let's walk towards the deer houses. You can pretend to be giving me my orders.'

The Duke smiled to underline the drollery of this. We walked in silence for a moment. I glanced about me. I suspected that some of the people I could see were his servants, ready to intervene if he desired.

'You've caused me a lot of trouble lately,' he said. 'I can't say I care for that. One of my favourite bawds is dead. My papers are stolen. A servant of mine is so maimed he's like to die. Even if he survives, I must count him useless. Another has his skull smashed like an eggshell while defending my property from a housebreaker. Every stone I turn, I find you underneath.'

'It's over, isn't it?'

'Don't be impudent, Marworm. Did I give you leave to speak?'

'Your riots are over.' I waved a hand in the direction of Wallingford House. 'Your attempt to build a party among the Independents and that crew. Men who long for the good old days. Your efforts to raise the City.'

For a moment I thought the Duke would hit me. Patches of pallor appeared on his skin.

He said, 'Is there any reason why I shouldn't have you flogged? It could be done here–now, in broad daylight–if I but click my fingers. It would make it clear to Arlington and his creature Williamson that I don't brook interference. It would also make it clear that I don't permit impertinence from my inferiors.'

'If I'm harmed or killed, sir, I have arranged for certain papers to be delivered to the King and the Privy Council.'

'Be damned to that. And your friends.'

'Mistress Catherine Hakesby —'

'That bitch.'

'She is innocent of any crime, Your Grace, but she knows something of your intrigue. If any harm comes to her, it will have the same consequence as if the harm was done to me. The King and the Privy Council will see the papers.'

'What papers are these? Do you take me for a fool, Marworm? I'm not a child to be frightened by things that don't exist.'

I rubbed my itching eyes. 'They include an early draft of the Whores' Petition written and amended in your own hand. It was taken from your desk in Cresswell's bawdy house in Dog and Bitch Yard. It will leave the King, his councillors and my Lady Castlemaine in no doubt that you were the original author. There's also a letter signed by the late Protector Richard Cromwell. He writes that you bribed him with money and promises of a pension to support your intrigues against the King and Parliament. His daughter Elizabeth has put her name to the letter as well, confirming the truth of what her father says. They throw themselves on the mercy of the King.'

'Prove it. Show me this draft petition you claim to have. And show me this letter.'

'They are safely lodged with a friend, Your Grace.' He wasn't to know that I meant my servant Sam, as I hadn't had time to find a safer home for them yet.

'I've only your word for this. I don't believe these papers exist. The more I think of it, the less likely it seems.'

'The draft of the petition has a line through it, Your Grace, and on the other side of the sheet is the document you wished to keep. It is a scene from a play called "The Rehearsal". I had not known you aspired to be a playwright as well. Let me quote you a line from it.' I paused shamelessly for effect. ' "By my troth, I have long'd as much to laugh with you, at all the impertinent, dull, fantastical things." Is that enough proof for you?'

'No. All it proves is that you've stolen a page from my play.'

I hesitated, groping in my memory for other words. 'Then let me remind you of a phrase you used in the petition, but later deleted. You informed my Lady Castlemaine that when the rioters seized her, she should expect "to be thrown on your back and roughly ravished by the grimy multitude". No doubt the King will want to share that with my lady.'

In the silence that followed, I listened to the cries of the little boys and the shouts of the horsemen. I watched the Duke. He was staring down the canal at Whitehall.

Suddenly he tore off his hat and stamped on it. The grey stubble on his scalp was greasy with sweat. He walked away, leaving the barrow standing among the trees.

I watched him. Worms can turn. So can Marworms.

CHAPTER EIGHTEEN

The Poultry House
Thursday 26 March–Sunday 19 April, 1668

Williamson had been dining with Lord Arlington. He was in a good humour because my lord had been in a good humour. My master was usually abstemious, at least where matters of business were concerned. But I could tell by his manner that he had taken more wine than was his custom.

I had reached Scotland Yard before him. He was humming an air when he came up the stairs. He beckoned me into his room.

He told me to close the door and flung himself into his chair. 'Where have you been?' He ran his eyes over me and frowned. 'You look unwell.'

'Cry your pardon, sir–a touch of fever. I couldn't get here sooner. I was —'

'Never mind that. How did you fare with your bawd in Dog and Bitch Yard?'

'I'm afraid she was unable to find anything

that linked His Grace with the riots. But I did call at Henrietta Street to question them about Mistress Hakesby's involvement with the Duke, and why she went to Wallingford House that evening. She said it was to do with her husband's business, and a mansion that the Duke has in mind to build in York-shire. Mr Hakesby was already there. But when she learned what the Duke was about with his dissenting friends, she insisted on leaving.'

'Do you believe her?'

I shrugged. 'I see no reason not to. The Duke's unlikely to have confided anything worth the hearing to a woman. I'm convinced she doesn't share her father's beliefs or the Duke's politics. Besides, she has other things on her mind. Her husband has been very ill. In fact he died yesterday.'

Williamson grunted. 'God rest his soul. But it was probably a false scent in any case. Not that it matters any more. The riots are all but over, and the ringleaders in prison. We'll hang one or two of them, and that will be the end of it. If the Duke had a hand in the affair, he's gained nothing by it. If anything, he's lost credit with his supporters.'

So that was the reason for Williamson's good humour. Though he did not know the full extent of Buckingham's intrigue, it had become increasingly clear that the Duke's failure to manage the King's business in Parliament had dealt a fatal blow to his political ambitions. Williamson could not resist confiding to me that, according to Lord Arlington, His Grace's voice no longer commanded much attention at Privy Council meetings.

'The King has his measure now,' Williamson told me. 'He lets the Duke amuse him. He lets him strut about court and pretend to be a great man. And he leaves the work of government to those who can do it. So all ends well, Marwood, thanks be to God.'

During the next fortnight, our lives resumed their even tenor. The issues of the *Gazette* came and went; letters were received, digested and docketed; other letters were written, copied into letter books, and dispatched to the four corners of the Kingdom; Mr Williamson and Lord Arlington walked slowly about the Privy Garden with their heads together, settling affairs of state and dispatching the business of government.

As for me, I bought myself a new peruke. I spent nearly ten pounds on it, for Chiffinch's jibe about my wearing two squirrels on my head had gone deep. It is a strange world where a man must pay through the nose to wear another's hair, yet also spend money on a barber to keep his own hair short enough for the inconvenience of wearing a periwig perched on his head. I also ordered a suit of clothes with a long coat and waistcoat after the new fashion.

Margaret raised her eyebrows at my extravagance. But the deaths I had witnessed during the last weeks had made me conscious of my own mortality. What was the point of laying up money in my strongboxes? Money is merely a means to an end, I told myself, and a man cannot spend it when he is dead.

On Thursday 9 April, I had the final fitting for my new suit. Afterwards, I took a hackney coach to Holborn and called on Mistress Dalton in her house by Hatton Garden. She was a stern, grim-faced woman. My arrival was understandably unwelcome to her. I had met her briefly once before, when I had visited the Cromwells here. She was scared of me, I think, and that made her dislike me even more.

She received me in the parlour. She asked me to close the door and speak soft.

I declined the chair she offered me. 'Have they gone?'

'He went to Harwich. He was hoping for a passage on the Hellevoetsluis packet. With luck he's in the Low Countries by now.'

'Had he money?'

She nodded. 'Enough for his passage, and more.'

'And where's the young lady?'

'In Hampshire. I had a letter from her this morning.' Mistress Dalton sniffed. 'She's tougher than she looks, that one.'

There was nothing more to say, so I went away.

'Goodbye, mistress,' I said as I left. 'Have a care of the company you keep.'

When I returned to my own house that evening, Margaret begged to speak to me. She followed me into the parlour. She was carrying a cloak over her arm.

'It's Mary, master. She miscarried this morning.'

'I'm sorry for it. And yet . . .'

I had had very little to do with the girl since I had brought her back from Dog and Bitch Yard. Mary had seen too much in the course of her short life. She had had too much done to her. Margaret kept her down in the kitchen where she did whatever she was told to do. But she would not say a word to anyone except Stephen, and then only in whispers. She shied away from Sam,

Margaret had told me earlier, though he would never lift a finger against her.

'It's better this way,' Margaret said, putting into words what I was thinking. 'Far better. She's no more than a child herself. What would she do with a bastard?'

'Can we send her back to her family?'

'She hasn't any, sir. But she has this.'

Margaret laid the cloak on the table. It was the one that had belonged to poor dead Chloris. I had given it to Mary when we fled from Madam Cresswell's house. Just before she died, Chloris had said that Mary should take it.

'She can keep it. I've no use for it.'

'It's more than a cloak.' Margaret folded back the hem and pressed the material together. The outline of a disc appeared. 'Mary unpicked the stitching–see: here.' Like a magician, she pulled out a gold coin. 'There are others. You can feel them in there.'

That was where Chloris had put the money I had given her. I had thought it lost for ever.

I said, 'Tell Mary to unpick the whole hem. There should be twenty pounds. Eight pounds is for you and Sam to share. One pound each for Mary and Stephen. You had better keep theirs in your charge, as well as

Sam's. Give the other ten to me.'

Margaret was staring at me. 'Master. God bless you. But what's it for?'

'Honesty.' I changed the subject before we embarrassed each other. 'What do we do with the girl?'

'We could keep her, see how she does. A scullery maid would give me another pair of hands in the kitchen. I could train her up to do more, given time. And she sews a little, and knows how to use an iron.'

'Very well.'

Margaret's eyes met mine. She gathered up the cloak and curtsied. 'Thank you, master.'

But she hesitated at the door.

'What is it?'

'I went to Henrietta Street again today,' she said.

During the past fortnight, Margaret had gone there frequently. Someone had to manage the household–Jane Ash, the Hakesbys' maid, was too young and too inexperienced to cope by herself. And someone had to tell Cat what a woman should do after a death. Death has rules and customs, like everything else, and the living can be censorious if they are not observed.

They had buried Hakesby decently but without undue fuss or ceremony in the

565

churchyard of St Paul's, Covent Garden. I had not realized that he had been so well respected. Dr Wren was one of the pallbearers. Dr Hooke and Mr May, the comptroller of the royal works, had followed his coffin, as had old Mr Poulton, the wealthy cloth-merchant of Dragon Yard. But afterwards I had not accompanied the other mourners to the sign of the Rose, where wine and biscuits had been provided.

'How is Mistress Hakesby?'

'She's taken it hard, master. Harder than I expected.'

'What will she do now?'

'I don't know. Nor does she, I think. She's hardly been out of doors since it happened.'

'Perhaps . . .' I said, and stopped. I cleared my throat. 'Do you think it might be beneficial for her to have some air? I might perhaps send Stephen to her with a note asking whether she would care to walk with me on Sunday.'

Margaret avoided meeting my eye. 'Perhaps, sir.'

'If the weather remains fine, that is.'

Towards the end of the second week of April, the body of a man was found on a piece of waste ground near the hamlet of Radcliffe to the east of the City. The man was tall, with unusually narrow shoulders and very long limbs. His body was clad in filthy brown rags. His feet were bare. He had been lying out in the open for some time. The body had attracted vermin and was already decaying.

The searcher who inspected the corpse could see no sign of a wound or plague sores. She told the parish clerk of Radcliffe that the man had starved to death.

The only possession on the body was a green leather case. It was empty, but the silk-lined interior suggested that it might once have held a quantity of valuable jewellery. On the lid, set into the leather, was a small gold shield engraved with a number of roundels.

As a young man, the parish clerk had accompanied an English ambassador to Florence. He recognized the arms on the shield as those of the Grand Duke of Tuscany. He considered reporting the matter. Presumably the dead man had stolen the case from someone. But the contents were long gone, and there was no point in making unnecessary work for himself. He prised off the shield with the tip of a knife, and later sold it to a goldsmith in Lombard Street for three shillings and eightpence.

The body was buried at the expense of

the parish. The empty case was sold for fourpence ha'penny to defray the cost.

Death was everywhere these days, Cat thought, inside and out. The thought of it fogged her eyes and fogged her thoughts. It made a mockery of the spring sunshine and robbed the food she ate of its flavour.

When Stephen brought up the letter from Marwood, she was in the Drawing Office, pretending to transcribe a list of almost illegible figures from Mr Hakesby's notebook. Brennan was at work on the Dragon Yard commission at his slope by the window. Mr Hakesby would have liked to see the job through himself. It had given him much pleasure. It was rare that he had so much control over a complete project.

'Of course Dragon Yard is small,' he had said to Cat, 'but at least it's ours. Let's hope it leads to bigger things. The future for us does not lie in palaces and public buildings. It lies in our cities, in the houses where people live and work. That is a far nobler ambition for us to pursue. Imagine what Inigo Jones must have felt when my Lord Bedford offered him the chance to design Covent Garden—the church, the piazza, the arcades, even the surrounding streets. Why, he had been granted a chance to create an entire world.'

She had liked her husband best at times like this, when he spoke with passion of his work, of the buildings he saw in his mind. He had a chest full of notebooks in his closet, and they contained forty years' worth of his plans and ideas. The chest had also contained his will. He had left his entire estate 'to my beloved wife Catherine'.

She did not answer Marwood's note immediately. She found everything hard to decide. Making up her mind was not something she used to find difficult. Indecision was a novelty.

When she next saw Margaret, Cat told her that her master had suggested they take the air on Sunday afternoon.

'I don't know whether to go or not,' she said.

'The air will do you good,' Margaret said. 'Master's got himself a new peruke, the Lord be praised. He's proud as a peacock about it. But at least he won't shame you in public.'

'But I'm in mourning,' Cat said. 'It's been less than three weeks.'

'No one will notice, mistress. And if they do, they won't care. Anyway, what does it matter? A widow may do as she pleases.'

The following Sunday, Marwood presented himself at Henrietta Street.

He bowed; she curtsied. They asked each other how they did. They went downstairs. Pheebs opened the street door and ceremoniously ushered them out of the house.

Marwood offered her his arm and they walked along Henrietta Street, he in his new finery and she in her widow's weeds. After the Drawing Office, the outside world was almost unbearably busy. Cat felt it strange that life should continue, oblivious to what had happened. It was as if Mr Hakesby had never existed.

'Where are we going?' she said.

'It's so fine today I thought we might go on the river. If you would care for it.'

'Will we find a boat?'

'There's one waiting for us at Salisbury Stairs. But we can leave it if you'd rather not.'

She was impressed by his forethought. 'No. I should like that.'

They turned down Half Moon Passage, crossed the Strand and went down to the river. Marwood had hired a tilt boat, with two pairs of oars. The watermen were squat, sour-faced men who looked like father and son.

When they were settled under the awning in the stern, the men rowed them out into the middle of the river. It was much brighter on the water, and she shaded her eyes against the glare.

'Where to, master?' asked the elder waterman.

'Barn Elms,' Marwood said. He looked at Cat. 'We can go ashore and walk there. It will be less crowded than the Park.'

Fewer memories too, Cat thought, remembering Ferrus running towards her from the Cockpit, his arms wheeling and his long legs rising and falling.

'The tide's right, Wanswell,' Marwood was saying to the waterman. 'We should catch the start of the flood on the way back.'

Inhibited by the presence of the boatmen, they spoke little during the crossing. At Marwood's order, they were brought ashore not at the public landing place near the village but in the fields half a mile upstream which were part of the estate. He told the boatman to collect them in an hour.

They were not alone–Barn Elms was a popular resort for Londoners on a fine Sunday afternoon–but there was so much space that people did not encroach on one

571

another. Further upstream, three couples were singing old-fashioned madrigals in perfect harmony while staring raptly over the water. A family had spread rugs on the grass and was eating a picnic. In the neighbouring field downstream, a party of apprentices was engaged in a violent, mysterious game which involved the possession of an inflated pig's bladder.

Cat stared at all this, at the people, the blue sky, the green of the fields and the shifting silver water. 'It's strange,' she said softly, almost to herself.

'That all this should exist in the same world as that?' Marwood gestured towards the far bank of the river: towards Westminster, Whitehall and London. 'Yes.'

She wasn't sure that was what she meant. But she let it go.

He looked about him. 'Shall we walk a little in those woods?'

It was cooler under the trees. The verges were strewn with the white stars of wood anemones and gleaming shoots of wild garlic.

'For me, it began here.' Marwood pointed through the trees with his stick. 'See where the trees thin? There's a field beyond. That's where Buckingham and Shrewsbury fought their duel. There was still snow on the ground.'

'You saw them?' she said, shocked.

'Mr Williamson sent me to observe the duel. It was a bloody business. I hid in the wood and watched them fight it out. I saw Shrewsbury fall. A young soldier called Jenkins was killed. But nobody really cared about him.'

In the blink of an eye, she was angry. 'Why bring me here? All that's done with, thank God, and better forgotten.'

He turned to her and smiled. 'Forgive me. I was curious to see the spot. But I'm glad we came. It's changed, you see. It's as if the duel never happened.'

She smiled back, for yet again her emotions had abruptly switched their course. 'The place has made a fresh beginning?'

'Yes.'

They turned and walked back towards the sunlit fields. The apprentices set up a great cheer for no obvious reason, and the pig's bladder rose high in the air. The singers were refreshing themselves with wine.

'What will you do now?' Marwood asked.

'I shall try to carry on,' Cat said. 'My husband left everything to me, not that there's a great deal. Brennan is willing to help, and we have Dragon Yard to finish.'

'And is there new work? Commissions in hand?'

She shook her head. 'Very little that can be depended on.'

'I have a suggestion.' Marwood hesitated.

She stopped, looking at him. She sensed his embarrassment.

'It's probably too small for you even to consider, too trivial, too.'

'What is it? I want work. Brennan and I would design and build a privy as long as we were paid to do it.'

'Mr Williamson mentioned something the other day. He had been talking with Lord Arlington. Did you know my lord has a daughter? She's barely a year old, and he dotes on her to the exclusion of all else. He wants to give the child a present. A poultry house.'

Cat burst out laughing. Marwood was smiling too. She could not remember when she had last laughed.

'This will be no common poultry house. Nor will it house vulgar hens. It's to be built of stone, and erected in the garden of Goring House, within sight of its windows. My lord thinks a small portico with pillars would lend it distinction in his daughter's eyes, and his own. Her name is Isabella, by the way. He calls her Tata.'

The bubble burst. 'But I have no connection with my lord,' she said. 'Or with Tata.'

'He asked Mr Williamson if he could recommend someone to provide some designs. I mentioned you.' Marwood was studying the ground at his feet as if the grass were particularly interesting on this spot. 'I may have given him the impression that you and Brennan had worked under Dr Wren and Mr May, as well as with Mr Hakesby.'

'Brennan worked under Wren. At Oxford.'

'There you are. So much the better. I also implied that poultry houses for ornamental fowl were of particular interest to you both, and you had made a study of the subject. If you wish, I could ask Mr Williamson to put forward your name.'

'I should be much obliged,' she said, her mind filling with pictures of a miniature temple with brightly coloured fowl scurrying about its pillars. 'Thank you, sir.'

They walked up and down the river and among the fields. Sometimes they talked of nothing much, but more often they were silent.

Their boat was coming back. Wanswell and his son had been refreshing themselves at the alehouse in the village. They waited for it at the landing place.

'That's a mighty fine peruke, sir,' Cat said

as the boat slid along the side of the jetty.
'Is it perchance new?'

HISTORICAL NOTE

In the early months of 1668, King Charles II and his allies tried to persuade Parliament to vote the money the government needed to service its ever-increasing debts, maintain the extravagances of King and court and fund the expansion of the navy.

The Duke of Buckingham was seen as a valuable ally, though he had shown himself reckless and unreliable on more than one occasion. But he had grown up with the King. He had immense wealth at his command and a considerable following in both houses of Parliament. In the past he had shown himself a friend to religious dissenters; that and his flamboyant generosity had earned him considerable popularity with the citizens of London.

Buckingham's duel with Lord Shrewsbury at Barn Elms, with its long-drawn-out epilogue, came as an unwelcome distraction. Its timing was significant, for the

Duke's affair with Lady Shrewsbury had been conducted so openly that it had been public knowledge for months. The duel clearly had a political dimension, and the Duke's chief political rival, Lord Arlington, would have had an interest in the outcome.

The Bawdy House riots occurred much as described, and some historians believe they were at least in part politically motivated. It is not known who wrote the tongue-in-cheek petition to Lady Castlemaine. It was designed to make political capital from the anti-Catholic feelings of the period and to embarrass the King and what Pepys called 'his great bawdy house at Whitehall'. Its text is as quoted, though the original is longer and the spelling has been slightly modernized. Later in the year there were several equally pseudonymous and satirical replies, including one purporting to be by Lady Castlemaine herself.

Christopher Wren's plans for a permanent headquarters for the Royal Society at Arundel House have not survived, though we have a description of what he intended in a letter he wrote to Henry Oldenberg, another member of the society. The Royal Society voted for a less expensive version of the Solomon House put forward by Robert Hooke. In the end the entire project was shelved for lack of money. In July 1668, however, Wren received news that more than compensated for any disappointment he might have felt: it had been decided to rebuild the fire-damaged St Paul's, and Wren's designs would be used for the new cathedral.

As for the last Protector, Richard Cromwell, it is strange how little is known of his life in exile between 1660 and 1680. During those twenty years he lived in straitened circumstances on the Continent. Apart from a handful of letters and one or two glimpses in other contemporary sources we know nothing about how or where he lived. In 1680 he was at last allowed to return to England, where he lived in obscurity under a false name until his death in 1712.

ABOUT THE AUTHOR

Andrew Taylor is the author of a number of crime novels, including the ground-breaking Roth Trilogy, which was adapted into the acclaimed TV drama *Fallen Angel,* and the historical crime novels *The Ashes of London, The Fire Court, The King's Evil, The Silent Boy, The Scent of Death* and *The American Boy,* a No.1 *Sunday Times* bestseller and a Richard & Judy Book Club Choice.

He has won many awards, including the CWA John Creasey New Blood Dagger, an Edgar Scroll from the Mystery Writers of America, the CWA Ellis Peters Historical Award (the only author to win it three times), the HWA Gold Crown Award and the CWA's prestigious Diamond Dagger, awarded for sustained excellence in crime writing. He also writes for the *Spectator* and *The Times.*

He lives with his wife Caroline in the Forest of Dean.

Twitter: @AndrewJRTaylor
www.andrew-taylor.co.uk